A Bit of Magic

A Collection of
Fairy Tale Retellings

The display type was set in Goudy Bookletter 1911.
The text type was set in Garamond.

Published by Rowanwood Publishing, LLC.
www.rowanwoodpublishing.com

First Edition

Introduction

We are the Just-Us League, an international group of friends dedicated to the craft of telling stories.

Though we come from different backgrounds and have different styles of writing, we share a common passion for storytelling.

Once upon a time, not so long ago, we decided to publish an anthology. The theme chosen was fairy tales, a theme we revisited with our fourth anthology. Now, we return with another volume of yet more twists upon old favorites, an anthology full of chaos and pride and love. Each author has chosen a story to adapt and make their own. Some are well-known. Some are obscure. All are reimagined.

Without further ado, we present to you the *Just-Us League Anthology: Volume Five*. Please enjoy.

Sincerely,
The Just-Us League

Table of Contents

Vanity

Kristy Perkins

Arabella didn't mean to almost murder her stepdaughter. It just sort of…happened.

Queen Arabella was not a natural maternal figure, but she still knew that Neve's first ball needed to be something special. Even if the girl was too airheaded to realize it herself. Honestly, what girl was happier flitting around the garden than attending a ball?

Neve was happier, though. A shame, because she had features designed for display, a natural beauty in spite of the spell her mother supposedly recited over her at birth. "Skin white as snow, lips red as blood, hair black as ebony." Arabella thought it was hogwash, even if the chant did match Neve's features in a poetic way. Of course, it didn't rule out magic being involved in Neve's excessively innocent personality or that ridiculous talent with birds.

"Are you sure that gown will fit?" Neve asked dubiously, eyeballing the elaborate dress spread across her bed.

"Of course it will. We're going to make it fit." Arabella pulled a corset out of the dark depths of her stepdaughter's closet. "You've worn one of these before, right, dear?"

"No, not really. Whenever I tried it was always so uncomfortable I took it right off."

Arabella paused in her examination of the princess's meager cosmetics supplies. "In any case, in you go. We'll get it on you, give you some time to adjust, then finish the rest of it." Arabella, of course, was already prepared. That was what potions were for. Potions and maids and three hours of prep time.

Neve would have to make do with half an hour and Arabella. She put on the corset, fastened it, and situated it around her waist, then looked to her stepmother, clearly bewildered and a little uncomfortable. "Now what?"

"Now you hold on to that bedpost, and I'll cinch it for you." Arabella wrapped the laces around her fingers. "Ready?"

Arabella didn't wait for the go-ahead but gave a good strong pull, worked the laces tighter, briskly repeated the whole process a few times, then tied off the ribbons. Neve made tiny squeaking noises throughout. "Now move around a bit, to get used to the feel of it, then we'll get that dress on."

She gave the girl a moment to adjust and turned her attention to the nearby mirror. Earrings, straight. Hair, still perfectly curled. Nose, in need of a quick powder. Arabella just barely caught Neve's movements out of the corner of her eye.

The girl walked in a circle. Wavered a bit, put a hand out to steady herself, but missed and tumbled to the floor. The thump was loud enough that a guard dashed into the room, only to turn red at the sight of the princess in her undergarments. Arabella snorted and reapplied her lip paint.

Neve didn't get up. Which was strange, and it was also strange that she didn't move when Arabella walked over. She cautiously nudged Neve with the tip of one golden shoe. The girl was turning blue.

She gestured angrily at the guard. "Well? Help her!"

***

Neve was revived quite easily, of course, but she got twitchy after the Corset Incident. The girl seemed cheerful enough, but she trembled whenever Arabella got close, and even Neve's birds twittered and chirped angrily whenever they noticed the queen. The princess never appeared for meals anymore, and when she was forced to, she made use of the enormous tables and sat far, far away.

Arabella fell into a panic when Neve disappeared a month after the mishap. At first it didn't seem like something to fuss about, but when Arabella spotted one of the little wrens pecking forlornly at a well-stone, she knew something must have happened. As she swept through the castle, the servants scurried out of her way until she finally made it to her chambers. She locked the door and yanked away the cloth that concealed her secret weapon.

"Mirror, Mirror, on the wall, tell me what happened to my stepdaughter!"

The large golden mirror on the wall shuddered, and then a face that was something like a caricature mask of a smiling man appeared. "She left the palace is what's happened."

"Mirror!" Arabella took a deep breath. "This is not the time for semantics, you foolish piece of furniture. I need to know how to get her back before she gets hurt."

The mask raised a paint-like eyebrow. "Really? You've never shown much in the way of maternal urges."

Arabella's eyebrow twitched, but it was an accurate statement. King Delbert had married her for her beauty, and after he died, she was much too busy figuring out how to run a kingdom on her own to bother with a little girl. Neve was a human child, and those were generally pretty self-sufficient after a certain age. Arabella had assumed she would be okay.

"Just because I wasn't much of a mother, it doesn't mean I want anything bad to happen to her." She set down her crown on the dresser and picked up an elaborate, gold-bound book. "Now, tell me why Neve ran away, before I smash this through your face!"

It was no idle threat, and they both knew it.

"It was Lord Morfran! It was him! Don't hit me!"

Oh, no. Morfran. Duke of the Western Isles, Lord of the Hunt. Drunken idiot who wouldn't take no for an answer. Delbert hadn't exactly been the love of her life, but Morfran asking for Arabella's hand in marriage less than a week after the funeral was just tacky. She hated tacky.

Sitting there furiously lacquering her nails, she heard Mirror's tale of how the man had convinced that ridiculous girl that Queen Arabella wanted poor Neve dead, and Lord Morfran was very sorry but the queen had ordered him to kill the princess and she had best run away. Which of course was a lie because it would have to involve Arabella talking to the man long enough to give those orders.

Arabella fumed. "Why would she think that about me?"

"You have to admit, the corset incident probably didn't help her opinion of you all that much."

"I wasn't trying to hurt her! Every girl her age should be wearing a corset. I just…shouldn't have made the laces quite so tight. Anyway, the guards cut the ribbons and she was fine."

Mirror made a hrmm noise, and Arabella scowled.

"Well, now I have to tell the guards to go get her and straighten this whole ridiculous mess out." She cleared her throat. "How do I look?"

"You look lovely, your majesty. Almost as lovely as Princess Neve."

Arabella pursed her lips. Mirror certainly knew how to irritate her, but she could allow a few untrue insults since, after all, she had threatened to smash it.

****

The guards were muttering in the corner again.

"That went better than I expected."

"The queen's not a complete monster, you idiot." The other guard scowled.

"I know!" The first guard pulled a face. "But I was afraid she might start throwing things. Jacob says once she pitched a candelabra all the way down the promenade. And she did kick the princess when she fainted."

Arabella scowled as she bit down on her lettuce. They didn't realize the throne room was designed as a whispering gallery, which meant she heard every word. It was the only reason she consented to eat in such a public setting. She dabbed at her mouth with the napkin after every bite.

The officer reporting looked like he thought she might start chomping down on his head or something of that nature. "So you see, Your Majesty, there was nothing to be done. After she clubbed Sir Andrew, she ran, and we were unable to catch her with all the brambles in the way."

Well, that was troubling. Arabella chewed viciously at her salad, using the otherwise wasted time to think. If they admitted to the brambles, they must have given up very easily. Which meant they didn't want to bring back Neve. Which meant they might just believe the rumors about Arabella's supposed assassination attempt.

One of the guards fidgeted. The officers at least pretended like they weren't unnerved by the pause.

Stupid salad. Stupid diet. Arabella swallowed. "Where. Is. The princess. Now?"

"We believe she's taken refuge in the Southern Forest. Probably near the mountains, but we cannot be sure of that."

Arabella jumped in her seat. The Southern Forest encompassed the lower ranges of the Vasting Peaks, which were the particular home of… "The dwarves!" She gasped, and then hoped that no one heard her.

Arabella wasn't always the most careful person when it came to interpersonal relationships, so she had left a fair few offended and jealous behind her. Too much to accomplish, no time to soothe egos. But the dwarves, that was a mistake, and she acknowledged it and the fact that they hated her now.

She hurled her water goblet as hard as she could. The water splattered on the floor, and the goblet clattered and rolled along the paving stones until it clanked against the far wall. One of the chatty guards whimpered.

It was into this tense scene that Prince Arthur emerged. Not to be confused with the Arthur who ran Camelot and rambled on about equality and brotherhood, Prince Arthur was Neve's fiancé. Arabella didn't pay much attention to it. At least the girl was happy about something that wasn't birds or scrub brushes. Arthur was a competent enough royal, but he had a bad habit of getting exceedingly lost. His father had expended small fortunes in getting the young man out of troll dungeons and dragon lairs, and finally had settled on teaching Arthur to be tough. He still got lost; he just fought his own way out of situations.

Right now, though, he wasn't lost, even if he probably took a wrong turn on his way to the throne room. "Where is Neve? What have you done to her?" For someone with leaves in his hair, he sounded awfully threatening.

Why did everyone seem to think Arabella did something? Tempting as it was to let Neve stay out there since it was clearly what she wanted, the people were starting to question Arabella's capabilities as a mother, and from there it was only a few steps toward questioning her capabilities as queen. It was especially dangerous since she was only queen in the first place by virtue of marrying Delbert. The soldiers clearly couldn't keep up with the girl, and it was doubtful that Arthur over there would be able to find his love. Arabella was going to have to manage this herself. Which she could do, because she was powerful, in control, and the fairest of them all.

She stood up to her full regal height. "Princess Neve is still missing. My guards have searched everywhere, but all they know is that she's in the Southern Forest. Prince Arthur, I beg you, find my stepdaughter and bring her home." She swept out of the room before anyone could question the gleam in her eye. That would keep him out of the way for a good long while.

***

Arabella knew exactly where the dwarves lived. The problem was, they also knew what she looked like, so it would take a bit of preparation before she could show up and whisk Neve away. She absolutely had to snatch the girl up before anyone else filled her head with ridiculous notions of filicide. There was no guarantee that Neve would listen, so it was best to just grab her and explain later.

Mirror complained about being moved down to what Delbert had always referred to as Arabella's dungeon. But there was only the one raven skull, and so what if Arabella preferred to be underground? It wasn't as if she'd ever tortured anyone to death down there. It took her a good week to create all the required potions and she needed the company. By the end of it, she had horridly orange fingers and she'd nearly smashed Mirror twice, but it was worth it.

A drop of purple potion would change her face and body to that of a wrinkly old hag when the time came; the idea of which nauseated Arabella to no end but there was no helping it. A quick trip to the servant laundry netted her some garb appropriate to an aged peddler of dainty hair things. Arabella slipped out the kitchen door. Hurtful as it was, very few people would probably notice her disappearance until it was time for the weekly meeting with the court advisors. Her habitual beauty retreats were common knowledge.

After walking for a day and complaining the entire time to whatever woodland creature would listen about blisters, Arabella made it to her destination. And sure enough, like she'd suspected, her escapee stepdaughter was right there with the seven dwarves, living in their tidy little cottage. Just as Arabella took up a hiding spot in the bushes, Neve appeared in the door with an armful of laundry.

There were a lot of dwarves in the Vasting Peaks, but most of them stayed under the mountains. Of those few that ventured outside of their safe delves, most stayed well away from humans. There were, however, seven brothers who hadn't entirely eschewed the company of taller beings. They'd paid for it, though, when Arabella…

Never mind that. The important thing was she'd found the girl and she could fix the mess if only she could get Neve back to the dungeon and explain things before someone else got the wrong impression. And if the only way to get Neve back was by tricking and drugging her, then so be it.

Lord Morfran stepped out of a little tent right next to the cottage. The popping noise his spine made when he stood up properly was something even Arabella could hear.

"Be careful, dear girl," he said, putting an overly familiar hand on Neve's arm. Not offering to take any of the laundry from her, though. "The queen is as intelligent as she is evil and treacherous. You might be far from home, but you are not entirely out of her reach. I would not be surprised if she had some way to strike at you, even here."

Arabella was torn between rage and bemusement. On the one hand, Lord Morfran was a philanderer. On the other hand, Neve could barely be attentive when she was trying, and, by the way her gaze followed the butterfly flitting past, she wasn't even making that much of an effort.

Morfran trailed off and, with an oddly menacing look, stalked away to his horse and rode away. Arabella fell back a ways and prepared her plan.

In ten minutes, the newly disguised queen walked into the cottage clearing. Arabella had transformed herself into a blotchy peasant stain on the cheerful meadow, and the stump-stump-stump of her walking cane scared away the birds. Neve bounded over straight away and by the twitch of her arms had to restrain herself from giving an apparent stranger a hug. Naive, even for her. The girl must have been starved for company.

"Welcome! Oh, it's so nice to have a visitor. What brings you to the Dwarf Cottage?"

Arabella sighed. So innocent. "I'm but a weary peddler. Might I spend a moment by your fire and rest my poor aching feet?"

Neve beamed, the brilliant reflection of her teeth nearly as blinding as her usual dazzling skin. "Of course! Would you like some tea? Or maybe a scone? I baked them myself."

Arabella let the girl lead her in, subtly measuring Neve's muscle mass as she went. The princess had put on a bit of healthy weight, and Arabella fretted that her carefully proportioned sleeping potion might not be strong enough. She went through the numbers in her head as Neve fussed over her and generally made much of nothing. Her plan was still going to work.

The homely wooden cottage hadn't changed much since Arabella had seen it last. There was a long, low table with eight chairs arranged around it. The kitchen pump stirred occasionally in the breeze from the window, giving off a squeak. A basket of potatoes sat by the fire. The stairs were covered in tread marks of long ground-in dirt.

About the only thing that was different was the bowl of flowers on the table.

The scone was delicious, which didn't quite make sense with Neve's usual attention span, but Arabella was hungry so she ignored that little point. "That was lovely, dear." She paused to cough. Elderly croak was hard on the vocal chords of the young. "You must let me give you a gift, to show my gratitude."

The girl blushed. "You're too kind."

Neve probably didn't even realize that people only used "you're too kind" to mean "tell me more about how amazing I am." Her humility was dumbfounding. Arabella hefted her peddler's basket and displayed the lovely items inside. All taken from Arabella's own dresser, and in wide variety in case anyone decided to look more closely at the basket.

"Oh, look at the ribbons! They're lovely. That red one is just the sort I've been looking for." Neve reached for an admittedly eye-catching crimson satin ribbon.

Arabella snatched it back. "No, no, no. Your kindness is worth far more than a ribbon. Please, take one of these combs. My finest work, you know."

After that the conversation turned into a rather tedious argument in which Neve demurred and insisted on taking something less valuable, and Arabella insisted she look at the combs. There was some tugging involved. Eventually, she resorted to pointing out the window and snatching away the ribbons entirely while Neve was distracted.

The girl finally noticed the right item. Her hand stretched out toward a slightly tarnished silver comb set with dull yellow topaz. Not one of Arabella's favorites, but the scrollwork was lovely, and Neve had always gravitated to that one when given the chance.

"Oh! This looks just like a comb that belonged to my mother. She died when I was a girl, and my father was always afraid I would lose her things so he kept them locked away until he gave them to my stepmother." Neve had tears budding in her eyes, but that perpetual smile was still in place. "She puts them to good use, though. My stepmother always looks lovely."

Arabella hadn't expected the surge of tears that came to her eyes. She'd never realized how much importance Neve had attached to those old things. Delbert gave them to her and she'd accepted without much fuss.

"It would look lovely on you, my dear," she said, not faking the tremble in her voice. "Here, let me help you put it in your hair." Arabella held out a hand.

It took a while, because she couldn't help but arrange Neve's lovely long dark locks into a pleasing hairstyle first. Even if the comb was a trick, it was no reason not to do it up properly. In case something happened. And because Arabella couldn't help it.

The girl waited patiently, chattering with Arabella and then with the birds when Arabella stayed silent. It was charming, adorable. Annoying when the birds kept landing on Neve's head and getting in the way. She had to settle for a half-up twist just to be done with it and, with deft fingers, stuck the comb in right at the top.

"It's beautiful!" Neve squealed.

With a sigh of longsuffering, Arabella handed her a mirror so she could actually see. The princess squealed again. "This is wonderful!"

Arabella cautiously patted the hairdo and then twisted the secret knob in the comb. The hidden needle jabbed into Neve's scalp. Just a pinprick was all that was needed. A little tiny opening to let the potion effects go straight to her bloodstream. The girl jerked her head around.

"What was that?" she asked, voice trembling.

"It must have been the comb. Sometimes the prongs are a little sharp. We'll just shift it around a little and position it so it feels more comfortable. Won't that be nice?"

Arabella's tone must have been just a bit too shrill, because for the first time in her life Neve did the sensible thing and backed away slowly, bumping into the low table behind her. "No, I can do it myself." She reached up and wriggled the comb around until Arabella could see the sharp point of the needle poking through the girl's hair.

One of the birds that had hovered nearby landed on Neve's shoulder, which made the girl sway a little. The flying pipsqueak jabbed itself into the needle point, almost like it wanted to be pricked. With a faint chirp, it slipped off and tumbled to the ground with an overly dramatic thump. The little thing even had its wings splayed out across the floor.

Neve cried out and leaned over to check on the birdie. "Oh! Sir Bumblebee! Are you all right?" She bumped her head on the table as she went.

Arabella rolled her eyes at the name but got cautiously to her feet and backed slowly toward the door. Neve was busy fussing over the unconscious goldfinch. In spite of her seeming density at times, she wasn't stupid. Nor was she literally dense, and as such she should have been knocked out well before that bird. It appeared Arabella had misjudged exactly how much sleeping potion would be needed.

Neve blinked at her. "Stepmother?" Arabella froze. The transformation couldn't have worn off already, could it? A glance down at her hands revealed disgustingly gnarled, age-spotted hands. How could she know?

And then Neve crumpled. Thank goodness for delayed reactions. But why the burst of recognition? Had she really known it was Arabella, or was it perhaps a brief hallucination?

Arabella picked Neve up and put her on the table. As an afterthought, she put the bird on the mantle. The girl's slender limbs were actually a bit of a challenge to arrange properly, but it wouldn't do for her to look a mess when they arrived. It was bad enough that she'd run away without making her look like she'd been mistreated on the way back.

When she was satisfied, Arabella fished around in her pockets for her escape plan. She was powerful and in control, the fairest of them all.

The door smashed open. "Stop! Get away from Princess Neve."

She flinched and looked over at where the seven dwarf brothers clustered in the doorway. Then she swore and swigged the contents of the tiny black bottle she was holding, grabbing blindly for her stepdaughter. A purple smoke surrounded her, and two sniffs and a sneeze later, she was back in her dungeon. Arabella dropped the bottle and fell into a coughing fit.

She took a moment to breathe and take a few drops of elixir to negate the old woman look. She was just starting to brush out her hair when she realized her mistake.

"By the blasted broken anvils!" Arabella hurled her hairbrush. It smashed against the far wall.

She had grabbed the table instead of Neve. Since she wasn't touching the girl, the potion didn't take her, and so after all that effort Arabella was right back where she started. It would take her at least three months to brew more getaway potion.

Drat. If only she hadn't panicked, this would all be over with. She'd have Neve, so she could convince the girl—and eventually the rest of the country—that she didn't want the princess dead. Murder was a terrible thing to be accused of, but kidnapping could be almost as bad, and that comb was infused in sleeping potion. Now she had to hope that Neve didn't remember a thing of it, and that no one realized what Arabella had tried to do.

She rested her head on her worktable with a sigh. That wasn't going to happen.

***

With her escape potion all used up, Arabella was

forced to make the subsequent treks to and from the cottage on foot, which thoroughly exhausted her tolerance for dirt and sweat. She meant to use the same disguise as before, trusting in Neve's inability to see through any kind of trick, but when she arrived back two days later, Lord Morfran had just finished setting up his little campsite within the clearing.

He looked handsome in his woodsman's tunic and rough leather gear, with his ax at his belt. If she'd seen him in this lighting before, she might have been tempted to accept his proposal. Just as well, then, because his personality more than soured the image, as did the bottle in his hand.

"Never you worry, my sweet princess," he bellowed at the cottage. "I'll make sure the evil queen gets nowhere near you. She won't harm you while I'm around."

Neve appeared, saying something about possibly being quieter. Arabella didn't get the exact details, because she was confounded by an unfortunate fact. Someone had actually cut off Neve's hair to get the comb out. Some thoughtful soul—probably Luke, since he was the only one of the dwarf brothers with any sense—had gone back and evened it up into something a bit more chic, but it still made Arabella stare because the comb had just been resting on the top of the hairstyle. They could have just slid it out, easy as pie. Honestly, those men.

Morfran bowed, almost low enough to be mocking. Neve brushed him aside to go about her work.

Now, Arabella had at least fourteen deadly poisons tucked away in various cabinets back home, but murdering a lord of the realm for irritating her would be somewhat uncouth. Not inappropriate, just impolite. Reminding herself of that was the only thing that kept her from dumping a whole bottle of nightshade extract in his wine sometimes. Of course, she'd never actually murder anyone, but sometimes it was fun to daydream.

At least the man's obvious goal, to marry Neve, was out of the question. The girl loved Arthur, and she had a nose for sniffing out terrible suitors. Arabella knew this mainly because she'd thrown every young man she could find at the rank of knight or higher at the princess. Every time, it would take a day or less for Neve to uncover whatever unsavory hobby the gentleman in question might have and then reject him and possibly find enough evidence for Arabella to have him arrested. She wasn't even doing it on purpose, as far as Arabella could tell. It was probably those birds of hers, poking their beaks into everything. There was no way Morfran's intentions would survive that kind of assistance, if he ever made his move.

Since murder was out of the question, even for Morfran, she would have to go back to the castle and come up with a different solution. Since she was a fan of simple plans, she decided she would just make an extra sleeping potion to dose Lord Morfran. Perhaps Neve would recognize her, but Arabella was confident she could overpower the girl and dose her anyway. She'd just have to find a different way.

She stepped on a twig, and half a dozen woodland animals bolted. Morfran's gaze snapped to the tree Arabella was behind, and he drew his sword. She didn't wait for him to arrive, but ran away at breakneck speed.

She waited until she was steady on her feet then stomped on home and brewed up something new. This one was the right approach. She could feel it. All those nobles with their wary sidelong looks could go eat nightshade.

Mirror was not as enthusiastic for her plan as she was. "You know she'll see right through you. Neve may be ridiculous, but she's still your stepdaughter, and she'll know it's you. And you've already used up your best disguise. Why not just let Arthur find her and take her away before more rumors spread?"

"Don't make me regret moving you down here,

Mirror," Arabella told it after the elixir was safely in its vial.

"Obviously you already regret moving me or you wouldn't have said that," it said. "Regardless, it's still a bad plan."

"It'll be fine."

Mirror sighed, as much as an oval reflective surface on the wall is capable of sighing. "Just remember that I did tell you. And before you ask, you'll look just as lovely as ever once the smoke clears and your eyes stop watering."

***

Arabella was sunburned and itchy and her stomach was swirling by the time she made it back to the little cottage in the woods. If only she hadn't eaten those berries before she left. Stupid diet. Stupid food poisoning. She couldn't even contemplate how she might look in a mirror. In any case, she was there, and it was time for her plan to go into action. She swigged a green potion.

Arabella was unnaturally beautiful when she glided into the clearing, even for her standards. When she tested the potion in the lab, Mirror had gasped. She glowed with a faint emerald light, and tiny leaves sprouted from her neck and hands. Lord Morfran drew his sword, but when he got a good look, he dropped it to the ground and fell to his knees.

"A dryad! Here to visit me, of all people," he murmured. "My mission is blessed."

Arabella swallowed her disdain and smiled as warmly as she could. "Accept this gift from the forest," she intoned.

She pulled the apples from her pocket and held the green one out for Morfran to take. He knocked over his wine bottle in his hurry to snatch it away. He gnawed at it hungrily, smiling maniacally at her through the juice that dribbled down his chin. She kept her smile frozen in place, despite her crawling skin.

The moments before he collapsed into unconsciousness were the longest seconds of her life. He sprawled in a heap of limbs and apple sludge that leaked from his drooling mouth. Reluctantly, Arabella checked to make sure he was still breathing and there was nothing obstructing his airway.

Neve came out just as Arabella finished shoving Morfran to the side of the cottage, out of view. The girl gasped and darted back inside. Arabella smiled winningly. "Oh, dear girl, I'm here to help you."

It took a long time to convince Neve to let Arabella in the cottage, and it took even longer to persuade her to hold the luscious red apple.

"Why do I need to eat this apple?" Neve kept turning the apple over and over in her hands, and Arabella prayed that the potion residue wouldn't come off on her skin.

"You look positively starved, and I thought you might like an apple." Arabella huffed. "You seem like the sort of person who would enjoy one, and dryads love to give people fruit."

"Well, yes, but—" Neve cut herself off. "I'm sorry. My stepmother has been hunting me, and everyone keeps telling me to be careful. I'm not normally so mistrustful." She stopped shifting the apple. "I don't like not trusting people. Thank you for your generous gift."

And she chomped down. Spent a few moments blinking rapidly and then grabbed at her throat and slid to the ground gracefully. Arabella waited for Neve's eyes to close before getting to work.

Something was wrong.

Neve wasn't breathing, and that wasn't right, because it was just a simple sleeping potion and it wasn't supposed to do that. But what if Arabella had perhaps somehow accidentally done something? She'd gotten tired, impatient. What if she had, without realizing it, made something else?

Had she mixed up the valerian with white snakeroot? Was the dosage wrong? What had she done?

The princess still wasn't breathing.

What could she do? What could Arabella do to stop this from happening? She had no ideas, no way to know what kind of poison she'd created. Even if she had a way to make an antidote, it might not be the right one.

Arabella fell to her stepdaughter's side, trying to find a heartbeat. She felt Neve's heartbeat slow to a standstill and finally stop. Thunder boomed, and the slow, even sounds of a heavy rainfall began.

The girl looked so lovely, lying there on the floor. So peaceful. And the cottage was undisturbed. No signs that anything whatsoever was wrong. Just the pristine body on the ground.

Dead. Not asleep, dead. The whole country would be out for Arabella's blood for sure. She choked on a sob. Neve would never be anything more than a simple princess, never change or learn the wisdom that could have made her a leader.

Arabella stumbled out of the cottage, her hands numb. Her muscles unresponsive to commands, merely instinct. Her gaze fell on Morfran, and her hands reached for the knife at her belt. The blade gleamed in the lightning that flashed. She stalked closer, raised the knife higher.

She nearly drove the knife straight through that treacherous fool's heart, but she held back at the last minute. Morfran hadn't been the one to kill Neve. Arabella had. All by her own arrogance.

The queen sobbed as she ran.

***

Arabella cried on and off the whole way home. The enormity of what she'd done would hit her at odd intervals.

The twitter of a bird, the flash of a bright red flower, and the guilt would come crashing down, sending her to her knees. She would gather herself, breathe, let go of the loss, and walk again, only to falter at the next flutter of a wing. The faster she moved, the more she could feel that she was almost outrunning Neve's death.

She stormed into the palace, not even caring whether the guards saw her. Let them see her grief. Let them understand that something horrible had happened. The dryad potion had worn off hours before, leaving only sunburn, scratches, and a face swollen from weeping.

She made her way straight to her dungeon and barely locked the door behind her before sinking to the ground and sobbing. Somehow, there were still more tears to be shed. Her mind drifted back to that moment by the cottage, and then back further still. Neve's life was such a vague sequence, and Arabella cursed herself for how little there was for her to remember.

What was she supposed to do now? No one liked her. Pretty soon she'd be overthrown, and then she'd be dead or in exile and her feet would get all calloused like Neve's. Poor Neve. Why did she run? Why did she have to die like that? She couldn't be gone. Arabella's mind moved in circles, from the loss of power to the loss of Neve, and then back to the loss of power because it was easier to scream over something selfish than something that mattered.

When she did stop weeping, it was mainly because her body had run out of expendable liquid and not because the flow of emotion was done. Arabella felt drained, like a broken bottle, unable to carry anything more than dregs. She choked down a calming potion and hoped that even if it was mild, it might soothe her spirit or at least tamp things down to the point where she could function again.

"Well, I take it things didn't go well."

Arabella scowled. Her eyes were sore and swollen, and it was hard to focus her vision. "Not now, Mirror." She sniffled. "Not ever, in fact. My hubris has killed my stepdaughter, and nothing will be right ever again." The verbal admission of what she'd done had a galvanizing effect on her soul. Time to clean up from her long run home, ready herself for the undoubtedly endless questions about Neve, and somehow find a way to move on.

If it was even possible.

She brushed out her hair, took out the tangles and brambles from her run. Next, she cleaned her hands. After that, she changed into a clean gown and set about unpacking the things she'd taken with her.

"I for one am glad you're back, your majesty. I've been entirely alone down here. Not even a servant to spy on in this dreary place." Mirror did his best to sigh. "I wish you would consider putting in a few tapestries. Or else relocating to the north tower. There are some lovely views."

"Silence!" she snapped. "Useless appliance." The prattle was unbearable. Mirror could be irritating at the best of times, and now it was simply...

The apple was in her knapsack. Neve's single bite mark was easily visible, and the potion had preserved the fruit perfectly. It hadn't even gone brown, the white of the apple flesh stark against the deep red skin. Red like blood.

How did it even end up there? What madness possessed Arabella that she picked up her own murder weapon and brought it home with her? Bile rose at the back of her throat, threatening to choke her.

"But on the bright side, once those scratches heal, you'll be the most beautiful woman in the land again." Mirror gasped, realizing the misstep.

Arabella saw red. She threw the apple with all the force she could muster.

It was supposed to hit the wall, but Arabella's aim had never been half as great as her strength. The apple slammed into Mirror's face, and as Arabella watched, horrified, the glass cracked and then shattered into a thousand pieces.

"No! Mirror!" She stumbled against her worktable. "No." Her voice faded, and she sank to the ground. No tears fell, because there were none left. She was exhausted and it felt like her heart was being torn from her chest. Mirror's destruction was a final weight, and Arabella sank to her knees. She had nothing left but the pain of failure and loss.

***

"What do you mean, Prince Arthur's getting married?" Arabella demanded, fingernails digging into the armrests of her throne. Her temper had not gotten any better in the month since Neve had died. At least her figure was flawless, since her beauty regimen was all she had left and the temptation to eat anything beyond her diet was gone.

The guard stood tall. "She's supposed to be even more beautiful than you, Your Majesty."

Well, that was just a rude thing to say. Arabella hurled everything she had at hand. "That selfish." Her scepter. "Ungrateful." The footstool. "Boy!" A plate of strawberries. "How can he even think about getting married?" The napkin. "His fiancée isn't even cold in the ground yet!" Her crown hit the wall hard enough to knock a gemstone loose. The guards backed away slowly.

Well, she would just have to fix that.

Telling someone about a wedding two days before it happens is generally a sign that they are not really wanted in attendance. Naturally, Arabella set out immediately, only taking the time to put on a black gown that wouldn't show travel dirt once she arrived. The coachman had fled, so she drove the horses herself.

Arthur's palace was a gloriously boring white edifice decorated by an excess of flowers on poles. Arabella knocked over a lot of those poles as she stalked through the palace. Most of the servants scurried out of her way, except for a few who brandished serviettes like blades. Let them scowl. She knew her own true crimes.

Arabella burst into the wedding, shoving aside the massive doors to the banquet hall like they were nothing in the face of her wrath. Knocked over a few guards, too. Which was just as well, because she didn't technically have an invitation.

The room was crowded with royals and nobles and all other sorts of people besides. The grand room was thick with the smell of nature, courtesy of the plethora of flowers covering nearly every surface. A grandiose fanfare died in cacophony, and a few of the ladies closest to Arabella's entrance screamed in terror. One gentleman fainted clean away, and nobody had the presence of mind to catch him.

A path was cleared down the middle of the crowd, and Arabella had arrived just after the ceremony was completed. Arthur and his new bride stood at the other end of the room, clinging to each other in sickening affection. A startled priest backed slowly away from the duo. Arabella stalked forward. By the time she was halfway to the happy couple, a few people had started screaming in terror.

Arabella observed all this, but she didn't care. "Arthur, how dare you disgrace Neve's memory? It's despicable! I thought you were more honorable than that."

In the middle of all the shouting, it occurred to her that barging in wearing a black gown probably made her look like the bad guy. Oh, well. Time to own it. If being the villain they always assumed she was would give Neve some small justice, then so be it.

She glowered at the person usurping a place meant for a much better young woman. "I promise if you go through with this I'll—"

The lady who stood next to Arthur was very familiar.

Short black hair, pale white skin, lips painted with an exquisite red color. Her usual vacant look was gone, though, which accounted for why Arabella didn't recognize Neve in an instant.

Before anyone could stop her, Arabella had swept Neve into a gigantic hug. It wasn't until Arthur pushed her away that she realized something might be wrong and that Neve was squirming to be released. She cleared her throat and took a few steps back. Neve moved back likewise until her new husband's arms were wrapped around her safely.

"How are you alive?" Arabella asked, wringing her hands. "I checked, and I didn't…"

"The apple lodged in her throat," Prince Arthur said, a bit more coldly than necessary. "When I kissed her farewell, the motion jostled her enough to dislodge it, and she could breathe again."

"Of course! And with it caught in her throat the sleeping potion would have metabolized much slower, so it would have kept her in a kind of stasis that would have preserved her life until the apple could be knocked loose, thus allowing her to breathe and wake up!" Arabella did a kind of skip-dance right there. Then she frowned. "You mean you actually managed to find her?" Arabella gaped. "I didn't think you could manage it."

Arthur looked a little hurt, but he recovered himself with the help of a pinch from his new wife. "I may have spent a while wandering around the forest, yes, and that bit with the dragon was my business entirely, but I found my love just in time." He kissed the top of her head.

After that, no one seemed to know what to do, exactly. There was a lot of milling around, a lot of guards gathering at the edges of the room, but no one had arrested Arabella yet and no one was screaming for her summary execution, so that was a positive. She felt somewhat left out, actually. No one had bothered to tell her that her own stepdaughter was alive and getting married. It hurt.

A ripple of murmurs caught Arabella's ear. She caught one hateful look and then another. The circle of people around her wavered and flickered, caught between curiosity and loathing.

Arabella didn't flinch. Her lip paint was perfect, and even though her hairdo was unraveling a little, she still looked amazing. She was powerful and in control and they couldn't touch her. She was the fairest of them all. It didn't matter if it was true or not, just so long as it remained her shield.

When the guards clenched their weapons tighter, she started to think maybe she should have made an escape plan.

It was Lord Morfran, of all people, who chose to break the circle and approach her. He staggered up, getting close enough she could smell the stink of his breath. "My Queen! I didn't think you would come today. As always, you are a vision of loveliness."

Arabella raised an eyebrow at him. After all his lies, he thought he could still ingratiate himself to her? She frowned. The longing look in his eyes was a familiar one. He'd worn it at Delbert's funeral. It seemed just as inappropriate now as it did then.

"Oh, my Queen, I can wait no longer. Marry me, Arabella!" Somehow, Morfran managed to go down to one knee without toppling altogether. There was a wine stain around his mouth. "Marry me, and we'll rule the kingdom together." The wedding guests went still.

Not this again. Arabella cleared her throat. "Lord Morfran, I've only ever been a regent. The rule of the kingdom falls to Neve, now that she's married and settled. I will never be a queen while she's alive." She wanted to turn down the proposal outright, but it seemed more important to make it clear about the line of succession first.

"Oh. I'll kill her, of course." He took a swig from the wine bottle he carried and then leaned in close like he was trying to be subtle. His voice still carried around the room. "All I ever wanted was for you to be free of the burden of motherhood. Should I put her heart in a box as a memento? No, you're much too gentle. You never understood when I hinted for you to make the girl disappear."

What? What was he saying? Was he...? "That—"

"I tried so hard. Got her to trust me, lured her to the forest, but then the dwarves protected her and I could never do anything and get away with it. Sorry." The idiot actually looked contrite. "I know that was inconvenient, everyone thinking you were a murderer. You would never hurt anyone, my sweet! You couldn't even poison her. Spent all those hours making sleeping potions. But you were the only one she really believed could do it."

Neve gasped. Arabella didn't look, because she didn't want it to hurt any worse. Neve, sweet innocent little Neve, had truly believed Arabella would hurt her.

"So, when shall we marry?"

The sheer arrogance. The dumbfounding, pretentious, egotistical narcissism of the man was enough to freeze Arabella with shock. It didn't last very long. He had the drunken audacity to smile at her.

Then she balled her hand into a fist and punched him hard enough he flew backward a few yards, landing with a squeaky thump on his backside. His cape was wrinkled, and a thick flow of blood came out of his nose. Morfran staggered to his feet, fumbled for the ornamental saber at his belt.

Arabella stalked across the floor. "You horrible excuse for a human being, how dare you threaten her? Did you think I would be grateful to you, framing me for murder? For leaving that death on my hands? Did you think I would be stupid enough to wed someone who would kill an innocent girl? Did you?" she screamed.

When his fingers finally found purchase on his sword hilt, she punched him again. The insufferable man fell to the ground, blinked dazedly for a few seconds, and then fell unconscious.

When she came to her senses, Arabella was isolated next to Morfran's body. All but one person had backed away. Neve handed her a handkerchief to clean away the blood from her knuckles. What a clever girl. Always thinking of the little details like that.

Once she felt presentable again, Arabella curtsied deeply. "My dear Neve, I hope you have a wonderful wedding, and I beseech you to forgive me for my interruption."

Neve, impossibly kind Neve, reached out and took Arabella's hand, squeezing it warmly. "Of course, Your Majesty. It is already granted."

***

Of course, even if Neve was safe and sound, Arabella's reputation was somewhere south of an underworld latrine, so one dark night, she packed up all her favorite things and slipped out the kitchen door before the angry mob could find her. Not a single potion went with her. She didn't regret leaving, just like she didn't regret marrying Delbert in the first place. But it was time to go home.

Before she left, she put a packet just outside Neve's room. Inside was the queen's crown, and all the combs Arabella could find that once belonged to the girl's mother. If only she'd realized sooner how much they all meant to the poor girl. They were just combs to her. Delbert had bought her dozens of new ones that she'd used far more frequently. Neve would have put them to much better use. Now she would have the chance. She'd have a time of it learning how to run the kingdom, but it was her place and not Arabella's at all, and they both knew that now.

Now Arabella needed to go to her destination, and

her footsteps lagged with each passing mile. What would the dwarves think of her?

The cottage was dark on the outside when she finally arrived one evening. Part of her wished she was still taking her regime of potions, but the larger part knew that it wouldn't make any difference.

Before she could lose her nerve, Arabella knocked on the door, hard enough it echoed, and the birds fluttered away.

It was the youngest, Erik, who yanked the door open, his shirt on backward as usual. He gasped and slammed it in her face. There was a lot of chatter, a lot of yelling and banging and stumping around on thick boots before the door swung open again, and they all spilled out. All seven in a row.

"You've got some nerve coming back, after all you did." It was Nash who said that, the oldest of the brothers. Arms crossed over his beard, eyes dark and scowling.

"It's not nerve. I just know that this is where I belong, now Delbert is gone." She'd rehearsed that line the whole way. It was all she could come up with to say that made any sense at all. "I'm not going to apologize for wanting what I did. I was the most beautiful." She stuck her chin out. "I still am."

Luke looked her up and down through his glasses, finally looking her in the eye with an unreadable expression. "You stopped taking it. The potion."

"I didn't need to be tall anymore. I could just be…" She sighed and looked at the ground. The vanity that had always sustained her was fading rapidly.

"You could be our sister again." Somer yawned when he said it, but he always stayed up too late reading, the sleepyhead.

"Yes, well, I never stopped being that." Arabella flushed red. Her hands had clenched into fists, and she forced herself to relax.

Nash wrapped her in a hug. Then Erik, Luke, Felix, Somer, Enos, and finally shy little Tanton curled around the outside of the great hug lump. All seven of her brothers, all together at last. It was wonderful. How did she ever give this up?

Felix beamed at her. "You look as lovely as ever, Arabella. Those infernal potions haven't made one lick of difference. It's wonderful to see."

Enos sneezed. "It is wonderful!"

"And I can still out-mine any of you," Arabella said primly.

"Still freakishly strong, eh?" Nash grumbled. "Well, that'll be useful when it comes time to take the gold to market."

"I'm not—" Arabella cut herself off and huffed. That was Nash. The grumpy one, who always made everything pessimistic.

"I'm glad you're home," Erik said with his dopey little smile.

"There is one other thing." Arabella reached into her pack and pulled out a cloth bundle. She unrolled it on the table to reveal Mirror's remains. "I didn't shatter it. Well, I did shatter it, but not until a few weeks ago, and I feel terrible about that, but you were going to melt Mirror down and that was horrid and I'm not sorry I stole him. But in any case, he's my only friend, and I'd like it if you would repair him."

Her brothers looked at each other and did a lot of whispering the way they always did when they planned to gang up on her.

"We'll do it," Felix chirped. "But you'll have to do all the cooking and cleaning until he's done. As a payment, you know."

Arabella tried to scowl, to hide the smile that was creeping up on her. They knew too well that she hated housework, but she knew them, and even if it was "payment" for Mirror, they'd end up doing it for her anyway like they always did. She was an alchemist, not a housekeeper.

"And when it starts chattering, you have to put up with it," Nash added.

Arabella nodded, heart and eyes full. They wrapped her in another hug.

"You're not going to throw a cauldron at my head again, are you?"

"That was one time, Erik! One time!"

The Measure of a Princess

Rebecca Mikkelson

"Father, I do not wish to go." Adelena crossed her arms over her chest, the blue and gold brocade wrinkling under the new pressure. A single brow arched high with her refusal.

With puckered lips the King of Calaphine leaned back in his plush chair. The dancing light from the fire brought a warm tone to his cheeks, making him look healthier than he had in months. His white-speckled brows rose a fraction of an inch. "You do not have a choice, Adelena. It is my command that you go. The King of Magonia has sent word to all the kingdoms in Saleres that his son has agreed to wed, but only to a princess of the highest quality. You are one such princess."

Adelena was able to resist the urge to roll her eyes because of her governess's teachings. She sank onto the stool next to her father's chair, heavy silk skirts pooling over her feet as she gripped his arm with her well-manicured hands. "Surely, Father, you do not want me to marry a man who calls for us like chattel? 'A princess of the highest quality'—it is an insult! Perhaps he should put forth higher quality for *me* to judge. My sweet sister should be thankful she is not old enough to be married."

The King closed his eyes, gripped the curved armrests with bony fingers, and took the time to inhale slowly. "I curse the day your mother made you so high-minded."

Grinning, Adelena kissed his whiskered cheek. It was something he said often, as she frequently disagreed with him. "You do not. Elsewise your kingdom would fall to fools."

"Will you not go, if only to please your dear father, Adelena?"

"And what of my charges?" Adelena narrowed her eyes. "What will happen to them if I am not here to see to their health?"

"Someone else can take care of them, Adelena." He looked toward the window, heaviness pushing his shoulders down. "I know you want to continue your mother's work, but you will have to let other people help you eventually. You must marry and produce heirs for your husband and your kingdom. You will only be regent for so long before your brother comes of age and you will need strong allies. Allies that marriage can bring that will help you keep Calaphine from being taken from you before your brother ascends the throne."

"Father—"

He held up his hand, the bags under his eyes seeming to deepen before he spoke again. "I will not be around forever, Adelena, and there has never been a female regent before. My advisors were not happy when I appointed you the first."

"It will never come to my being regent. You will outlive us all on stubbornness alone." Looking at his sunken face, Adelena's resolve melted. "I will go on the condition that you make me a promise first."

"And what would you have of me?"

"I would like your word that if Prince Anders chooses me for his bride that I may refuse him if I find him to be lacking in substance and virtue."

After a long moment, he nodded. "I will make you this promise."

***

Adelena tossed a red gown made especially for the event on the bed with a growl. It sighed as it slid from the bed, the heavy silk billowing as air rushed from the skirts.

Eleanor rushed forward, picking up the dress before it could wrinkle. "My Lady, is there something weighing on you? I've never seen you in such a foul mood."

"I have just put Lady Karyn in the position to care for my charges."

"What is wrong with Lady Karyn? I have heard she is quite skilled."

Rolling her eyes, Adelena grabbed another dress to pack. "She is, and she was prompt to tell me how much better she would be at caring for them, the insipid little witch."

"My Lady!" Eleanor's eyes widened, her mouth hanging slightly open.

Adelena had the grace to look chagrined, her eyes lowering. "That was unkind of me, I know. She just sets my blood to boiling."

"I believe this trip already has you ready to assail anyone who crosses you, my Lady," Eleanor excused. "I know that you do not wish to go."

"Not in the least." Adelena pursed her lips. "I am sure you have heard by now exactly how we were summoned."

"I did. It was tastelessly done."

Adelena threw a shoe in her traveling trunk. It plopped with barely a sound on one of the dresses that nearly filled the trunk with its accompanying petticoats. "I should be the one testing to see if he is worthy of me, not the other way around."

Eleanor calmly folded a petticoat. "You should."

"I should," Adelena agreed. "Will you help me?"

Eleanor blanched. "Me? How could I help? I am

only a lady's maid."

Adelena slowly examined Eleanor. Her shoulders were slim like her own, they shared the same blue eyes, and she had her sister's petite nose. "You have the same name as my sister, and you have the look about you that you could be one of my kin. We could say that you *are* my sister and Calaphine is putting forward two brides instead of one. You could help by being more appealing than myself so I can see this Prince Anders's behavior unhindered."

"And what if His Highness chooses me?"

Adelena smiled, her eyes crinkling and a single brow quirked. "Does this mean you will pose as my sister?"

"Yes," Eleanor said after a long pause, "but the question still stands."

"We don't know if he will choose either one of us. We will cross that bridge when we come to it," Adelena said with a wave of her hand. "Now what shall we test?"

Eleanor closed one of the full traveling trunks. "You can only search for so much in a short period of time."

Nodding, Adelena said, "I will test him three times only, then. It should be what I feel is most important in not only a husband but a king." Adelena chewed on her lower lip until it started to hurt. "I should think it will be his generosity, his courtesy, and his respect for a woman's honor."

Closing another trunk, Eleanor said, "All good qualities to have, my Lady."

"Indeed, they are." Adelena sighed, looking around the room. Two tapestries hung on her stone walls depicting the wonders of Calaphine. One showed the local fauna frolicking in the meadows spring brought, and the other depicted the harsh winters they faced yearly. Some would even last for up to six months if they had an unusually hot summer. She didn't mind the longer winter—she rather enjoyed the cold weather forcing everyone close to the fires where they would tell stories of their adventures.

She tried to commit as much detail to memory in case she did not return. "Pack my finer gowns for yourself, Eleanor, if you please. I want Prince Anders to have to see one of us finely dressed and one of us adequate."

***

Adelena and Eleanor arrived at the royal palace in Magonia after four long days of travel. Their hosts, Prince Anders and King Eckland, waited on the steps of the palace. Once a footman opened the carriage door, Adelena stepped out with his help. The carriage had been well-sealed to keep the cool air that their Winter's Breath charm produced. She'd offer one to the royal family, but it would be useless as their palace had no windows to keep the cool air in. Adelena let out a strangled noise when the heat hit her. She wore a plum silk dress with black buttons up to her collar—a choice in wardrobe she now regretted. Sweat already pooled at her neck.

Her drab clothing had the effect she wanted, though; Adelena saw Prince Anders's face transform from a pleasant smile—well-practiced with dignitaries, she assumed—to a bland expression with no upturn of his mouth whatsoever at the sight of her, to a dimpled grin when Eleanor came into view. Her blue jewel-toned gown shined in the light. The crystals sewn into her bodice and the diamonds around her neck sparkled, making her smile seem brighter.

Prince Anders raced forward and offered his hand, which Eleanor took. Her hand looked unearthly pale against his darker, tanned skin bronzed by the hot Magonian sun.

Adelena nearly scoffed. Her subdued appearance would most certainly work to her advantage. Now she only had to wait for the right opportunities—or create them—for her tests.

"You must be tired from your journey, my Lady." The prince spoke only to Eleanor as he led her toward the steps of the palace. "Allow me to escort you to your chambers."

Eleanor looked back at Adelena before answering the prince. "Yes, my sister and I are weary from the travel. Might I ask that we share chambers? We are not very often apart."

"Sister?" Prince Anders snapped his head in Adelena's direction. "My apologies, my Lady. I did not realize."

King Ecklan hobbled forward to escort Adelena, his girth jiggling with each heavy step. "My Lady, we bid you warmest welcome," he said as she dipped into a curtsy. He offered his hand to help her up. His hands were not nearly as dark as his son's, showing he had not the time for leisure out of doors.

Adelena took it, a smile dancing on her lips. "Thank you, Your Grace. The kingdom of Calaphine was pleased to receive your invitation. We would be most honored for one of us to be chosen as the bride of Prince Anders."

"Calaphine?" King Ecklan's black brows furrowed. "I was unaware that King Edward had more than one daughter of marrying age."

Keeping the smile on her face, Adelena cursed herself for not thinking of an excuse for this discrepancy. "Princess Eleanor has reached her majority only this year, my Lord."

"I see, I see." He nodded, jowls bouncing, accepting her answer while he patted her hand.

They followed Prince Anders and Eleanor to the rooms that she and Adelena had been assigned.

"We will give you the rest of the evening to yourselves, Princess Eleanor, Princess Adelena. Should you need it, we have maids available to help you dress and make your time here more convenient. You can meet the other princesses in the morning." Prince Anders bowed over Eleanor's hand before leaving.

Once in their room Eleanor turned to Adelena, a wide smile on her face. "He seems quite charming, my Lady. I'm sure he'll prove worthy of you."

"We shall see."

***

Adelena and Eleanor met the other princesses in the morning and waited patiently for the herald to finish addressing them. The princesses would apparently have this day and the next to familiarize themselves with the palace grounds and recuperate from their journeys before the events started. Prince Anders would inform them following tomorrow night's feast of what the events would be so that they would be able to start on equal footing. Thankfully there were not many princesses—only eight of them—in Saleres as there were in their neighboring continent, Hadrial. It would make the process all the shorter.

When Adelena saw Prince Anders walking toward them, she glanced at Eleanor. Her face brightened, and a smile creeped up her cheeks. This might complicate things in the end. Adelena couldn't have Eleanor telling Prince Anders what she was doing because of doe-eyed infatuation.

Eleanor was the first to curtsy, Adelena slowly following suit. "Your Highness, it's wonderful to see you so soon in the day."

"Yes," Adelena agreed, "but I wonder if we might go for a walk in the city?"

"It would delight us greatly if you would escort us." Eleanor looked at him hopefully.

Prince Anders swept Eleanor's hand up in his, kissing her knuckles lightly. "It would be my pleasure, my Lady."

Adelena smiled. It was time for his first test. "We will meet you before the end of the hour in the courtyard." Linking arms with Eleanor, she led her away, whispering,

"We will be giving the prince his first test."

"How will we do that?" Eleanor furrowed her brow.

With a sly smile, Adelena answered, "You will see."

***

Prince Anders arrived in the courtyard clad in brown, supple leather. Adelena made considerable effort to hide her scowl. She had no idea how he could wear such heavy clothes in this abominable heat—she was slicked with sweat standing outside for all of ten minutes, even with her sleeveless gown. She had even requested, quite scandalously, that Eleanor remove her petticoats. Behind him stood four guardsmen in light blue uniforms, two sets on each side.

"Are the guards really necessary, Your Highness?" Adelena raised a brow. "Surely your city is safe enough for us to take a walk?"

"I would feel much better having them with us—for your safety as well as mine."

"That is very kind of you to worry for us, my Lord," Eleanor said before Adelena could say anything else. "Shall we go?"

Anders offered his arm to Eleanor. "We shall."

Once they entered the city, Adelena turned to Prince Anders. "Might we give alms to the poor while we are here?"

Prince Anders looked at her skeptically. "Surely you would not enjoy that."

"Oh, could we?" Eleanor leaned in to him, her eyes pleading. "Every city we go to we visit the poor and the sick. It helps ease Lady Adelena's ache of being away from her ill charges when we travel."

Prince Anders hesitated only a moment more. "If it would make you happy, my Lady."

He led them to the section of the city where the beggars resided. They lined the streets, some in threadbare clothes and others in tattered rags that hung from their thin frames. There were more than Adelena had ever seen in a single city before. The roads had nearly crumbled to dirt compared to the pristine sandstone roads near the palace. Almost everything in the city, including the palace, was made from the mineral so prominent in the country. The lower city was a bland beige, while the areas that housed the wealthier merchants grew more colorful until it reached the palace, which was made of blindingly white sandstone to repel some of the heat from the sun's rays.

"Do you not have sanctuaries for your poor?" Adelena looked at him incredulously.

Prince Anders moved away from one that came too close. His arms were only skin and bone, his skin darkened like a roasted hazelnut from sun exposure. He also seemed to be missing most of his teeth. Prince Anders noticeably flinched looking at the poor man. "Why would we? They're a scourge on our city."

Adelena thought the only scourge on the city was the nobility that did not care for their people—*all* of their people—simply because they did not like the way they looked. "Perhaps you and your guards should return to the castle if you do not feel comfortable here."

Glancing at Eleanor, he sighed softly. "We will remain here for your protection."

"Protection?" Eleanor turned to Prince Anders, her blue eyes wide. "Are they very dangerous here, then?"

Adelena waited to roll her eyes until her back was turned. "They are probably driven by hunger." She handed Eleanor a small coin purse. "Go to the bread seller we saw around the corner and tell him we will be purchasing all his wares."

"Are you sure?"

"Yes," Adelena snapped. "Now go, Eleanor."

While Prince Anders, Eleanor, and two guards went to the bread cart, Adelena pulled out another coin purse and began to hand them out. When they returned, Adelena saw the owner of the bread cart in tow, wheeling his cart toward her.

She went to stand by it before calling out to the people, "Please, come if you are hungry. We will feed you for as long as supplies last." Adelena broke the first loaf of bread in half and handed each to a different beggar, and Eleanor and Prince Anders followed suit.

"God bless you, my Lady," one of the homeless uttered while he gripped her hands over the bread.

Adelena smiled, bowing her head to him. "It is my pleasure, friend."

When he pulled his hands away, several stains had settled on Adelena's pale skin that she would rather not inquire what they were. She wiped her hands discreetly when she reached for another load from the vendor.

"Get off me!" Prince Anders yelled, pushing away one of the dirtier among them. Two of the guards pushed the homeless man farther back and stood in front of their prince to offer him more protection.

The man stumbled on the broken road, falling into the crowd. "M'sorry, milord!"

"Prince Anders!" Eleanor cried, putting a hand on his arm. "Are you all right?"

"Give that man a full loaf of bread," Adelena commanded the vendor. Her face pinched, she turned to Prince Anders. "I believe we have kept you too long from your duties, my Lord. I am sure the others are feeling your absence already."

"But—"

"We will be fine here, Prince Anders. Please, do not let us keep you any longer. We will be back before the evening bell."

Prince Anders looked toward Eleanor, but she kept her eyes to the ground. "I will leave three guards to protect and escort you back to the castle when you are finished here."

"That is very kind of you, my Lord. We are grateful for your thoughtfulness."

Once Prince Anders had left them, Eleanor turned to Adelena. "Why did you send him away, my Lady?"

"I would not risk the safety of these people, nor a riot with his behavior," Adelena whispered, glancing at the remaining guards. "Any man who will scorn another for his situation is not one I will tolerate."

"Does this mean that you have already made your decision?"

Adelena hesitated. "I still have two more tests for him and will not make my decision until all three are complete."

***

The next night, Prince Anders held a feast, filling the dining hall with roses of every color and petals scattered between each podium of flowers. Adelena raised a brow at the other princesses who gasped in wonder, impressed the roses were there in the "winter" season. Adelena's expression remained neutral; she had read everything she could about Magonia on her journey from their political and social history to their unbearably hot climate so different from Calaphine's perpetually cool one. Their summers, though hot to the Calaphinians, would still be a chilly spring to the Mangonians. She knew the Magonian royal family employed Growers from the Southern Isles to keep flowers at the castle year-round. Her father had considered them for their services once, but their price was too steep.

"Princess Eleanor," Prince Anders called, a toothy grin brightening his face. "You and your sister will sit next to me."

"Do not forget to be disagreeable toward me this evening," Adelena whispered as the prince came toward them.

Eleanor curtsied to him. "You honor us, Your Highness."

Prince Anders offered his arm to Eleanor, escorting her to her seat. Adelena trailed behind, counting the number of Princesses still left. Only seven remained, including herself and Eleanor. One had already been sent home, possibly for her appearance. Adelena ran through her knowledge of the nobility of Saleres. Princess Tanesha was the least attractive of all of them. She had the misfortune of having inbred parents, causing her face to be elongated to where she resembled a horse and her lower jaw jutted out just enough that Adelena noticed she continually pulled her lip up to cover her teeth. At that point, she wondered if it was worth keeping the bloodlines pure.

After only pulling the seat out for Eleanor, Prince Anders sat. Adelena twitched her mouth into a discreet scowl and reached for her wine. In her haste she tipped it over, the maroon liquid seeping into the white tablecloth. She stood quickly, her heavy wooden chair screaming against the floor.

"Be careful, Adelena, you will get us both sent home for making a fool of yourself."

Adelena's brows shot to her hairline, giving Eleanor a withering look. To her credit, she did not quail. "My apologies, *sister*. I was parched."

"Perhaps you can contain yourself next time. I daresay Prince Anders will have something to say about it, then."

Prince Anders, remaining silent through the whole ordeal, stood. His chair remained blessedly quiet when he moved. It must have been well padded. "Princess Eleanor, you would have to worry more about your unkindness than her clumsiness. Would you speak so brazenly if we had guests we meant to impress before negotiations, I wonder?" He retrieved the goblet, setting it right before he picked up one of the floral arrangements and moved it over the worst of the stain.

Eleanor cast her eyes down, a blush coming to her cheeks. "My apologies, sister."

At the raise of Prince Anders's hand, one of the servants came to refill Adelena's cup. "Thank you," she said to both the servant and the prince.

Smiling into her cup, Adelena was pleased to see that the Prince of Magonia had at least one redeeming quality she could hold on to: courtesy. If she was chosen and did accept him, she could exploit it until it bled into the rest of him.

The first course, a sweet fish, was set in front of them without delay. Adelena eagerly picked up her fork, cutting into the flaky white meat. The creamy sauce topping the fish spilled onto the plate, flooding the cavern left in the fork's wake.

"Careful not to overeat, Adelena," Eleanor warned, a smirk curving her lips. "You will never attract a husband if your waistline starts expanding."

Adelena paused, fork poised in front of her mouth. "I beg your pardon?"

"Your waistline, my dear. Tailor will need to let out your dresses soon."

"I think a woman who is sturdier will bear better—and more—heirs," Prince Anders said, looking between the two women. "What do you think, Princess Adelena?"

Setting her fork down, she answered, "I agree, Your Highness. Our grandmother was a sturdier woman—as you put it—and she bore fifteen children for our grandfather."

"Your point is well taken, sister," Eleanor mumbled.

"I should hope we do not hear more of this from you tonight, my Lady." Without waiting for confirmation, Prince Anders shoved a large forkful of fish into his mouth.

Adelena continued with her meal, smiling to herself.

***

When the evening meal was over, the two said their goodnights to the table and returned to their chambers. A warm breeze came through the open windows, billowing the diaphanous white drapes toward their beds. Adelena wondered if the things Eleanor said were things she had always wanted to say to her, but because of her station never could. She hoped not. Adelena would have to ask her and clear the air.

"Eleanor?"

"Yes, my Lady?"

"Did you mean what you were saying tonight?"

Shame clouded her face, color darkening her cheeks. "Of course not, my Lady. I was only doing as I was told: do what I can to test his courtesy."

Adelena inhaled deeply and let out a sigh, pressure releasing from her chest. "Thank you. I would hate to think that's the way you really felt about me."

"Of course not, my Lady!" Eleanor caught Adelena's hands up in hers. "I could never think that of you."

Squeezing them, Adelena let Eleanor's hands go. "Thank you."

***

The next morning, Prince Anders was resplendent in a red doublet, gold stitching scrolling up his sleeves, vines and leaves spreading into his chest. He smiled at each woman who entered the great hall, waiting until they were all seated before he spoke. "Your Highnesses, as much as I have enjoyed your company, it is time for you to prove to me that you are princesses of the highest quality and would serve not only me well, but Magonia and her people."

Murmurs erupted between the women. Adelena remained silent, knowing had her mouth opened, she would have brought shame to her father. She waited impatiently for him to explain himself while Eleanor stared at the prince in rapt attention.

"Each of you will host a dinner, entertain the room, and display your grace," Prince Anders continued. "It will be explained further to each of you when the time comes for you to be host. We will go by order of arrival."

Adelena breathed a sigh of relief. She and Eleanor would be going last. "Make sure to watch carefully so we can see what *not* to do," she told her maid.

***

Five dinners passed and three of the princess had been sent home. The first for the inability to entertain the room; she had attempted to play pianoforte while they had after-dinner drinks, but was so poorly skilled that the piece sounded as though the hunting dogs had choked on a bone and hastily tried to evacuate it each time her fingers strayed from the keys they were supposed to be on. The second for not being able to make a menu without the help of someone else; she took full advantage of her position and forced the kitchen staff into making Prince Anders's favorite meal with the threat of that or no dinner. And the third for forcing the entire production onto the servants, staying in her room while the servants she brought with her scurried around planning the whole thing for her.

"Who should go first?" Eleanor asked.

Adelena picked up her tea and looked to Eleanor. "Do you know how to plan a dinner?"

After hesitating, Eleanor admitted that she did not.

Adelena took a sip before saying, "I will go first then, and you can see how it's done. Or we can ask Prince Anders to allow us to entertain together."

"That hardly seems fair! All the other princesses have had to plan and execute on their own. He would certainly not allow it."

Adelena shrugged. "The answer will always be no

until you ask the question. It's quite possible he will decline our request, but it would make it easier on you if we can."

"It would be." Eleanor sighed. "When should we ask?"

"We will seek out Prince Anders now to ask his permission and then we will go to the kitchens to visit the cook." Adelena set down her finely painted cup before she stood. "Come along, then. We have quite a bit to do today."

They journeyed outdoors to the small, flat plateau that was divided by a net. Prince Anders and another one of the Magonian royals played a game with a small white ball and long thin racquets where they hit it back and forth between them. Both men were drenched, their linen shirts clinging to them.

Adelena caught the eye of the other nobleman, and he flashed a charming smile. "Prince Anders," she called, lifting her hand only slightly higher than her shoulder. She did not want to seem overeager by extending her arm all the way.

Prince Anders turned toward them, wiped the sweat from his brow, and shielded his eyes from the sun. "Your Highnesses, what is it I may do for you?"

Moving closer so they would not need to shout, Adelena asked, "Prince Anders, might we beg a favor of you?"

"If it is within reason, I will grant it," he said, slightly out of breath.

"We were wondering if perhaps you would allow us to host a joint dinner, as we are from the same kingdom," Adelena asked sweetly, her head turned slightly to the side.

"I am afraid I cannot allow it, my Lady, in the interest of fairness to the other princesses that had to plan on their own."

Nodding, Adelena curtsied, and Eleanor followed suit. "Thank you, Your Highness. If you will excuse us, I have a dinner to plan."

He waved his hand dismissively. "Good day to you, Ladies."

"Come along, Eleanor." They made their way down to the castle kitchens, the hearths still blazing from the morning meal. Servants curtsied and bowed as they journeyed to the heart of the kitchens. "Where is your head cook?" Adelena asked one of the kitchen maids.

"She'll be the one with the blue apron, m'lady." She bobbed a quick curtsy before scurrying on her way.

A plump woman stood behind a wooden table, her blue apron dusted with flour, kneading dough until it bounced back. She looked up and nodded at Adelena and Eleanor. "Yer Highnesses. What can I do for ye?"

"I would like to discuss a menu for tonight's meal with you." Adelena smiled, making sure to keep her skirts away from the floating flour dust. "Might I ask what is in your stores?"

"We've everythin' ye can think of, Yer Highness."

"Everything?"

With a lift of her chin, Cook confirmed, "There isna a thing ye can think of we wouldna have, m'lady."

"I am pleased to hear that." Adelena smiled at Cook. "I do believe we will work quite well together."

A small smile graced the otherwise unpleasant face of Cook. "Aye, m'lady, we'll work well together. What will ye be wantin'?"

"Nothing at all like the previous. I would like to have a dinner much closer to that of my country. I would like roasted boar—made with garlic and rosemary butter; nothing else will do—and an au jus. A hearty potato soup— roast the potatoes first for better flavor—to start and smashed potatoes to be served with the boar as well. String beans for a side, asparagus roasted with garlic. To finish the meal, I would like bread pudding with three options of topping: butter and whiskey sauce, warm cream flavored with a small dash of nutmeg, and cream whipped until it is stiff."

Cook nodded along, scribbling on loose parchment as quickly as Adelena instructed her. "An' what kind o'wine d'ye want served with yer dinner?"

"A bold red, I think. Serve a dram of whiskey with dessert, but give the option for a sherry if they cannot handle the other."

"Verra good, m'lady." Cook put down her charcoal stick and nodded. "I dinna think we'll have any trouble, but I will send one o' my girls to find ye if there is."

Eleanor followed Adelena out of the kitchens. "My Lady, the bread pudding takes two days to make!"

She shrugged. "If it is not possible for mine, you can use it for your dinner tomorrow evening, but I did see that there were several loaves of bread that I doubt will be used before the evening meal."

"Where will we go next?"

"To the Growers. The table will need to be appropriately decorated."

They found the Growers behind the palace in a building solely dedicated to their craft. It was made of glass to let in as much light as possible so their blooms stayed warm and full of color. Dirt and grass gathered on the lower panes from the rain and frequent cutting.

Upon entering, they were blasted with hot, moist air that smelled prominently of dirt and slightly of mildew. Adelena scrunched her nose, lifting her tongue to touch her soft pallet, hoping to stop the smell from going any farther. It was not long before a Grower spotted them and approached. His fingers were stained green and dirt gathered under his nails. He wore pants made of soft brown cotton, an apron with several tools occupying the pockets, and an open cotton shirt that clung to his sweat-drenched arms and chest.

"Your Highnesses, welcome to the Growery. What is it we can do for you?" he asked with the soft lilt to his voice that all Southern Islanders had. All the Growers came from the Southern Isle, where everything was green and blooming year-round.

Adelena smiled a smile that reached her eyes. Her order would be rather extravagant compared to the others. "I would like to request an arrangement for the table tonight—several, actually."

"Do you know what you would like?"

Adelena hesitated. She had never used a Grower and did not know what they were capable of. "No."

"Come in further, then, and tell me if anything strikes your fancy."

He led them to the heart of the Growery where the flowers that were fully grown were gathered. There were flowers from every country represented in Salares. Nothing particularly struck Adelena as a must on the table. "How quickly can you grow the plants using your talents?"

"It depends on the flower—each one is different and has a different set of needs. What did you have in mind?"

"I would like to have fir branches, holly berries, and white and red cyclamen to surround just the boar, and summer foxglove native to Calaphine to surround the rest of the room."

"You…want us to grow a tree?" The Grower's brows endeavored to reach his hairline.

Adelena's cheeks darkened from more than the hot air when even Eleanor raised a brow in her direction. "If it is possible, yes."

He ran a hand through his dark, greasy hair as he thought. "It would take all of us, but I believe we could do it."

"Would it be in enough time to have before the table is set for the evening?"

"We will try very hard, my Lady."

"Could you just grow the branches to make it faster?"

After a long pause, the Grower said, "I am afraid not, Your Highness. You need the tree for the branches to grow on first."

Eleanor hid a laugh behind a cough, turning to look at some of the flowers.

"I should think that we will be in the way if we stay in here much longer. We will leave you to your work." Adelena grabbed Eleanor's hand, nearly dragging her from the greenhouse. Eleanor erupted into a fit of laughter once they had left, earning a glare from Adelena.

"You know he wanted to ask if you knew how trees grew, but he was too polite," Eleanor barely got out before gales of laughter made it impossible.

Adelena glared at her harder. "Mind your own manners, Eleanor."

She struggled to compose herself before she could respond with, "Yes, my Lady."

***

Adelena adjusted a spoon on the table, making sure the cutlery was perfectly aligned. She inhaled deeply, letting out a contented sigh. "Perfect."

One of the footmen stepped forward. "Will there be anything else you need, Your Highness?"

"No, thank you, everything looks wonderful."

The Growers were able to accomplish their task and fir branches rested under the platter the boar would be placed on. Red and white cyclamen alternated on the table while more summer flowers of blue and yellow foxglove were placed every five feet around the room.

Adelena returned to her chambers to change, her dress already laid out on her bed. One of the newer dresses made for her as soon as she agreed to travel to Magonia, it was red silk with gold stitching, displaying the wonders of Calaphine. The skirt held four large pines, the tips of the trees ending at her waist. Her cuffs held several different species of bird that looked like they were flying through the forest when she held her hands in front of her and continued up her sleeves. The shoulders held other fauna regularly seen in her kingdom: bears, wolves, and deer.

Sighing as the silk slid over her arms, Adelena adjusted the fit of the sleeves while Eleanor laced the bodice in the back. Once she'd finished, she sat for Eleanor to do her hair. It was a simple style of four braids pinned back—two started at her crown, the other two starting just above her ears—the rest of her hair simply remained curly. "Thank you, Eleanor. This looks beautiful."

Eleanor smiled. "Thank you, my Lady."

"Take some time for yourself and I'll meet you at dinner."

"Very good, my Lady." Eleanor curtsied quickly before leaving the room.

***

Adelena heard a giggle from the hall to her left as she walked toward the dining hall. Raising a brow, she peeked around the corner before quickly darting back. Eyes wide, she peeked around the corner again. Eleanor had her back against the wall, and Prince Anders stood closer to her than propriety called for, a lock of her hair twirled around his finger. Adelena darted past the corridor toward the dining hall.

She shook her head, wondering if she should go back and separate the two of them. It would do none of them any good if they decided to have a tumble in a dark corridor and had an accident they would both regret for years to come. That would certainly be interesting to explain to her father who had no idea of her plans. Adelena bit her lip, glancing behind her. She assured herself that they would soon tire of their clandestine meeting and make their way to the dining hall and began walking in that direction.

Music reached Adelena as she entered the corridor to the dining hall. She'd conscripted a minstrel from the city to entertain the guests because she could neither sing nor play any form of stringed instrument. Adelena doubted that Prince Anders would appreciate where her true talents lay, in politicking and talking back. Adelena stopped short of the door where a herald waited to announce her and any other guests. She cleared her throat and smoothed her skirts as she bided her time. Ten minutes passed before she started to tap her foot.

Perturbed, she glanced down the hallway. If they carried on kissing for much longer, Eleanor would not have a face left. Adelena stepped up to the doors. She could not wait for Prince Anders to escort her any longer; she was far past fashionably late. "Announce me, please. Princess Adelena of Calaphine, the host for the evening."

When the herald opened the door, she saw a crowd already gathered in front of the singer. Smiling, she knew she made the correct decision. "Your evening's host, Her Royal Highness Princess Adelena of Calaphine."

The music paused and the peerage of the room turned to her and curtsied or bowed, clapping as they had done for every other host. What had not been done for her, however, was Prince Anders escorting her into the room because he had been too preoccupied with another woman.

Since she'd left to change, the Growers had added more flowers around the room and wreaths of pine over the lintels and peppered them with the same red and white blooms that also adorned the table. Adelena inhaled deeply, closing her eyes blissfully. It smelled of home. If anything, she hoped that Prince Anders did not pick her so that she did not have to leave her home permanently. It had barely been two weeks and she could already feel the longing to return to Calaphine. It was too hot for her tastes in the southern country, and the air too humid. She desperately wanted to return to the cool, dry air of her homeland.

Prince Anders walked in behind her with Eleanor on his arm. "His Royal Highness, Prince Anders and Her Royal Highness, Princess Eleanor of Calaphine," the herald announced at the door.

Adelena's back stiffened at the sound of their names together, her mouth forming a thin line. He did not even have the courtesy to enter the room by himself, instead coming in with the woman he ignored her for.

The music paused, and the group turned to greet the heir to the throne with bows and curtsies.

Adelena bobbed a quick curtsy herself, bowing her head to keep the prince from seeing her irritation. "Welcome, Prince Anders."

"You should have waited for me to escort you in, my Lady," he said with the audacity to look hurt.

"My apologies, Your Highness, but I waited as long as I could after finding you otherwise occupied." She glanced quickly at Eleanor before lowering her eyes demurely.

Looking around to hide the blush on his cheeks, Prince Anders said, "This is a lovely room, Princess Adelena."

"Thank you. That is very kind, Your Highness." Dipping her head, she kept her lashes lowered demurely. "It is a taste of my home."

"It seems a lovely place."

"Oh, it is, Prince Anders," Eleanor gushed. "The most wonderful place."

"Perhaps I will see it one day."

"We would be delighted to host you." Adelena smiled. "Will you lead us to the table?"

"It would be my pleasure." Prince Anders offered his arm to Adelena and escorted them to the head of the table, one on each side of him. The rest of the room followed suit.

Footmen peeled themselves from the walls to pull out chairs, pushing them in as everyone sat. The music resumed with a gentler tune that would not disrupt the conversation.

"I am looking forward to this evening's meal." Prince Anders looked as excited as he sounded.

Promptly, the potato soup was ladled into their bowls. Adelena let out a low moan, leaning over her bowl to smell the rich garlic and meat. Cook had added bacon without needing to be told, making it even more appetizing.

"So, Prince Anders, what do you think a princess should be?" Adelena asked.

"She should be confident in her position, but demure. A delicate lady who will win the hearts of any dignitaries that come to negotiate policy. She should be gentle and kind and soft-spoken, and always ready with undeniable charm." Prince Anders spooned a bit of soup into his mouth. "And she should be sensitive to the slightest thing out of place."

"The slightest thing?" Adelena raised her brows, a smile playing on her lips. "Should we have the cook send up a bowl of peas to put under our beds?"

Before he could answer, the boar was brought to the table, stealing the attention with a bright red apple in its mouth.

***

One more princess had been sent home after Adelena's dinner for her poor behavior, drinking to excess until she fell asleep at the table. Only four remained and Adelena needed to give her final test. "Eleanor."

She pulled her attention from the book in hand. "Yes, my Lady?"

"Prince Anders seems to be quite fond of you."

"He does, my Lady."

Adelena watched as color spread across Eleanor's cheeks. "I have yet to test Prince Anders a third time."

"What will you test him on this time?"

"Perhaps his honor." Adelena shifted uncomfortably, looking away from her lady's maid.

Eleanor paused. "And how will you be doing that?"

"Well…" Adelena cleared her throat, color spreading down her neck. "I saw you the night of my dinner in a dark corridor with Prince Anders… I thought perhaps you could let him know you were hoping you would be selected because you were, um, well, looking forward to the wedding night."

"You want me to *seduce* him?" Shock flitted across Eleanor's face, her mouth dropping open and her eyes widening.

Silence settled between them. Adelena avoided eye contact with Eleanor, the back of her neck prickling. She did not feel good about asking Eleanor to do such a thing. "Yes, but you do not have to agree. This is far outside the realm of your duties."

After inhaling deeply, Eleanor's cheeks darkened further. "I will do it."

"You will?" Adelena snapped her eyes to Eleanor's. "You in no way need to go through with it. All I need to know is if he has any integrity and will respect your honor."

"I know, my Lady."

***

Eleanor's dinner went smoothly. Much smoother than Adelena's, to her annoyance. Perhaps it was because Eleanor was always on the service side of these that she had pulled her event off seamlessly. She catered to Prince Anders's whims, paying homage to Magonia with their comfort foods and decorating the hall with the roses that were frequently seen around the castle. Eleanor had even requested the Growers create a new breed of rose that was streaked with red, gold, and white to pay homage to

Calaphine. After the dinner had finished, Adelena watched Eleanor and Prince Anders sneak off together while the others were returning to their rooms.

Adelena did not wait for her to return.

The next morning, Adelena woke to the sound of her door opening. She groggily gazed in its direction, spotting Eleanor walking in with her hair tangled about her face. Her dress was rumpled and looked like it was laced closed with one hole off, giving her a lopsided appearance. "You were successful, I see."

Eleanor jumped, putting a hand to her chest. "My Lady, you scared me."

Sitting up, Adelena continued, "Was he amenable to the seduction?"

Eleanor's cheeks flamed red. "Very much so, my Lady."

"I see."

"What does this mean for Prince Anders?" Eleanor wrapped her arms around herself, not looking at Adelena.

"It means he has proven himself easily persuaded by a woman's wiles. What would that mean for me? Would I have to worry about the people of Magonia suffering because he wanted to please a mistress with lavish gifts, paid for by the royal coffers?" Adelena shook her head. "There are too many questions that won't have answers until the damage has already been done."

Inhaling deeply, Eleanor finally returned her gaze to Adelena. She looked somewhere between hopeful and distressed. "And what will happen if he chooses me this evening?"

After a long pause, Adelena said, "We will have to tell him you are my lady's maid. He cannot marry you thinking that he's marrying a daughter of King Edward and gaining a political alliance when he is not. It could dissolve relations if we do not tell him. If he still chooses to marry you knowing this information, then I am more than happy to give you my permission."

"But, my Lady, if he's unworthy of you, how are you happy that I should marry him?" Eleanor furrowed her brow. "Should you not be unwilling to grant your permission?"

"You seem to be quite smitten with him, and if you are not bothered by his faults—and you do not seem to be— then why should you not benefit from this experience? You would be a queen one day if he wanted you!" Adelena pulled the covers from herself, sitting up. "But we should not worry about that now. There is no sense in fretting over what we do not know will happen. Go and clean yourself up, and we will start the day."

"Yes, my Lady." Eleanor bobbed a quick curtsy before leaving for the washroom.

***

Adelena waited impatiently in the Great Hall with the two other remaining princesses and Eleanor. Prince Anders and King Eckland were very rudely tardy to their own announcement. After thirty minutes of waiting, the two finally entered the room. All of them curtsied deeply to the King, and the Prince, rising when he gave his leave.

"Your Highnesses, our apologies for keeping you waiting for so long." King Eckland sat on his throne, putting his chin in his hand. "After a long debate, Prince Anders has chosen his bride, and I have given my approval."

The princesses shifted uncomfortably on their feet, waiting to see who was chosen and who was to be rejected. A heavy silence hung over the room until Prince Anders spoke, "I have thought long and hard over, and I have chosen Princess Adelena of Calaphine."

Adelena's stomach sank and before she could stop herself, "Why?" slipped from her lips.

"*Why?*" Prince Anders's brow furrowed. "Because I

have found you the most worthy."

"Prince Anders, I do not think—"

"May I speak with you privately, Princess Adelena?" The prince was already walking toward her, his arm extended to usher her away from the others.

Adelena held up a hand to stay Eleanor and let Prince Anders lead her into the corridor. "Prince Anders, I cannot accept your decision," she said before the prince could say anything.

"I beg your pardon?"

"I cannot marry a man who would sleep with my sister and then choose another woman the very next day. It's abhorrent."

Anders let out a short laugh. "She too willingly gave up her virtue—what kind of wife would she be?"

She let out what sounded like a snort, rolling her eyes directly at him. "I have tested your own worthiness of *me* since I arrived here, and I cannot in good conscience marry a man I have seen behave so." Adelena had a hard set to her jaw as she glared down Prince Anders.

Raising a single brow, he asked, "And just how have you tested me and found me—the heir to the richest country in Salares—unworthy?"

"The only reason you are as rich as you are is because of the poor quality with which you treat your people! Do you think if you invested in the constituents of Magonia there would be so many of the poor you detest?"

Prince Anders leaned against the stone wall, crossing his arms over his chest, an amused expression settling on his face. "And was the only reason *you* gave alms to the poor of Magonia to test me? Would you have done it otherwise?"

"Perhaps, perhaps not, but I am not the one under scrutiny here."

"Are you not? Is that not your sole purpose for being here?"

Adelena's mouth hung open briefly before she

continued. "My next test you passed, when Eleanor berated me in your presence."

"Small mercies, I am sure." He shifted from the wall, beginning to pace in front of her. "And I assume there was another test after that?"

Her eyes followed him as she crossed her arms in front of her. "I saw your infatuation with Eleanor and bid her seduce you, to test your honor regarding women."

He stopped pacing, looking at her incredulously. It was the first time Prince Anders looked shocked. "You bid your own sister to bed me and *I* am the one who is unworthy?"

"She is not my true sister; I would never treat my sister so." Adelena glared at him again. "She is my lady's maid."

Prince Anders took two bounding steps to stand in front of her, his face inches away from Adelena's, anger darkening his eyes. "Even worse! You have lied to me since the moment you arrived and now you tell me that you willingly abused your power over your servant just to test me? You deliberately looked for and found fault in my person so that you would not have to marry me."

Adelena stepped back, her eyes wide. "I—"

He straightened, folding his arms over his chest. Prince Anders scowled at her, his lip nearly in a snarl. "I am happy that you have told me this, Princess Adelena. Truly, I am, otherwise I would have never seen you for the distasteful, pernicious woman you really are."

Adelena blinked several times. "I beg your pardon?"

"I happily accept your rejection, *Princess*," he said, spitting the word. "Very happily and I will pray that your father lives a long and happy life and your brother comes of age under his tutelage, because I assure you I will not come to your aid if you ever become regent of Calaphine."

She reached out to stop him. "Prince—"

He waved his hand dismissively, turning to the side

as if to leave. "You may go, Princess Adelena. Pack your things and leave with your lady's maid. I hope to never see you again, but if I do, I sincerely hope that you have improved upon yourself."

Adelena curtsied and quickly turned down the hall toward her chambers. Her cheeks flamed red with her embarrassment. Prince Anders was correct: she had abused her power over Eleanor to find the faults she wished to find in him. In her efforts to pass judgment on him, she had blinded herself to her own behavior and tarnished her character. Even worse, her people would suffer for her pridefulness.

She had made herself unworthy.

Monsieur Puss

Heather Hayden

"Pip! Pip!" A gentle hand on his shoulder shook the young miller's son from his daydream of flying above the cottony clouds as a dragon. He looked up into the beaming, freckled face of Em, his best friend. Her auburn curls bounced as she straightened.

"You were drifting again," she said, half-scolding and half-laughing. "Did you forget I was coming?"

"No." He got to his feet and brushed dirt from his trousers. "You're late."

Em's smile faded a bit. "Sorry. I couldn't get away any sooner."

"It's fine." Pip stretched and glanced around. "Where's Puss?" His father's mouser had followed him to the field as usual, but was now nowhere in sight.

"I don't know." Em cupped her hands around her mouth. "Monsieur Puss! Where are you?"

A plump orange tabby trotted out of the field's thick carpet of wildflowers. The cat headed straight for Em, who knelt in the grass to stroke his head. Soft purrs vibrated down the cat's body.

"Who are we up against today?" Em kneaded the cat's back. "Pirates? Ogres? Giants?"

The mention of his favorite pastime made Pip grin. "That depends on you, my cunning sidekick, Em the Brave! Perhaps goblins from below have come to capture you and

Monsieur Puss, and the brilliant Marquis of Carabas must save you!"

"Maybe mermaids should sing the Marquis off the bow of our ship," Em retorted, her blue-green eyes dancing with excitement. "Then Puss and I can stage a rescue."

"Prrt!" The tabby lashed his tail and pulled away from Em with a sharp look.

"He doesn't like that idea." Pip laughed. "How about you two plot to rescue me from an evil witch instead?"

"No, I want to be a mage rescuing you from a dragon!"

The tale unfolded as they fell into their roles, Puss offering amusement and aid as the moment required. Hours passed by, and eventually, imaginary foes all defeated, they collapsed among sun-yellow dandelions, laughing as a few seed puffs drifted off and stuck to the tabby's fur.

"All this gold is ours," Pip claimed, gesturing at the flowers. "We shall buy a thousand castles and fill them with mice for Puss to chase."

The cat purred in contentment, curled up between the two children. His tail twitched, tickling Pip's arm. Em stroked the cat's back, the silver ring she always wore flashing on her finger. The sparkle made Pip think of a story he'd heard of the sea, how it stretched out for miles and miles to the horizon, how the sun danced sparkles upon the water's surface. It seemed so far away from his sleepy little village where no one else ever dreamed of magic or adventure.

"Pip!" Em nudged his shoulder gently. "Don't drift again." Something in her voice made him sit up and focus on her.

"What's wrong?" he asked, seeing a glimmer of tears in her eyes. "We defeated the ogre. I'm sorry I didn't let you get in the final blow, but next time—"

Now the tears were slipping from the corners of her eyes, sliding down to vanish into her curly hair. Pip patted through his pockets, searching for a handkerchief. He found one and offered it to his friend.

Em sat up and blew her nose, then reached out and dragged Puss into her lap. The cat normally hated forced cuddles, but today he nuzzled her arm and licked at her tears.

"What's wrong, Em?" Pip asked again, desperate to know what had made his normally cheerful playmate so sad. "Do you want to be the Marquis of Carabas next time? I don't mind. I could be Pip the Brave or—"

Em shook her head and scrubbed at her face with the handkerchief. "I have to leave."

This wasn't the first time she'd had to cut their playtime short. Pip tried to hide his disappointment. "That's fine, Em, I'll see you tomorrow—"

Another shake of her head, this one so slow her curls barely stirred. "I'm leaving Beaumont. I don't want to, but Father says I must…" The tears came flowing back, and she hugged Puss. Hissing in protest, the cat twisted from her grip and darted a few feet away, where he sat and began to lick one of his paws.

Pip slid across the grass and wrapped his arms around his friend. Sobs shook her frame, and she buried her face in his shoulder. He breathed in her familiar rosemary scent and held her close, wishing he didn't have to let go.

"Why?" Pip didn't know much about Em's family—nothing, really, other than that she wasn't very happy at home, which was why she snuck out as much as possible to play with him in the hidden field of wildflowers.

"He says I must," Em mumbled. "I wish I could stay here with you."

For a moment, Pip imagined bringing Em back to his home and begging his parents to let her stay. But they already had too many mouths to feed, and they didn't know about her. If his parents found out he neglected his chores to play with a stranger, Father would lock him in the mill overnight. The thought made him shiver.

Em hugged him tighter.

He wriggled a bit. "Will you come back?"

She shook her head, her curls tickling his nose. After another choked sob, she pulled back and looked him straight in the eyes. "Will you forget me?"

Caught in her sharp gaze, Pip shook his head. "Of course not! I'd never forget you."

Sniffling, Em narrowed her eyes. "Even if I never ever come back? Even if you find someone else to play with?"

"Never," he vowed.

Em looked away, watching Puss wash himself as she played with her silver ring. Then she pressed her lips together and tugged the ring off. "Here. Take this." She held it out, her hand shaking. "That way you'll have something to remember me by."

Pip hesitated. "But I won't need it. And it's way too fancy—"

Em grabbed his hand and pressed the ring into it. "I don't want you to daydream so much that you forget me." Her lower lip trembled.

Pip curled his fingers around the ring. "All right. I'll keep it safe. I promise." He could feel tears pressing against his own eyes now. "Are you really never coming back, Em? I don't want you to leave."

"I don't know," she whimpered.

As the two of them hugged and cried, Puss trotted over and curled up beside them, a low rumble in his throat.

***

Six years later, Pip sat under an oak tree, wishing he was anywhere—or anything—else. "Maybe a frog," he mused. "That would be a nice change. I'd love all this water coming down. Or a fish. Half the ponds and brooks we've passed have been overflowing. It's the perfect time to be a fish. I wonder if I could find a mage who'd be willing to transform me. Although I suppose they could just make the rain go away instead."

Puss sneezed miserably and dug his claws into Pip's leg. Three days straight of pouring rain had put the cat in a poor mood. He was huddled against Pip's side, under the youth's thin coat.

"I'm sorry, Puss." Pip dug in his pocket. "We might have a bit of ham left…" He found a scrap and split it, offering the greater half to the cat, who was already looking thinner. Had they really only left home a few days ago? He should have left Puss behind, but the cat had refused to stay…and besides, Puss was the only thing Father had left Pip in his will.

They'd spent a lot of time walking through the oak forest these past few days, sometimes in circles. Pip had never been one with a head for directions.

Puss snapped at the meat, nearly taking Pip's fingers with it.

Pip chuckled and chewed his own portion slowly to savor it. "We're going to have to find work somewhere soon, Puss, or we'll both starve. I've only got a few coins left." There was the ring on the cord around his neck as well, but he would never sell that. It was all he had left of Em, that and the long-faded memories of the stories they'd created.

"Don't worry, Pip. I have an idea."

Startled, the youth looked around. "Who is there?" It was early in the morning, but still dark from the storm clouds overhead, making it hard to see anything.

Puss twitched his ears. "Don't be dense, Pip."

Frowning, the youth peered at his cat. Was it his imagination, or had the cat opened his mouth slightly when the words were spoken? No, surely not. Pip licked his lips, wondering if the ham had been a bit off. Maybe it was making him hear things.

"Pip! Pay attention." Puss's paw landed on the boy's

leg and claws dug through the cloth, pricking his skin.

"Ouch! Watch it, Puss." Pip nudged the cat's paw away with his hand.

In response, Puss ducked out from under the jacket and reared back on his hind legs. "Listen to me. I have a plan, but you must do something for me first."

Pip stared. His cat really *was* speaking. And standing, like a human. "You can talk?"

Puss leapt forward, landing with a thump in the boy's lap. He kneaded Pip's thigh with his claws, rougher than before. "Clearly. Now, focus, Pip. I need you to go into the next town we reach and purchase a pair of boots and a hat for me to wear."

"Boots and a hat?" Pip laughed. "Why would you need something like that?"

"It's important," Puss insisted.

"Food is important too."

"If you do as I say, I'll catch you a nice fat fish for dinner."

That made Pip laugh even harder. "I don't think you've ever caught a fish in your life." His laughter hissed to a stop when Puss dug his claws in.

"Just do as I say," Puss snapped, his tone deep with impatience.

"All right, all right." Pip got to his feet and brushed off his clothes. "How are you able to talk? Did someone enchant you as a kitten? Have you always been able to do so? Can other cats talk as well?"

Puss flicked an ear and trotted off into the trees. "Let's go."

The next few hours were spent walking in the lessening rain. Pip's questions continued to fall to the ground, unanswered, and eventually he stopped voicing them out loud, though they still danced merry jigs through his mind.

He was imagining a mage blessing Puss with the gift

of speech for ridding a house of giant rats when Puss butted his leg. "We're almost to Perrault. Do you remember what you need to get?"

Pip blinked, then nodded. "A hat and boots."

"Sized for a cat." Puss raised a paw, pointing through the trees at a glimmer of water. "Meet me by the pond there. I'll fish while you're in town."

Excited by the prospect of dinner, Pip strode into town and headed straight for the seamstress's shop.

"You want what?" The tall, skinny woman behind the counter laughed as she continued sewing a tight line of stitches down a dress hem. "Get out of here, you ruffian, and find some honest work for those idle hands of yours. Clothes for a cat!" She scoffed.

Pip scurried out. The town was only big enough for one seamstress; where else could he try? His gaze fell on a tiny shop bearing a colorful sign that read TOYS.

Perhaps the owner of a toy shop would be kinder. He ventured in and discovered that it was owned by an older couple. The husband, George, carved beautiful toys and his wife, Anne, fashioned clothes for them. When Pip explained he was looking for clothes for a cat, they shared a look, then Anne smiled.

"Of course, dear. I have just the thing." She drew out a handsome leather tricorner hat with a jaunty plume the color of solid sunshine tucked into its gold ribbon band. Its brim was the width of Pip's spread fingers. "Will this do?"

"Yes, it's perfect!" He accepted the hat, admiring the stitching as he turned it about.

"As for boots…" Anne tapped a crooked finger against her pursed lips.

"Perhaps these?" George reached behind a half-finished doll and drew out a small pair of leather boots, cunningly fashioned with hard leather soles and shiny buckles.

"I don't know…" she murmured, but Pip nodded

enthusiastically. "Well, I suppose they would do," she concluded. "But I haven't quite finished the stitching around the top yet."

Pip sat on a stool and watched George carve while Anne finished the boots. The man's knife skillfully shaved off bits and slivers from the round piece of wood he held, forming a strange shape—half cat and half fish.

"What is that?" Pip nodded at the carving.

"A seal," George replied. "They live in the ocean, far from here. I've heard that some can turn into people."

Pip's eyes widened at the thought, but after hearing Puss speak, perhaps such an idea wasn't so fanciful after all. "You're really good," he remarked. "It looks so real."

The man smiled, but the cheer didn't quite reach his eyes. "Thank you kindly. I love to see the children's faces light up when they receive them… We often wish we could have had our own child to play with our toys."

Unsure how to respond, Pip picked up one of the finished dolls, admiring the careful details of the face. "This one could be a princess. But she has a bit of sadness in her eyes…maybe she's been searching for her prince and hasn't found him yet?" He selected another, this one a boy doll dressed in a simple tunic. "Maybe he's the prince, but in disguise because he's being chased by an evil mage…"

As he continued spinning a tale from his imagination, the air in the shop grew lighter, and by the time Anne had finished her stitching, both she and her husband were chuckling. Pip could see the love between them clearly in their shared glances and bright smiles, and it made him happy and sad at the same time. He could remember laughing like that with Em, once upon a time.

The toymakers insisted on giving Pip a generous discount on the clothes, but the transaction still took every last penny the boy had in his pocket. Though grateful for their kindness, without which he'd have never afforded the hats or boots, he hoped Puss actually did manage to catch a fish, or they'd both go hungry tonight.

"Are you a storyteller?" George asked as he shook Pip's hand, completing the deal.

Pip shook his head.

"You would make a wonderful one." Anne smiled. "Perhaps next time you pass by, you can stop a while and share a story with the children of the town. They would love that, I'm sure."

Pip's eyes widened at the thought, and he spent the entire walk back to the pond daydreaming about traveling through exotic countries, sharing stories with anyone who would listen. What a life that would be. He was so caught up in the idea, he barely even noticed that the rain had finally stopped.

He found Puss curled up in a patch of sunshine, napping. A silvery pink trout lay in the grass beside the feline. Pip's stomach growled at the sight, and he reached for the fish.

Puss leapt up and batted at the boy's hand. "Let me see the boots and hat."

"I'm starving," Pip grumbled, but he drew out the clothes and set them on the ground for the cat to inspect.

"Marvelous." Puss batted gently at the feather. "What a lovely hat. Well done, Pip."

Pip grinned and began gathering materials to build a fire. As the fish roasted, he became lost in the daydream again, not stirring until the smell of burnt fish broke through his thoughts.

It was only a little scorched, thankfully, but as he began to eat, Pip realized that Puss had vanished along with the boots and hat.

"I guess we won't continue our travels tonight." Pip yawned. "Tomorrow, we can set out for the border. Perhaps the southern one? No, the northern one, by the sea. I'm sure they could use a storyteller in the kingdom where the land is shrouded in shadows for months upon a time. And they have lots of fish there, so Puss would love it. Perhaps I'll even see a seal…"

It had been a long day, and the grass was soft. Warmed by the fire's glowing embers and his fiery imagination, he curled up and fell asleep.

***

Puss was a tough cat with a gentle heart, and he'd always seen Pip as a human sort of cat, at least in terms of being able to relax and appreciate the world and its wonders. The boy was definitely no hunter, but he could doze and dream like the best of felines. Unfortunately, his family had always seen it as laziness.

Just like they'd called Puss a "lazy cat" for not deigning to chase mice. As if a feline descended from a long, long line of talented cats would spend his days catching rodents! Well, Puss would show them. He would focus all of his cunning on a plan to provide a life of luxury for his adopted master, and, of course, for himself. Although he'd been sold as a kitten to the miller, he'd picked up a few tricks along the way. And thanks to some news he'd overheard in Beaumont before they'd left home forever, he had the perfect plan.

With the hat balanced on his head, the boots on his back paws, and a fine, fat fish clutched delicately between his teeth, Puss made his way to a large stone building a few hours' walk from Perrault. He'd spotted it the day before; Pip had been too soaked and miserable to notice. But Puss knew exactly what it was—the king's summer palace, a beautiful place of pink granite and white marble that looked like a freshly decorated cake tucked against the dark velvet of the forest.

Even better, Puss knew the king was in residence. That was what had sparked the idea that led to the plan he was now setting into motion.

Getting inside the castle was easy enough, despite the fish weighing him down. Puss plopped through an open window into a long hallway. The stone was cool on his front paws. His ears swiveled, picking up sounds. The clanking ahead was likely a guard on patrol. The giggles echoing down the hall were mixed with the scent of baking bread; likely scullery maids preparing for the morning meal.

Following his nose and sticking to the shadows, the cat moved away from the tantalizing scents of the kitchen, toward the more elegant parts of the castle. Long tapestries woven with scenes of battles and celebrations lined the hall. Their tasseled edges begged to be played with, but Puss forced himself to ignore them. For now. His plan needed to be set in motion soon, as the king would not be in residence for long.

He headed toward the king's chamber, following the scent of sandalwood soap—too rich a choice for anyone but royalty. The strong aroma of rosemary caught his nose as he passed by a closing door. Through the narrowing gap, Puss caught a glimpse of the princess. Her eyes were teary and red-rimmed, no surprise given the whispers he'd heard while passing through the halls.

With a tail flick, he moved on. She wasn't his target today.

A single guard stood at attention by the door leading to the king's chamber. Leaving the safety of the shadows, Puss rose onto his hind legs, took a few steps forward, and set down the fish.

"Excuse me," he said, using the imperious tone he had practiced for just such an occasion. "I am here to see the king."

The guard stared at the cat standing in his hat and boots. "What?"

Puss ground his teeth and repeated the message. Why were humans always so dense?

"I... Ah..." The guard hesitated then rapped on the

door. "Sire? You have…a visitor."

Puss's sharp ears picked up the eventual response. "Send them in."

Shaking his head, the guard opened the door.

Puss picked up the fish and trotted in, balanced perfectly in his boots despite the growing ache in his hind paws. The hat made his ears itch, but he ignored his discomfort as every eye in the room turned to him.

The king was seated in the antechamber, eating a light repast while servants tended to various duties, such as polishing his crown and arranging his hair. He stared at the cat for a moment then burst out laughing.

"What could this be? A cat or a man?"

His servants chuckled quietly, though they continued to work.

Ignoring the insult—he was certainly not a human!—Puss set down the fish and gave his best bow, the feather bobbing in the corner of his eye. His tail twitched slightly; the feather made him want to stop and chase it, but he needed to focus.

"Sire, I am Monsieur Puss. My master, the Marquis of Carabas, has sent me to present you this fish with his compliments."

"A single fish? But presented by a talking cat. What a master you have, Monsieur." The king gestured to a servant boy, who stepped forward and picked up the fish with only a slight wrinkling of his nose. "Please ask the cook to prepare it for my breakfast," the king requested. "And perhaps send a saucer of cream for our new friend."

Puss offered another bow. "Tempting as that is"— and it was quite tempting, Puss *loved* cream—"Sire, I must depart without delay."

"Then please take a few coins for your trouble." The king gestured again, and a servant produced a handful of coins, gold and silver, which was passed to Puss.

"Thank you for your generosity." Puss bowed for a

third time. "I hope you have a lovely day." Taking the coins in his mouth, he left the room, only returning to all fours once he was far down the corridor.

Out of the castle he ran, returning to the pond just before Pip began to stir. Puss dropped the coins in the grass, kicked off the uncomfortable boots, and curled up for a nap.

***

Pip yawned as he sat up and stretched his arms over his head. He was sore from sleeping on the ground, cold, and hungry. There was a little fish left from dinner, which he had kept for Puss.

Looking around, he spotted the cat sleeping nearby.

"Puss?" he called.

A slight ear flick, which meant the cat was trying to nap and didn't want to be disturbed. Deciding the cat would have eaten the fish if he'd been hungry, Pip devoured the remaining scraps and licked his fingers. A glint in the grass near Puss caught his eye, and he collected the cool metal coins with trembling fingers. There was a small fortune pooled in his palm, enough to feed them both for months.

"Where did this come from?" he wondered aloud.

"It's all part of my plan." Puss released a sharp growl, clearly annoyed by the interruption of his nap. "If you must insist on being noisy, would you please do so elsewhere?"

"I'm sorry." Pip tucked the coins in his pocket and sprawled out by the pond's edge. Early morning sunlight glistened on the edges of puffy white clouds. It was a beautiful day, he had no chores to do, and his stomach was—at least currently—full. He wriggled around until he was comfortable, then made up stories in his head about this cloud and that one. Battles waged overhead, dragons roared, princes and princesses rushed to the rescue of their dear ones. The occasional cat wandered through, chasing a fish and a mouse.

What plan did Puss have for him? Pip was grateful for his cat's support, but also curious. The feline seemed disinclined to explain, however, leaving Pip's curiosity burning a hole in his mind like the coins in his pocket.

***

The fish had been well-received, but Puss needed to keep the king's attention. So, instead of taking his regular afternoon nap the next day, the cat left his master daydreaming by the pond and headed off to hunt. It didn't take long to find a plump rabbit, and soon Puss was headed for the castle.

The king smiled upon seeing Puss again, this time in his elegant throne room. "Welcome back, Monsieur Puss. I see your master has sent another fine gift for my table."

"Yes, Sire." Puss took a step back to allow a page to gather the rabbit. "He sends his best regards to you and your daughter. We hope you are having a pleasant stay."

"Indeed I am. My daughter is as well." The king's gaze drifted briefly to the smaller, empty throne sitting beside his. "She has been ill and the country air is good for her."

Ill, was it? Puss withheld a growl of annoyance. According what he had overheard, she was unwell because the king had arranged her marriage with a local duke, a man as cruel as he was wealthy. If the rumors were correct, Duke Ocher had in fact forced the king's hand by threatening a civil war the little kingdom could not afford. The king and princess had come to meet the duke in person before the upcoming nuptials.

It took effort to keep his ears tilted in a friendly manner, but Puss managed a polite bow. "I must depart, but please pass both my and the Marquis of Carabas's wishes toward her good health."

"Thank you kindly, Monsieur Puss." The king gestured for another page to step forward. "I noticed that your cap has a simple canary feather in it; I hope you don't mind my offering this feather to replace it?"

The page held out a bright red cardinal feather. Puss had to restrain himself from leaping for it—cardinals were a favorite of his to chase, though they were also too fast for him to catch. What a thoughtful gift from a human.

He bowed again. "Thank you for your generosity, Sire." The fluttering of the feathers as the page tucked the new one into Puss's hat called to him, but Puss kept his unblinking gaze on the king.

The king nodded. "I assume you must be on your way again? If not, I could send for some cream."

"Unfortunately, I must depart again. My master requires me by his side."

"Very well. I hope to see you again soon, Monsieur Puss." The king gestured for a guard to escort Puss out, and the cat trotted alongside the man until they reached the castle gate. Only once he had reached the deeper shadows of the nearby woods did Puss sprint off, tail swishing. He was not surprised when the guard attempted to follow him, but it was easy enough to give the man the slip. Humans were so clumsy and slow on their two feet.

Perhaps due to the boots they wore, Puss reflected, kicking off his own. He picked up hat and boots and carried them back to where Pip lay in the grass. A loaf of bread and a paper-wrapped wheel of cheese sat by the boy's side.

The cat set down his burden and sniffed. "Didn't fetch anything for me?"

After a moment, Pip blinked slowly and turned to Puss. "Oh, you're back! I got you something." He reached behind his back and pulled out a smaller package, wrapped in waxed cloth. The smell of beeswax clogged Puss's nose as Pip unwrapped it, only to be overpowered by a familiar scent—sausage!

Puss gave a small nod and flicked his tail as he turned slightly away. "That will do."

Pip's expression fell. It wouldn't do to lavish him with praise, but Puss relented a little. "Thank you, Pip. It smells delicious."

The lad's face brightened with a smile, and he set it down for Puss to nibble at. "Where did you go?"

"Here and there."

"I was thinking we could head north. With the coins you found, we could easily have food and shelter for the trip, and—"

Puss cut him off before the daydream got too far out of hand. "We need to stay here a little longer."

Pip's eyebrows pressed together like nesting birds. "Why?"

"You'll know soon enough." Puss couldn't reveal the truth, not yet. He'd overheard the servants in the halls talking today, and he knew what his next plan of action would be. The princess's engagement was to be made official in a few days, once she recovered. However, Puss had listened closely to what the servants said in fearful whispers, and he knew there were other, darker rumors about Duke Ocher floating around the local countryside. Some even suggested that he wasn't a man at all, but a demon or ogre in the form of a man.

Given the way the man's mansion had reeked of dark magic when Puss had passed by earlier that day, the cat was almost certain those particular rumors were true. Which fell perfectly in line with his plans.

The cat grinned smugly to himself as he settled down for a quick nap.

***

Puss arrived at the castle the following afternoon with a beautiful pheasant. He had taken care to kill the bird swiftly and carefully so as not to mar its lovely feathers, and his neck had quite the crick in it from carrying the bird all the way to the castle without stirring up too much dust and dirt.

"How delightful!" The king beamed as he had a page gather up the pheasant. "Thank you, Monsieur Puss. It is a shame my daughter is not feeling well; I had hoped she might get a chance to meet you. Perhaps you could stop by again tomorrow? With your mysterious master, if possible?"

"I am afraid my master is too busy running his lands to visit," Puss replied smoothly. "But he has suggested that your daughter might feel better if you took a carriage ride tomorrow morning. The fresh air and sunshine would do her good."

The king nodded. "I haven't been able to coax her out of her room, she's been so ill. But perhaps I can suggest a ride. Her future fiancé lives nearby; maybe we can visit both him and your master. Whereabouts is the Marquis's home?"

"My master is a private man," Puss said, dodging a question he hadn't expected and didn't have an answer for. Yet. "I must be off."

"Wait!" The king held out his hand. "I have another gift for you." He gestured to a page, who brought forward a small, thin-bladed sword. It was a rapier, complete with grip and guard, but doll-sized.

Or cat-sized, Puss realized, bemused. "Thank you, Sire, but without thumbs, I can't wield a blade. Besides—" he held up a paw and flexed his sharp white claws "—I carry my own with me."

The king chuckled. "The blade isn't even sharp; I thought you might like to wear it, however."

"Ah." Puss allowed the page to buckle the scabbard belt around his middle. The leather rubbed his fur uncomfortably, and the page took the liberty of stroking his back, but Puss suffered in silence. He would have much preferred a bowl of cream.

"You look positively dashing." The king clapped his hands and smiled. "Thank you, Monsieur Puss, for your delightful visits. I won't keep you longer, but I do hope we have a chance to see you again, and meet your master, before we must depart."

"I hope so as well." Puss bowed, the sword tip scraping against the stone floor, before he departed the throne room.

The guard escorting him tried to follow him once again, but even with the ungainly sword dragging him down, Puss still managed to give the man the slip. The king thought he was being clever, trying to make it easier to track him, but Puss wouldn't give him the satisfaction.

"You look amazing!" Pip exclaimed when Puss arrived at the pond. "Wherever did you get such a little sword?"

"It was a gift," Puss replied. "It's all part of my plan."

Pip sighed. "Will you ever tell me what that plan is?"

"All I can say for now is that tomorrow we should head off again. We can't stay here forever."

"Wonderful! Are we going north, like I suggested?"

"No." Puss shrugged off his human contraptions and curled up for a well-earned nap. "Get some rest. We have quite the journey ahead tomorrow."

"I do wish you'd tell me what this plan of yours is." Pip stroked Puss's head gently, kneading his neck in just the right place.

Puss purred, ignoring the boy's request.

***

Walking on the road was easier than through the forest, but the sun beat down harder and the packed dirt was rough on Pip's worn shoes. Newly formed blisters stung with each step. He winced and glanced at the sky. It was barely midmorning, but already he was tired. The rippling sound of a nearby stream caught his attention, and he gazed longingly through the bushes at its sparkling water.

"Can't we stop for a rest, Puss?"

The cat was trotting along, dragging the sword and carrying his hat and boots in his mouth. Pip had offered to carry everything, but Puss had refused, saying it was all part of the plan. It still made no sense to Pip, but then, he was taking advice and directions from a talking cat. If nothing else, he'd have quite a story to tell the villagers of the next place they stopped, wherever that might be.

"Puss?"

Puss halted, set down his burden, and raised a hard stare. "We haven't been walking for that long. Did your legs stop working?"

"My feet hurt." Pip sat down and tugged off one of his shoes, wincing at the twinges shooting through his foot. "See?" He held out his foot, showing off the blisters forming on his sole.

Puss wrinkled his nose, either from the smell or the sight or both. "That must be painful. Perhaps you should rest a while. Maybe take a bath in the stream? It would be perfect for cleaning up."

"Do I need a bath?" Pip sniffed under an arm and grimaced. Yes, perhaps he did. A proper storyteller should keep up appearances, after all. And a dip in the cool water would be nice after the sun's blazing autumn heat. "Are you taking one too?" He grinned as the cat's hair stood on end.

Puss spat. "Not likely!"

Pip found a good spot in the stream to bathe. The water was deep and slow-moving, and bushes screened it from the road. He folded his clothes carefully and tucked them by a rock, then ducked in. The chill was bracing, and he was soon washing up, feeling better than he had in a while. Even Em's ring, hanging on its cord around his neck, was shinier than it had been some time. He cradled it for a moment, recalling the bittersweet memory of the day she'd gifted it to him. Did Puss remember her? Miss her? The cat was often an enigma, impossible to read or question. But at least he was a faithful companion.

Smiling, Pip looked up and found both Puss and his clothes missing.

***

Puss kicked a few more leaves over Pip's clothes. They would be easy enough to locate by their reek if his plan failed; otherwise, they'd eventually rot and become a part of the soil. Puss left the coins behind as well, but took his boots, hat, and sword with him.

The cat headed back down the road toward the lane that would lead him to Duke Ocher's mansion. Under different circumstances, it would have been a pleasant walk, with the fields lining the road offering plenty of amusements along the way. He could hear the rustling of small rodents, could see birds flitting amongst the crops. His tail lashed as a particularly bold sparrow swooped by overhead, but he continued down the road.

All too soon, the dark mansion belonging to the duke loomed ahead, with no fields separating it from Puss. The feline trotted up, his hackles rising as he approached the large house. Elegance dripped from the eaves onto the carved granite staircase leading to the front door, but underneath it all was the smell of something rotten.

Magic. Puss sneezed. He wasn't a fan of magic, especially not the twisted kind that lingered in this place. Steeling himself, reminding himself of the young lad dependent on his skillful mind and claws, Puss rapped the doorknocker once and waited.

A butler opened the door, and Puss let himself inside. The man stared down at him with a vacant gaze.

"I'm here to see Duke Ocher," Puss announced in the same imperious tone he'd used to speak to the king, and the butler shuffled off without comment.

Time crept slowly past, marked only by the shifting sun and the unshakeable itch in Puss's fur. There was no time to waste—where was Duke Ocher?

The butler returned. "He will see you in the parlor." After escorting Puss there, the man shuffled off again.

"Your hired help seems a bit tired," Puss remarked, entering the parlor. "Perhaps you should give them a day off now and then."

Duke Ocher looked up from his armchair, glaring. The man was tall, even sitting down, a looming shadow of a monster with crow-sharp eyes and shaggy red hair. He reminded Puss of a wolf. Or perhaps a fox. Puss stared back, holding the man's gaze until Duke Ocher's expression shifted to dark amusement, and he laughed.

"When my butler told me there was a talking cat here to see me, I thought he was going insane like the last one. Well, well, what are you doing here, my little swashbuckler?" The man's teeth were just a tiny bit sharp as he smiled.

The whole room reeked of dark magic, and the source of the smell was Duke Ocher. Time for the most dangerous part of Puss's plan.

The cat flicked an ear. "I came to see if the stories were true, that a creature of the night had taken the form of a man to live in luxury. It seems you've done well for yourself, ogre."

"Ogre? Pft. You shame me with such a title. I'm a shapeshifter, a master of disguise." The man threw out his arms to gesture to the entire room. "Do you see the splendorous place I've created for myself? My brethren can only dream of such glory. And I have even convinced the king of this land to give me his daughter's hand in marriage." His smile became sharper. "I can't wait to drain her essence, too."

That confirmed Puss's suspicions. This man was indeed an ogre, a creature of dark magic who required the life force of others to keep its own magic burning. It explained the butler's appearance and the fear of those living on the duke's land.

Puss swished his tail. "If you are a shapeshifter, does that mean you can become anything? Why be a human then? Aren't there far better forms? Or can you only change your human appearance?"

The duke laughed again. "I can become anything you can imagine, little kitty."

Puss's fur bristled, but he forced it to smooth again. "Can you become something of any size?"

The duke jumped to his feet. "Of course!" In rapid succession, he became a large bull, snorting and pawing at the priceless carpet, a magnificent stallion, releasing a shrill whinny, and a stout mastiff, growling at the cat.

Puss dug his claws into the carpet and bowed. "What a magnificent display, Duke Ocher. But those are all large animals... Can you become something smaller? A cat perhaps? Or a bird?"

"Easily," the duke said, his voice a deep rumble coming from the mastiff's throat. The dog's form shimmered and shrank to that of a goose, then a cat that looked almost identical to Puss—not nearly as handsome, though. "See?" the duke purred, licking a paw. "I'm the most talented shapeshifter in the world."

"That's impressive. But you're still pretty big. I bet you couldn't shrink as small as a finch."

"Of course as I can!" Fur bristling, the duke puffed out his chest and shrank. As his body grew round, feathers spread across his hide, and his mouth stretched into a beak.

Puss didn't have to think about his next action. Pure feline instinct drove him forward to pounce upon the bird. The duke shrieked and tried to shift. His form became slippery and soft as shadow beneath Puss's claws. Snarling, the cat bit at his prey, but the monster's reaction was even swifter.

With a yowl, an enormous wildcat with bright orange and black stripes flung Puss across the room. He slammed against the wall, the impact shaking the strength from his bones. Panting, Puss tried to focus on his enemy, his gaze clouded with pain.

"You think you're so clever, little kitty," the duke growled, stalking closer, his form shifting from wildcat to mastiff to bear as he approached. "I hate cats. You think you're superior to everyone. Better than everyone else. Time for you to learn your place."

No one spoke to him that way! Puss hissed and flexed his claws as he clambered to his feet. Despite his brave front, his body swayed from the effort. Baring sharp teeth, he braced himself as the duke raised a massive paw.

***

Pip was shivering from the cold. Puss must have dragged his clothes off somewhere; a thorough search among the bushes near the stream's edge had revealed no sign of them. Or the cat, for that matter. At least ten minutes had passed, and Pip was beginning to worry Puss had abandoned him for some strange reason.

"Is this part of your plan?" he whispered to the absent feline, his mind filling with increasingly creative words to use when the cat returned. He was particularly pleased with "bumblekitty bigfoot." It rolled nicely off the tongue.

Another few minutes drifted by like the rippling stream, and Pip's teeth began to chatter. A distant rattling sound grew closer, catching his attention. A wagon? It was the first he'd seen today. Perhaps the travelers would be willing to spare him some clothes. Whatever Puss's plan was, Pip couldn't understand why it required his clothes.

The sounds of creaking wood and leather, rattling wheels, and snorting horses grew closer. Wrapping his arms around his chest, Pip crept up the hill and peered out from behind one of the denser bushes. His eyes widened—this was no farmer's wagon. It was a carriage, richly bedecked with carvings and gold leaf.

Swallowing hard, he raised one hand above the bush and waved. "Please, I need help!"

The driver glanced in his direction and frowned, snapping the reins to make the horses pick up their pace.

"Please!" Pip shouted.

"Halt the carriage!" The call came from inside the rolling contraption, and though the driver frowned, he drew up the reins. Another man stepped down from the back of the carriage.

"My king, I don't think—"

Pip's heart skipped a beat and his eyes widened. This wasn't just any carriage he had tried to flag down, it was the king's! What was the king doing here in the country? And for that matter, why would he stop the carriage? Questions flew through Pip's mind as the kind face of a middle-aged man wearing a thin golden circlet peered out of the carriage's window.

"Giles, be a good man and offer the poor lad your cloak. He's dripping wet without a stitch on him."

Pip blushed, glad the thick bush hid his lower half from the road. The guard came forward and held out a richly embroidered cloak, frowning as he politely averted his eyes.

"Th-thank you." Pip wrapped himself in the cloak, welcoming its heavy warmth. Still in a daze, he let the guard escort him to the carriage.

"What are you doing out here without any clothes?" the king inquired, offering a gentle smile. Curiosity shone clear in his eyes.

Pip lowered his gaze to the ground, heat rising to his cheeks. What could he say? "They were taken."

"Stolen? Do we have thieves in these parts? I'll have to speak to Duke Ocher about that." The king pushed open the carriage door. "Well, we can't leave you standing here, especially not with Giles's favorite cloak. Get in. We can drop you off at your home."

"Oh, that's really not necessary—" Pip hastened to say, concerned that Puss wouldn't be able to find him again.

"I insist."

How could he refuse royalty? Pip climbed up the steps into the carriage. He stopped, startled to discover the king wasn't alone. A young woman sat on the cushioned seat across from the king, her hands folded in her lap. Her crown rested upon a blue veil, which hung down over her face.

She had to be the princess. Pip was well-aware of his lack of dress and manners. Clutching the cloak tight, he managed a slight bow and a choked "good morning".

"Nice to meet you," she murmured in a quiet voice. "Please, have a seat." She gestured at the seat next to her.

"Th-thank you." Pip settled on the cushion, careful not to drip water on her fine silk dress.

"I must admit to having an ulterior motive to offering you a ride," the king said as the carriage began to move again. "You are a local to these parts, yes?"

Pip shook his head. "I was only traveling through. I'm headed north, to see the ocean."

"How unfortunate." The king sighed. "I was hoping you might have heard of the Marquis of Carabas, who lives near here. I'm not familiar with him, but I've had the most intriguing visitor at my palace the past few days."

"I haven't heard of him," Pip said, but even as he spoke, the name stirred a memory from his childhood, the stories he'd played out with Em. He swallowed hard. They'd made up that name; where could the king have heard it? Did Puss have something to do with it? But what would Puss be doing, visiting the king?

"It is all right," the king said, misreading Pip's

concern. "Why don't you tell us about the town where you live, to pass the time until we reach Duke Ocher's home?"

"I come from Beaumont."

"I know the town!" The king's eyes sparkled. "I have a small hunting lodge there. My daughter actually spent some time there when she was younger—"

"I remember." The princess's words were soft and sharp at the same time. She turned her head to gaze out the open window.

Pip edged a little away from her, getting the sense she didn't want him in the carriage. Maybe a story would help pass the time until they reached this Duke Ocher's place. Then he could take his leave as quickly as possible, find Puss, and head north.

"I don't know this Duke Ocher, or the marquis you speak of, but I am a storyteller," he started. "If you like, I could tell you a story about a knight who befriended a dragon."

"Wonderful!" The king gestured for him to continue, and Pip did as he was asked.

Spinning a tale from bits of ideas was a comforting activity, and Pip began to relax as he unfolded the story of a poor knight who rescued a dragon and became rich, only to realize that money wasn't what he sought, but love. With the help of the dragon, the knight fended off the bejeweled ladies seeking his hand and was able to propose to the barmaid who had been his friend since childhood.

The king chuckled and sighed and gasped in all the right places, the perfect audience. Only the princess remained silent, still as stone as she stared out the window.

Pip's tale had barely finished when the carriage came to a stop. "We're here, my king," Giles said as he opened the door.

Pip's jaw fell as he stared at the mansion. Tall stone walls and glass windows formed an imposing structure. It almost seemed like a small castle. Whoever this Duke Ocher might be, he was certainly rich.

"Odd, I would have expected the duke to greet us." The king frowned as he helped the princess out of the carriage. "Perhaps he is out. Giles, be a good man and knock?"

As the man took a step forward, a loud yowl rang out from one of the open windows on the lower floor. It was closely followed by a sharp hiss, and Pip's heart skipped a beat. He would know that sound anywhere—that was Puss! The cat was in trouble.

Abandoning caution to the wind, he dashed across the grounds toward the window, shouting his friend's name. "Puss! I'm coming!"

The large window had a low sill, and Pip peered over it, his breath catching in his throat at the sight of a bear towering over the cat. The beast was about to smash a paw into the feline.

"Puss!" Pip's shout distracted the bear, which turned and growled at him as he scrambled over the sill. The cloak caught and he yanked at it. The heavy fabric tore, and he flung it off and over the bear's head.

Rather than back away from the obstacle, the bear charged, its form shifting like smoke into that of a human, who brushed away the cloth before shifting again into a large striped cat that struck out at Pip.

He barely had time to dodge, the tips of the cat's claws scratching dark lines down his left arm.

"Pip!" Puss darted across the room and leapt onto the wildcat's back, claws digging into the beast's flesh. The larger cat yowled and twisted, trying to throw off its unwelcome passenger.

Whirling, Pip searched for a weapon. His arm stung and his mind was swimming in confusion and fear. There, a poker against the wall by the fireplace. He darted over and grabbed the cold metal rod. Whirling, he swung the poker by instinct just as the wildcat pounced.

The heavy iron bar thudded against the cat's jaw, knocking it to the side. It tumbled over itself, form already shifting again, but Puss pounced, his claws digging into the beast's throat. In rapid succession, the creature changed from cat to dog to bear, but Puss held on, snarling.

"You can't defeat me," the bear growled as it tried to bat Puss away. The cat dodged and leapt again, this time at its face.

If he hadn't just seen the creature change form multiple times, its speech might have startled Pip. Instead, he simply raised the poker and dashed forward with a sharp yell.

The bear, blinded by Puss's slashing claws, turned and tried to strike at Pip, but its paw went wide. Pip slammed the poker against the creature's nose.

Once again, the monster shifted, this time shrinking faster than the eye could follow. Pip saw a mouse dash for the corner of the room, and struggled to follow, but his feet were clumsy and his hands stung from the impact of the poker.

Puss was faster. The cat streaked across the room, an orange blur of hunter's instinct, and his pounce was followed by a sickening crunch.

The mouse lay beneath Puss's claws, its back broken. Pip dashed over, raising the poker in case the beast shifted again, but this time, the odd creature simply faded away. A moment later, it was as though it had never been there.

Puss let out a purr of satisfaction and started licking a paw.

Footsteps in the hallway sent Pip dashing for the cloak on the floor. Though torn, it at least covered him. He clutched it to himself, suddenly terrified. What would Duke Ocher do to him upon seeing the devastation in this room? True, the creature had caused most of the damage, but what if no one believed him? The only evidence of the monster's existence had already vanished.

It was Giles who flung open the door, the king only

a few steps behind.

"What happened here?" the king demanded as the guard moved aside.

For once lost for words, Pip glanced at Puss for guidance.

The cat flicked one ear.

"Monsieur Puss?" The king gasped. "What is going on here?"

Puss lowered his paw and dipped his head in a bow. "Sire. Please allow me to introduce my master, the Marquis of Carabas."

"What?" Pip and the king said in unison.

Strutting across the room, Puss leapt up onto the desk and sat, curling his tail around his paws. "I see my master kept his identity a secret. No wonder, given his current appearance. But rest assured, Sire, this young lad saved your kingdom a great deal of trouble today by defeating Duke Ocher. Did you know that the duke was an ogre?"

"An ogre?" The king's eyes widened. "Here, in my kingdom?"

"Unfortunately, yes. But my master learned of your plight and vanquished the monster."

"I am delighted to hear that." The king bowed his head to Pip. "Thank you, Marquis. You have done me, my kingdom, and my daughter a great service today. If it would not trouble you, I would ask that you take over ruling these lands in the duke's stead; I believe you will serve the people here far better than he did."

Stunned, Pip simply stared at the king. Surely he wasn't serious?

"My master seems awestruck by his good fortune." Puss twitched his ears. "May I suggest a celebration to honor this glorious occasion?" At the king's nod, the cat jumped from the desk and trotted toward the door. "I will inform the cook to begin immediately. Come, my master, we must find you some clothing better suited to your status."

Pip followed Puss to the kitchen. The cook seemed a bit dazed by the turn of events, but readily agreed to have a light repast prepared in an hour's time. She also provided bandages to bind Pip's injured arm. Next, Puss led the way to a room in the east wing of the mansion, where Pip found a suit that would fit him well enough.

"What's going on, Puss?"

"You are the Marquis of Carabas," Puss replied. "Duke Ocher was that evil creature you saw in the study, and now that he has been vanquished, all this land is now yours." He paused for a moment, lashing his tail, before finally adding, "I thank you for your aid in vanquishing him."

"Is this what your plan was?" Pip sat down on the edge of the bed, folding his hands in his lap. "I don't want to rule this land—"

Puss snorted. "Nonsense. My plan is not yet complete. Now hurry up, we can't keep the king waiting."

Pip stumbled back down the stairs to the dining hall, where a veritable feast awaited them. Puss dipped his muzzle into a bowl of cream while the others ate bread and cheese, roast chicken, and vegetables in a variety of delicious sauces. Pip did his best to be friendly and entertaining for his two royal guests, though the princess remained quiet and ate little.

Finally, the king sat back with a satisfied smile. "When I originally arrived here, I expected to meet the man who forced my daughter's hand in marriage. Instead, I encountered, through an odd turn of events, the man who would defeat the creature holding this part of my kingdom hostage. I thank you, Marquis of Carabas, for your assistance."

Pip's face reddened. "I couldn't have done it without Puss."

Puss raised his head proudly, cream dripping from his whiskers. "Nonsense. I did little of note, save distract the duke until my master arrived."

The cat's unusual humility concerned Pip—what was Puss plotting now? But the lad was distracted by the king again as the older man raised his drink in a toast.

"To the Marquis of Carabas, may he live long and well." The king bowed his head to Pip. "You charged into the fight without even a thought for your own wellbeing. A person of such initiative is one I would be grateful to call my son. In gratitude of your service, would you do me the honor of accepting my daughter's hand in marriage?"

Pip's jaw dropped and he glanced at Puss, who merely licked cream off his whiskers. Was *this* what Puss had wanted? "S-Sire…" The youth's hand rose and grasped the necklace around his neck. He couldn't marry the princess. "I-I'm honored by the offer, but I must refuse. My heart belongs to someone else."

He drew up the cord, revealing the silver ring on it. "A long time ago, someone very dear to me gave me this before she left. I gave her my heart in return. I'm sure the princess has someone dear to her as well; shouldn't she have a say in who she marries?" He held his breath, unsure how the king would respond.

It was the princess who spoke first, however. "Pip!" She flung back her veil, revealing blue-green eyes and familiar auburn curls. Her face was paler than he remembered, but there was still a smattering of freckles.

"Em?" He gasped, not believing his eyes. It couldn't be her… But it was. They leapt from their seats and clung to each other.

"I wasn't sure it was you at first," she whispered in his ear. "And when I knew, I couldn't think what to say… It had been so long… And I thought you'd have forgotten me."

"Never," he murmured in reply. His eyes flicked to Puss for a second; the cat wore his usual smug look. "When you left that day…"

"Father sent me away."

The king rose from his seat. "You know each other?"

"We met when we were children." Em rested her head on Pip's shoulder. "He was my best friend."

"Is that why you threw such a fit when I sent you away to your aunt's?" The king sighed. "My poor dear child. I had no idea. How curious that you two have met again, under such fortuitous circumstances." He glanced at Puss, who stopped washing his face.

"Don't look at me," the cat retorted. "You've got a wedding to plan, and I have a nap to take."

Puss leapt down from the table, leaving behind his hat and boots. "Oh, and have one of the servants put those on display somewhere. I am *not* wearing those again."

"Not even for a wedding?" Em begged. "Please, Monsieur Puss?"

The cat's tail flicked, but his stiff ears sagged a bit. "Perhaps for you, princess. But *only once*."

Laughing, Em turned back to Pip. "I probably should have asked you, or let you ask me first, but would you—"

"Yes." Pip sealed the promise with a kiss, and it was sweeter than any daydream, better than any story he could have told.

***

After a quiet local ceremony at their joint request, the king left to prepare a more lavish one in the capital. Pip and Em would join him soon, but first Pip had a few things he wished to take care of.

The first and most important one was Puss. Pip found the cat lounging on the grass in the sun.

"There must be something else I can do for you," Pip said. "You gave me everything I could have asked for."

The cat sniffed. "I didn't give you anything. Just

made sure the world would send you where you needed to go. Now, if you want to do me a favor, stop blocking the sun and send someone out with a bowl of cream. My feet ache from wearing those awful boots."

Pip chuckled and went to do as the cat asked.

A few days later, he and Em departed. Puss was left in charge, something no one commented on despite the oddness, because at this point, everyone was becoming used to the talking cat. Em promised to bring him the best catnip she could find when they returned from the capital, and Pip offered to bring him a new hat, a suggestion met with a sharp hiss and dark look.

"Get on with you," Puss said, flicking his tail. "I've got everything under control."

And on they went. One of the first places they stopped was the little town of Perrault. The toymakers were delighted to see him again.

"Here," Pip said, drawing a pouch from his satchel. He held it out. "This is for your kindness to a young lad searching for his own story."

"Did you find it?" George asked, accepting the pouch. His eyes widened at the weight.

"And then some." Pip fingered the crown, also stashed in his satchel. He wasn't used to its weight yet. "Would you like to hear the story?" When they nodded in unison, he smiled. "It's about a fanciful young miller's boy who became a storytelling prince, thanks to a very clever cat."

Rapunzel and the Toad

Renée Harvey

Once upon a time, there was a beautiful lady. She had silky golden curls that framed her oval face. Her green eyes sparkled, and her cheeks were healthy pink. She lived in a modern colonial-style mansion set on ten acres of property. The driveway was freshly paved, the shrubbery was precisely sculpted, and the lush green grass on the lawn was exactly one and a half inches tall. The lady loved rampion, so the plants bordered the driveway, dotted the rolling landscape in carefully gardened plots, and outlined the red brick mansion itself. She spent her mornings going for walks in her gardens, breathing in the tart, yet fresh, fragrance.

The only things she loved more than her rampions were her dear husband and cheery-faced daughter. Her days were filled with helping her husband keep his records and meetings organized, and in all the time in between, her daughter, named for her beloved flowers, was by her side. They played hopscotch, dress-up, even rode horses together, and the little girl with her mother's short golden curls had everything she could ever want.

That was once upon a time.

The lady got sick and laughed less; her pink cheeks were pale one day and flushed the next. The horseback rides fell by the wayside, the games of hopscotch were less enthusiastic, and the husband's record-keeping got sloppy. The husband took his precious wife to all the best doctors and witches, seeking anything that could help, but none knew what to do.

In a sterile hospital with monitors beeping, nurses rushing in and out with clipboards tucked under their arms, and a small rampion stem in the window being kept alive with a touch of fairy magic, the lady died.

Her husband, Goethe, tried to give their daughter everything she wanted, just as the lady had. There were horseback lessons, art classes, lavish birthday parties and more, but Rapunzel, caught between sadness and anger as she entered young womanhood, rebelled against her loving father. She stomped out of riding class never to return, threw the easel and paints out the highest mansion window where they landed in the mud, and locked herself in her room when fifty guests arrived for her sixteenth birthday party.

"Rapunzel," Goethe demanded as he knocked furiously on her bedroom door. "This behavior is unacceptable. All your friends are here—even Kelso. Should I tell them to return all their gifts?"

Goethe didn't want to send all the guests away. He couldn't care less about the mountain of gifts now piled on the entry table in the ballroom, but if they had a chance of making his heartbroken daughter laugh again, he would invite another fifty guests. Even another Kelso or two.

Kelso was a boy from Rapunzel's school, a handsome young man, tall, with dark, stylish hair, and who happened to be the elder son of Goethe's business partner, Rudyard. But he was a boy, and Goethe didn't want his precious daughter growing up too quick.

Still, Rapunzel and Kelso had been friends since they were babies, and Goethe had stacked the deck in his favor to make this birthday one Rapunzel would happily remember. There was a modern rock band, the entire agricultural team from school (a team which Rapunzel had insisted on joining after leaving behind her horses), and a disco ball hanging amid sparkling streamers and marbled balloons from the rafters. A tiered strawberry cake with banana frosting waited beside twenty gallons of double dutch chocolate ice cream in the kitchen, and enough pizza, soda, and crinkle-cut potato chips to feed three football teams lined the buffet tables.

Rapunzel threw her hairbrush against the door. "Just go away!" she yelled. And so, shoulders drooping, Goethe did.

He went back down the mahogany-lined hallway, descended the grand staircase with its polished handrail and Persian runner, and entered the ballroom where Rapunzel's guests danced to the band's music. One of the students, a freckled boy with wire-rimmed glasses named Luke, had his wand out and pointed at the streamers, making them twist and twirl in fancy patterns that made the rest of the crowd cheer.

Rudyard met Goethe against the wall. He nodded toward Luke and spoke loud enough to be heard over the band. "I didn't think you approved of Ms. Snatchelworthy's students."

Goethe couldn't say anything. Rudyard had another, impish, son, Henry, who was a student at the witch's school. Some called it a blessing. Goethe found it fortunate that Henry was, sadly, too busy with his coursework to attend. At the last camp out their families had taken together, Henry had thought himself clever when he lit up his sleeping bag in an eerie green light to see his way in the dark instead of just using the flashlight, and that wasn't his first episode of strange thinking.

Besides, Goethe, after seeing that magic held the same lack of cures for his wife as modern medicine, considered the study of magic a waste of time.

Rudyard changed the touchy subject to another sore spot. "You couldn't get Rapunzel to come down, hm?"

"Rudy, you know I've tried everything with that girl," Goethe replied, crossing his arms as he watched the door. "I even told her Kelso was here."

Rudyard laughed a deep belly laugh that drew Kelso's attention from across the room.

Kelso rolled his brown eyes, embarrassed, but left his friends to seek out Rapunzel. This was her party, after all. She had to show up at some point so everyone could eat the cake.

The band was just finishing a floor-shaking piece when Rapunzel, who had snuck downstairs after she was sure her father had left her room, realized through a gap in the ballroom doors how grand of a party he'd thrown for her. She clenched her manicured hands tightly. Clad in her flannel princess pajamas and pink bunny slippers, Rapunzel trembled in anger. "There will be a few guests," her father had told her a few weeks ago. "Dress comfortably. These are your friends."

Rapunzel spotted Luke manipulating the streamers with his wand. Those in that ag club could hardly be counted among her friends. This outfit would embarrass her in front of the entire school! One of the girls, Deidre, caught Rapunzel's eye and smiled.

Rapunzel faked a smile back but inwardly seethed. Her father would pay for embarrassing her like this. She pushed the ballroom doors wide open, strode straight ahead, and stole Luke's elm wand. He complained, but she ignored him.

She had a knack for magic, though Goethe wouldn't admit it, and she'd watched Luke practice with his wand before. She took the tool, magic end forward, and aimed it right at Goethe.

"This, dear father, is the end of the road.
I use your 'gift' to turn you into a toad!"
The magic shot out of the wand with a bright golden stream of light, and everyone watched in horror as the beam headed straight for Goethe.

Well, not quite. Kelso happened to be walking by, hoping Rapunzel had been hiding somewhere near their fathers and just needed some encouragement to come out. The beam hit him, and he disappeared in a brilliant flash.

Rapunzel's jaw dropped. She hadn't meant to hit her friend!

"What did you do?" Rudyard yelled, turning red in the face at the loss of his son.

Rapunzel fell to her knees, searching all across the floor beneath everyone's feet for Kelso. *Where did he go?* she thought. *What did I do to him?* She had only visualized her father as a toad, sipping his beverage as he lounged outside a café in Paris. *I haven't sent Kelso all the way to Paris, have I?*

"Call the police!" Deidre yelled.

"I'm getting out of here," another boy, Kirk, declared. He headed straight for the exit, and everyone else ran after him. Luke snatched back his wand on the way out the door.

Rudyard was so angry he shook. With that part about the "road" in Rapunzel's spell, Kelso could be anywhere in the world now, lost, alone, and confused. He stomped out of the ballroom, slamming the door shut behind him so hard the stained glass windows rattled.

Goethe scanned the room for any sign of a toad while he waited for the band members to exit. He knew the spell had been meant for him, and something had to be done about his daughter. He had let her behavior go unchecked for far too long, she had turned against him, and, in the process, had hurt her friend. His thoughts flew to an ancient tower hidden in the middle of the nearby forest, safe, and far away from anyone. Rapunzel wouldn't be able to harm anyone there.

"Rapunzel, you are out of control," he said, forcing himself to speak rationally as she searched in every corner. "I'm taking you to Isobel Tower. You must learn that this behavior is unacceptable. I will have the butler bring the car around, and the maid will pack your bag. We will leave immediately. You may come home after we have located

Kelso."

Rapunzel protested all the way to the Cadillac, bargained as they drove down the highway, and fell into a surly pout by the time they passed the swamps that lay around Isobel Tower.

Goethe led Rapunzel up the tower's narrow steps and let her fall in the middle of the room's gray stone floor. He parked her rolling suitcase beside her as he fingered an old, tarnished key that fit the lock on the door.

Rapunzel watched that tarnished key closely. If she could take it from him, then she could lock him in this dank, dark room, throw away the key, then head off to find Kelso herself. She had a few ideas of where to start.

"You are to stay here," Goethe told her. "Caretaker will check in on you. I will give her the key. Oh, and just in case you decide to pick the lock…" He pulled a pouch of pixie dust from his pocket and tossed a pinch of the sparkling dust on the door's handle.

"The rest of the tower has other charms to prevent escape," Goethe added, then moved to exit.

"Daddy, wait!" Rapunzel pleaded. "How will you tell me when you're coming back or when you've found Kelso? You took my phone."

With a small smile, Goethe pulled a brass hand mirror from his shoulder bag. "We will talk via this."

Rapunzel accepted the heavy mirror. The glass was smooth. Roses were engraved along the frame, and four pearls were set into the back. The handle was too small for her, as if made for a child instead of a teen. It seemed very unremarkable.

"How does it work?" she asked, eyeing him suspiciously.

He laughed. "You kids can figure out smartphones in less time than it takes to pour a bowl of cereal, and you're asking me how a simple a/v mirror works?" He chuckled again, then rested his hand on the doorknob. "I love you,

Punzie. Just as much as your mother did. I hope one day you can see that."

Goethe gripped the handle.

"Father, wait! Please, can't I—" She wanted to give him a hug and sneak the key out of his hand.

Goethe pulled the door shut. There was a faint clicking on the other side. Rapunzel rushed forward and twisted the handle, but it held firm. She banged against the door, shouting his name in frustration, but it was useless.

Rapunzel refused to cry. Wiping away a stray tear, she whirled around.

The room had stone walls that matched its floor, all of it cold gray with bits of moss in the dark corners. There was a plain, but clean, twin bed against the left side with fresh bedding at the foot. A coal-burning stove was on the right, with a blackened barrel on one side and another lidded barrel on the other. Four wooden pillars held the roof up. Directly across from the door was a large window. A heavy brown curtain hung from a silver rod above. Rapunzel rushed to the window and peered out.

Four stories below was the great forest that surrounded Isobel. The stairs up to this room had seemed to go on for ages, but it was nothing compared to the total lack of civilization in the trees before her now.

At the base of the tower, Goethe emerged. Rapunzel shouted to him, desperate for one last chance to change his mind, but he simply shut the tower door, got into his Cadillac, and drove back down the dirt lane.

Rapunzel squared her jaw. First step: find someone to help her get out of this tower. Second step: get to an airport and take the first flight to Paris, using Goethe's frequent flier miles, of course. Kelso had to be there.

Behind her, right beside her suitcase where she'd dropped it, was the mirror. The pearls were only minorly scratched from the rough fall, but the glass was still perfectly intact, no doubt protected from damage by magic. She flipped the mirror over and over, looking for how to make it work, but it didn't come with an instruction manual.

She smacked it in frustration. *If only Kelso were here*, she thought, but she quickly put it out of her mind. No amount of wishing would make him appear.

But Hillary would know what to do. She was a cheerleader friend who knew how to worm her way out of tough situations.

The mirror shimmered in Rapunzel's hands, the glass glistening like the sun rising from behind mountains until Hillary's perfectly made-up face appeared in the reflection.

"Rapunzel? Hey, I heard about your party. I'm sorry I couldn't go." Hillary looked at her reflection off-screen as she fixed her cherry lip gloss. "Did you find Kelso?"

"No, and for it, my father locked me in Isobel Tower," Rapunzel complained.

"In Isobel? Isn't that a bit extreme?"

"Who knows?" Rapunzel replied. "Can you help me get out of here? Maybe help me find a way around the magic?" She turned the mirror around, aiming it to show Hillary the tower's interior.

"Wait, so did your father ground you? How come you still have your phone?"

Rapunzel turned the mirror back to herself. "I don't have my phone. This is a crazy old mirror. Your family doesn't have one, too?"

Hillary shook her head, eyebrows slightly raised to make her look amused and vaguely interested. "Nope. You're on video chat right now."

Rapunzel had more pressing concerns. "Cool. Will you help me see if there's a way out of here?" She turned the mirror back around to show the room.

"Actually, it's almost time for cheer practice," Hillary said. "Chat another time?"

Before Rapunzel could turn the mirror around, Hillary was gone.

"Well, *she's* no help." Rapunzel dropped the mirror on the floor, trusting the protective shield on it to once again protect it from harm. She turned to the door itself. "Father *said* it was protected, but maybe it was just a show?" She pulled a bobby pin out of her chin-length curls and straightened it out to make a pick. Then, she rested one hand on the brass knob and inserted the pin.

Or would have, except for the tingling that zipped up her fingers, hand, and forearm. The bobby pin skittered across the floor.

"Ouch."

Next, she climbed to the rafters and any hole in the magic up there, but the air itself seemed to shock her as she reached for the nearest rafter, making her tumble all the way back down.

"Ow! Really?!"

She tried throwing the bench against the door, but she could barely lift the wood, never mind slam it hard enough to break anything. She got a bruised foot from dropping it.

She poked stones until she got bored of trying to find a loose one.

She tried swinging her legs outside the window where the breeze tugged against her princess pajamas, but there was another zappy field just below the ledge and around the window's frame.

"Ow!"

Rubbing her tingling hands, she plopped down on the bed, ready to give up for the night. The sun was setting and she was tired.

Then, a toad croaked from within the room.

***

At the moment Rapunzel's magical spell hit Kelso, he felt strangely suffocating, like every cell in his body was expelling all its extra space. He shrank much smaller as the magic tossed him against the wall behind the table. There, he had avoided the stampede of classmates leaving the ballroom. After realizing that he was now a toad, he heard Goethe's plan to take Rapunzel to Isobel and hopped into the Cadillac. At the tower, he had jumped one step at a time, all the way up the stairs to Rapunzel's room, landing inside just as Goethe locked the door.

Now, determined to be freed from the spell, Kelso sought out the only means he knew to help himself out of his predicament. He hopped onto the magical mirror and thought hard of his brother at Ms. Snatchelworthy's school. The mirror shimmered beneath his webbed feet.

Rapunzel leaped up. "Get off that, you toad!" Kelso leaped away as she scooped up the mirror.

The image in the mirror lightened until it was filled by a boy with spiky red hair and freckles across his narrow nose. It was Kelso's little brother, Henry. He took after his mother.

"Hiya, Punzel!"

"Henry?" Rapunzel was confused. *How did a slimy little toad manage to call him? Or did Henry call me? Does he already know what I did to Kelso?* "I thought you were at school."

"Ms. Snatchelworthy's Institute for Phantasmagorical Adolescents?" Henry asked, grinning cheekily, too happy for knowing about his brother being cursed, even for him.

Rapunzel frowned at his smugness. "You don't have to rub it in."

Henry laughed. "But it's so much fun to say!"

"Is Ms. Snatchelworthy in her office?" Rapunzel asked sharply. An idea worked its way into her mind—one that would undo the magic that kept her locked in this cold, dark tower, freeing her to go find Kelso before Henry found out about his brother.

Henry shook his head and showed her the rest of the room. There was a vast collection of mason jars filled with all kinds of plants, animals, and bones scattered across the wooden tables. A fire crackled merrily in the fireplace against the far wall.

"She said she'd be back in the morning. Some rich guy hired her to keep an eye on someone. Is there some way I can help?"

Rapunzel was disappointed, but Henry was Ms. Snatchelworthy's student—a student of magic. She would have to tell him what had happened and hope he could help. The sooner she got out of this tower, the sooner she could fix everything. Reluctantly, carefully, she related her tale.

"I just want to get out of here," she explained. "Once I find Kelso, I'll figure out how to put everything right."

Kelso listened earnestly from beside the nearest support post. *Rapunzel's sorry?* he thought, but he didn't believe her.

Henry thought long and hard, chewing his bottom lip as he stared at a dark corner of the room. "I can think of one recipe that might get you out of the tower. Wave your hair around."

Rapunzel obeyed.

"Wasp stingers and poison oak," Henry said with a grin on his face.

"Excuse me?"

"I'll need them for the potion. I'll get it to you by morning."

"Really?" Rapunzel asked. "How?"

Henry grinned and showed her an apple. Then he snapped his fingers. The apple disappeared from his hand, and Rapunzel heard a *thunk* on the floor beside her. It was the apple.

"Magic," Henry replied, and the mirror's surface went dark.

Rapunzel bit into the little apple. It was tart and crunchy, but very juicy. In the dim light, Rapunzel saw Kelso still nearby. His buggy eyes looked hungrily at the apple. "You want some, too?" she asked. She didn't know if toads could eat apples, but she bit off a little piece and scooted it toward him. Kelso munched at it as if it was the sweetest honey.

The next morning, Rapunzel woke up as the sun poked its head out from behind the distant tree line. Her short blond hair was frizzy from a night of tossing and turning, but she had slept better once she discovered her favorite blanket in the suitcase. It was threadbare and very faded, but she could still make out the pink and purple hearts all over it. Mother had given it to her for her fourth birthday.

Next to the door was a platter filled with food. Scrambled eggs, toast and marmalade, hash browns, and apple juice. Rapunzel shared some of the egg with Kelso, who was at the foot of her bed, just as trapped as she was. He snapped up the egg appreciatively.

Then she noticed a vial she hadn't seen earlier next to the platter. It was a small glass vial tinted in purple with gold trim. There was a note tied with twine around the vial's neck.

"Use six drops of this potion to wash your hair every three hours. Call me again tomorrow with the results. Henry."

Rapunzel squealed, giddy as a birthday girl. Here was her ticket out to join the search for Kelso!

She took the vial to the stove, where she'd found that the second barrel was filled with clean water. She'd drank a bunch yesterday, but the barrel still seemed completely full. She used exactly six drops of the potion like shampoo before rinsing the spicy-smelling brown stuff out.

All day, Kelso stayed nearby, following her around like a puppy or mournfully watching out the window. *The best Henry could come up with is shampoo?* he thought.

Rapunzel wasn't sure how a toad pulled off such a

mournful look, but how else would one describe how the eyes seemed to droop so much and the lips were so down turned? Was Kelso, wherever he was, just as sad?

Probably not. Kelso's much better about getting himself out of trouble than me. He's probably already human again, and on his way home.

Though she waited for her father's call, she followed Henry's directions exactly. Except for the time around noon where she thought she miscounted the drops and added another for good measure. The next time, she thought she'd made a mistake and only used five drops.

"How much difference can one drop make anyway, right?" she asked the toad as she washed her hands. He didn't reply, but he was the only one around to listen; Goethe had yet to call.

There was something pokey in the potion, along with something that made the watery solution feel silky on her fingers. Henry had said something about hornets and poison oak, and she didn't want to get a rash, so she used extra lye soap available next to the never-draining barrel of water.

She woke up as often as she could through the night to wash her hair, and the constant interruptions to her sleep meant she got up for the day after the sun was fully risen. At least she was certain she hadn't missed a call. *What if Father is making me stay here longer just to teach me a lesson? What if Kelso is really still missing?*

Rapunzel ran her fingers through her hair as she ate the French toast and sausage that had appeared by the door, more determined than ever, now, to get out and find Kelso, or at least figure out what was going on. What was the potion supposed to do? If anything, her hair only felt more staticky than before. *How am I supposed to get out with static hair?*

Worried, she called Henry.

"I don't think it worked," she said when his freckled face appeared again in the mirror. He looked sad. "Hey, are you okay?"

Henry swallowed. "Fine. Father hasn't heard anything from Kelso. I'm worried. You really did a number on him with that spell of yours."

Guilt gnawed at Rapunzel's soul like termites attacking a wood plank. "I'm sorry, Henry. I'm going to fix it. I can't do anything until I get out of this tower, though."

Henry furrowed his brow. "You said the recipe didn't work? It should've. Let me check." He went away from the mirror, leaving Rapunzel to look at a portrait hanging above the fireplace. It was framed by a heavy rose-engraved border. The portrait was of a woman, tall and regal, comfortably dressed in jeans and a sweater. She had a brown mole on her chin, and her brown eyes looked on in patience as Rapunzel had often seen in her mother.

Kelso croaked again from the floor, eying Rapunzel with a doleful gaze. She reached out to pat her companion's bumpy skin. He wasn't as slimy as he looked.

Kelso appreciated the gesture. *But it still doesn't make up for turning me into a toad and worrying my family.*

There was something he had read before, something he was missing about Henry's potion…

Henry reappeared with a thin book opened in his hand. "I found it, and I followed it exactly. You should've noticed the effects by now."

"What was it supposed to do?" Rapunzel asked, reaching again for the gentle little toad.

"Wait, there's something in the margins. Use toad secretions…"

Kelso remembered now. He'd helped Henry study for his exams and knew what his newfound secretions were supposed to do. A bit gleeful, he leaped high in the air, landing squarely on Rapunzel's head, and began clawing at her hair.

Rapunzel squealed. She batted at the toad, but his little paws clung to her hair, tugging painfully at her scalp when she tried to pull him off. He was secreting something slimy and warm. "Henry, help, it's so gross!"

Kelso completed his work and hopped down. He curled back up on the floor to wait.

Rapunzel tried to pull the goop out of her hair, shuddering as she realized her hands were covered in what felt like slimy boogers. "Ew, ew, ew!"

She pulled and pulled, desperate to cleanse her hair. She ran her fingers to her tips and little blobs of goop landed on her shirt. *The maid is going to have a cow about having to clean this...*

She pulled her hair from roots to tips, roots all the way to tips, roots all...the...way...

Rapunzel's hair was longer. Her tips were a couple inches past her shoulders. She pulled her fingers through the glistening strands again to be sure, and the tips nearly reached her elbows.

"Henry, what is this?" She combed again in front of the mirror, stretching her hair even farther.

Henry's stunned expression turned upward as he laughed. "That's it! It's working! What happened?"

"It was the toad." Rapunzel turned to Kelso, who sat, eyes closed, on the floor.

"The secretions, of course!" Henry smacked his forehead with his palm. "Toad secretions make things slippery, allowing them to stretch and mold their shape. It's what the stingers and poison oak needed to be activated! While your hair is wet, you can make it grow long enough now that it'll reach the base of the tower, and you can just climb down."

Rapunzel hadn't forgotten about the zappy field around the window. "How am I going to get past the charms?"

Henry waved his hand. "I added a bit of dung to the potion. Pixie dust to rise and cling to the air, pixie poop to fall and cling to the ground."

Rapunzel took her hands away from her hair

instantly. Now the brown color made sense.

"You'll have no problem getting around the enchantments." Henry sighed. "When you get down, call me again, and I'll see if I can help you track down Kelso. Ms. Snatchelworthy left a few minutes ago to speak with the guy who hired her. I'll have to wait for her to get back to ask, but it's my brother. It should be fine."

Rapunzel cringed and began pulling at her hair again, her determination to find her friend inflamed. "See you soon, Henry. We'll find him."

Henry ended the call quickly, and Rapunzel looked around the room, trying not to think about the stuff now spread all over her hair. *It'll hurt like crazy if I tie my hair to the ledge or one of those posts and rappel down, but what if I use some ties to make a rope?*

Piles and piles of shiny blond locks were gathered under the window sill, and Rapunzel finished twisting a barrette at the base of her neck. Several minutes later, she found the hair ends, the strands now dry, and tied them around the nearest support post. She pulled hard and was satisfied when the knot held firm. Then she picked up the mirror and returned to the window. Looking all the way to the ground four stories down, she took a deep breath to calm her thudding heart. It was time to help Henry find out what happened to Kelso, figure out how to turn him back the way he was, and apologize for the rest of her life.

Kelso croaked as he leaped over to Rapunzel. He didn't want to be left in Isobel any more than she did. By jumping on the ledge, he made it more difficult for her to descend the tower without him.

Rapunzel smiled. "You want to go too, Toady?" She tucked the mirror into her belt and Kelso into a knotted pouch she tied into her shirt, then tossed all the rest of her hair out the window. It cascaded as a wavy blond waterfall halfway down the tower. Henry hadn't exaggerated how long she'd be able to stretch it. Grabbing the makeshift rope, she twisted herself out the window. Kelso pressed himself as flat as he could inside the makeshift pocket.

The zappy field's tingling bothered them for just a moment but faded once they were down a few feet. Rapunzel went faster after that, reaching the ground in no time.

"Well, that was easy."

Kelso jumped out of the pocket, glad to be back on solid ground. He sucked in the sweet air of freedom. Now, he needed to find some way to get Henry to realize he was the toad everyone was looking for.

Rapunzel pulled out her mirror to call Henry as she'd promised. The mirror, with its heavy face, fumbled in her hands and fell to the ground.

The glass cracked into several pieces.

Rapunzel gasped. She reached for the mirror, but her hair caught; it was still tied to the post four stories above her.

Rapunzel screamed in frustration.

I could leave her here, Kelso considered. *She* did *turn me into a toad, after all.*

Still, she hadn't shunned him in the tower, and she had brought him back down. She might again be able to help him reach Henry faster to undo the spell. He wasn't far, but humans could run faster. He hopped over to the mirror. Very uncoordinated, he pushed it closer to Rapunzel's foot.

When she realized what the toad was doing, Rapunzel cheered and kept urging the little critter on. The handle came just within reach of her foot, and she flipped it up just enough that she could grab it.

The surface of the mirror was cracked like a spider web. It reflected Rapunzel in broken chunks. She tried with all her might to call Henry—to call Hillary—to even call her father!—but the sunset colors never shone. Sighing, she tried to sit down. Her hair wasn't quite long enough to manage that, and it refused to stretch any farther.

Kelso croaked.

"What are you looking at?" Rapunzel asked, feeling very sorry for herself. *I'm all alone at the bottom of this tower, and the toad has the nerve to croak at me! And what's with that smug expression on that fat little face?*

"Oh, just go away," Rapunzel complained. She made as if to throw the mirror at it. The glass shifted. Pieces fell off and flew to the ground. With a sharp breath, Rapunzel froze.

Then, she realized that those shards could be used like a knife. She drew the mirror back to her and gingerly picked out the largest piece of remaining glass, which had been laid on top of a wooden back. Gently, she tossed the rest of the frame away and gripped her hair. The glass sliced through the golden locks with a ripping sound.

Freed, Rapunzel cheered. "Come on, Toady. Let's get out of here and go find Kelso." She tried to scoop him up, but he hopped away, taking four big leaps down the overgrown road before Rapunzel could catch up.

Together, they traveled the paths that cut through the forest, seeking the exit, but the day grew later, and the sun set before they reached the edge of the woods.

Rapunzel hugged herself tightly, shivering hard as she stumbled forward in the darkness. "T-toady, are you s-s-still there?" She could hardly see more than a foot or two ahead of her. The trees above her were too thick to let much moonlight through.

Somewhere off to the side, Kelso croaked. She couldn't tell for sure, though. She'd heard several other toads around the ponds they'd passed. Still, Rapunzel veered, hoping to find him again.

"He's probably headed to a bog," Rapunzel grumbled to herself, but at least a bog was better than tripping over tree roots she couldn't see.

Her foot sank into a hole, and she fell forward with a shout. Deep, aching pain ignited in her ankle. Her cold fingers gripped the dirt as she began sobbing.

"I'm hurt." She gasped. "I'm hurt, and I'm lost in this stupid forest far away from that stupid tower, and no one will ever find my stupid self again." Gingerly, she curled into a ball on the ground, feeling the dirt beneath her cheek and scraping against her arm. "Toady, are you still there?"

There was a croak right above her head, and she rolled her chin up to see.

Kelso watched her, waiting for her to get back up so they could keep going.

"Toady, I need help," she whimpered. "Do you understand? Please."

Kelso heard her anguish. He sat still, an uncomfortable ache filling his belly and chest as he realized Rapunzel had gone as far as she could.

Rapunzel curled her arms around herself. "I know you'll probably just hop away now, but it's cold, and I'm tired, and now I've done something to my ankle." Warm tears ran across her face as she realized she might die in the woods. She didn't want to die. Not here, all alone. *Father will never get over it, especially not after losing Mother, too. He doesn't deserve that.* "Please, Toady. Can you help?"

Kelso remained in his spot, unblinking, his mind spinning. He thought he knew where he was. Help might not be that far away.

Sighing, Rapunzel curled back up to try to repress her shivering. A *toad* couldn't help her. Her eyes were heavy. Her ankle ached. Her stomach rumbled from missing a meal. When she looked back up again, her only companion was gone. Just like Mother, just like Hillary, all her friends, and just like Father. "Please, Toady," she whispered, as if she could beg him to reappear.

It was hours later when several voices brought her out of a restless sleep.

"Rapunzel!"

"Rapunzel, are you out here?"

"Punzie, please answer!"

The calls sounded as if coming through a fog that coated Rapunzel's ears. There was a toad croaking, too.

"Punzie!" Goethe called again. Henry was with him, too, and the woman from the portrait.

"Father?" Rapunzel opened her eyes and uncurled, trying to see where they were coming from. Her ankle twinged, making her gasp.

"Rapunzel?" Henry called.

"I'm over here," she replied with a scratchy voice. Nearby lights flickered.

"Over here!" she tried again, and the lights turned toward her. She was saved! Tears streamed down her face.

"Punzie." Goethe dropped his flashlight and scooped her up, rocking her in his warm, comforting arms. Rapunzel cried out as the movement jostled her ankle.

Alarmed, Goethe examined her length. "She's hurt."

"Ah, a twisted ankle, I see," the woman replied in a no-nonsense tone. Rapunzel felt a gentle pressure around her foot where the woman inspected the damage. "Henry, bring me the potions."

"Yes, Ms. Snatchelworthy."

The area around Rapunzel was bathed in light. She sat up in her father's lap and saw she was surrounded by thick trees. The ground was relatively clear but pockmarked. There was no way to know which hole she'd stepped in. The light came from what looked like clear half-size bowling balls and lit the area as if it was the middle of the day.

Ms. Snatchelworthy, with her hair tied back, finished applying a paste to Rapunzel's ankle. "There, that should do it. Just be careful how you walk for the next few days while it heals."

"Can't you just heal it now? I hired you to watch over her, Hepzibah," Goethe growled. He remembered how little witches like Hepzibah had been able to do nothing for his wife, but perhaps this witch had a yet unknown skill. With Rapunzel nursing a wound, his quest to find Kelso for

Rudyard would be stalled.

Hepzibah Snatchelworthy smiled apologetically. "Magic only goes so far, Goethe. You should know this. The potion can minimize the pain, but the wound has to heal on its own."

Rapunzel sniffed, drying her tears as she felt the potion work. She thought she could move her ankle more freely now, if she so desired, but she remembered Ms. Snatchelworthy's warning to be careful for the next few days.

Kelso croaked and leaped into her lap. His wide eyes stared straight up at her, and Rapunzel recognized Toady.

"Get off, you!" Goethe said, reaching out to move the creature, but Rapunzel pushed his hand away.

"Father, no! He's my friend."

"He came right up to the door of the hut and started smacking himself against it," Henry said. "It was Ms. Snatchelworthy who realized he was trying to tell us something."

Awed, Rapunzel stared at her friend. "You saved me," she whispered. She laughed, joyful, scooped him up, and kissed his cheek in thanks.

There was a flash of gold light that blinded them all. When they blinked away the bright spots, they found a handsome young man sitting in his party attire in the middle of them all.

"Kelso!" Henry and Rapunzel shouted together.

Kelso laughed, overjoyed to be back to his normal self and very glad to not have to croak or jump against a door to get anyone's attention anymore. "Thank you," he said to Rapunzel, feeling his cheeks burn as he recalled the kiss, but then Henry tackled him.

Relieved he was okay, Rapunzel giggled, then turned to Goethe, humbled.

"I'm sorry, Father. I didn't mean for it to happen."

Goethe hugged her tightly. "You and I both miss your mother very much, don't we? But...can't we try again to make our little family work?"

She thought about the party, the relatively comfortable tower, the mirror, the care, and even the search for her tonight. Goethe had proved over and over again that he loved her just as much as Mother had. She had been a child not to see it. Blinking back tears, Rapunzel wrapped her arms tightly around his neck. "Please, let's try again."

And so they did.

The Scarred Shepherdess

Kelsie Engen

~ I ~

The wild birds mock Clara as she flies across the rocky ground of the King's Forest. Blinking away her tears, she pulls at her fur-lined cloak as a tree branch rips at it. All too soon, she will be huddled inside its warmth as the first cold, lonely night of her exile sets in.

Clara ducks her head and forces her slipper-clad feet to move; she cannot be caught here, neither by those watching, nor the tempestuous Fae. She travels until her feet are bleeding, until she leaves the King's Forest and enters the Edormiscan Forest. Only then does her mad pace slow— although the danger does not end.

The cheery sunlight filtering through sparse branches turns to a dark forest floor shielded by a thick canopy of leaves. Clara casts a lingering glance over her shoulder at the Edormiscan Forest as she disentangles her gown from the grasping branches.

Staying within its borders is impossible with the grave accusations against her. If she stays, she dies. So she treks on, tugging her dress and cape free every few steps.

Shivering, she pauses at the base of a tree with human-sized leaves to shelter her from the rain drizzling down from the sky. Darkness envelops her, allowing her to see only a few feet ahead of her path. Heart hammering in her chest, Clara presses on. A minute later, she gasps as the smooth expanse of a wooden house appears before her, stretching out as far as she can see in either direction.

Cautiously, one hand upon the rough-hewn oak, she tiptoes alongside the wall until she finds a door. No light peeks out from within, and Clara bites down hard on her lip. Does she knock? Hoping it is a friend and not an enemy within? Or does she pass on, hoping whoever is within does not see her?

She dabs at dry lips with a dry tongue. She's found no water she can trust yet, so her tongue only cleaves to dry teeth.

Hesitating, she lifts her hand and knocks.

And knocks.

And no one answers.

Disappointment wars with relief within her at the home's abandonment. The knob turns under her hand, and she pushes her way inside. A candle tilts crookedly on a wooden table inside, and Clara lights it with a match from a nearby box. She takes the sputtering candle with her as she scours the kitchen cupboards, discovering dusty bottles of fermented gooseberry juice. She drinks her fill, for it is far safer than any water she might find in this area of Edormisco.

Setting down an empty bottle, she turns and gasps at the sight of a ragged woman with cuts crisscrossing her face wearing a dirty gown. Clara staggers backward and so does the woman. She lets out a breath. It's her.

Raising the candle, she walks closer to the mirror, inspecting herself in the cracked glass. She had been at the King's ball the night she'd fled, wearing a faery-made gown of the softest silk. That was the night everything went wrong. The night of the attack upon King Effrenatus. The night of her arrest.

She leans forward, and the teenaged girl in the mirror does the same. Raising a hand, she touches it to the fresh wounds upon her face. They were not there the morning of the ball, and yet they already look half healed. With a shake of her head, she turns her gaze upon her body instead. The bottom of her faery-made gown is in tatters, though her faery attendant could turn it back into the beautiful gown it had been with a flick of her wings, or even something completely new.

But she cannot keep traveling in it. Thoughtful, she takes the candle and finds the bedroom. A trunk at the foot of the bed stores a few articles of clothing, but the only one that will fit her is a simple, gray wool dress.

She changes into the dry clothes and stretches out upon the dusty, mouse-nibbled bed. In moments, she sleeps the sleep only a prisoner on the run could sleep.

***

Clara stumbles out of a copse to the edge of a low rock wall. A humble cottage of rock stands a quarter mile away, black and white sheep dotting the landscape between her and it. She has never welcomed such a sight before. She had almost begun to believe that all of Edormisco had abandoned her.

Lurching over the rock wall, she points herself in the direction of the cottage. At the door, she drops her sack and knocks, swaying.

There is a rustle inside, a babe crying, and a young woman opens the door. She blinks at Clara, her astute gaze sweeping over the princess before saying, with great hesitancy, "Can I help you?"

"I—" Clara stops and bites her lip. "I am a traveler weary from days on the road. Do you have any clean water?"

"Of course. Faery's teeth, you look ill. When's the last time you had something to eat?"

Clara weaves in place. "Five days? I couldn't trust anything in the forest."

"The forest? What forest?"

"The Edormiscan Forest," Clara manages.

The woman's face blanches at her words. "You came from the forest? From Edormisco?"

"Yes." For the first time, a hint of panic probes at Clara.

Her eyes sweeping over Clara's face again, the woman takes her time in answering. "Five days? Come in. Sit down. You need food." Taking her by the arm, she helps Clara to the table before returning to the door and picking up her cloak-sack. "I have some fresh bread and sheep's milk. You must eat and drink, regain your strength."

Clara barely finds the strength to shovel the bread and tip the milk into her mouth.

"What is your name?"

Clara takes her time swallowing the sheep's milk. "Vera." As she speaks, she experiences a pang of guilt at the half-truth. "What is your child's name?"

"Clara."

Clara starts, grateful to find the woman distracted in giving her daughter a tender smile.

"I am Dulcis," she adds.

Breath returns to Clara, and she takes another bite of bread to hide her worries. "Thank you, Dulcis. For the food."

As Clara finishes eating, Dulcis gazes at her, bouncing baby Clara absently on her knee. "I thought for a moment you were the prisoner on the loose." Her gaze seems both hard and soft at once.

Panic trembles throughout Clara though she fights to stay calm. "Prisoner? No. And I saw no one on my way here."

Bottom lip between her teeth, Dulcis nods slowly. The baby gives a cry, and her mother resumes her bouncing, shaking a wooden rattle in the shape of a sheep before the baby's blue eyes.

Clara considers the slender woman, with her dark bags under sky blue eyes. She wears a simple wool dress in blue a shade darker than her gaze.

Clearing her throat, Clara pushes back the plate from before her. "I wish there were some way for me to thank you. I cannot imagine how long I would have traveled without meeting anyone."

Dulcis shakes her head with a rueful expression, shifting the baby onto her other shoulder. "You wouldn't have lasted much longer."

She nods thoughtfully. "Where am I?"

"You're in Ostium. About an hour's ride from the capital."

"I am?" Clara bites her lip at being in the land of what had once been considered an enemy. Were they still? Dulcis, whatever her opinion on Edormiscans, seems kind. "I wonder…where to go now?" Clara murmurs to herself.

Dulcis gives her a curious look, her gaze lingering on her left cheek. "Are you looking for work?"

"I—yes. Though I am not trained in much." Clara almost laughs.

"Well, can you keep house? Cook?"

Clara bites her lip, all humor gone. "No. I'm afraid my education was lacking in that."

"Can you tend sheep?" Dulcis asks.

"I—" Clara closes her mouth. *How much can there be to tending sheep?* "I can try."

Dulcis's eyes glint. "It is not difficult."

"I am a fast learner."

"I will speak with my husband when he returns. It would help us greatly to have a shepherdess."

"Thank you. In the meantime, can I help you somehow? With the baby?"

"Thank you." Dulcis hands over the baby, and Clara takes her, smiling. *Perhaps I am not so useless after all.*

~ II ~

Under the heat of the sun, Clara revels in the sights of green grass and blue skies, thick clumps of trees and fields of colorful flowers. Despite the lack of faeries and all traces of magic, there is a magic here in nature she has never seen before.

Even with its hardships, she enjoys her newfound freedom. She sleeps before the fire in the cottage, rises early to take the sheep to pasture, and returns late bringing them home. It is a dirty job, being a shepherdess, but Clara finds a satisfying simplicity in it.

The sun beats down upon her, in less than a month having turned her skin from the color of cream to sand. She has learned much in her exile, including how to wield a needle and thread, but all of Dulcis's cooking lessons have failed to teach her a thing.

Sheep bleat around her, ewes with their lambs frolicking nearby or resting in the shade of the trees along the edge of this pasture. Nearby is a pond of such clarity that Clara first saw the extent of the curse she had brought upon herself. Then tears had sprung to her eyes at the sight of the scars crisscrossing the left side of her face. They have not disappeared. Not that she's held out much hope, but in quiet moments of reflection, she still wishes for the face she once had.

Today, she ignores the still surface as she stows away her mending in her sack, rises and brushes off her skirts. As she does, her fingers snag on a rip. "Heavens. Another one? How am I going to manage that?" She only has the one dress, except—

Soon after she arrived at the cottage, she hid her cloak and faery-made dress under a rock by the pond. Dulcis and her husband can never discover Clara's secret.

She makes her way toward the pond, inspecting the surrounding pasture and trees to make certain that no one has stumbled upon her. When she reaches the pond, she unbuttons her wool dress and shakes herself free of it, leaving her white shift on. She casts a glance at the pond then back at the sheep.

It is early morning, and the sun already scalds. A swim will be the perfect way to cool off. Her mending can wait a few minutes. She swims deep, enjoying the cold, refreshing water as it embraces her. When she finally climbs out, her skin is chilled and her flesh is like a goose's freshly plucked. She shivers but wrings out her long hair and raises her scarred face to the sky, knowing she will warm quickly.

Thoughtful, she pulls out her faery-made dress and shakes the creases from it. Just the sight brings back a hundred memories of better days, and she can't resist: she steps in.

As she smooths the dress down over her thighs, she thinks she hears a little tut of disapproval. It sounds so much like her faery attendant, Alma, that tears spring to her eyes.

"You'll never get those wrinkles out. Not without me."

Great. Now I'm hearing her voice, too. Clara sighs and abandons her attempt at smoothing the dress. *They won't come out. That much is true.*

"Here," the voice says in her head. Then there is the familiar warmth of magic at work, and Clara gasps as her faery assistant materializes before her.

"Alma!"

The little faery smiles, bobbing in front of her face.

"How did you get here?" Clara demands. "Have you been exiled? How——?" She's so thrilled she could smash the faery in her arms but restrains herself. Barely.

"I followed you," Alma says, eyes glinting with pride.

"But… Why now?" It's been weeks since her exile.

Alma's entire body dims, even her faery dust losing some of its sparkle as she flutters in the air before Clara. "Your father—he's set a bounty upon your head."

The entire world goes cold. "What? But why?"

Alma's face falls. "I don't know. But soldiers have been sent to find you. I think…I think it's Prudens's doing."

Clara's sharp inhale breaks the silence at the news of her sister's continued misbehavior.

Clara's exile had started with a spell…Prudens's spell. And when she had cast it, Clara had been forced to cast a spell of her own, hoping to stop the effects of Prudens's curse. Only Clara's magic wasn't powerful enough against her sister's. Prudens's curse, enhanced by the Edormiscan tiara she wore, had succeeded. Clara had suffered the magical backlash, and Prudens had convinced their father that Clara was at fault.

"She has dabbled in dark magic too long." Alma bites her bottom lip, her eyes glimmering in concern. "It has taken a grave hold of her, Clara. Which is why I left to find you."

"What am I supposed to do?" Clara's mouth works over ideas she cannot fathom. "Go back? I don't have the magic to defeat her."

Alma shakes her head. "No. We must find some way to stop her. Together."

"Without having her discover your help," Clara adds grimly. "Or else you'll have a death sentence upon you as well."

"I already do," Alma answers. "For crossing the border. You know the laws as well as I." She gives a tiny shrug, and her faery glow swells. "Now. I'm starving. Would you like some lunch? I've been practicing my cooking and think I can whip up an excellent feast." She gives a wink. "I find it's all in the quality of salt you use. And luckily, I brought some of the best Edormisco has to offer."

Without another word, the faery sets to work creating a feast, and a few minutes later, Clara is eating like a queen.

***

"That was excellent," Clara says, leaning back against the large rock by the pond and patting her stomach. "I can't believe how much you've improved."

Alma flutters her wings in thanks.

"Did you—"

"Shh!" Alma hushes her, her wings going transparent in her alarm, a Fae defense mechanism.

Clara bolts to her feet just as a man rides a horse around a clump of trees. Her stomach clenches. It's not Ovis, Dulcis's husband.

"I'm so sorry, I didn't mean to startle you," he says, his round face warming in amusement.

Clara gapes at him, too shocked to speak. Half his face is shaded under a wide-brimmed hat, though he seems familiar to her. He wears the simple attire a servant might, plain brown trousers and a sand-colored tunic. She cannot know him.

"Are you all right?" he asks, looking around. "Was there someone else here?"

"No!" bursts out of her before she closes her eyes with a flinch. *Alma has her own protection, especially against humans.* "No, you— I am not— I mean, I was startled, but it is all right. I was merely surprised to see you— Someone— Here. Behind me." She takes a deep breath.

He answers her stammers with a patient smile. "Do you mind if I sit and refresh myself at the lake?"

She shakes her head, granting him permission, so he drops the reins to his horse, who shuffles off to graze alongside the sheep.

He steps to the shore of the lake, a short distance from Clara. To keep her fingers from trembling as her mind races, she picks up her wool dress and begins to repair the newest hole.

"Are you a shepherdess?" The man dips his hands

into the water and splashes his face.

"I am." She peeks at him from beneath her sheet of brown hair, still attempting to conceal her face. "What brings you to my pond?"

He chuckles. "I am just out for a ride through my country."

Her grin flares up, too quick to hide. *His country indeed.*

"In the midst of searching for the escaped Edormiscan prisoner."

Shock wipes the grin from her face. "Oh?"

He gives her a reassuring smile. "I wouldn't worry too much. Some prisoner escaped a few weeks back, and King Effrenatus thinks that perhaps she has made her way into Ostium." He rolls his eyes and brushes off a smudge of dust from his trousers. "There are many out searching."

"Such as you?" She chews the corner of her lip, wondering if they have a description of the prisoner.

"Don't worry." The man shakes his head dismissively, not even bothering to inspect her. "They have assured us she is no risk to the public."

Her dress becomes a little looser as she lets out her breath and bends to her mending. Automatically, she brushes the hair that falls into her way behind her ear.

The man's breath hisses over his teeth.

Clara fights back a grimace. He's noticed her scars. Surely the information on the escaped prisoner mentions her scars? But he clears his throat and his breath returns to normal. "Do you have any sisters or brothers?"

Clara hesitates. "Yes. Several sisters. You?"

"Two younger brothers." He sighs. "Parents?"

"Father. My mother died years ago."

"Ah. My father has died, my mother lives."

Even though she tells thinly veiled lies, she relaxes in his presence. *He must not have meant to find me. He's so distracted…*

"What can I call you?" he finally asks.

She gives him a crooked smile, careful to hide her scars behind her hair. "Are you sure we should share our names?"

"Why ever not?" His deep laugh spreads warmth through her.

"I don't know," she answers, pretending to mull over the decision.

"Come now. What are secret meetings in the woods good for except abandoning propriety?"

His words, which should concern her, instead have her giggling. "Well, in that case, you can call me Vera."

"Vera. Lovely. You may call me…" He hesitates. "Laetus."

"Laetus." She bites her lip as she steals another glance at the man. *Why is there something so familiar…?*

"It's a terrible name, I know." He laughs uncomfortably.

"No… It's…not." *Terrible?* She remembers another time hearing that. A memory beckons her as she stares at that familiar face.

"Help yourself. I'm sure you're hungry after my father's lecture on the country." Clara smiled at the visiting prince of Ostium.

Prince Albus's lips twitched. "Oh no, it was terribly interesting."

"Or just terrible, perhaps," Clara said before she could stop herself.

He choked on a laugh. "No, no. It's not true. I am fascinated."

Biting back her gasp of realization, she throws her visitor a reassuring smile that quickly falters. *The crown prince of Ostium. Prince Albus Laetus Aeilius of Ostium.* It is—it *must* be—him. She stands and turns her back to him, clutching her wool dress in her hands. "I—I must get back to my sheep. I am sorry."

He stands with her. "I'm sorry—did I say something

to offend? Should I not have given a name at all?"

"No. That's not it at all. But I must attend them." She sweeps a hand toward the sheep. *I must get out of this dress before Dulcis sees me.* "I am afraid I must go."

He rises and brushes his trousers off. "Then I will leave you to your pasture. You must have many tasks to complete, and I have many miles to ride." He brings his fingers to his lips to call his horse over; when the animal arrives, the prince mounts and is gone.

Clara finds herself staring after him, wishing she had had the courage to ask him to stay.

***

"I had hoped to run into you again today," comes a familiar, refined voice.

She straightens as both joy and confusion rush through her. *Good thing I put my faery dress on again. And thanks to Alma for giving it a different appearance.* A smile pulls her lips up before she remembers her scars. *How can he make me forget these cursed scars so easily?*

"Do not be foolish, Clara," a little voice buzzes. Alma, making herself as small as a fly, settles upon Clara's ear.

"I do hope I'm not intruding," Albus says.

Clara turns, careful to keep the left side of her face hidden. "No. I am pleased to see you." Her cheeks burn as he beams at her.

"I'm starving," he says. "I've brought some cold roasted pheasant with me. Would you like to share it with me?"

"I would be delighted. I wish I had something—" She breaks off as a familiar magic warms her. She half turns and finds a basket, undoubtedly full of Alma's exquisite faery food, sitting behind her. Her smile widens. "Join me in my midday luncheon?"

"I would be delighted," he echoes.

***

Is she an Edormiscan faery playing a game with him? She appears like a sprite in the woods, dressed in such finery and supplying Albus with such decadent foods.

"You are an amazing cook. I've never tasted anything so delicious." He shakes his head. Not even the food at the Edormiscan ball was as mouthwatering as the lamb chops he just devoured. "Where do you come from? How did you learn to cook like this?"

She smiles mysteriously. "From far away."

He refrains from pressing her to say more. *Let her keep her secrets, and I'll keep mine.*

A bleating of the ewes interrupts his thoughts, and Vera starts to her feet. He follows suit only to see a pair of riders. *Bounty hunters.* A stab of guilt attacks him. *I should be out searching for that escaped woman, and yet, here I am, all but having forgotten her.*

Vera steps back, away from the rough-looking men on their shaggy horses. Not eager to run into men who might recognize their prince, Albus follows suit.

"Who are they?" she asks him.

"Probably bounty hunters."

He can almost feel her chill as she shudders and moves closer to him.

"Don't worry. They won't hurt you." He gazes down at her, finding her concern over the prisoner endearing. "I won't let anyone hurt you."

The riders pause to water their horses, their voices a low murmur, when a loud crack issues from the woods on the other side of the lake. The two men exchange a glance. "That way!" They rein their horses around and dash into the woods.

Albus leads Vera back to the lake, his hand upon her

elbow. "Don't alarm yourself. They're long gone. Besides, they're not interested in a shepherdess."

She smiles and shakes her head. "Of course not."

Sighing, she stretches out before the lake, resting back on her hands, but the cloud of concern doesn't lift from her brow. He mimics her position, his hand brushing hers as he reaches back. She doesn't pull away, doesn't shy from his accidental touch. He doesn't either.

For hours they chat, and every few days, the same happens. He rides hard for an hour to find her waiting by the lake in beautiful gowns, looking as though she should be at a ball instead of herding sheep. And, day by day, he looks past the scars on her face that she tries to hide behind her hair, looking instead into her clear eyes and bright smile. And finds himself undeniably enchanted.

***

"Alma," Clara says one day, "I have been thinking."

The little faery perches upon the large rock by the lake, sheep bleating in the background. "About what have you thought?"

"We must do something about Prudens." Clara picks at a hole in her wool dress.

"Yes," Alma agrees.

A cracking of a branch from the nearby woods draws both of their attentions. A ewe trots out from amongst the thick brush before Clara continues her conversation. "I am going to go home. I already told Dulcis that I cannot stay. This was never meant to be permanent."

"Home?" Alma's entire body betrays her alarm. Her face glows dark amber, her wings quake, and she rises several inches into the air. "You will die if you go home. There is a bounty upon your head!"

"Yes, but an entire nation will die if Prudens continues down this path with dark magic." She sighs, the weight of responsibility dragging her down. "There has been no news from Edormisco, which makes me believe she has suppressed the throne. I cannot let her succeed."

Alma sinks in the air, settling upon Clara's knee. "I understand."

"Thank you. I expected—"

"But I cannot let you go."

"—that." Clara sighs. "I knew you would say that. But I must go."

"No." Alma rises into the air before Clara's face and reaches out a tiny hand to touch her ward's cheek. "I will go for you. It will be safer for me to go, and I will find out what we need about Prudens."

"But Alma—"

"If I have to bind you to a tree to keep you safe, I will, Clara." Alma's threat is anything but empty.

Clara chews on her lip. "Why couldn't we go together?"

"You will not return to Edormisco, not while your sister is determined to kill you. It will do you no good to die or be imprisoned for the rest of your life."

Bowing her head, Clara succumbs to the truth of Alma's statement. "But you are in just as much danger—"

Alma gives a sad little smile. "But I am not as valuable."

"Alma, of course you are. My life would be tasteless without you."

Rising into the air, Alma flutters in front of Clara's face then lands on her shoulder to give her an embrace. "Thank you for saying that, dear, but we both know it's not true."

"If you fail, if you get caught—or killed—I will have no one to help me defeat her." A tear slips down Clara's cheek, and Alma brushes it away with a wing. "I don't want you to die. I don't want her to die either."

"I know. Which is why I go to find her weakness."

Clara hugs her arms around her knees, sorrow rising into her throat.

"But while I am gone, you must make me a promise."

Clara sniffs. "What is that?"

"You must not see him anymore." Alma's wings flutter in the air, lifting the ends of her long, blond hair from her shoulders as Clara whirls to look at her.

"What? Why ever not?"

Alma flutters in front of Clara's face, kissing her cheeks with the breeze from her wings. "Even if we defeat Prudens, as we intend, there is no guarantee that the people of Ostium will want you as their queen."

Clara bites her nail at the snare of Alma's truth. She loves Albus, but, with the bounty upon her head, would she ever be fit to marry him?

"Please, Clara." Alma's expression is gentle. "I say this for your own good. To protect you."

Despite knowing Alma to have her best intentions at heart, the sting of the faery's words is too much for Clara's heart to bear.

~ III ~

Clamor from the great hall reaches Albus where he paces in a nearby chamber. She has not come to the lake for weeks, nor has there been sign of her sheep. *There is only one possibility: she does not love me. And I am a fool.*

Weeks more pass, but Albus does not stop seeking her. He returns to the lake whenever he can. He goes morning, noon, and night, but at no time does he find her.

"Darling, what is it that bothers you so?" his mother finally demands. "You have been in such a state… You aren't eating, your clothes hang upon you. Are you ill?"

He pushes the choice lamb chop around on his plate, his stomach turning. This poor excuse for supper is nothing like Vera's. "No. I'm not ill, Mother."

"Then explain what is wrong. Does this have something to with the rides you have been taking?"

"I—"

"Has your valet been inadequate again? Or is it the meal? We can hire a better cook, one that—"

"No, Mother, I—" Albus broke off as a thought occurs to him. "Yes. There *is* someone I might employ… A new cook…"

His mother straightens. "We'll conduct interviews at once—"

"No." He fixes his mother with a smile. "I know exactly the girl."

"Who?" The Queen's glance is sharp.

"I'm…not sure." He shakes his head. "I don't know where she lives. But she cooks the most exquisite lamb…"

She peers at him with that keen, motherly stare which penetrates everything. When she has finished, her lips twitch into the barest smile. "Tell me who she is. I'll find her."

As if I haven't been scouring the hills, Mother? He just shakes his head. "How?"

A smug smile lifts her lips. "That needn't concern you, son."

***

A week later, two of the Queen's guards appear upon Dulcis and Ovis's doorstep.

"You must comply with the Queen's proclamation," one guard says, his dark mustache quivering over his lips as he speaks.

"What proclamation?" Clara's heart trembles. *Oh, I wish Alma were back. Where is she? What am I to do?*

"The proclamation for all shepherdesses to report to the Queen. You must obey upon pain of death," the other says. A scar across his right eyebrow and continuing over his eye gives him a dangerous appearance.

"Do you refuse to present yourself willingly to the Queen?" the first guard demands.

Behind her, there's a fearful intake of breath from Dulcis.

If I don't go with them, it won't just be my death, will it? She asks the question of the first guard with her eyes, and she thinks she sees the confirmation in them. She bows her head. "I'm willing."

"Then present yourself to the Queen by this time tomorrow, or suffer the consequences." The bushy mustache trembles smugly.

***

The next morning, Clara trudges along the road to the palace with the two Ostiite guards behind her.

Dulcis had taken Clara aside the night before. "Please don't go with them, Vera."

"But I must," Clara answered. "You heard the proclamation."

"I don't believe it. You should go now. Flee."

"Where? It would put you in danger—I couldn't—"

"Forget us. Or tie us up and go, we can pretend you overtook us. Save yourself."

"Fine." Clara frowned at Dulcis. The baby reached for Clara, and she swept the babe into her arms. "I'll go in the morning."

But morning had been too late, for the guards had arrived before daybreak.

Pausing, she takes a minute to wipe her brow and drink from her canteen. The sun beats upon her head, but neither guard has offered her a ride. As they walk on, the capital on the horizon grows larger ahead of them. Behind her, the guards joke back and forth.

Clara cannot shake her unease. If Queen Sapphire of Ostium had truly issued a proclamation to all shepherdesses, then shouldn't there be another shepherdess making the trip alongside Clara?

With the scrutiny the two guards give her, Clara cannot find an opportunity to escape. She can just pray to the Great Fae that Alma will return and help her—as she did once before.

She focuses instead on the city as they enter. The crudely made brick buildings are the color of mud and quite ugly compared to Edormisco. Smaller buildings crouch alongside them, quiet, unassuming homes made from rough wood with small windows.

The palace, another pale, brick building, towers above the rest, a quarter of the size of the Edormiscan palace she grew up admiring.

At the large doors, the guards dismount and usher her inside, dirt, sweat, and all.

A servant leads them through the expansive entrance with its grand stairway and down a wide hallway lined with statues and portraits. She trails behind, taking in the modest palace.

At a door, the servant stops and mutely motions with a sweeping gesture for them to enter.

"Thank you." Clara steps inside, finding a large room with a gentle breeze invading from two open windows. Several couches and chairs have fleece sheepskins draped over them. Before Clara can do more than absorb the warmth and hominess of the room, a woman enters from a side door and stops short.

Her mouth opens as if to speak, then her gaze slides to the guard standing at the door. "Ah."

Clara flicks her gaze over the woman, from the top of her head to her hands and feet. When she returns her gaze to the woman's round face and unusual eyes, Clara finds the confirmation she desired: this is Albus's mother.

At the last moment, Clara remembers herself and dips into a curtsy. "I am a shepherdess answering your summons, Majesty."

The Queen purses her lips and surveys Clara. "You may leave."

Clara blinks, but when she turns her head, it's to witness the heels of the guard as he slips out the door, leaving the women alone.

"Turn around."

A frown not far from her lips, Clara obeys. Her mind races over possibilities for the Queen to have summoned her and only her. It is either because of Albus, or else because she's a prisoner. She bites her tongue, hoping it is the former.

A noise halfway between disgust and disapproval issues from the Queen's throat as Clara completes her turn. "If you are as you say, I have a job for you."

The frown settles upon Clara's lips, weighing them down. "I am already a shepherdess."

The Queen's lips twitch. "We both know that there are better jobs."

Wariness worms its way into Clara's stomach. "And

the one you are offering…?"

At her question, the Queen's smile turns down at the ends. "You will make my son a meal. If it is not the best he has ever had, then he will never know you were here."

Clara hesitates then says, "Is there a reason you are requesting shepherdesses to come cook for him?"

The Queen draws herself tall. "Every woman should be able to create at least one meal. In order to please her future husband."

You didn't answer my question, Queen, Clara thinks.

"You will be given whatever you ask to prepare a feast for my son—but the main course must be lamb with a port glaze. If he likes it, you shall meet him."

Biting her lip, Clara closes her eyes. *Where is Alma when I need her? The Queen asks the one thing I cannot do. And now I will lose him because of it? But perhaps it is for the best… Alma may be right. If I marry Albus, I cannot hide my true identity.*

"Do you accept these terms?"

Eyes closed, head shaking slightly from side to side, Clara says, "How can I not? When you have been most generous."

"Excellent." The Queen sounds pleased with herself. "Then rise, and my servant will escort you to the kitchens. You have three hours before dinner. You must feed seven." The Queen does not wait for a response, but turns on her heel and disappears through the same door she entered through.

Dread washes over her as the queen exits. *Even Dulcis couldn't teach me to cook. How am I to win this challenge? I will fail, and Albus will never even see me.* Clara pushes herself to her feet as a guard appears in the other doorway.

Determined, she smooths down the skirt of her wool dress and steels her expression. *After all, what have I got to lose?*

***

Two hours later, Clara is near tears. She has an entire lamb, along with vegetables and herbs from the palace garden. She has flour and eggs and milk, and still she has nothing that resembles a finished—or more importantly, edible—meal.

The minutes tick down, and Clara's gravy boils over on the stove, spilling half. "Faery's teeth," she curses, dragging the heavy pot off the stovetop and thumping it on the countertop. "Why did I agree to this?" Tears burn her eyes. *I will never see Albus again. The Queen will make certain of that.*

"Don't despair," comes a little voice to Clara's right.

She jumps, looking around for the origin. "Alma?" Incredulity washes over her at the sight of her faery attendant sitting atop a bowl of flour. "What are you doing here? *How* are you here?"

The little faery grins. "I returned to the cottage this morning. I overheard Dulcis and Ovis talking about where you had gone. Ovis was most disappointed that you were forced to answer a summons. Apparently he must watch the sheep while you are gone." Her eyes twinkle.

"He will be eager for my return then." Clara's chuckle quickly dies. "Which will not be long…"

Wings fluttering, Alma lifts herself into the air to peer into the pot's contents. "What is it you must do?"

When Clara explains, the faery gives a shrug and pushes up the sleeves on her tiny faery gown. "Then it's a good thing I am here. For I have found a way to satisfy both your desires and defeat your sister in the process."

***

"Another shepherdess cooking tonight?" Albus sinks into his chair at the long, oak table. "Mother, you won't find her. And why not just bring her out, instead of subjecting me to more horrible food?"

"As crown prince, you have more important things to do than inspect a parade of shepherdesses. Have you seen how dirty they are?" She shudders before producing a smile and stepping toward the table. "Besides, appearances can be misleading, especially if there's a crown prince involved. Now, shall we eat?"

Albus doesn't move at his mother's explanation. "Mother—wouldn't it just be easier to skip din—?"

"Darling, just try it," she says impatiently. "Women will go to no ends in order to capture a prince, but not all of them can cook. Besides, we must eat anyway." She motions a servant who brings in a roast lamb and sets it on the table before them.

His gaze lingers on the lamb, roasted to perfection, just the way Vera cooked it. A port glaze gives it a reddish hue and fills the air with its heady scent. His stomach growls. He sighs, knowing he'll give in to the Queen's demands— again. Despite her tough outer shell, he's always known his mother to be a romantic at heart.

"Mmm. It smells divine. Have you ever seen a more impressive feast?" His mother watches him with the utmost care as he inspects the meal. "I don't think I have."

"No. I can't say I've seen anything better."

"Try some," she urges.

He hesitates, gaze on the port glaze. *Could it be possible?*

The scent lures him into cutting a bite and placing it on his tongue. As flavor explodes across it, he closes his eyes. He remembers sitting before the lake, eating lamb chops and fresh bread. On the side sits a port glaze so exquisite, Albus wonders how she had made it.

His eyes fly open. "Where is she?"

Stoic, his mother turns to the servant by the dining hall door. "Bring in the cook."

The servant disappears though the door as the Queen takes a generous bite of lamb.

A minute later, the door opens and a young woman trails in behind the servant. Albus's heart stops as he recognizes the scarred face above a wool gown. "Vera." Her name leaves his lips in a breath.

She gives him a shy smile. "Good evening, Prince Albus."

He rises from the table, dinner forgotten. He streaks his napkin across his chin and drops it onto his chair, eyes on Vera. "How did you come here?"

"Your mother's proclamation," she says.

"Did you—did you know me all along?"

A hint of concern creases her brow. "Not immediately, no."

Smiling faintly, he shakes his head. "It's all right. I've never been happier to see you."

"Truly?" Her eyes sparkle as she turns her face up to his. "Even though I forgot to curtsy?"

"I never want you to curtsy to me. Ever. You're the only woman I could see as being my equal." He glances to his mother, who tilts her head in a sort of amused approval. He turns back to Vera. "Marry me?"

For the first time, her expression dims. "I—I have to confess something. Then perhaps you can ask me again. If you want."

Albus's heart stutters against his ribs. "What could change my opinion of you so?"

"Why don't you two go and speak privately?" the Queen suggests from her seat.

"No, Your Majesty," Vera says before Albus can answer. "This will concern you as well."

At that, the Queen lays down her fork and dabs her napkin to her lips. "Then continue."

"I am not who I told you I am, Albus. I am Princess Clara Vera Notio of Edormisco."

The Queen's breath slices through the room. "*Princess* Clara? The Edormiscan *prisoner*?"

Albus steps back. An image of the twelve princesses of Edormisco at the ball in the palace dances in his mind. The faeries flitting over the table of mouth-watering food. Dancing with Princess Clara amidst the glittering lights and faery music. And then the shouts rudely pulling him away from the dance he had been coerced into.

He stepped back from the princess to find King Effrenatus and his youngest daughter, Prudens, shouting at one another.

Clara raced to them, trying to placate them, but Princess Prudens gave Clara such a look that even Albus shuddered. Then the King demanded of her, "How much do you love me? The one who loves me the most gains my kingdom."

Prudens had given her answer, "You are the apple of my eye."

The air steamed, reminding Albus of a fire burning in a small, unventilated room.

The King shook Clara by the arm. "Answer me!"

She whimpered. "I—I love you like the salt in my food."

Instead of answering, the King gave Princess Prudens a glazed look, blinking slowly and nodding. "Yes. Yes." He faced Clara. "You insult me."

Prudens smirked.

"Father, salt is the best thing in life—" Clara said, but he was not listening.

"Take her away," the King said.

Clara turned to her sister and raised her hands, a look of determination upon her features. Without warning, a small explosion rocked the ballroom. Albus couldn't remember anything after that moment, even now.

Albus blinks at the woman standing before him. She has the same coloring, the same petite frame, but the face is so different, even looking past the scars. Older and weathered. Tired and yet at ease. "You are Princess Clara?"

"Yes." Clara's eyes close. "I'm sorry I couldn't be honest with you before, Albus. Even the family I lived with knew nothing of who I once was." Her shoulders sink in defeat. "My father disowned me, thinking I used magic against him, when it was my youngest sister who did so. And, at his ire, and the bounty upon me, I didn't have the courage to return. I cannot explain or counteract my sister's influence over him."

Albus leans down, but she won't look up at him. "Vera. Clara. I was enchanted with you the first time I saw you. That first time…by the lake."

As his meaning dawns on her, she looks up, a slow smile growing upon her lips. "Then?"

"Only then. Had I known who you were when I saw you then, I wouldn't have returned. But you being…who you are…" He shrugs. "You enchanted me."

"Only then? Not at the ball? Even with this face?" She motions to her left side with a hand, giving a tragic, uneven smile.

He takes her hands in his. "No. Not then. Then you were just another princess, to strengthen our kingdoms or perhaps divide them."

"And now?"

"Now, you're the only woman I would ask twice—"

"Just a moment, Albus," the Queen interrupts. "As delighted as I am to see you having found the woman you love, you are forgetting that if we allow her to stay, we start a war with Edormisco."

Albus frowns, glancing back at Vera—no, Clara. "That's a risk we must take then, Mother. As she explained, she did no wrong."

The Queen's lips curve into the slightest smile, then she lifts her fork and pokes another cut of lamb. "Then by all means, continue with your question."

With a surge of elation, Albus turns to Clara. "Where was I? Oh yes, you are the one woman I would ask

twice…three times?…to marry me."
Her uneven smile blooms, and his heart lurches.
"Does that smile mean you accept?"
"Yes." She pauses. "On one condition."

~ IV ~

Two months later

Clara stands before a mirror in her bedchamber, examining her bridal gown, a dress the shade of pale Edormiscan gold.

"You look absolutely stunning." Albus comes up behind her and puts his hands on her shoulders, kissing her left temple.

"That she does," Alma says, flitting around Clara's head to smooth stray hairs.

Clara smiles her crooked, sad smile at her husband's reflection.

Something shadows his face as Alma pats a final, stubborn hair on Clara's head into submission. After a little shake of her wings, thus spreading her faery dust over Clara's hair, Alma, with a bob at Albus, says, "I must get to the kitchens."

"Are you sure this is the wisest plan?" Albus asks after watching the faery flit away. "I'll give you anything you want, but...after what she's shown herself capable of doing?"

At his words, she forces herself to examine her own face in the mirror, taking in the full result of Prudens's curse. Three jagged scars crisscross her left cheek, from eye to ear to lip, puckering the skin that was once as smooth and unblemished as the right. She has endured her share of taunts and names from the Ostiite people. Although they dare not say them directly to her, she hears the whispers and knows of the edict forbidding such whispers as treason.

"I must face her, Albus." Clara touches a finger to her lip, where the scar ends. "If not now, her power will only grow. I must attempt to thwart it."

In acceptance, he leads her out of her bedchamber. Her time in the Ostium palace has accustomed Clara to the hand-polished stone and its servants, but she would be lying to say she didn't miss the palace she once called home.

When they enter the dining hall, everyone stands and applauds, cheering their beloved prince and his new bride.

Clara takes a deep breath and prepares herself, then turns to Albus. "Let me introduce you."

Her husband's face clouds when she makes the introductions, and his arm hardens under her hand before she lets go to embrace her sister.

Discomfort plays over Prudens's features underneath the Edormiscan queen's golden crown. Clara's uneasiness grows at the sight of the gemstone-laden ornament. Pushing aside her emotions and casting aside typical princess protocol, Clara pulls her youngest sister into a hug, as she would have done before that fated ball.

"I'm so pleased to see you," Clara murmurs into Prudens's ear. She releases her sister to address her father. Half a step forward, and she has to refrain herself from falling into his arms. He may have come to the bridal feast today, but he does not embrace her as daughter yet. His eyes are dark, closed to her welcome.

So she dips a slight curtsy before him, aware of her renewed status as princess, this time to a different throne.

"Princess Clara," he says in his booming voice. He lifts her by the elbows with large, firm hands. "You—you—" He trails off, letting go of her left arm to reach toward her cheek with his hand, sorrow creasing his features as he battles something darker.

Clara's heart sinks. *He is still under her spell then.* She shakes away her sorrow and bolsters herself with a smile. "Let us eat."

She gives Albus a meaningful look, to which he squeezes her hand in reply before he seats her at the table. He whispers in her ear the answer to her unasked question. "Yes, the kitchens received and followed out your orders. Alma is, of course, supervising."

She casts him a thankful smile and sits beside her

father, spreading her napkin over her gown as he begins his meal. "How are the people of Edormisco?"

He spoons a heap of smashed potatoes into his mouth. His lips twist before he schools them back to a neutral expression. He tries a bite of bread next, but his reaction is the same. Lifting his napkin, he spends too long wiping his mouth and clearing his throat. "Your sisters are doing well." He motions to Prudens. "As you can see."

She waits until he takes a few more reluctant bites, until his expression begins to lighten, then asks, "And how are you finding the meal?"

His mouth twitches, but his eyes grow brighter. "It's…well…"

"It's awful!" Prudens says from his other side.

She smiles knowingly. "Your Majesty, I have a confession to make."

He lifts his napkin again. "And what is that?"

"Why your food tastes so awful is because I requested the kitchen to refrain from adding salt to it."

Under her watchful eye, his face grows blank and then his eyes widen.

"As you do not care for this food without salt, so do I not care for my life without you. You give my life flavor as the salt flavors this food." She reaches a hand out toward his, where it sits on the table between them. "You once asked me how much I love you. Do you remember how I answered you?"

Prudens shifts in her seat, eyes upon their father. Anger glints in her gaze as she clenches a fist around her wine goblet.

King Effrenatus stares down at his plate, confusion tightening his brow. "You said you loved me…like salt in your food." He lifts his gaze to hers. "I don't understand."

"Yes." Clara motions to the plate of bland food set before her father. "I answered that way not because I love you little, but because I love you too much to endure life without."

The King's expression falters. As if from under the depths of a deep lake, awareness begins to surface. "Clara? Wha—what has been happening?" He turns to Prudens.

Prudens does not bother attempting to pacify her father, but stands at her place, fists clenched.

In a moment, Ostiite guards are beside her, hands upon the hilts of their weapons.

Prudens goes still, but her eyes glint with fury.

"I still don't understand." King Effrenatus motions to the three-quarters of his food he has not been able to stomach. "Why then did you try to curse me?"

"I never did. And I bear these scars as testament to my honesty." She fixes her gaze on Prudens, who seethes from the other side of their father.

"What do you mean?" The King's voice is uncertain.

"If I had cursed you, I would never have been able to endure these scars. I would have sought every forest in Edormisco for a sorcerer or Fae to heal my face. Instead, I endured your exile as a shepherdess."

Prudens leans forward, her face puce. "How dare— of course you cursed him, you—" She breaks off, inspecting her hands as though expecting them to be filled with something and finding them empty.

With a half a glance at her father, now blinking in confusion at his surroundings, Clara withdraws a small vial from the folds of her dress. "And this is what was *added* to *your* food, my sister. A potion that temporarily steals your magic as you attempted to steal our father's throne."

"What?" The King's voice cracks. "Prudens?"

"The culprit you seek does not sit on your right, but on your left, Your Majesty. This potion broke her spell over you. I hope you will forgive this use of magic, but I promise you, it is the only magical potion I have ever used, this prepared and given at the hands of my faithful faery attendant, Alma."

"Why are you—? 'Your Majesty'?" His eyes clearing, he draws in a breath that straightens his spine. He locks his gaze upon Clara's, speaking as though he has just seen her for the first time in years. "It was not you, Clara. You never cast that spell."

Clara smiles gently. "No."

"Don't listen to her, Papa," Prudens says. "Why would I curse you? I have never had magic like that. I love you."

Clara watches the truth dawn on her father's face.

"Clara— Father, Clara's lying. This isn't true, I—"

"Silence!" the king snaps. "I see it all now. It is as if scales have fallen from my eyes." His face darkens, but his eyes remain bright and clear. "I have dealt with your schemes for long enough, Prudens. You have plotted against me, hoping to call my throne yours, but that will never be." He breathes heavily out through his nose before turning to Clara. "Darling daughter, it's only right that you choose her punishment. What would you suggest?"

"Me?" Clara sits back. "I have never desired her punished, Father, but only fairly treated." She considers a moment before saying, "I suggest only the same punishment that I was given: exile."

"And scars to match," her father growls.

Prudens's eyes widen as she draws away in terror. "Please—"

Their father beckons for his guard, whose hand goes to his sword hilt.

Clara finds her voice. "Father, no."

He holds up his hand to his guard. "What?"

"I do not wish her to suffer my fate with these scars." She motions to her face. "It might be fair, but I wish mercy."

From her other side, Albus squeezes her hand.

Her father's face hardens briefly then softens. "Then mercy it will be."

~ Epilogue ~

It was many happy years before Prince Albus became King Albus of Ostium; by then, he and his wife had many princes and princesses of their own. By the time King Albus and Queen Clara died, she had lived far beyond her nickname of "The Scarred Princess," and she was much beloved by the people of Ostium, who had adopted the Edormiscan as their own. Princess Prudens served her sentence in exile, but failed to learn her lesson. However, that is another story, and not this one.

Reed Girl, Fire Girl, Cloud Girl

Lynden Wade

Long ago, in the heart of an ancient forest, there lived a young man called Yanek.

He was the strongest man in his village. When felling timber, he needed just one swing of his ax to topple a giant pine. When building a house, he could throw the roof beam up to the man sitting on the bare rafters. When bandits attacked the village, he fought them off single-handedly, knocking the leader unconscious with a single blow of his fist. He was the youngest of his family and won his father's land back from their unscrupulous neighbor with his amazing strength—in fact, not only his father's land, but also a cup that never emptied and an everlasting loaf.

This is not the story of how Yanek won these gifts. It is the story of how he lost them.

One night, his father announced, "I am not getting any younger."

Yanek, who had been tidying away the remains of supper, looked up in surprise. True, he was the youngest by far of his brothers and his father had been nearing old age when Yanek was born, but just now they'd been talking of the new foal.

"All this will be yours one day, lad. Yes, yes—your brothers? They won't get a thing. You were the son who stayed and helped me look after the farm. You were the son who defended our lands from that villain, Pavel. So I've been thinking. You need to marry. That way you will have someone to help you look after the house and the herds when I'm gone. Someone to give you sons, too, who will inherit the farm."

Yanek had never thought of settling in this way. In the evenings, when his father dozed before the fire, Yanek would indulge in his secret dream. It was not to sail the seas, like his oldest brother, or ride over the plains as a soldier, like his middle brother. He privately yearned to search out his soulmate: a girl who did not know he'd been the dunce at school and would not laugh at him, a girl who would look into his eyes adoringly. He would never admit this to his father, though.

"I can manage the farm on my own, Father. Why would I need a helper when I can do the work of five men myself?"

"Manage on your own! You think all you need is muscle? No, you're a good boy, but you have a brain the size of a bean. You need a woman to make the decisions for you. So I have found someone."

"Found someone?" Yanek gasped. "Who?"

"Zhenya, Sergey's daughter. Good hips and lots of sense. I arranged it with Sergey this afternoon."

Zhenya had grown up with Yanek, but she always smirked when she saw him and treated him like a child. All the village girls were patronizing, knowing that Yanek's strength was his only attribute and that he was as thick as the logs he threw about, but Zhenya was the worst.

"No," Yanek said rather loudly.

His father's eyebrows shot up. "No? Since when did you decide to disobey me?"

"Father," Yanek said, "I have done everything on the farm the way you want. But I will not obey you on this. I will not marry Zhenya."

His father leapt out of his rocking chair and started to shout, but a coughing fit overtook him. Yanek thumped him on the back and helped him back into his seat. When his father had recovered, the old man began again. "You must. You cannot manage on your own. I lie awake every night worrying about what you will do when I am gone."

Yanek sighed. "I will marry one day, I expect, Father. But let me choose my own wife."

"No, no. You must do it now. Zhenya is the one for you, I know it."

"Father. Let us sleep on it. We can talk again in the morning."

The old man argued some more, but his mutterings grew fainter as he drifted off to sleep by the fire.

Yanek gazed into the embers and pondered his problem. He had no idea where to look to find the bride he dreamed of. He could hardly wander the countryside looking for a girl who might adore him, could he?

In the heart of the forest lived Baba Yaga the witch. She sat in her huge mortar to fly through the night air. She knew things ordinary mortals did not, and many sought her advice, dangerous though she was to approach. Some she helped, others she ate for breakfast. Yanek had been one of the fortunate ones; she had helped him before when his father was sick, giving him the elixir that fought off the disease. He would ask for her advice once more.

When his father's head lolled, Yanek slipped a hand under the old man's armpit and guided him to bed. He arranged the covers over his father then pulled on his boots, coat, and hat. Next, he wrapped a round of cheese in a cloth and tucked it under one arm. Taking up his lantern, he let himself out quietly and strode into the forest at the edge of the village.

It was a cool night, a hint of a colder one to come. A sickle moon sat thin and pale above the tops of the pine trees, giving little light. He scanned the forest for the glint of wolf eyes, his ears pricked for the sound of breaking twigs. The pine needles on the forest floor muffled the sound of his footsteps. An owl swooped suddenly over his head, and when he straightened again, a glow between the tree trunks announced he had found the witch's house.

His approach had been detected. The menacing quiet of the forest was broken: "Man! Man!"

The shrieks came from a row of hollow skulls, their jaws clacking as they clamored. Since his last visit, Baba Yaga had replaced the mossy heads with fresh ones, hair and withered skin still clinging to them. They served as lanterns, and fire shone through the eye sockets. Each one topped a sharpened post in a palisade of pine trunks, which stood shoulder-high around the cottage. The house, a two-room hut, sat on a giant disembodied chicken leg, which hopped in circles on the spot with its huge claw.

"Shut your traps!" a cracked voice shouted, and the skulls fell silent. The door slammed open, and a skinny figure darted out, white hair flying from her head in every direction. Her eyes, sharp as her twitching nose, fixed to his. She broke into a smile that was more ghastly than her glare.

"Yanek! Come to see how this poor old woman fares? You've taken your time. I could have died and you'd never have known."

"You can't die, Old Mother," Yanek reminded her.

"Huh! That's hardly the point. I suppose you want my help again? Want, want, want—you men are always after what you want, never mind an old woman's needs."

"You sought me out last time, remember? Because you wanted to show off your powers after the doctor said you were just a crazy old woman."

"Bah! It was no fun in the end. You should have let me tear him up and eat him. The quack deserved no better. Enough of the small talk. What do you want of me?"

Yanek explained how his father wanted him to find a mate. "I need to find a wife of my own choosing. But not one of the girls in the village."

"Pah! What a silly task. Do you think I just sit here in

the forest waiting for you to come and ask me for help with everything? Wait—do I smell cheese?"

"You do." Yanek lifted the huge round of cheese to show her. Made of goat's milk, it was one of the specialties of his father's farm. A greedy grin broke Baba Yaga's face in half, and she started forward.

"Wait. Help first, then cheese."

Baba Yaga scowled. "I could just take the cheese."

"A skinny old woman like you against a strong man like me?"

She turned and shuffled back into the hut, her mutters fading as she retreated.

Yanek waited before the palisade, wondering if she had decided against the cheese. He would make her help him somehow. He had just retreated in order to take a running jump over the gate when she appeared again at the door, holding her pestle and mortar. One spring of her bony legs, and she was at his side.

"I'm not able to help you find the perfect wife," she said, "but I can show you the person who can."

She put the pestle down. Water sloshed inside it. She stuck her mortar in and began to stir it round and round into a storm. The chill of the night sucked the warmth out of Yanek as he stood waiting, puzzled.

"Now look," she barked, yanking the mortar out so water drops flung at his cheek.

"The first face you see here will be your helper in your quest. Hurry up! Don't keep an old woman out of her bed."

He leaned over obediently, wondering what he was supposed to look at. The water rocked from side to side, settling slowly. His face, shattered by the ripples, came together again on the surface—and another, too, looking over his shoulder. It took a moment for Yanek to recognize this other face, as he didn't come into the village much— Anton, who had a child's mind in a young man's body.

Whether it was the loss of his parents that had made him like that, or if he had been born that way, no one knew, but his stare and his silence unnerved the village folk.

Yanek straightened with a start. "Mother! You can't mean this! What use is Anton?" The man couldn't even fend for himself. He lived in the forest with his little sister, who was even crazier than him.

But Baba Yaga had upended the mortar and seized the round of cheese. With a hop, she bounded back into her cottage, muttering through mouthfuls of cheese that Yanek was more of a fool than Anton.

A young woman's voice came from behind him. "Anton! What are you doing? It's very late to be wandering around the forest."

Yanek turned to find himself face to face with Anton's stare—and, coming up behind the boy, Anton's sister Nika, half her brother's size but just as disconcerting. He knew her from her trips into the village to sell lumps of honey and wild mushrooms. It was said that the two lived in the hollow of a tree and covered themselves with leaves at night. As always, she wore a man's tunic hitched up with a belt, giving her a lumpy appearance. She wore her hair all tangled and twisted into knots, held against her head with twigs.

Nika's eyes met Yanek's and widened briefly as if in surprise. The next minute, though, her brows lowered and she gave him a curt nod. She stretched her hand out to Anton. "Come along. Let's be getting home."

Anton flapped her hand away and shook his head. Sounds writhed out of his mouth.

They made no sense to Yanek, but Nika clearly understood, for she said, "Yes, I remember. Yes, it's Yanek, who saved you when those boys threw rocks at you."

She turned to Yanek. "He wants to know if your wound healed. Where one of the rocks hit you."

"Oh. Yes, it was just a scratch." Had she been there

too? He vaguely remembered a female voice, but he'd been blinded by the blood running down his face, and when he'd wiped it off, there was no one left in the market place.

Anton babbled some more, his face lighting up with a big grin. He pointed to Nika and then to Yanek. Nika flushed.

"What's he saying now?"

Nika said, "Just nonsense. Enough, Anton."

Anton's mouth drooped. He looked at her sideways and made another string of noises.

Nika listened carefully, her brows tightening in concern. She turned to Yanek.

"Is this true? He says Baba Yaga's given him the task of helping you find a wife."

Yanek looked around for the old witch, but the cottage and the palisade had gone. The only glow came from his lantern, which puttered as the flame sucked the last of the oil. He wanted to laugh at the thought of this boy as a matchmaker. But then he remembered that he'd laughed when Baba Yaga told him what was in the elixir she'd brewed to heal his father.

"It is, yes." What a slow journey this would be with this timid, crazy man-child. Who would lead whom? Yanek could not see how this could ever work. He opened his mouth to say he'd changed his mind, but Anton burst into garbles again.

Nika interpreted. "Anton says it's important for us to know what you want in a wife before we set out."

Adoring, he thought. He wouldn't say that. Nika might curl her lip, or burst into laughter, as the other girls in the village would. "Beautiful," he said instead. "I want a girl that's beautiful."

"But what's your idea of beauty?"

"Slender." His eyes slipped to Nika's thick waist. She raised an eyebrow then turned to Anton. They carried on a curious conversation, Nika asking her brother questions,

Anton gesticulating with sweeping hands and wild nods, his jaw working away at the strange noises he made.

Nika turned back. "The Reed Girl is the one for you, says Anton. She's the daughter of the Marsh Guardian. You need to seek her out in the bogland that's one day's journey west of here."

A bogland. With Anton. Yanek made a decision. "You will need to come with us. To interpret."

Nika raised an eyebrow. "Whoever said I'd let you take him without me?"

"Tomorrow, then. At daybreak."

Nika nodded and slipped her arm into Anton's to lead him away. They disappeared from the circle of lantern light. A crackle of a twig and they were gone.

Yanek picked his way back through the forest. All the while he swung between elation and amazement—elation at a chance to escape his responsibilities at the farm and amazement at himself for even thinking of such a quest. When the farm came into view, his eyes ran over the fields and enclosures. Another ten years of delivering slimy foals, milking goats, and sacking up turnips for the cows? No, he'd take the opportunity to roam the marshes with two crazy things. His friend and neighbor Vadim had five workers for his farm; he would send a few over to feed and water Yanek's livestock while he was away.

At dawn, he made his arrangements with Vadim. Next, he packed his cup of plenty and his everlasting loaf. Waking his father and explaining the quest was a tricky task, and the old man was reaching new heights in peevishness when finally there was a knock at the front door. Relieved, Yanek went to open it.

His eccentric guides stood there waiting for him. Anton seemed to be very excited about the trip, waving his arms and squealing. Nika looked even crazier by daylight. Today she had added an apron stitched out of leaves dried to mere skeletons. A necklace of acorns hung around her neck.

She held a bundle slung over her back.

"Goodbye, Father," Yanek called over the old man's protests and the young man's squeals. He picked up his ax and his bundle and pulled the door closed behind him.

The way west took them along the main track out of the forest, but as the trees thinned out, the road curved north. There, they broke away from the road to keep going west. The sun trailed a path over their heads to sink below the horizon. When it was too dark to be sure of where to put their feet, they stopped for the night.

Yanek got out his cup. He'd packed in haste, but now he wondered whether he'd have done better to bring a flask of water or milk. The cup served beer, ale, or wine; you never knew which it would be, but it was always alcohol for him and his father. What effect would that have on the boy? He passed the cup to Nika, wondering what to do.

She gave it to her brother.

"Wait, that's—"

"Your cup of plenty. I know. Everyone in the village knows."

She watched serenely as Anton drained the cup, wiped his mouth, and passed it back. Yanek watched him closely as Nika drank and returned the cup, but Anton did not sway or hiccup.

"Water." Nika nodded at Anton. "Water for me too. It was beer again for you, Yanek, wasn't it? The cup gives each person what he needs."

"How did you know it would?"

Nika smiled. "I know all sorts of things."

She emptied her sack of provisions—a bundle of nuts and a honeycomb for food, and three blankets for covers for the night. Yanek chopped wood to make a fire, splintering a fallen tree in three deft blows. The fire and the blankets kept them warm, but it was not a restful night. Anton muttered and squealed through the night, and Nika hushed and soothed him. Yanek pulled his blanket over his ears.

In the morning, they set out once more. The open land was shrubby under a gray sky, with a stream or two lurking in ditches behind a haze of rushes. A "V" of wild geese flew overhead. The ground grew boggier as they went on, squelchy mud circling clumps of drier grass. By noon they had to pick their way carefully between the rills, keeping to the higher clods of earth. At last they came to the edge of a great expanse of open water that reflected the dull sky, broken only by ducks rocking on the ripples. Bulrushes waved their fluttery heads as the breeze whispered through them.

Anton stopped and pointed, his head rocking, noises jerking out of his mouth.

"He says that's your bride," Nika said.

"I can see only reeds," Yanek replied, puzzled.

"The tallest one is the Reed Girl," Nika said. "My brother says you must cut the reed down and split it open. He says her father the Marsh Guardian is powerful and fierce and kills anyone who approaches her."

Yanek looked again doubtfully. How could a girl come out of a reed? True, now that he shaded his eyes with a hand, he saw that these were bigger rushes than the ones from the village pond. So he took off his boots and coat and picked his way over the mushy terrain. He was light on his feet as well as strong; he cut the reed at the first whirl of his ax without losing his footing. Turning, he made himself take the steps back just as slowly, irritated by Anton's stare.

"It will be safe to split it open now," said Nika.

Holding the ax near its head, he inched it along the reed then prised it open with two thumbs. In a slither like egg white and yolk coming out of a broken shell slid a damp, delicate thing. Yanek knelt on the ground and stared. It was a girl, curved eyelashes closed onto pale cheeks, long wet hair clinging to her neck. She was probably a head shorter than him and slender as a wand.

A scream and the sound of pounding water burst behind him. He spun around to face a monstrous gray creature erupting out of the panicking waters, part lamprey, part fish. A long, spiny fin ran down its shining black back, its mouth yawned wide round dozens of tiny, sharp teeth, and he bellowed with a man's voice.

"GIVE ME BACK MY DAUGHTER!"

There was a squeal behind Yanek. Nika's retreating voice called after her fleeing brother. With a "wump" of its snaking body, the Marsh Guardian heaved itself onto the shore before the youth, blocking out the sun. The mouth stretched wider and the head jerked back, ready to strike, screaming all the time. Yanek's fist struck under its eye, and its head swayed. Quick as lightning, the Guardian's tail lashed around Yanek and tightened, crushing the breath out of him. His vision blurred. His head rang with the creature's screech. He gripped its jaws and strained to keep the sucking maw away from his face. The Guardian thrashed, and Yanek slipped in the mud, falling on his back. The fall surprised the creature, and it slackened a moment. Yanek tightened his grip and the screaming turned to a choke and a whisper. All he could see was the thick, gray neck of the Guardian. Under his hands, he felt the creature jolt madly then go limp.

In the sudden stillness, Yanek pulled himself up. Nika's voice, getting louder as it gave out a low stream of reassuring noises for her brother, told him his companions were returning.

His vision cleared, but his throat still burned, and he gasped in breaths of air. He struggled over to where the Reed Girl lay. Her eyes fluttered.

Behind him, he heard Nika say, "The Marsh Guardian is dead."

"Yes. It tried to kill me. Anton was right, it was very strong."

Yanek had hoped for praise, but he got none from Nika. "Look! The marsh!"

There was a sucking sound all around them, and before their eyes, the marsh water sank into the ground. The mud dried and cracked until it looked like a brickfield stretching to the horizon. A waddle of ducks launched themselves into the air, quacking in alarm. Eels and fish lay gasping on the hard bed. Yanek surveyed the scene of disaster, aghast.

"Water! Water!" The voice was faint and unfamiliar. He looked down at the Reed Girl. Her eyes had opened, pupils large and dark. He slipped his hand under her head. Where was he to find water now?

"Water, water!" The girl was shrinking before his eyes, lashes fluttering, skin taking on a cobweb pattern like the leaves on Nika's apron.

Nika nudged Yanek's arm. He turned to see she was holding out his cup of plenty. But it was too late. With a faint wail, the Reed Girl faded and blew away like a leaf. Yanek watched her until she was a speck against the clouds. He hoped she'd felt no pain, but the waste of her life disturbed him.

The sun rode high in the sky and blazed down on the backs of the questers. Yanek flung his coat over his shoulder. Anton pushed his hair back off his brow. Nika pulled at her belt, rolled the tunic over her head, and bundled it up. Underneath, she wore a long-sleeved gown with an unraveled hem. Without the tunic, she was half the size she was before.

He gestured at the mud, the wilting plants, the staggering reeds. "What happened? What went wrong?"

Nika bit her lip and turned to her brother. "Anton? Do you understand?"

Anton screwed up his face and bunched his fist under his chin in concentration. Nika waited while he muttered to himself. When Yanek thought it would go on all day, Anton suddenly raised his arm and let out a string of noises.

"He says it is because you killed the Marsh Guardian."

"It attacked me. What was I supposed to do? Let it kill me?"

Anton babbled some more.

"He says you should have talked to it. Asked its permission to court its daughter."

"Talk to it! I'm no good with words. I'm only good with my fists."

The pair regarded him silently. Nika tilted her head at the scene of devastation.

He still did not know how he could have avoided the situation, but the dry marsh bed, the dying eels, the scorching sun accused him nevertheless. "What shall I do? What can I do?" The cup still in his hand, he waved it at the marsh bed.

Anton took the cup, looked inside, and handed it back, babbling. Yanek looked over to Nika, who translated. "You can give the cup of plenty to the marsh creatures."

Unsure how to do this, he picked his way over the uneven ground to what was once the deepest part of the marsh and poured a trickle from the cup onto the cracked earth. A slurp and it turned to mud, then a pool. He retreated and poured again. The water rose. He put the cup down at the water's edge, and the waves rippled out, lifting the eels in, where they wriggled and dove down. A splutter of honks above told him the ducks were flying back. Looking up, he saw behind the birds the Reed Girl, eddying down on the breeze to land at the water's edge with a sigh. So she was alive. He was glad he hadn't killed her, but he made no attempt to reach her. She seemed spiritless and no longer attracted him.

Nika was looking at him with an expression he was struggling to read. Hardly admiration, but perhaps some grudging acceptance that he had done what he could.

"So what now?" Yanek asked. "Do I have to fetch

the Reed Girl back? I don't think she is the bride for me. "

Anton made more noises.

"He says you should think again about what you want in a bride."

Yanek didn't answer straight away, his head bowed in thought. "Grace. I want her to dance like—like…"

"Like a flame." Nika's eyes followed his, and he realized he had been looking at her feet in their clogs. Shame washed over him that she should notice, but surely most men preferred a light, pretty ankle to stomping feet?

"So it's the Flame Girl for you. She's the daughter of the Fire Toad, and she lives east of here in the forest on the other side of a chasm."

He'd not heard of the Fire Toad's daughter before, but he liked the sound of her. A flame girl had—well, fire and spark. He was surprised and impressed by his own poetry.

"You have to remember, though," Nika went on, "to ask the Fire Toad for her hand."

Yanek nodded then said, "But will a toad understand the human tongue?"

Nika just raised an eyebrow and slung her bundle over her shoulder. The three companions set off in an eastwardly direction. After an hour's walk and much persuasion, Nika let Yanek take her bundle as well as his.

By nightfall, they reached the edge of the chasm and camped a little distance away from it. Nika shared some nuts she had, and Yanek got out his everlasting loaf. Anton found it intriguing. He tore it in half again and again, and every time it multiplied, he gave a shriek of delight. After five minutes of this, Nika gently took half out of his hand and passed it to Yanek. Yanek tore it and gave half to Nika. Anton crammed hunks into his mouth, his face working from curious to amazed to contented.

"It's good bread, this," Yanek said to Anton.

Anton responded with squeaks.

"He's never had bread before," Nika said. "Not from wheat."

"What do you eat then? Surely not honey and nuts all the time?"

"No, that would be boring. All sorts of leaves. Berries, of course. Roots. Some can be ground and turned into flour. Then we can keep it for the winter."

"How about meat? Do you hunt or trap wild animals?"

"No. Anton won't let me. I trapped a rabbit once, when we were quite small. I was going to stun it with a rock, but Anton just screamed and screamed. I had to bandage its leg and make it a bed next to us. It died anyway, two days later. After that we stopped eating meat. I buy cheese and curds from the market, though. My honey fetches good prices."

Yanek had bought honey from her himself a few times. His father loved it; it went very well with the everlasting loaf. Yanek would buy several combs at a time, barely glancing at her as he passed over the coins, assuming she didn't have the wit to understand words or to reply. How wrong he'd been! He turned his face to hide the flush of embarrassment he could feel creeping up his neck. He knew what it was like to be thought stupid.

It was good bread as ever, fresh and slightly warm as if just out of the oven. They washed it down with water from a nearby stream. Yanek cut wood for a fire again, to ward off any wild animals.

The next day, they made their way down one side of the chasm, across the river at a fording point, and up the other side. Pine trees clung tenaciously to the walls of the chasm. At the top, the trees thickened, and the light dimmed as the branches crisscrossed the sky. Their feet crushed pine needles underfoot, making more scent than noise. The shreds of sky behind the branches turned pink as the sun sank. Yanek wondered if they should camp for the night, but

Nika said, "No. We will see the Fire Girl best by night. Look out for the flames."

Sure enough, not many steps farther on, a flicker between trunks made them slow down. They inched toward the light until they found themselves looking into a clearing circled by fire. In the middle, where nothing burned, danced a graceful figure.

Anton gesticulated energetically, and Nika interpreted. "He says you need to take this branch and call, 'Fire Toad, Fire Toad! Hop on my bough.' The branch will burst into flame, and you will see the Toad in the fire. Then you must talk to him."

Yanek grasped the proffered branch and took a step into the flames. A spurt of light and heat told him his coattail had caught alight. Rapidly, he beat at it with the branch and put it out. He strode on, his eyes fixed on the girl in the clearing. Her hair, a red-gold, whipped around her face and neck as she twisted and leaped like a flame, flickering and fierce. As she twirled, he caught her eye, and she smiled.

Why call on the Fire Toad? he thought. *He may try and fight me like the Marsh Guardian. Look how that worked out! Better to bypass him altogether. She looks as if she likes me.* He lowered the branch toward the Flame Girl and said, "Fire Girl, Fire Girl, light on my bough."

Instantly, she vanished and the branch burst into flame, throwing up light and shadows until the trees around seemed as tall as towers.

Yanek carried the flaming branch out of the circle. As he did so, there was a deafening bellow from the darkness around them and out waddled a warty toad with eyes the size of a child's head. Flames belched from its mouth. Heat surged out and burned Yanek's face.

Holding the flaming branch away from him, Yanek stepped back. Behind him, Anton shrieked, and Nika soothed her brother.

"Fire Toad! I mean no harm. I want to marry your

daughter."

The Toad rolled the flame back into its mouth as if it were its tongue and barked, "You? Marry my Fire Girl? A peasant like you? Ha!"

"Run, Yanek!" Nika cried.

He didn't want to run. That would be coward's behavior. He stood his ground. Branches snapped behind him and Anton's wail faded as the boy fled.

The Fire Toad roared again and darted forward. Flames scorched the earth at Yanek's feet. He jumped to one side. The Toad twisted and darted at him again. Yanek dashed to the left just in time; the flames blackened a tree trunk instead. This was crazy. Was he just going to let the Toad drive him in circles all night?

The creature thought the same, clearly. With a spring, it cleared the space between them and landed on his chest. Claws scratched at his eyes, powerful legs kicked him in the stomach, winding him. Burdened with the torch, he only had one hand to defend himself. Each time he seized one of the Toad's limbs it kicked out of his grasp. A claw raked his face just below his eye. Desperation gave him new strength. He closed his fingers around the Toad's back leg and yanked. A sudden release told him the creature was flying through the air. A mighty thunk said the Toad had crashed into a tree.

Flames leaped out of the pine needle matting as the Fire Toad hit the ground. Yanek grabbed the branch and ran after Anton. Nika hesitated then ran too. The flames sprang after them, bounding up trees and along fallen logs, flicking at their heels just as they got to the river. There, it fell back, and the travelers splashed their way through the ford.

Yanek had carried the branch high all the way, and not a drop of water had touched it. But as he climbed the other bank, the branch crumbled into hot embers in his fist. He dropped them with a grunt. The glow faded, and the embers collapsed in a heap of ashes. Yanek bowed his head.

He looked up to see Nika watching him. "Is she

dead?" he asked.

"I don't know."

"I've killed her father, though, haven't I?"

"Yes."

Yanek scanned the burning forest beyond the water. "I only meant to defend myself."

Nika turned away.

They found a hollow in the riverbank to spend the night. Nika took Anton down to the river to help him wash—he'd slipped in the mud in his panic to flee the flames. Yanek stood outside the hollow and watched the fire. It had consumed all the trees on this side of the forest and now it was hunkering in bushes, as if considering its next leap.

Garbled noises came from behind the rooty trees that were protected by the water. It was Anton's voice, but it almost sounded like laughter. Curious, Yanek shifted along the bank. Yes, they were both laughing and splashing, the sound free of care for the moment. Nika had rolled up her gown at the arms and hitched it at the waist. Without her clogs and woolen stockings, her calves were slim and strong as she jumped back and forth in the mock fight.

The snap of a branch under Yanek's feet made the siblings look up. The laughter in Nika's face turned to a scowl, and she pulled her tunic down.

No one wanted to light a fire that night; besides, the heat from the Fire Toad's flames lingered. They ate from the everlasting loaf and went down to the river again to drink.

"What am I going to do now?" Yanek asked.

"I don't know," Nika said. "It's your quest." Her mouth was set in a hard line.

Yanek put his chin in his hand. "I think my strength is my handicap in this quest. The trouble is, I've been used to solving everything with my fists."

The hard line of Nika's mouth softened. "So use something else."

"I don't have anything else. Father says all the porridge I ate built my muscles, not my brain."

"There's more to life than muscle and brain," Nika said.

"Wealth? I don't have much of that."

"Heart, Yanek. It's heart that made you rescue Anton when the boys were throwing stones at him. I wanted to thank you when you next bought my honey, but you still would not say a word to me."

"I am sorry. I—I suppose I thought you were like Anton, unable to talk."

"He can talk! It's just that no one else understands." She bunched her fists and pushed them against her hips.

"I stand corrected. Now tell me about the stories they pass around in the village. Is it true you two sleep in a tree hollow covered in leaves?"

Nika snorted. "Only if Anton has wandered a long way from home. Sometimes, by the time I find him, we can't get back before dark."

"So where is home?"

"Our parents' hut."

Yanek knew where it was, deep in the woods—their father had been a charcoal burner—but Yanek hadn't been to the spot in years.

"That's no better than a hollow tree. The roof's fallen in."

"We've mended it. Anton helped me. If you tell him what to do, he can do it."

"Isn't it lonely, stuck out there with only…" He was going to say, "someone who can't talk," but checked himself in time.

"There's Father and Mother in the garden. I talk to them sometimes." She threw him a look that was a challenge—*go on, say I'm crazy.*

"They're buried there? Why didn't you bury them by the church like everyone else?"

"Mother wouldn't let Father be taken away. It was hard enough to persuade her to let us bury him at all."

"Us? You and Anton?"

"Yes. And Mother, too. No one would come close to us after Father's death. Don't you remember?" She shrugged one shoulder. The gesture was half accusation, half acknowledgement that he was too young at the time to be blamed for not remembering. "They didn't like how crazy she became, and they shunned her when she went to market."

Yanek had a faint memory of their mother bringing Nika and Anton to the market. He would have been maybe seven then, and Nika... He glanced at her, trying to assess her age for the first time. His memories were of a girl younger than him by perhaps a year. Six, to bury your father! And her mother had died a few years later, doubtless buried by their children like their father.

As the night drew on, it grew colder. Nika made Anton lie down to sleep, but she and Yanek took turns to watch, wrapped in their blankets. They sat back to back, to keep warm and so one could doze propped up by the other. As she dozed, her spine pressed into his through the felt.

He woke from an uncomfortable slumber to the forest in daylight. It was a terrible sight. Blackened stumps studded the hillside across the river, and ash grayed the bushes on the riverbank. Two squirrels pattered over the ground, scratching uselessly for something to eat. Overhead, birds screeched and wheeled. This was his doing. He had destroyed their home. Now the animals had nowhere to shelter and nothing to eat.

He jumped up, surprising Nika, and pulled out the everlasting loaf from the bag. The river froze his bare feet as he waded through. At the top of the bank on the other side, he broke the loaf and pulled off hunks to throw into the ruins of the forest. Sharp, suspicious eyes watched him. With a last throw, he hurled the entire loaf and scrambled down the riverbank, through the water, and back to camp.

When he looked back, a bird had dropped to the forest floor and was pecking at the loaf. Two more swooped down and seized a piece each, winging up again. As the birds flew away, a spray fell from each loaf hunk. Yanek thought it looked like crumbs, or seeds.

A garbling noise from behind him told him Anton was awake and up, and watching too. Yanek looked around to see if Nika had also noticed. Of course she had—she missed nothing. He turned back, and the forest had transformed. Where the spray had fallen, green leaves shot out of the ground, exploding into branches, leaves rushing up to the sky. The crisp smell of pine needles filled the air. The squirrels bounded up the side of one tree, chattering to each other, and two birds came to perch on a bough, lifting their throats to sing in liquid notes. A flicker caught his eye from the spot where he'd dropped the flaming branch. A flame sprang up, blazed out heat for a second, and took the shape of a dancing girl, who lifted her heels and ran away into the heart of the forest.

"That's better," Nika said.

"Do I go after the Flame Girl?"

Nika raised her eyebrows.

"I don't think she'll want me now that I've killed her father." And what future was there with a wife who'd collapse into ashes?

"No," Nika agreed.

"We've nothing to eat now."

He picked his way down the bank to the river and scooped up handfuls of mountain water, drinking some, washing his face with the rest. The sting of the cold water woke his brain up. He'd tried to find the perfect bride but failed both times. Maybe it was time to give up.

Go back home? To clean out byres and milk cows? No, not yet. He was savoring his freedom. He hadn't slept well out in the wild, and he was hungry, but it was an adventure. A quest to find a princess, like in the tales the old women told. He wiped his face with his sleeve and climbed back up the bank to Nika and Anton.

"So what now?" Nika asked.

"I've been a fool," Yanek said. "What's the use of girls who dry up or burn out? What I want is someone strong and brave."

He wondered where this thought had come from. He turned. "Would you ask Anton? And then you'll want to go home. You've given me enough of your time. I'll carry on the search by myself."

Odd. From her expression, you'd think he'd slapped her in the face, not let her go home. He tried to explain. "I've learned from you what Baba Yaga wanted me to learn. That fighting and taking from Nature isn't the way to do things."

Her face hardened. She placed a hand on her brother's arm, muttering low. Anton's mouth crumpled into worry; he pawed her shoulder, making mewling sounds. She put a firm palm over his hand to still it and turned back. Her words came through clenched teeth.

"You've not learned half of what you need to learn. The Griffin's daughter, the Cloud Girl. The mountains to the south. Come, Anton."

The Griffin must be fearful indeed, thought Yanek, judging from the stricken look on her face as she turned away. Before he knew it, they'd gone. Well! She could at least have said goodbye, after all they'd shared.

Yanek pulled on his boots and coat and set off south. He had little idea how he would find the Griffin, but as he walked, he told himself he didn't need that strange, infuriating pair to guide him. He couldn't miss a mountain, could he? And hadn't he given up his cup and his loaf to repair the damage he'd done to the marsh and forest? Of course he'd learned. Whatever happened, he would not kill the Griffin. If the Griffin killed him instead, so be it.

That night he lit his own fire, but he was still very cold. With no one to talk to, he stared into the dark patches in the bushes. He found berries to eat and scratched around for some roots. They were very bitter, and he wondered if they were poisonous, but in the morning he was still alive, so they'd been safe to eat after all.

He tramped all day, and by sunset his tongue stuck to the roof of his mouth from not talking. As he made camp again, a cracking of branches made him think Nika had followed him after all, but when he looked, it was a falling bough. He told himself he was relieved it wasn't her.

On the third day, there was a smudge on the horizon, and by noon he was sure it was the mountains. On the fourth day they loomed high, white and blue, the foreground ragged with boulders and scraggy small pines. Midmorning, he began to climb.

Scree slipped under his feet, making him stumble and catch his balance. The sun rose and baked him. There was no water, and he had no food. He took off his coat and laid it carefully over a boulder, hoping he would find the same way back. His neck began to burn. He ignored the heat, ignored the sweat running into his tunic, and kept climbing.

Some twenty minutes later, the temperature began to drop. Looking up, he saw he was nearing the edge of the cloud around the peak. Three steps closer, it gathered itself into a tight mist and glided over his head. Bullets of rain fell and drenched him. When it had plastered his hair to his forehead, it stopped abruptly, and the drops flung themselves together, the outline of a girl showing on the mountaintop. She was tall and dark and glorious. It was worth every drop of sweat and rain for him to be able to gaze on her.

He would do this right. He was going to learn from his failures. He would ask, not take. Aloud, he said, "Cloud Girl, you are very beautiful. I am Yanek, son of Ivan. I have come to ask your father for your hand in marriage. Where can I find him?"

The Cloud Girl laughed and pointed to a spot beyond his shoulder.

A wind swept his hair off his brow as great wings beat overhead, and a huge shape threw its shadow over him. He looked up at the curved beak, the black and white feathers, and the lion's body. The Griffin was here. It flew south and glided down onto the peak ahead.

Yanek set off to cover the last bit of the distance, but caution made him hunch as he got closer and circle around to approach the Griffin. This way, the breeze blew his scent behind him, not toward the nest he could now make out.

"I can see you, you know. You can stop darting around like that." This new voice held an edge of amusement, despite the narrow iris its owner fixed on him.

Yanek straightened and walked up to the Griffin. It pushed itself to a standing position and cocked its head at him.

"I haven't seen a human in a hundred years. What brings you up here? My jewels?"

Yanek's eyes flickered to where the sun caught a spark of red, another of green. The nest held not eggs, but precious stones, each as big as Yanek's fist.

"No. Your greatest treasure of all, I would expect. Your daughter."

The Griffin ducked his head in appreciation. "My daughter! You are an ambitious man indeed! And what makes you think you are worthy of a Griffin's daughter?"

Yanek was silent. He thought about how he'd killed the Marsh Spirit and endangered the marsh. He thought about how he'd slain the Fire Toad and brought devastation to the forest. He thought about how he'd sent Nika and Anton home.

The Griffin opened his beak and let out a harsh chuckle. "Ha ha! You know you don't deserve her! Well, I like you for being wise enough to see that, and there's merit in wisdom. Perhaps I may be persuaded to consider your suit after all. What is your greatest treasure? What can you offer me in return for my daughter?"

This question was little better than the last. He had nothing to offer. Even his eternal cup and his everlasting loaf would have been paltry gifts for a Griffin with a nest of jewels. He searched his mind in vain.

"My cup of plenty? I've lost that."

The Griffin snapped his beak in laughter. Yanek kept well back.

"My everlasting loaf? I lost that too."

"Think! You need to give me the thing that you prize most."

Yanek was speechless. What was dearest to him? His father? His farm? The farm was a duty rather than love. Nothing he owned meant much to him. Wasn't this why he had pursued his quest for a wife? Someone slim and graceful, strong and brave, someone with twigs in her hair...

What? Where had that idea come from?

The shriek of laughter from the Griffin sliced through his eardrums. "Yes! Yes! That's right! Not a thing, but a person. That's who's dearest to you! You will bring her to me in return for *my* dearest one!"

"Someone who's dearer to you than me?" The voice came from above Yanek's head. He looked up at the Cloud Girl, floating above him. Her brow was drawn into a sharp "V" of distrust. "You call yourself a suitor? Who is this person?"

She was magnificent, and he'd walked miles and climbed a mountain to win her—but a little voice in his head said she didn't stir his heart. "Her name is Nika, one of the villagers. She wears a man's tunic and a string of acorns around her neck. She is a brave and loyal sister to her brother, and the wisest person I have ever met."

The Cloud Girl drew her breath up through her nose with a hiss. "A peasant girl? You'd spurn me for a peasant girl?" Her hair whirled round her head and she rose into the air, whipping round until she'd become a blurry black cloud again. Rain fell like knives then turned into hail that hammered onto his head.

"Bring me Nika!" her voice called from the cloud. "Then you'll see what happens when you insult the Cloud Girl."

"I can't! She's not mine to command."

A cutting, buffeting wind from above blew him into the rock outcrop. He landed against sharp corners and stumbled, grazed and bruised.

"Bring me Nika!"

He gasped his breath back. "Why would I do that? You only want to harm her. She's on her way back north now, and she'll be safe home in a day or so."

Abruptly, the wind dropped, the hail stopped. He looked up and saw the Cloud Girl, in the form of a woman again, triumph on her face. "You've told me where to find her now. I was going to loose the floods on you, but I'll loose them on her instead."

"No!" he shrieked. "Kill me if you must, if that will avenge your pride, but leave her alone."

The rain fell as if a river had flooded its banks. A bolt of lightning cracked above his head.

"Stop!" It was the Griffin.

The rain stopped.

"Daughter, enough. I'll not have killing on this mountain. Maybe the man is a fool for not wanting you, maybe not. I think he's been acting foolishly for a long time, but I also think he knows it now. Time to be off, young man."

"Yes. I need to find Nika."

"Hop on my back, and I'll take you. It'll save you days of walking. And you are bruised and soaking wet."

"No, thank you. I need to think."

"Plenty of time for that on the flight. It's self-interest

that makes me offer. I don't want you bumbling around on my mountain all afternoon. A Griffin needs his peace and quiet. You too, daughter—you've made enough noise for one day. Go and bother some bandit down in the gorge below, and don't come home until you've blown yourself out."

The Griffin was right about thinking time on the flight. Clinging to the beast's feathery mane as the wind rushed past his ears, Yanek watched the mountainside, the plains, and the forests glide below them as they flew. He wondered if Nika would have him. She didn't need a man; she took care of her brother single-handedly. If she did have him, she'd want Anton to live with them too. Yanek didn't know if that meant working the farm together, adventuring on the roads, or living in the woods, but he was happy with any of those options if she was with him.

"Down there!" he cried suddenly. Below lay a plain, with two figures tramping across it, one small, one tall and lanky.

"Your dearest treasure?" The Griffin sounded doubtful.

"She doesn't belong to me, but she is very dear. Will you put me down over there, in the coppice? I don't want her brother to take fright."

The Griffin complied, alighting stylishly on the other side of the trees. Yanek scrambled off with hurried thanks.

"Yes, yes. Off you go, now."

Yanek crashed through the coppice and began to run. The two figures before him trudged along, their pace easy to catch up with. Nika's shoulders sagged, and her head bent forward. He sped up and shouted her name. They both spun round.

Joy flashed on Nika's face, then disbelief, then puzzlement.

"Yanek. Didn't you find the Griffin's daughter? Please tell me you didn't kill the Griffin."

"Look. Up there. He's just flying away."

Nika and Anton tilted their heads back. The Griffin was wheeling above their heads, his wings beating slowly, his magnificent head outlined against the cloudless sky.

"And his daughter?"

"She can't compare to you. Dearest, I've nothing to offer you. I've lost my treasures, and I'm a fool. Well, I was a fool, but I don't want to be one anymore. Will you be my wife?"

She looked back at him silently. Was she going to refuse? It was not much of an offer. He held his breath. He couldn't bear to think of a refusal.

A smile slowly spread across her face. She took his hands and raised her lips to his. As Yanek kissed her, Anton clapped and roared. Yanek thought it sounded like approval.

Goodbye, Gigi

Louise Ross

The man leaned down to Gigi's cheek. His nose came into view. Cigarette smoke mixed with sweaty armpit and spittle, and she turned in the chair. A thick hand pressed harder on her shoulder, stopping her from escaping the smell, pinning her in front of a desk and two more men.

"I could break all her fingers." The fingers on her shoulder flexed and tightened down one at a time.

Goosebumps popped up along her arms. It might have been the threat or it might have been how his breath moved her hair, sending a chill down her neck. Her upper lip lifted in disgust, but she kept her mouth shut.

"No, Junior. We can't do that." A younger man dressed like a banker and wearing a model-perfect pout rested with one leg on the desk in front of her. A perfect crease divided the center of his pant leg. His black and gray wingtip shoe rocked back and forth, marking the time as she waited to hear her future.

"What do you suggest?" the man behind the desk asked. He seemed the most normal, a khaki and polo guy with slightly mussed hair and not magazine-ready. He leaned forward like the man in charge. If he was, she needed him to be on her side.

Widening her eyes and dropping her mouth open, she pleaded silently with him. If the scared little girl act didn't work, she'd switch to crying. Crying almost always worked. The man behind the desk didn't turn his head or look away, but he also didn't sigh and tell Junior to release her.

"She could pay for the damage. Once she's evened up, she can go her own way." The banker smiled, displaying perfectly straight teeth. As she watched, his eye teeth lengthened into fangs. If he wanted to paw open her stomach and tear into her flesh, she'd kick him in the balls. No way would he be getting his teeth on her. She shuddered.

The third man nodded. "You've heard your choices. Which do you choose?"

Gigi tried to lean forward, but the hand held her in place. Tears moistened her eyes. She glanced down, feigning innocence, and looked back up slowly, hoping to project that she would do anything for him if he only saved her from the situation. "Isn't there any other option?"

The man clasped his fingers in response. "Absolutely. We could do the responsible thing and turn you over to the cops."

"But—" she began her denial.

"No." He shook his head. "Let's review the evidence." He pressed several buttons and held up a tablet. "Exhibit 1: The inept thief comes out of the tree line and runs directly up to the deck in direct view of a security camera. Notice how clearly I can zoom in and see your face. Very stupid."

Her cheeks reddened. "I—"

"Exhibit 2:" he continued without regard to her, "the thief shines a light inside the glass door, activating the motion setting of the internal camera, so that we can watch her break in." He paused the video playing on the tablet. "What were you even trying to do? Is that one of those movie glass cutters? You thought you could cut a silent circle in a window pane? One that wouldn't shake the glass enough to set off the security alarms? That's the center window panel. Look at how ridiculous you look shoving your arm through that hole. I'm surprised you could reach the handle at all, but lucky for us you did." He paused with dramatic effect. "Which means we have your fingerprints."

She sat straighter. That glass cutter worked perfectly, and she got through their door. Fancy alarm system aside, she broke in.

The man in charge continued. "Sticking your arm through that hole tripped the internal alarm system. From that moment on, all surveillance became active. So what do you do? You raid the kitchen as if you have all weekend to rob the place. Were you so hungry you couldn't leave without taking a bite out of an apple? You stole a bag of pears. The kitchen knives on the counter are more valuable than a bag of pears. I have no clue what was going through your head."

Her fist clenched. The pears had been laying on the counter. It wasn't like a bag of pears would make a big difference considering everything else she planned on taking. Besides, she had been hungry. She still was. And knives. Well, they didn't sell well and would be heavy and potentially dangerous in her escape. Light or valuable, that's what she was after. Cash would be best, but priceless art or jewelry would work. Thinking about the pears, her stomach growled.

Junior leaned over her shoulder and growled in her ear. His muzzle extended right next to her cheek, and the ick shudders overtook her before she realized that nose had been human moments before. She leaned away.

"Exhibit 3: You chose to steal a metal and stone mosaic icon from the living room. To get it, you pull over a chair. There is a thick, rustic chair feet away, but you pull over a 1700s spindle-legged cloth-seated chair and stand directly in the middle of the ancient fabric. Somehow you manage to pull the icon down from the wall, adding even more weight. Didn't you feel the chair giving way? Watch."

On the video, her right foot tore through the seat of the chair. She fell to the side, shoving the chair the opposite direction. Its legs collapsed under her, breaking from the seat. Her elbow landed on a sideboard, knocking a painted vase onto the floor where it shattered. Her shoulder turned to regain balance, but she over corrected, slipped onto her knees on top of the broken chair. The icon slammed into the sideboard. The green gem that made the eye of the saint popped out. A crack split through the pieces creating the figure. A corner fell off. She tossed the piece on the ground. She detangled from the chair and kicked it. Twice.

Her accuser moved the slider back thirty seconds to replay. His fingers shortened and widened out. Two inch cylindrical nails tipped the stubs. She looked away. The chair was a mistake. One that she would not make in the future.

"Exhibit 4: You then search the house, stopping in every bedroom to lift up the mattresses. Do you think we distrust the banks? That we store wads of cash under the mattress? Were you checking for softness? Absolutely ridiculous." His voice deepened and became gravelly.

She clenched her jaw. The tears had dried up with her embarrassment. People hid all sorts of interesting stuff under their beds. Her mom kept her money there. Aunt Cecelia kept a gun under her mattress. She didn't like this third beast at all.

"Exhibit 5:" He reached for a coil of rope in his drawer. His deformed hand took two paws at the rope before he plopped it onto the desk. "You open a second-story window, tie a rope around your middle, and jump out. You didn't stop to measure the length of the rope, didn't check the sturdiness of your tie off, and didn't look out the window to see where you were jumping. A half-competent thief would have avoided this house or at least come up with a manageable plan. Instead you come in," his mouth lengthened into a muzzle, "destroy our property, attempt to leave with nothing but a bag of pears, and end up being found hanging five feet from the ground in your own getaway rope."

His paw smacked the desk. "There is more than enough evidence to let the police deal with you. The court will lock you up, and you will be treated like the criminal you are for the rest of your life."

The rope had been an idea she'd considered trying for a while. It had too many pitfalls to be useful in the future. Acid boiled in her stomach, and she shifted in her chair. "I—"

"I think of myself as a fair man."

Biting her cheek, she avoided laughing. The t-shirt-wearing grizzly sitting behind the desk didn't resemble a man at all, but he didn't resemble a stuffed teddy bear who'd brush off her laugh either.

"My brothers and I tend to disagree and if we vote amongst ourselves, each option would likely have one vote. In this instance, the fair thing would be to let you have a vote. You have your options. If you vote for any option but the ones presented, I will cast the deciding vote. So, as a recap, we could: cause you physical harm, force you to pay us back, or turn you over to the cops. Choose."

The paw on her shoulder pressed down. Five long nails indented her skin. It caught the edge of her curls, and the hair pulled on her scalp. It stung, and she shifted her head to avoid the pain. There was no real option; she wouldn't sacrifice her fingers, and she wasn't going back to jail.

She huffed and slumped down. "I'll pay you back."

"Good. You have until Friday. On Friday, I will send these videos to the cops, and Junior will hunt you down. If Junior finds you, don't expect him to stop with your fingers."

Junior laughed, a staccato of low bursts reminiscent of a machine gun in slow motion. He ripped the cap off a marker with his teeth and wrote on her palm. Message written, his hand released her.

Gigi hopped up and jogged for the door. "Friday,"

she shouted in acknowledgment over her shoulder and broke into a run.

***

Gigi ditched her apartment and crashed on the sofa at Pete's house. Which is how she woke up to a naked six-year-old running through the room.

The girl waved her underwear above her head and screeched like a banshee. Pete blocked the living room doorway with his arms crossed. On the second pass of the streaker, he grabbed the demon child by the waist and carried her off. The shrill siren continued another five minutes. Ten minutes later, just as the warm fuzzy sleepiness pulled Gigi back into oblivion, a princess in white dress shoes and a yellow ladybug dress skipped to the front door.

"Never have kids," Pete groused and watched the chirpy child stand at the end of the driveway, waiting for the bus to pick her up.

"Gotcha. No problem." Gigi turned over and nuzzled her nose into the stench of wet dog. "Yuck. Your couch smells." But it was too much to turn over again, so she stayed nose to dog couch.

"Then don't come over to sleep. Stay at your own place." Pete shut the door and flopped into a blanket-covered high-backed chair.

"I gotta hide for a while." Putting action to words, she pulled the afghan over her head.

"What are you hiding from?" Pete didn't actually jump up and down on the couch and dump water on her face, but he wasn't letting her sleep either.

"Who. I'm hiding from a who."

"Okay. Who are you hiding from?" The TV clicked on. A crowd cheered. A news anchor welcomed everyone to another beautiful morning.

From somewhere deep inside, Gigi gathered the

energy and strength together to flop on her backside and turn her head to Pete. She groaned, loudly.

"Come on. You've crashed on the couch. Time to talk to your best friend Pete. Tell Pete all about it, and he'll make your problems go away."

"Pete." One arm fell off the couch. Her palm opened up and a number was written across her palm in black permanent marker. "Do you have this much money stored in your mattress?" Her hand waved back and forth.

Pete didn't even lean forward. "Damn, that's a big number. With a number like that, you have to count the commas not the zeros. You buying your own island?"

"If I bought my own island, you think I could make people shut up and let me sleep?"

"Ouch. That hurts." He came across to the couch. "That hurts so much, I think I might faint." With a drama queen wrist to the forehead, he collapsed on top of her. His boney elbow stabbed her in the ribs and his butt crushed her thighs.

"Come on! Get off!" She squirmed and pushed at him. "Ugh."

Ooching backward, he wiggled his butt between the back of the couch and her thighs, leaving her no options other than to roll off. The ground wasn't as comfortable.

"Alright. Now that you're up, let's hear it." Pete's foot rested on her hip and jiggled her back and forth. "What's the money for?"

"I broke some ancient piece of art and the world's flimsiest chair." The floor smelled worse than the couch. "Do you have a dog?"

Pete tilted his head to the side. "No, why?"

Gigi groaned. "Because your house reeks of wet fur."

"That hurts too. Maybe I don't want to help you."

"You don't have the cash and you're not living in a mansion. You can't help with the money, so just let me lay low and sleep. That's what I want."

"Not until you tell me who you are hiding from and what happened." He crossed his arms over his chest.

"Ursines." She coughed the word into her fist.

Pete's foot pressed down hard on her hip. He choked on the idea. His hand tapped the couch cushion.

Rolling away, she sat up and watched him struggle to accept her answer.

"Please, please, please, please, please, don't tell me you broke into a bear's home. They own half the city, Gi, and financed the other half." He gasped the words between gagging fits.

Since she wouldn't lie to him, she sat there and watched. Eventually his gagging turned into hiding under a pillow and breathing heavily.

She waited.

He mumbled behind the fabric. Like a light switch coming on, he sat up straight and stared at her. "Gigi, you can't stay here. I got a family. They can't come here."

"Where else am I supposed to go?"

"You can't go anywhere. They will find you. Wherever you go. That can't be here."

"Well, it's not like I can pay them back. What am I supposed to do?"

"Throw yourself on the mercy of the cops. Ask them for witness protection."

"Don't be an idiot, Pete. I don't have information on the Ursines. I don't have anything to give the cops. They don't protect thieves. They lock thieves in a cell and scrutinize their every movement. I'm not going back to jail. Besides, one of the Ursines gave me that option, and I opted out."

"Then run away."

She lifted her eyebrows and looked at him.

"But not here. Go somewhere else."

"I'm not spoiling for options here, Pete. I can go visit my mother or my sister. I might have a connection or two in another city, but I'm not exactly overflowing with places to go."

"Then you got to pay them back. Get a job and send every paycheck to them. Maybe after a lifetime of work, they won't come after your family to pay off the balance."

"Friday. I have until Friday to pay them or they'll start breaking my fingers."

"Offer your left hand."

"No." She tucked her hand in her armpit. "Hell, no. It's my hand. I need it." She flopped back on the carpet. "Damn it. I got to find something valuable to steal. If I hock it or offer it in trade, maybe I can save my fingers."

Pete shook his head. "Haven't you learned. Stealing sucks. First you land in jail, then you have the Ursines after you. Get a new career goal."

"No. I can do this. I am a cat burglar extraordinary. I will succeed. I just need to learn from my mistakes."

"Gigi." He leaned over the couch and stared straight into her eyes until she wanted to squirm away. "There is no one that would have something that valuable. Do you plan on robbing the Ursines again to get the stuff to fence to make back the money? Stop being stupid. Give up the life of crime."

"That's it." She closed the gap and kissed his cheek. "I'll rob the Ursines to get the money. You're brilliant. What do you know about Junior Ursine?"

***

Gigi crouched behind a battered pickup truck with rusted side panels and watched Junior Ursine's house. Junior technically still lived at home according to the internet, but Pete's friend Jasper's second cousin had bought some weed from a guy who boasted that his supply came direct from Ursine and that he was banging Junior's girlfriend. The whole thing seemed ridiculous except a black and silver hog leaned on its kickstand under the carport. The license said "BIG BEAR," and the helmet hanging from the side featured a yawning bear with people-ripping fangs on display. Junior was the oldest brother and a bear. That seemed like a good sign that weed-seller was right; this was Junior's home-away-from-home, his girlfriend's place.

The Ursines didn't like how she approached their house? Well, she could do better. Pete dropped her off at the corner, and she worked her way back to the house. The outside looked poor, well, not as poor as her own shabby apartment, but definitely not hiding lost treasures of the Golden Valley. It was a slab house with slat siding and a two-car metal carport. Since Jasper's second cousin's drug connection was probably right, there might be drugs or drug money stashed in the house. If he was wrong, then maybe she could blackmail Junior with something she found.

The house wasn't a fast-paced convenience store with a parking lot full of cars and five-minute turnarounds, but Gigi counted three vehicles that pulled up to the curb. Once, when a shiny red mustang with two white racing stripes down the center pulled up, Junior himself came out to the car window. He machine-gun chuckled at something the driver said and patted the car door twice before the mustang peeled out. With Junior's confirmed presence, Gigi crept closer.

A chain-link dog enclosure ran along the side of the house. A wide-skulled, short-nosed dog slammed against the fence and barked at her until she ducked behind an overgrown lilac bush.

Her stomach growled, demanding lunch or dinner or a pear. Dusk darkened the yard, but the house lights didn't flick on. She duckwalked over to the house, staying below the windows, and pressed her back to the siding.

Junior stepped out of the side door into the carport. The door thumped shut. The motorcycle roared to life. The engine revved. The headlight lit the driveway, and she flattened tighter to the house and thought two-dimensional thoughts. Two people rode off on the bike. The oversized frame of Junior and a tiny-waisted, long-haired figure.

Crossing her fingers, Gigi ran to the back door, hoping that no one remained inside the dark house. The door was flimsy. Its cheap standard doorknob lock could be picked in minutes, but she didn't even need to try. The door had a hole for a bolt lock that was stopped up with an old sock. She poked the sock out, squeezed her hand through the hole, and unlocked the door from the inside. Too easy.

Inside, dirty dishes, discarded boxes, and ashtrays littered the kitchen. Her shoes stuck to the linoleum as she snuck into the living room. A coffee table with a single open spot directly took up the middle of the room. Stacks of magazines piled around it. Nothing looked recently moved. If they were dealing drugs or stashing money, it'd be somewhere they could access it.

She skipped the bathroom, which smelled like the fragrance section at a department store, and slipped into the bedroom. Clearly, they cared about the bedroom more than the rest of the house. A clean carpet path ringed the bed. The purple and silver cover matched the pillow cases. A lamp and an alarm clock lay on the otherwise open dresser top. The walls even had posters decorating the space.

In the bottom drawer of the dresser, she found a small lockbox. She didn't waste time opening it. She wrapped it in a shirt from the drawer and skedaddled. She was back to successful robberies just like that. Mission accomplished.

***

Pete refused to let Gigi return to his house. Instead, he arranged to meet her behind the gas station. He pulled into the parking space next to dumpster.

She waited for him to turn off the headlights before

she shimmied out from behind the metal container and slid into his car.

"So, what'd you get?" Pete made grabby hand motions.

Holding back her smug face, she solemnly placed the t-shirt in his hands.

Pete's nose wrinkled, and he kept his arms at full length.

"I brought you the grimy workout clothes of a hairy beast. Behold."

Without looking away, he rolled down his window and tossed the wad of cloth out. "Very funny. Was that it?"

"Golly, Pete, I went through a lot of effort to get you that. My thighs burn from staying crouched all day." She grinned at him. "But I got this too." She untucked her shirt and pulled out the box.

"A cash box?" His thumb clicked back the latch slider, but the top didn't pop open.

"A locked cash box," she agreed.

"Okay. Let's see what's in it?" He opened the glove box and pulled out a long flat bar.

"What's that?"

"It's a Slim Jim. To get into locked cars."

Her mouth fell open. "You gave me the guilt trip about stealing, and you got carjacking tools in your glove box? So not cool. Not cool." She popped him in the arm with her elbow.

The bar slid into the slit on the box. The handle levered up, and the box lid twisted and popped open. "I don't carjack. Believe it or not, a lot of people get locked out of their cars, and having the right tool on hand at the right time is a quick way to earn twenty bucks. I'm a savior." He grinned.

"When you're not stealing cars," she agreed.

"Duh, duh, dun!" He opened the box. The cash tray had a collection of pennies in one compartment and two dimes in another.

"Damn!"

"Yep, totally anticlimactic." He lifted the tray up, but there was nothing under it either. "So how does it feel to be the most incompetent burglar ever?"

She punched him in the arm. "I'm not incompetent. I got in and out without being caught."

He nodded. "This time."

"Eff. You. Pete."

"You've robbed the same guys twice and ended up with nothing both times."

"Yeah, well, I got to try again. I need the money to pay them back. Unless you have a better suggestion?"

They sat in silence. Pete chewed on his lip and scratched his nose.

"Naw. I got nothing."

She banged her head on the headrest. The robbery part she could do. Get in, get out. With something simple, where the door already had a hole, there was nothing valuable to steal. If she really wanted the kind of money to pay off the Ursines, she needed a big loot. They wouldn't gift a million-dollar painting to the two-timing mistress of a thug like Junior. Those pieces would be on display. Somewhere they could show them off.

"Where do they keep the valuable stuff. The stuff I can sell off and get the cash I need?"

"Like jewelry?"

"No. Like fine art."

"You can't sell off fine art."

"I can too. There's got to be a market for it or they wouldn't sell for 1.3 million dollars."

Pete shrugged. "And to get those prices it has to be verified and they'll contact last owners for chain of custody and stuff. Plus, you've never robbed anything big solo. You're a partner. A sidekick, Gi." He sighed loudly like the drama queen he was. "And the good stuff is probably at one of the three mansions."

"Okay. Where?"

"The wood house. I'm guessing that's the one you already robbed. The Pine Palace, which is where the main family lives, and a mansion out in Hide Park where the second brother lives."

Gigi narrowed her eyes and turned in the seat. "How do you know so much all the sudden?"

"I'm not stupid, Gi." He pulled out his phone and pulled up a search on the Ursine family. "You hide out in my house, potentially bringing them into my home, and expect me to not research? Tough luck, cookie. I'm not going to my grave because you got in over your head. I got a wife and a daughter. You endangered them too. Why the hell did you try to rob the Ursine mansion to begin with?" His calm voice rose in volume until it filled the passenger compartment.

She leaned back from him, pressing her shoulders into the door. "You're yelling at me." Her muscles jerked; trembling rattled the broken lockbox she held in her hands.

"So. Give me an answer. Why'd you do it?" The dashboard lights highlighted his over-sized nose in blue the way movies side lit skulls in horror movies. She'd have nightmares of his snarl.

"I'm panicking here." She held up her trembling hand for him to see.

He smacked it down. Her hand stung, but the shock kept her huddled in the corner of her seat.

"Maybe you should panic. You're screwed, Gi. You're dragging me into it, so I want to know why. What started this?"

She needed a good lie, something to make her sound noble or at least intelligent, but she wouldn't lie to Pete. She wanted to throw up, but it was too great a probability that throwing up in his car would get her kicked out. Maybe that was okay. She opened the car door and swung one leg out.

Pete's hand wrapped around her arm and kept her

inside.

"No." Pete's voice was hard. "You are not running away this time. I need an answer. Did you need the money?"

She shook her head.

"Was it for the thrill? Were you coerced?"

She shook her head and slumped back into the car. Pete was the annoying brother type, always getting into her business, but she had endangered his family. Maybe he had the right to be angry with her.

At the time she broke into the house, it made perfect sense. Earlier that day, the landlord had stopped her on the stairs and demanded she pay at least part of her rent, but her thousand bucks in back-owed rent didn't justify breaking into the Ursine house. Jo, her sometimes partner in heist, had dinged her that afternoon for being a screw-up. They'd broken into a house, but she'd tripped an alarm and they'd had to run. That wasn't the first time Jo called her names.

After the landlord and Jo, she'd needed to get away. She'd taken the bus to the lake, walked around until the thoughts in her head overwhelmed her, and then hiked into the woods. When the trees cleared, there it was. Garden lights lit the thing like a movie premiere. From statues in manicured flower beds to large pieces of furniture in plain view of the patio doors, everything about it advertised wealth, luxury, and ease. It was everything she ever wanted. She wanted to walk around and pretend that it was her life. The windows were dark. The driveway was empty. She already had some of her gear in her backpack from the house break. The stars aligned, and she did it. She didn't have a good reason, or at least, not one Pete would accept.

"I just did it." She pulled the door shut.

"That's a stupid reason, and you should get smart quick." Pete released her arm. "Here." He typed on his phone. Her phone pinged an incoming text. "That's the address for the house in Hide Park. If I were you, I wouldn't even try it."

She slumped back. Her muscles relaxed, leaving her feeling light, while her hands trembled and her neck stayed bent holding back the millions of pounds of pressure. She had to get in, get something valuable, and get out.

First, she had to get some sleep.

***

In twilight, the Hide Park mansion didn't look like the right opportunity. In a neighborhood of stone and brick villas on display for the whole neighborhood and aerial surveillance, the mansion couldn't even be seen from the street. Rows of bushes covered the front of the house as if shielding it.

The yard, which wasn't wide enough or deep enough to park a single-wide, had two strips of mowed grass and wide flower beds. If she did it right, she could stay under cover from the street to the front door.

An alley cut up right behind the house. From there, it was clearly a single-story home. A dog lay on the concrete pathway from the back door to the private parking. Its head popped up as she walked past, and it watched her. She pulled her hoodie up and kept walking.

The next house had three stories above ground and stone arch windows. The parking spots had "his" and "hers" signs and red brick lining cobblestone. Large clay pots with lush ferns sat on the corners of the path. The house across the street had tricolor gingerbread hanging over a wraparound porch. A stained glass window above the back door had a large lily flower and curving filigree. The door had carved panels with animals, three locks, and large black hinges. It looked like it protected something old and valuable. Every house in the neighborhood looked more likely to hide treasure. If the Ursine mansion was a bust, she'd try one of the others.

The Ursine house might not have looked like the

National Museum of Art and Culture, but it didn't look like Junior's girlfriend's slab house either. She strolled back to the main street and jogged in place, pretending to be taking a moment's break before jogging into the neighborhood. As a jogger, she had a reason to be in the ritzy neighborhood. She started down the street to the mansion. Two houses away, she slowed to a walk, stretching her arms out, hiking her knees up to her chest, and twisting. When she came up to the Ursine house, she jogged up the two steps and toward the house.

Lights flooded the little green patch. It blinded her with brightness, stealing away the shape of the house, the dark green bushes, and the sidewalk. It disoriented her until she worried that if she lifted her foot, the ground would disappear from beneath it.

A red light pulsed into the overwhelming white. A dog barked. She pivoted on her toes. With the lights behind her, the world reappeared, and she ran. Done with the jogging charade, she gripped toe to pavement and didn't stop until she'd made it three bus stops away.

Sirens then flashing lights then city police sped past her. The house probably had surveillance. The whole neighborhood probably did. They could follow video from one house to the next and find her roaming the neighborhood. When they searched the streets for her, they'd be looking for her long blond hair, her black and red Widow's hoodie, and her backpack.

She stripped off the hoodie and tossed it and the backpack in the trashcan beside the bench. Her hair hung in a ponytail. She pulled the band out, braided her hair in a thick French braid, looped the tail a few times before banding it all back together. Hopefully, no one would notice she hid the length of her hair in the loops. There wasn't much else she could do except walk calmly as if she had never considered robbing a house in her life.

She waited in a fast food joint eating a dollar burger

until she was sure the cops weren't focused on her and contacted Pete. They rendezvoused in a strip mall near the loading docks.

"Heya, Gi. How'd the cat burglary go?" His teeth gleamed in the parking lot lights. His grin annoyed her.

"How do you think?"

Pete laughed.

"Not cool. Don't laugh at me." She crossed her arms and squeezed her sides for comfort.

"Sorry. I told you to avoid that one. Did you get in? Did they have anything cool?"

She sank down in the seat and pressed her knees to the glovebox. "I didn't even get to the window. It was too difficult, too well protected."

Pete leaned back in his seat and pulled a pack of cigarettes from the console. The box tapped twice on his palm before he ripped open the packaging. He pulled a cigarette and offered her one.

She shook her head.

Flipping open the top of a silver lighter, he lit the cigarette. He inhaled a long breath and released a cloud of smoke into the car.

She rolled down the window.

"It's Thursday," Pete observed, taking another drag.

"I know." Her fingers applied more pressure to her ribs one at a time, reminding her that they were all there and functional.

"I've been asked to give you this." He extracted an envelope from the console and tossed it on her lap.

The envelope had loopy script with her name across the front. Pete's handwriting was all sharp up-and-down spikes, nothing like this. The flap was sealed and stamped at the point with a red bear paw.

"What's this?" She flipped it over. It had raised bumps halfway through which fell from one side to the other as she tilted it. It wasn't likely to be a bank card with a gazillion dollars on it, but she hoped it was.

"Don't get mad at me. You're the one who brought the freaking Ursines to my house, Gi. They knocked on my door like the local evangelists." He leaned his head back. His jaw bulged, and he closed his eyes. "Bobby Ursine came by my house and gave me that to give you."

"Bobby Ursine?"

"Looks like a banker, acts like he owns the world."

"Oh. The restitution one." Her stomach clenched low, and she curled tighter in a ball. "He must really want his money to chase you down." Holding the envelope on her knees, her fingers worked their way under the edge of the flap at the corner. She ripped the flap open in jerks.

The small item was a card with Robert James Ursine typed on it, no number, no address. On the back, it repeated the horrible million-dollar number still inked into her palm. She pulled out the trifolded piece of copy paper.

"What's it say?" Pete took another hit from the cigarette and stared at the car roof.

"Dear Ms. Incompetent Thief," she read aloud.

"Wow," Pete's voice slid up and down a scale of sarcasm. "His insults are so clever."

She cleared her throat. "Thank you for coming to visit me at my home today. I apologize that I was not there to receive you, but my security company advised me of your visit. I have left my calling card at your home and have asked your friend to deliver a second card to you directly. I expect to see you Friday by five. If you are prepared to make restitution before that time, you know where I live. Bobby Ursine."

Gigi sank lower in the chair and turned on her side, curled tight between the seat back and glove box, and groaned.

"How'd they find you?" She whispered the words into her legs.

"They're the Ursines. They can find anyone.

Anytime. Anywhere."

"They were at my house."

Pete stubbed out his cigarette and opening the pack for another. "You were at their house."

It came out as a fact, one she couldn't argue because she'd visited three of their homes now. Still, she'd never feel safe in her apartment again. She needed to fetch her clothes and escape. She needed to pay them back so they wouldn't follow her.

"How do I get out of this? Help, Pete." She had less than twenty-four hours left. Whatever happened, it had to happen quick. Her next hit had to score big and either be cash or something she could sell quick.

"You need a fast turnaround. Drugs, jewels, electronics. Hit the gadget stores and take every laptop and music player you can."

She shook her head. One memorable heist where Jo and she hit a cell phone store and were arrested when they pawned the phones was enough to teach her to stay away from electronic stores. "Electronics are out. Unless your convoluted information channels have another tip, I don't know where to steal or sell drugs. Bank robbery or jewel heist. That's my options. So jewels. Will you help?"

Pete coughed a laugh. The cough rolled on and on until she sat up and scooted out of the way in case he barfed on her. His head shook back and forth. When the coughing slowed, he choked out a quick, "Hell no."

"Some friend you are."

"Yeah, well, give up the life of crime, Gi. You'll find I'm way more helpful. Right now, you are lucky I'm still willing to meet you."

Lucky was not how she'd describe it. They were lurking behind buildings in a totally conspicuous way. He hadn't let her crash at his place since that first night. His ideas were fruitless. He was even hand-delivering letters from the Ursines. He probably called them and gave them updates on her actions.

"Bet you didn't try to protect me from the Ursines." She pouted.

"Bullshit, Gi. Bobby shows up at my door asking if you're there, and I told him no. He asks when I'll see you next, and I shrug and tell him I have no idea. He gives me a letter for you, and I let him know I'll give it to you the next time we meet. He leaves. That's it. I didn't lie for you, but I didn't give you up either."

The answer was too vague for her liking, tricksy and too much of a play with words. "You ever thought of being a lawyer, Pete? You might be good at it."

"Ha ha." He flicked his lighter to life then flipped the lid closed. "I should go home. I've already been out too long. Where do you want to be dropped?" His seat straightened up. The keys turned. The engine started. The conversation was over.

"I'll get out here. See ya, Pete. If I don't, remember me." She hopped out and jogged across the lot. It wouldn't be the first time she slept under the overpass, but it might be her last.

***

She chose a store based on location and size. The jewelry shops in her neighborhood were mostly gold and pawn items. Her chance of getting enough to make her payment was too small. The mall had three jewelry stores she could hit back to back, but the longer she stayed there, the greater possibility she'd be caught. So she caught the bus out to Golden Ridge. Hamlet Construction, a subsidiary of the Ursines, had built and developed the tiny mansions, including a plaza of strip shops. The shops ranged from fast sub sandwiches to museum art. The only thing they didn't have was a car lot.

When she got there, the shopping day was in full

swing. Cars drove up and down the winding paths, parking in metered parallel parking spots or slipping into small lots only big enough for a dozen cars. A man sat on a five-gallon drum and pounded out a rhythm. The shoppers walked wide around him, as if the music scared them off. Air conditioning burst out on the street as shop doors opened. The whole time, rising plateaus of mansions stared down at the bustle, scrutinizing. Pine Palace, the Ursine main house, was among those homes.

Her neck itched, and she kept to the sidewalk under the awnings. Her path started and stopped as shoppers crossed her to get in and out of shops. The air currents forced her to smell herself. Her hand smoothed back her greasy hair, and she wished she hadn't thrown out her hoodie the day before.

She stopped on a corner to let a car turn into a lot, and a man stopped her with a hand. "Here, miss." He shoved a wrapper in her hand. "God bless you." He walked off.

She unfolded the paper to find half a panini. Torn between yelling at him that she wasn't a beggar and her growling stomach, she ate the sandwich. It was good, and it gave her an idea. She grabbed a collection of silverware from the outdoor patio of a restaurant. She stashed the knives and forks in her back pockets and found an open spot close to a corner jewelry store, one with two floors that shared space with a fancy handbag designer.

At close of day, she'd find a way in, grab the bags, stuff them with jewelry, and get out. She used the spoons to clink out a rhythm. It wasn't as confident or polished as the bucket guy, but the crowd gave way, giving her a bubble of space. The crowd ducked their heads and avoided eye contact. She watched the shop, identifying the roll cage that would come down over the front window and the bars that would pull across the door.

A walking security patrol came around and told her

to move on. She crossed the street and circled behind the jewelry store to check out the back. She sat in the back alley, chewing on one spoon and peering into dumpsters as an excuse. It'd be a long climb, but there were no bars or protections on the second-story windows. The store had small decorative circle windows on all four sides.

An employee came out the back door of a shop. She ducked her head and escaped back to the main street to restart her spoon session. She switched between her spoons and pretending to look in dumpsters until the shopping area cleared out. The stores switched to security lights. Bars and roll-down coverings locked into place. Gaggles of employees walked to their cars, stood in the parking lot chatting, and finally drove off. The walking security turned to car patrols. It was time.

Gigi waited beside the building until the patrol car passed. She ran across the street to a coffee shop where a metal half fence separated the crowd from the drinkers. They'd stacked one table upside down on the next. She slid a table off. It weighed a million pounds and slipped from her grasp onto the concrete. The top hit the half fence, and a metal-on-metal clank rang through the street. Shifting her grip and hoisting the thing on her shoulder, she hustled across the street. No patrol car circled back, but she waited at the side of the building until the nausea stopped.

The dumpsters had flimsy plastic lids. Even if she managed to pull the table onto a lid, it'd collapse. The store beside the jewelers was a farm-to-table restaurant. It was a single-story building with a sharp peaked roof. It touched the side of the jewelry store.

Its dumpster was walled off by a wood fence, and Gigi measured the gap between the fence and the dumpster to be less than the table width. Plus, the fence was easier to climb than the dumpster. It had cross boards to step up on.

Perched on the lid of the dumpster, she pulled the table up, balanced it between the dumpster and fence, rocked it back and forth to gauge her likelihood of falling, examined her potential fall distance, and took ten long solid breaths. If she died from the fall, it wouldn't matter how many fingers Junior broke. She shimmied up onto the table, pulled herself onto the roof, and crawled up the gable to the second-story window of the jewelry shop.

She had dumped her equipment after the Hide Park incident, so this would have to be a smash and grab. Pressing her nose to the glass, she estimated the drop to the ground, the run to the purse display and back to the jewelry counters. She planned the vault over the glass, the display piece she'd grab to pry open the locked sliding doors of the cabinets.

When the plan looked smooth and feasible in her head, she took one of the knives out of her back pocket. The metal gleamed in the security lighting. She touched the tip to the glass, removed it and set it against the glass again, visualizing the tip piercing through the pane and shattering the glass. With all her power and speed, she stabbed the knife into the glass.

The tip scratched the surface then broke under pressure. She stabbed a second time before she worried about triggered alarms and the possibility of failing on the second try.

The glass changed from clear to translucent foggy white, cracking like safety glass. With her elbow, she shoved the majority into the store until it was wide enough for her to slip through. She ran the heist one last time in her head. In and out.

She jumped in, landing hard on a display table, breaking it. Jumping up, she ran for the purses. Anytime, the patrol cars would see the broken window or the cops would respond to the silent alarm. She couldn't help but grin. This heist felt right, not some too-simple, no-gain bust like Junior's girlfriend's house or the front lawn shakedown from Bobby's house. This would work.

The purses were on display on shelves along the wall.

Each one sat alone, and she shoved her arm through a bunch of straps and began pulling the stuffing out as she raced back to the counter. A large bag with stiff piping on the outside snagged on the counter, making her leap less graceful, but she made it across the top and behind the counter.

Using the tree displaying costume necklaces, she pried the cabinets open. She counted as she grabbed the display pieces and grabbed the stock boxes. Twenty. Nineteen. Eighteen. Seventeen.

She pried open the next door. Sixteen. Fifteen. Fourteen. And tossed its contents into the next bag. Thirteen. Twelve. Eleven. Ten. Nine.

Sirens sounded on the street. She glanced around. Eight. Seven.

She zipped the purses. Six. Five.

Vaulted the counter. Four. Three. Two.

And sprinted for the window. One.

A beam backlit the window. They'd found her entrance. Her heart stopped. Her breath caught. Then she moved.

It didn't matter if she was caught inside or outside, but she couldn't escape if they trapped her inside. She leapt for the window.

The light stayed centered on the window, and she burst into it, bags hanging off her arms.

The light came from the back where her dumpster table waited, but there was no time to mourn the loss. She slid down the roof to the front and dropped into the restaurant patio.

"Stop!"

She knew better than to follow that command. If she stopped, it was over. She wove around the tables and bolted for the open sidewalk.

Footsteps pounded out behind her.

"Stop." The voice wheezed.

Her breath was fire in her lungs. Her arms pumped, and she ran. She was not going back to jail. They could shoot her first.

She ran toward the hill. Toward trees. Toward the big houses. Toward their landscaping sheds.

A second set of footfalls came out of an alley between a toy store and kitchen store. These were closer and accompanied by the sound of clinking metal.

She glanced over her shoulder. Two cops chased her. Both heaved for breath. She zagged.

Her foot rolled off the sidewalk into the gutter. Her ankle twisted to the side. Her arms flailed as she lost balance. Her other leg lunged out, steadying her. It didn't take long, but it slowed her down long enough for the cop to grab at her.

His hand caught a purse. She ripped at it, but he didn't release.

He yanked harder and grabbed another purse. If she didn't drop the purses, he'd get a hold of her. If she dropped the bag, her last hope to repay the Ursines would slip away with it.

She didn't have much: a crappy apartment she couldn't afford, an accomplice or two, and Pete the traitor. The cops would take even that from her, shoving her into a small cell, but she couldn't stay in the Ursines' territory.

The cop grabbed at her back.

She screamed and loosened the purses.

The cop ripped all of them from her arm and fell back into his buddy.

Freed of the jewelry, she ran, using the pain in her ankle, the fear of the Ursines, and the pounding beat of the cop's pursuit to keep her running.

The cop's breath came faster, he stopped yelling to the others, and his footsteps faded.

She ran into the trees and past the mini mansions. There wasn't even a bike to steal, and she pushed herself to get out of the neighborhood and to a bus stop.

***

Gigi woke in the back of a bus. The bus driver stood over her, his arms hanging at his sides and large bags weighing his eyes down.

"End of the line, and I'm off shift. Get out of here." He followed behind her as she walked down the aisle and stepped out.

The bus stop had a large sign on a circular kiosk that read "Crimson County Depot." Four outdoor benches lined the road.

The bus pulled away and took a count of thirteen to pass a metal barn, the next closest building to the "depot." Turning in a slow circle, she counted three buildings; two were houses. All three buildings together probably had less wealth than Junior's girlfriend's house.

She had skills for breaking into homes, but this nowhere town had no home worth robbing. Her arm stung from where the purses were ripped from her. She'd have to sneak on another bus. Her phone had no service, which made it easier to destroy it. She couldn't have the Ursines tracking her by the phone.

She'd have to walk to the next town where she could blend into the street crowd and start rebuilding her life. Her ankle hated the idea, but she grinned. She'd broken into one of the Ursine stores and almost got away with treasure. She'd been thinking too small all along. When she got to the next town, she'd hone her skills and make the big heists. If she ever earned enough to repay the Ursines, maybe she'd go back and shove her success in Jo's face and tell Pete her story.

Gigi held her hands above her head, flipped off the life behind her and sauntered down the road.

The churn of car tires came up from behind her, and

she turned, her thumb already out for a ride. The black SUV pulled to a stop, and the desk-sitting Ursine in his polo and khakis stepped out.

"Hello again."

Gigi turned and ran.

Footsteps pounded up behind her, and a bear in midshift grabbed her around the shoulders and lifted her off the ground.

She screamed and kicked. They would not take away her escape.

The bear roared.

"Come on, Junior. Let's take her home. I promise you can have a leg bone."

Her legs flailed, but the bear's grip held tight. He dragged her back to the SUV, and they slammed the door shut on her hope of freedom.

Cursed Winds

Allie May

A loud thunk on deck disrupted the young captain's concentration. He glanced up from his map. Through the open porthole, the buzz of the docks thrummed in on a salty breeze that blew his long hair around his face. Grumbling, he slammed the porthole closed and knotted his hair at the nape of his neck.

By now, the crew should be loading supplies. They had been docked in Southampton for too long. If their ship was recognized… He refused to finish that thought.

After tucking away his map, the captain climbed up the ladder to the main deck of the *Swift Storm* and stumbled as his foot caught on a fallen bundle of ropes. He kicked them aside and scanned the familiar port.

He hadn't been home in five years.

A neighboring crew unloaded barrels of fish onto the dock, and one of the sailors waved to him.

He nodded politely, stepping closer to the gangplank. He loved the sea, but how he longed to step onto dry land again. The stench of stale rum drifted out of a bar nearby, followed by fresh bread and hearty stew, taunting him, tempting him to cross the threshold onto solid ground.

"Captain!" Winston, one of the lookouts, whistled as he ducked around the bustling crowds.

The captain cleared his throat and busied himself by retying the ropes with a forced smile. No one could know he only had a few days left to live.

***

Six hours outside of Southampton, Avery, the cook, approached the captain, twisting his knit cap in his hands. "Sir, it seems we miscounted our rations. I thought we had enough food for ten days when we left, but I just took stock, and—"

"How can that be?" Wentworth, the stodgy quartermaster, interrupted. "I triple counted before departure."

"Then someone took extra biscuits after dinner. And some pork and cheese, too."

Wentworth squinted at Avery while he cleaned his spectacles on his vest. "That's impossible. I've been on this ship twenty-eight years, and no one has ever touched anything without my knowledge."

"I'm just reporting what I know, sir."

Scratching his trim beard, the captain addressed the first mate, "Edison, keep to the helm. We'll be back."

Edison tipped up his sharp nose to check the breeze.

Ducking belowdecks, the captain lifted his eyepatch so he could see in the dark. "When did you notice the missing food?"

Avery led them into the galley. "After I finished my supper."

"How long were you out of the galley?" Peering down at the cook, Wentworth twisted up the tip of his graying mustache.

Avery shrugged. "Maybe a half hour?"

Wentworth opened his mouth, but the captain cut him off.

"Do we still have enough food for our venture?"

Avery replaced his cap on his head. "I always buy extra."

"Good. Wentworth, you can stay and total the rations."

Already counting, the quartermaster pulled out a notepad and started tallying the food.

The captain pushed open the door and Avery followed him out into the passageway. "That should entertain him for the time being."

"I'm really sorry, Captain…"

He held up a hand. "It's not your fault. Wentworth will surely find the thief and give them a firm reprimand that'll make them wish they never stole in the first place."

"Yes, Captain." Wringing his well-worn hands, the cook turned on his heel and trudged back into the kitchen.

The captain stared after him. Something was wrong. The crew wouldn't steal; they were a family, and Avery fed them well. So where would the food—

A loud thump sounded behind him.

He snapped his head around.

Silence.

Holding his breath, he stepped down the empty passageway.

Another scuffle echoed from behind the cargo bay door. And ragged breathing.

He opened the door and froze. "What the…"

A little girl cried out, clutching a teddy bear tighter to her chest.

He took a step back. "Hello."

She backed away from him, crawling farther into the dark.

"No, wait." He crouched to see her better. "What's your name?"

She gulped in air, despite her trembling. "Clara."

"Hello, Clara. What are you doing here?"

She twisted one of her braids in her hand and choked back a sob. "I was…I was…" Tears streaked her cheeks and she muffled a whimper with her teddy bear.

"Okay, umm…" The captain turned back toward the passageway. "Avery!" Avery had children. He would know what to say to this…small, skittish creature.

The cook came running. "Captain! What's wrong? What's—oh!" He skidded to a stop behind the captain, his shoes squeaking against the wood. "Well, hello there." He knelt next to the captain. "Mr. Bear, how on earth did you get on board?"

Confusion flashed across Clara's face.

Avery kept his eyes on the bear. "Really? What a story!" He shook the bear's paw. "Are you hungry?"

The corners of Clara's mouth twitched upward and she used her hand to nod the bear's head, then stuck the tip of her braid in her mouth to hide her grin.

"Well, hmm." Avery tapped his chin. "What do bears eat?"

"Fish!" Clara's hair, still in her mouth, muffled her answer.

"We've got plenty of fish around here, don't you worry, Mr. Bear!" Avery crept a few steps away from the girl.

"His name is Theodore." She crawled out into the passageway to close the gap between her and the cook.

"Very nice to meet you, Theodore. My name is Avery, and…" He feigned a gasp, as if he just now noticed Clara. "You brought a friend aboard with you. What's her name?"

"Clara." The captain cleared his throat.

Avery raised an eyebrow. "Thanks, Captain, but I was asking Theodore."

Clara giggled.

Avery stood and held out a hand to Clara.

She handed him Theodore and pushed herself to her feet, brushing off the knees of her black stockings.

"Well, Clara, I'll have to thank Theodore for introducing us. This is the captain of the *Swift Storm*." Avery passed the teddy bear over to the captain.

Clara shook Avery's hand then reached out to shake the captain's. "And what's your name?"

Awkwardly, he accepted. "They call me the Beast."

Her eyes widened as she recoiled from his grip.

Avery snorted. "Don't worry, Clara. He's not scary. It's just because he snores so loud."

The captain scowled. "Clara, did you take some food from the galley, by chance?"

Clara looked at her feet before pulling a half-eaten biscuit out of her coat pocket.

"Avery, if you don't mind making sure that Clara gets a proper supper, I'll inform Wentworth that we've found our misplaced rations."

"Of course, Captain." He held out an elbow and she accepted, following him to the galley.

The captain tugged on his ponytail. This…stray complicated things.

***

Seven hours outside of Southampton, Avery, Edison, Winston, and Harold met in the captain's quarters while Clara slept in Avery's bunk.

"She's an orphan on her way to live with her aunt in La Rochelle." Avery spoke for Clara, as he had been the only one to meet her so far.

"France?" Harold, the navigator, leaned over the map. His long, graying brown hair brushed along the paper as he scanned the French coastline. "It's a five-day journey, Captain, if the winds are in our favor."

"We can't return to Southampton; we took a big enough risk going there in the first place. But, we can't just drop her off somewhere in England." Edison sighed. "We have no choice."

"Do we have provisions to make it?" Drumming his fingers on the desk, the captain wished for an excuse to drop her at the nearest port and not look back.

Avery examined the quartermaster's notes before responding. "Wentworth will have a heart attack, but yes."

Edison waved his hand dismissively and tossed his dark hair over his shoulders. "I'll deal with Wentworth." They had been on the ship longer than anyone, and the first mate had the easiest time handling the quartermaster's angst.

Silence fell, as if everyone held their breath while waiting for a decision from their captain.

He sat at his desk staring at the map. As the youngest of the crew, he had never felt sure of his position. He didn't deserve it just because of his father. It should've been Edison in this cabin, weighing this decision and wearing this title.

Scraping his chair against the wooden deck, the captain stood. His dark blond hair hung loose around his shoulders, and he fiddled with his leather hair tie, wrapping it between his fingers as he paced. He stopped at the door and turned back to face the others. "Winston?"

The lookout straightened, though he towered over the captain even if he shaved his curly, red hair. "Yes, Captain?"

"Where's that list of ships from Southampton?"

"Right here." He pulled a crumpled piece of paper out of his pocket and handed it over.

The captain smoothed out the wrinkles and deciphered Winston's messy lettering. "This one." He pointed to one of the ships described on the paper, the *Raven*. "It's headed south to Spain?"

Winston scanned the paper. "Yes, sir. A merchant ship headed to San Sebastian. They were packing for a ten-day trip, at least. With a crew of around forty."

Edison picked at a fingernail. "Slower than us, and with that much product?"

"Cotton, wool, and silk?" Avery raised his eyebrows as he scanned the list over the captain's shoulder. "It'll make a good haul, Captain."

"If we can catch up to them before we reach La Rochelle. Otherwise we'll have nothing to bring in at port and we'll have wasted five very valuable days." The captain tossed the paper onto his desk.

Leaning over the map, Harold eyed the captain, waiting.

Winston tucked the list back into his pocket. "They had only loaded half their stock by the time we left. I'd say they're about ten or so hours ahead of us, if we turn 'round now."

He didn't want to abandon his crew in France, but it seemed he had no choice. "Chart the course."

"Aye, sir." Harold rolled up the map and tucked it under his arm.

"Avery, we'll slowly introduce Clara to the rest of the crew tomorrow if she's feeling up to it. I don't want her to be afraid for the next five days. And if she needs any extra food, take it out of my rations."

"That's very generous, Captain. I was going to volunteer Wentworth's." Edison cracked a smile.

Sighing, the captain rolled his eyes. "Everyone out. I'm going to take the wheel for a while. Get some sleep."

"Aye, Captain," the crew chorused before heading out the door.

The captain paused, taking a deep breath before following his crew out and climbing up to the main deck. He shooed the boatswain off the wheel and to bed, then waved to Clayton in the crow's nest. As grateful as he was for his loyal crew, he couldn't wait until they arrived so he could send them ashore and sail out on his own. Six days left. While he didn't believe in God, he prayed for favorable winds.

***

Ten hours outside of Southampton, Harold took control of the wheel. The captain yawned as he climbed belowdecks, anticipating the gentle rise and fall of the waves rocking him to sleep, but stopped when he saw Clara sitting in the passageway, hugging her teddy bear.

"Clara, what are you still doing up? You should be in bed. Where's Avery?"

She rubbed her eyes. "Hi, Beast. I couldn't sleep."

"Why not?"

"I'm not tired." She yawned.

"Of course not. What are you doing out here?"

"I got bored. So, I went to go find something to do, and I met Monty. He's got a scar!" With a grin, she traced across her eye to indicate Monty's scar.

The captain almost choked on his breath but covered it with a cough. Of all the people on the ship, she had to meet one of the gunmen.

She traced her finger around one of the knots in the wood at her feet then followed the grain up the bulkhead behind her. "I asked him what he does, and he said that he fights people. I said I didn't believe him so I made him show me his weapons. He's got lots of pistols." She nodded for emphasis.

He clenched his jaw. "Yes, I know."

"Do you have a pistol?" She tucked some stray hairs behind her ear.

He blinked.

"I didn't see one, but you're the captain and captains always have swords or something in case they need to fight."

He cleared his throat. "I do have a sword, Clara. And two pistols." He held up two fingers.

Her brown eyes widened, then she let out a big sigh. "Oh, good. Then you can fight off the Oceanid."

"The what?" His blood froze, and he found himself suddenly lightheaded. Lightheaded, like the depths of the turquoise glowing water were crushing the air out of his lungs as he watched a dark shadow being dragged down, wrapped in seaweed-entwined hair. He leaned against the bulkhead to catch his balance, acting casual.

"Monty said the English Channel is haunted by an evil Oceanid named Menestho. I don't want to get eaten."

He shook his head, reminding himself to give Monty extra chores tomorrow. "Oceanids don't eat people…"

Clara eyed him suspiciously.

This was a child; it was better to lie. "Menestho isn't real. You're safe."

"But Monty said Winston saw Menestho once."

"Winston is a lookout. He spends all day staring at the horizon so the rest of us don't have to. He could say he saw a Kraken and none of us could argue with him even though we all would know he was lying."

"What's a Kraken?" She tilted her head.

"Never mind." He needed to distract her. "Have you ever been in a hammock before?"

She gasped. "No!"

"Really?" Opening the door to his cabin, he pointed out his hammock strung up in the corner.

Her eyes widened. "Can I?"

"Of course." He picked her up and placed her on the hammock with Theodore on her chest. "Lay back and close your eyes. It's more fun like that."

She obeyed, and soon enough, her breathing became deep and steady.

Sighing, he settled into his armchair for a long, uncomfortable night and closed his eyes. At least he always had fleeting warmth in his dreams when memories of his childhood love, Rosemary, would come visit. He often wondered about her and what would've happened had he stayed behind on that one fateful voyage. Maybe by now they would've married and had a child of their own. Smiling, he let the flowery scent of Rosemary's perfume carry him off to sleep.

***

"My tummy hurts," Clara moaned.

Rudely awoken from his dream, the captain jumped out of his chair. Rosemary's image was replaced by the thought of mopping up Clara's seasickness. Scooping her up, he bolted to the main deck. "Out of the way!" He plowed past Edison and Wentworth, not stopping until he reached the railing at the bow. Gingerly, he leaned Clara over the edge, careful to keep her from dropping the bear into the churning water below.

"Uhh, captain on deck?" Edison appeared at his side.

"Find Avery. We need peppermint. Or ginger."

"On it, Captain." The first mate disappeared belowdecks.

Clara heaved, but nothing came out.

Rubbing her back, the captain held her in place until she finished. Ignoring her cries, he forced her back onto her left side, using her bear as a pillow.

Clara curled her knees to her chest, while crushing his hand with her tiny fingers. "It hu-urts."

Uncomfortable, he looked for someone else to take over and pried his hand from her grip. "Wentworth, what were those breathing exercises you used to have me do?"

Wentworth knelt next to them, stroking her hand. "Clara, focus on my face."

"I can't…"

Clammy sweat dripped down his neck. Overwhelmed by heat despite the breeze, the captain stood and backed away.

"Beast…help me." Her voice sounded weak.

A breath hitched in his chest.

Avery hurried over with a cup in his hand. "Sit her up."

Wentworth slipped an arm under her neck and shoulders, raising her head.

"Clara, I need you to drink this." The cook pressed the cup to her lips.

"Please don't go." She stared at the captain, her hazel eyes panicked.

He turned on his heel and darted downstairs to his quarters. He paced around the small room before someone knocked on the door.

Edison poked his head in. "Everything all right, Captain?"

"Not really." He ran a hand through his hair.

Edison raised an eyebrow.

"How old was I when my father first took me out to sea?"

"Not much older than Clara, if my memory is correct."

"I thought so." He paused before resuming his pacing.

"Is this about your father?" Edison folded his arms and leaned back.

"Well, I mean…" He sighed.

The first mate raised an eyebrow.

The captain stared at his feet. "He was always right there to help me when I got sick. He knew what to say if I couldn't sleep because I was afraid of the Oceanid, or—"

"The Oceanid? Who…?"

The captain waved a hand. "Monty."

Edison rolled his eyes. "Of course he did."

"That's not the point."

"Captain, are you scared of a little girl?" The first mate leaned against the door and a smile tweaked the corners of his mouth.

The captain frowned. "That's not funny, Edison."

He stifled a grin. "You know what I mean, Captain."

"I wish my father was here. He would take better care of Clara than I ever could."

"You're doing the best you can, Captain. Besides, it's

not your fault your father is dead."

"Right." The captain coughed to loosen the knot in his stomach.

"She likes you. Go sit with her. And maybe she'll feel better knowing that you got just as sick as she is."

Sucking in a breath of stale cabin air, the captain straightened his coat before making his way back upstairs.

Clara, now sitting up, copied Wentworth's breathing. She smiled when she saw the captain again.

"Thank you, Wentworth." He helped Clara to her feet and guided her back to the bow, placing Theodore into her arms. "Did you know that when I was your age, I used to get seasick, too?"

"Really?" Her eyes looked more hazel as they reflected the sea.

He paused, chewing on his lip, then he put a hand on her shoulder. "My father used to stand with me here because I felt better looking forward. I loved to feel the wind on my face, and if I was lucky, I'd get splashed when the waves hit. That's how I learned that I love sailing. And look." He pointed at the sparkling blue waves around them. "From here you can clearly see that there are no Oceanids."

She grinned and hugged Theodore. "You're right! See, Theodore? I told you there was nothing to worry about."

"Captain!" Clayton yelled down from the crow's nest and pointed.

The captain pulled out his spyglass and spotted the *Raven* off in the distance. He waved over Edison and murmured, "Tomorrow, nightfall."

***

Avery's peppermint tea worked its magic, and Clara recovered in time to assist in cooking lunch and serving it to the crew. Later, Winston and Clayton taught her how to climb the mast to the crow's nest, and a vexed Wentworth recruited her to count supplies and reorganize the cargo bay.

She woke the next morning and announced it was her turn to steer the ship. She shed her black overcoat, cinched her black skirt up to her knees, and sauntered all over the ship without shoes. Overnight, her bangs had fallen free from her braids and hung over her eyes.

The captain had actively avoided her since they spotted the *Raven*. Unsure how she would react to their choice of occupation, he decided it was better for her not to find out. Apprehensive, he stayed in his quarters, planning with Langston, the master gunner, and his two fighters, Rowley and Monty. Meanwhile, Harold and Edison maintained enough distance between the *Swift Storm* and the *Raven* so their prey remained unaware of their intentions.

Finally, the sun set, and he left his room with his cutlass and pistols hidden under his navy waistcoat. After collecting an apple from the galley, he meandered past the crew's quarters. He ate while Langston divvied up weapons to the crew as they prepared to board.

"Avery, where's Clara?" The captain took another bite of his apple.

"In the bay with Wentworth." Avery cinched the belt that sheathed his cutlass and daggers.

"You're sure she'll stay put?"

"She's young. Say it just how we rehearsed, and she'll believe you. And, maybe lock the door, just to keep her safe?" The cook pocketed some grenados and matches.

"We'll be in and out without her knowing the door is locked." The captain glanced around at the crew once more before heading for the bay, where he found Clara counting barrels and Wentworth overseeing her work.

"Excellent, Clara. You'll make a fine quartermaster one day."

"Nah." She shook her head. "I'd rather take charge and tell everyone what to do."

"And who says the quartermaster isn't in charge?" He puffed out his chest.

"I do." The captain crunched another bite from his apple and leaned against the doorframe.

"Of course, Captain." Wentworth bowed his head.

Clara snickered and skipped toward the captain. "What else can I do?"

"I'm glad you asked, Clara." He gestured down the passageway, and she fell into step beside him. "It seems that my walls are quite bare. Unfortunately, there are no artists aboard to draw pictures for me." He stopped outside the door of his cabin.

Clara gasped. "I could do it!"

Opening the door, he feigned surprise. "Really? You'd do that for me?"

"Of course, Captain!" She skipped inside and plopped herself down at his desk where he already had paper, a pen, and his inkwell waiting.

"Perfect." He slipped outside, locked the door behind him, and stashed the key in his pocket before joining his crew up on the main deck. Though it was dark, the stars lit the way. They were almost upon their prey.

"Captain on deck!" Edison approached and the rest of the crew turned toward him.

He finished the last of his apple before tossing the core overboard. "Men, tonight will be different. Be quick, and be silent. Clara does not know what we do, and I'd prefer to keep it that way. No cannons, and no pistols if possible. This is about stealth. After we have the cargo, we'll take out their masts."

"Captain, they've hailed us." Clayton swung down from the crow's nest.

"How many on deck?" He took the spyglass from Clayton and scanned the ship.

"Six, by my count."

"And the captain?"

"Belowdecks. He disappeared about two hours ago."

The captain passed the spyglass back. "Probably asleep for the night. Perfect. We'll be in and out without him knowing." He leaned over the port side, watching them skim over the surface of the water before he waved to Edison. "Drop anchor."

The splash of the anchor plunging into the dark water broke the silence. A few minutes passed before the ship slowed. Now they were close enough to clearly see the sailors on board the other ship as the *Swift Storm* closed the gap.

"Ready, men?"

The first boarding group climbed the ropes. Once everyone was in place, the captain nodded and they swung off, landing on the deck of the *Raven* and pulling out their weapons.

"Don't make a single noise." Langston held his pistol under the chin of the *Raven*'s first mate.

Gulping, the man backed against the railing.

Wood clattered as the gangplank was lowered, connecting the two ships.

"Raise the flag." The captain waved to Winston, who clung to the masthead.

Winston unfurled the black fabric bearing a horned skull with crossbones so it covered the white banner with the navy blue "W" that signified the shipping company that once ran the *Swift Storm*.

Once Wentworth placed their gangplank next to the *Raven*'s, the second boarding party crossed over, followed by the captain. Only Bradley remained behind at the helm.

"Gentlemen." The captain nodded at the *Raven*'s crew lining the port side of the ship. "We will be taking your cargo. Any objections?"

They all stared at him, but no one so much as shook their heads.

"Perfect." He turned toward his own crew. "Men?"

They hurried into action while the captain and Langston guarded their prisoners. Quick and quiet like the captain ordered, they loaded the crates of fabric over one gangplank onto their own ship, and returned empty-handed over the other. During the past five years, they had done this a hundred times.

Wentworth recorded the new inventory as the others carried it aboard, noting the value of each crate. Once most of the crates were loaded, he headed down to the *Raven*'s bay to see what else was worth taking.

The captain enjoyed the silence, the salty breeze against his face, and the knowledge that their last haul was a good one. He had served his crew well. He was going to miss sailing, though. He turned his back on the lower deck to face the wind.

"Captain!" Langston shouted.

He spun around to see the *Raven*'s captain charging toward him with his rapier brandished. Instinctively, he unsheathed his own cutlass and sidestepped the assault. With a swift kick of his boot, he knocked the other captain to his knees and sent his sword clattering across the deck. "Do you know who I am?" With his blade pressed against the man's neck, he circled the other captain.

The other captain scowled. "You're the Beast. We heard tales of you when we were docked in Southampton."

The Beast raised an eyebrow and chuckled. "You hear that, Langston? We're famous."

Langston sneered before grabbing the first mate's arm and dragging him over to the captain's side where he forced him down on his knees with a pistol to the back of his head. "We're almost done, mate. If you're good, we'll leave you alive."

The other captain glared. "But first you'll dump all our food overboard, set fire to our dories, and knock out our masts."

"At least it's better than what they did to the original

crew of the *Swift Storm*," the first mate muttered.

The Beast shrugged. "It's your choice."

"What did you do to the crew?" a soft voice squeaked from behind the Beast.

He whipped around to see Clara clutching Theodore. "Clara? How did you…"

Bradley clambered over the gangway. "Sorry, Captain. She got out. I don't know how." He grabbed for her, but she slipped away.

"The *Swift Storm* isn't your ship?" Her eyes filled with fear.

Wentworth guided one last crate up from belowdecks but hesitated when he spied Clara. Harold and Edison, carrying the crate, bumped into him, and almost dropped the goods.

"Clara, get back on the ship!" The captain pointed over the gangplank.

Anyone with free hands joined in the chase as Bradley attempted to corral her back to the *Swift Storm*.

The other captain lunged for his rapier while the crew was distracted.

"Don't even think about it, mate." Langston jammed his pistol into the first mate's neck so hard, the man whimpered.

The other captain froze, his hands in the air.

Avery snatched Clara and hurried over the gangplank behind the stolen crate. She screamed and flailed, squirming to free herself and making them wobble over the churning waves. Bradley came to the cook's rescue and helped drag the writhing girl on board.

Agitated but relieved, the Beast retrieved the other captain's sword. "This is a beautiful blade, Captain. It's a shame, really." He hurled it overboard.

Eyes burning with anger, the other captain glared but kept his mouth shut.

"Dump their food." He directed Rowley, Clayton,

and Monty back belowdecks. A minute later, they came back with barrels of dried meat and cheese, enough food to feed fifty for two weeks, and balanced them on the edge. The Beast nudged the barrel with his boot, sending it crashing into the waves below. Then the next, and the next.

"That'll do, men." He pointed back to the *Swift Storm* and the remaining crew clambered over the gangplank.

Keeping his pistol aimed at the first mate, Langston followed the rest of the crew back to the *Swift Storm*.

"Weigh anchor!" Last over the gangplank, the captain paused when he heard footsteps behind him. He turned back and pointed his pistol at the other captain. "Don't."

The other captain grunted and lunged for the Beast, trying to knock him into the water.

The Beast jumped to the side and instead shoved the other captain overboard. He pointed his gun at the first mate. "Do not follow us."

The first mate blinked, staring at the pistol instead of looking for his captain.

Walking backward over the gangplank, the Beast kept his pistol trained on the first mate. When he was safe aboard his own ship, his crew removed their gangplank and knocked the other into the water. The ship started moving again, the anchor now stowed back on board, and the Beast returned his pistol to its holster. "Take out their masts."

"Fire!" Edison shouted.

Rowley lit the fuse on one cannon while Monty lit another. With a crack, the cannons fired chain shots that splintered through the wood. The masts toppled over, scattering the crew.

Something soft smacked into the captain's back.

"You really are a beast!" Clara yelled.

He turned to find Theodore at his feet, and Clara standing a few feet away with her hands on her hips.

She squeaked when they made eye contact and

scurried belowdecks with her braid in her mouth.

The crew stared with slack jaws. Avery started after her but paused to look back at his captain for permission to leave the deck while on duty.

Angry, the captain ignored him. "What is everyone waiting for? We still have a job to do! Bradley, set course for La Rochelle. Crowd sail!"

The crew busied themselves with whatever they could find to avoid the captain's glare.

Edison appeared next to the captain but kept his eyes on the *Raven* fading into the distance. "I'll take over from here."

The captain grunted and snatched Theodore from the deck before stomping to his quarters. The door had been left ajar. He growled and slammed it behind him before returning his weapons to their shelf in his wardrobe. Just for good measure, he pounded those doors shut as well.

He sighed and leaned his head against the cool wood. Why was he so frustrated? They had taken in a great haul. Whether Clara knew they were pirates or not didn't matter. It was their last trip. He was dropping her, and the rest of his crew, in La Rochelle and that was it. Four days left.

Someone hiccupped behind him.

He turned.

Another hiccup.

He crept toward his desk. On top were childish drawings of Clara climbing the mast with Winston, cooking with Avery, and at the helm with Bradley. The last one was of himself standing next to Clara at the bow, pointing to the ocean.

A third hiccup squeaked out from under the desk, followed by a sniffle.

He pressed his lips together and took a deep breath before kneeling to find Clara curled underneath his desk. "Hello."

She crunched her knees up to her chest and looked

away.

"You seem to be missing something." He placed Theodore next to her.

Without looking at him, she pulled her braid tip out of her mouth and wrapped her arm around the bear.

"How did you get out of here, anyway? I locked the door."

She was quiet for a moment. "Rowley taught me how to pick locks."

"Of course." He shook his head, trying to hide his frustration.

"Why did you do that to those people?"

He sat down in his hammock and motioned for her to follow.

With her lips pressed together, she crawled out from her hiding spot.

He picked her up and set her on his lap. "Clara, have you heard anything from the crew about my father?"

She nodded. "He was the captain before you."

"That's right. My father, Gibson Williams, owned a shipping company. That's what the flag with the 'W' represents. He had ships that sailed all over the world to deliver people and goods to different places. But he also gambled. I traveled with him to help him with the business, and because my mother hoped I could stop him from gambling. Unfortunately, my father had too much debt to repay, and he died before he could pay them all."

Her eyes widened. "How did he die?"

He ignored her question. "One night when he was still alive, Wentworth sent me ashore to find him. Of course, he was gambling again. When I asked him to stop, he refused and we argued. Eventually, I got him back on board the ship, and we left. He died that night, and every day I feel guilty that I didn't tell my father I loved him one last time."

"Why did you steal all that stuff from those people?"

"I'm getting to that, Clara." He chuckled to hide the

guilt squeezing his stomach. "On our way home, we went through a terrible storm that blew us off course. It took us weeks to get supplies and repair the ship to make it home. By then everyone thought we had all died, and my mother had sold the company to pay off my father's debts. But the crew still needed work, and as their new captain, they were my responsibility. We couldn't make enough money with such a small ship. One time, we were even boarded by pirates and fought them off."

Clara's eyes bulged.

"It's true. That's how we got the idea."

She stared up at him, her mouth tweaked to one side as she thought.

"Clara, this is actually our last trip. After we drop you off with your aunt, we're done. We've made enough money to provide for the crew."

"Why did those men say you stole this ship?"

"We lied."

Her eyebrows crinkled in confusion.

"If people were scared of us, they wouldn't fight us and no one would get hurt."

"But you broke their ship!"

"It won't take them very long to fix it."

"But you threw their food overboard!"

"Here." He climbed out of the hammock, laid out a map on his desk, and pointed over the water. "This is where we are right now. And see this?" He pointed to the land nearby.

She followed his finger.

"It will only take them a few hours to reach this port to buy some more. We couldn't let them follow us."

She frowned for a second before nodding at him. "I get it, but you're still a bad man."

He snorted. "I agree, Clara. I'm not a very good man, but I did what I had to for my crew."

"I'm sorry I threw Theodore at you."

"No, you're not."

She thought for a moment. "You're right. I'm not."

He bit back a smile. "All right, Clara. I don't know about you, but Theodore is very tired and needs to go to bed." He scooped her up and laid her in his hammock.

She yawned.

"We'll turn out the lights and be very quiet so Theodore can sleep." He dimmed the oil lamp on his desk.

"Good idea." She lay back down with Theodore on her chest and closed her eyes.

***

The Beast awoke, sore from sleeping in his chair again. He stretched out his stiff neck and spotted his empty hammock. Clara must've gone up for breakfast already.

After donning a clean shirt, he ventured up to the main deck. The crew worked, as usual, but something bothered the captain. He walked over to the bow, pushing his long hair out of his face.

The wind usually blew the hair out of his face... *The wind!* He turned back toward the sails to see the lifeless banner of Williams & Co. dangling against the mast. No wind. And he only had three days to get the crew, and Clara, off the ship.

"Bradley!" He marched over to the helm.

"Aye, Captain?" Bradley leaned against the wheel.

"The wind."

Bradley shrugged. "It all but died overnight."

"How long until we reach La Rochelle?"

"If this keeps up, three days." He tipped the wheel slightly, keeping the ship on course. "Maybe more?"

The captain swore under his breath and stomped off to the galley.

Avery and Clara chatted as they cooked. "Captain!" Clara jumped off the barrel and ran to his side, grinning. "I hung up your pictures for you. Did you notice?"

"Hmm?" He looked down at her. "Yes."

She frowned. "Well, if you don't like them, I'll go take them down."

"They're exactly what I wanted, Clara. Don't take them down." He grabbed a block of cheese and a couple of biscuits, patted Theodore on the head, and returned to his quarters, where he locked the door behind him and didn't emerge until after suppertime.

The sun had already set, and Edison knelt on the bridge, teaching Clara about the constellations. She waved him over. "Did you know the stars tell you directions?"

He folded his arms, avoiding her eye contact and drumming his thumb on his shoulder. "Edison, has the wind changed at all?"

He glanced up at the still flag. "I'm afraid not, Captain."

"These cursed winds..." He growled and stalked back belowdecks. Time was not on his side. Frustrated, he tugged the leather hair tie out of his hair and discarded it on the deck, then threw himself into his hammock and closed his eyes, hoping for sleep.

A few minutes later, he felt a tap on his shoulder.

Opening one eye, he spied Clara watching him. "What?"

"Theodore thought you might be lonely since you didn't talk to anyone today." She tugged on her braid and placed the bear on his chest. "He wanted to make sure you were happy."

He swallowed the lump in his throat. "Thank you, Theodore."

She grinned, stuck her braid in her mouth, then scurried out of the room.

His heart twinged as the bear weighed on him. He couldn't let Clara pay for his sins. He would do just about anything to get her off the ship before it was too late. The wind had to pick up.

After a fitful night of sleep, his whole body ached, as if he had aged ten years overnight. He rolled out of his hammock and wandered to the galley where he grunted at Avery, picked out an apple, then trudged up to the main deck.

A gentle breeze brushed his hair out of his face and he spotted the flag fluttering and the sails distended.

Bradley whistled at the wheel. "Mornin', Captain! We should reach La Rochelle in no time, if this breeze keeps up."

The captain tipped his head at Bradley, a smile tugging at the corners of his mouth…until he spotted dark clouds gathering behind the Boatswain. "Bradley, is there a storm coming?"

"Aye, Captain. It'll probably hit soon, but it shouldn't deter our heading."

"Well, keep a weather eye on it." Something about the dark clouds seemed threateningly familiar, but he couldn't put his finger on it. He took a bite of his apple and shifted the thought to the back of his mind. Two days left, and they would reach La Rochelle just in time.

He busied himself by double-checking the knots and the sails before returning to the galley for a heartier snack. "Avery, have you—"

"Where's Clara?" the cook interrupted.

"I haven't seen her." He scratched his head. "I assumed she was with you."

"She told me she was going to find you hours ago."

They blinked at each other before bolting out of the room.

"Clara!" Their calls echoed around the small passageway.

The captain checked in his quarters, under his desk, anywhere she had previously hidden, but to no avail. Theodore was still in the hammock. With the bear now in hand, he met up with Avery again.

Shaking his head, Avery shrugged. "She's not in the crew's quarters."

"Well, she can't have gone far. We're in the middle of the ocean." He clambered back up to the main deck. "Has anyone seen Clara?"

The crew exchanged uncertain glances.

"Check with Wentworth?" Winston suggested from his perch in the crow's nest.

Avery shook his head.

"She likes to hide. She could be anywhere on this ship." The captain paced in a small circle before snapping his fingers and running belowdecks to the bay, Avery close on his heels.

Wentworth counted barrels and crates, marking notes on his paper. He straightened when he saw the captain. "Sir, I—"

The captain put a finger to his lips and slowed his steps, tiptoeing through the rows of cargo.

A sniffle broke the silence.

He stopped in front of one row and half-smiled before placing the bear on the deck and taking a few steps back.

A hand reached out from behind a barrel and snatched the bear.

The captain waved Avery and Wentworth out of the room before poking his head over the barrel. "Hello."

Clara looked up at him with tear-stained cheeks then buried her head between her knees.

"Did you hear that you're almost home? That's exciting, right?"

Her shoulders shook with a fresh wave of sobs.

Confused, he dropped down to her side. "What's wrong, Clara? Don't you want to go back to your family?"

She shook her head and wiped her tears with the bear's paw.

"Why not?"

"My sisters are mean to me." She hiccupped.

"I never had sisters, but there was a girl who grew up across the street from me. She wasn't mean, though she did enjoy playing pranks on people." He smiled at the memory of her dusty brown hair and taunting smile. It had been twelve years since he had last seen Rosemary, except in his dreams. He still loved her, but over the years, she had become a reminder that he was a dead man. She would never know how he felt.

Clara leaned against the Beast's arm and wrapped her tiny hand around his elbow. "My sisters told me they didn't want me to come with them. That's why they tripped me on the docks. They even hid Theodore so they could run away, and I couldn't find them."

"When did this happen?"

"In Southampton. I didn't know what ship to get on. Everyone came on board, and you left before I could get off."

"Well, what about your aunt? Don't you want to live with her?"

Clara shrugged through a shaky breath. "I don't know. I've never met her."

"Oh. Then how do you know you *don't* want to live with her?"

She blinked, thinking.

"I'll tell you what, Clara." He patted her delicate fingers. "If you don't like your aunt, I'll come back to La Rochelle and take you away." It was a lie, but she wouldn't realize that until he was already dead.

She smiled through her tears. "Really?"

He nodded, despite the growing pit of guilt in his stomach. "Now, come on. You can't hide in here all day, otherwise Wentworth will make you count all these crates for him." He pulled her up onto her bare feet. He'd have to find her shoes before sending her ashore in La Rochelle.

She giggled and ran out of the bay, dragging Theodore behind.

The captain sighed, trailing after. Up on the main deck, the storm had shifted closer, and the winds were now blustery and wild.

Clara climbed up the mast to sit with Winston.

A strong gust of wind shook the ship, and the first droplets of rain fell from the dark sky.

The captain's stomach churned in an unfamiliar sensation of apprehension. "Clara, come down from there!"

Winston nudged her and helped her out onto the mast, but as she let herself down, her grip slipped.

The captain's heart skipped. Though he would never make it in time, he lunged forward to catch her. He would do anything to keep her from getting hurt.

Winston swung down and grabbed her around the waist, slowing her descent until she dropped onto the deck, landing on her knees with a thunk.

"Clara!" the captain scolded, his anger covering his panic as he helped her up.

She tugged on her braid and stared at her feet.

Nursing a red burn on his palm despite the years of wear, Winston clambered back up to his post.

Shaking his head, the captain put a hand over his pounding heart and put his other hand on Clara's shoulder. "It's okay, you're safe. But I want you to stay belowdecks until this storm is over." He turned her around and nudged her toward the stairs.

She sighed and slinked off.

Facing the sails, he barked orders at the crew.

Bradley remained at the helm while Clayton, Edison, and Monty raced to furl the sails and secure anything loose on the deck.

The captain clung to the mast to keep his footing as the ship swayed. Though it was impossible, he was sure he had faced this exact storm before.

Then the water started to glow an eerie turquoise.

"Captain!" Edison called from behind.

"I see, Edison." He swore under his breath. "Menestho."

Edison ran to him, blinking in the rain. "Why is she here? Again?"

"She's come for me."

"What are you talking about? She saved your life. Why would she take it now?" Edison combed his dripping hair out of his eyes.

"You don't know the whole story."

Slowly, Menestho rose from the water, her green hair plaited with seaweed and her skin an ever-changing blue, as turbulent as the seas lifting her. "It is time, Beast." Her deep voice echoed around them, her yellow eyes glowing.

"You promised me five years, Menestho!" He stepped forward. "I still have one more day!"

"Your five years ends now."

"But…" He stared at his hands. Had he miscounted the days?

"What is she talking about?" Edison put a hand on his arm.

The captain brushed him off. "Please, I beg of you. Let me get my crew to safety first. Isn't that why you won't allow me to step on land? So I can't escape you?"

Her laughter churned the glowing water beneath them, precariously rocking the ship. "Bargaining again? Just like your father."

He couldn't speak through the guilt clutching his chest.

"I see you haven't told your trusted crew what really happened to their captain."

He spun around, his sopping hair lashing against his cheek, to find Edison and the rest of his crew staring at him, frozen in confusion.

"Allow me to explain." Menestho's hair swirled in

the wind, adding to her wild look. "Your beloved captain Gibson owed me a great debt. When I came to collect, Gibson and his son were thrown overboard, where I became fond of the Beast and gave him an opportunity—if he would choose to love me, stay with me as my companion for eternity, I would set his father free. But he refused."

"She gave me five years to change my mind, or die," the captain finished.

"Will you come willingly?" She grinned, baring yellow fangs encrusted in barnacles. "Or do I have to motivate you?" The boat careened violently, the hull tipping up before splashing back down, sending the crew sprawling across the deck.

"No!" Edison whipped out his pistol and aimed it at the Oceanid. "We won't let you take him!" He pulled the trigger, but it clicked and fizzled out from the storm.

"She's an Oceanid, Edison, you can't stop her. Let me go," he pleaded.

"Is this because you fought with your father that last night? You feel responsible?" Edison grabbed the captain's wrist.

The rain made it easy for him to slip out of Edison's grip. "I *am* responsible, Edison. He's dead because of me. Menestho was right. If I loved him—if I wasn't mad at him that night—I would've done anything to save him. But I didn't. That guilt is worse than death."

"I promised your father I would keep you safe," Edison pleaded.

"And I promised my mother I would keep him out of trouble. This is my punishment to face alone. Let me go, and you can all get to safety. Please, Edison, Clara is on board."

The ship rocked again, breaking Edison's pained stare.

The Beast ran to the starboard bulwark of the ship. "Menestho, you must promise to let my crew make it to safety."

As if he had caught her off guard, the storm eased. Then, it redoubled to add extra incentive to the captain's dilemma. "If you come willingly, it will make the next part much easier on us both."

"Give me your word that you will not harm my crew, and I will go with you." Using a rope to steady himself, he stepped onto the railing, ready to dive into the churning waters. The wind tossed around them, the waves dangerously rough.

"No!" Clara squeaked and ran toward him, slipping in the water. She reached for him just as another wave shook the ship, her arms missing their mark as she bumped her hip into the railing. Headfirst, she toppled overboard. "Beast! Help me!"

The same cry his father shouted when he tumbled into the waves, into Menestho's glowing grips, dragging his son with him.

Five years earlier, he had panicked, frozen between duty and anger. He chose anger, letting Menestho claim his father as she laughed, telling him he was next.

He wouldn't let Menestho win again. She could take his life, drag him down to the cold depths of the sea, keep him as a prize for eternity, but she wouldn't get Clara.

He dove into the frigid waves with the rope in his hand. Spitting out salty water, he scrambled for her tiny hands as Menestho's storm dragged her down. His lungs burned as he dove after her.

She thrashed against the current.

With one final kick, he tied the rope around Clara's waist.

The crew pulled on the other end, hauling her up the side of the boat as she screamed his name, clinging to his hand.

He let go and the waves carried him under.

***

He woke to an aqua glow. Blinking, he cleared his vision. He floated underwater, but he was still alive. For now.

Menestho floated in front of him, her eyes narrow and her finger tapping her chin. "I've always found the human spirit fascinating; mortals determined to change the world despite their limited life and abilities. Their capacity for fear, joy, and love…" Her expression turned dark as her lips pursed. "But you have me stumped, Beast. You were willing to die for this child, this girl you barely know, but you wouldn't save your father. Didn't you love your father?"

As before, he had no trouble breathing in the salty sea thanks to Menestho's magic. "We've already had this conversation, Menestho. I was mad at him, because—"

She rolled her eyes. "So you said, but you also said your heart belonged to another, this neighbor girl."

"Rosemary." He clenched his jaw. She deserved more respect from this demon.

"Whatever. It's just another excuse. Another way for you to avoid the truth."

Offended, he opened his mouth to speak, but one look from her cut him off.

"I'll let you in on a secret—I never planned to kill you. Now it's your turn to be honest." Her voice was cold but still colored with hope. "If you weren't angry with your father, would you have given yourself up for him? Would you have loved me?" One of her cerulean hands brushed his arm.

He recoiled in disgust.

Her green, forked tongue clicked once as her mouth contorted in disappointment. "Then why give excuses at all?"

Stunned, he blinked a few times as he processed the truth of what she said. He had been giving excuses all these years to justify what he did, but he simply didn't understand why it was his responsibility to keep his father out of trouble, stop him from gambling, and keep him from harm. Shouldn't his father have looked out for him that way, loved him and his mother enough to stop gambling on his own, protected their lives at the cost of his own?

"You never answered my question, Beast. You were willing to die for this child, but not your father?"

"My father's life was not my responsibility, but my crew's lives are, especially Clara's. I would do anything to keep her safe."

"Anything?" Menestho's long hair encircled him as her yellow eyes flitted over him.

He swallowed, keeping his gaze steady. "Anything."

"I am intrigued." Her blue lips puckered, then she sighed. "But I still do not understand. This is a kind of love I am not familiar with."

As her hair released him, he found his breath again and with it, a calm optimism he hadn't experienced in five years.

"How can you claim to know more about life than I? I don't like that, and I don't need a reminder of your so-called love. Take the girl home. Walk on land. I release you."

Before he could respond, a current lifted him out of the ocean, dumped him on the deck of the ship, and the storm dissipated as if it had never happened.

"Captain!" His crew dashed toward him, surrounding him and checking to make sure it was really him.

He tried to take a step but fumbled, feeling as he did when he walked on dry land after a long voyage.

Clara appeared behind him, wrapping her arms around him.

"What happened?" Edison asked as the crew clambered about him, checking him for injury.

"She... She let me go." He turned toward where Menestho once floated, but no trace of her remained. He picked Clara up and hugged her tightly, fighting the urge to smile.

She pushed away from him. "You lied to me!" She poked his shoulder.

"What?"

"You told me Oceanids weren't real!" She pouted and crossed her arms.

He laughed. "I'm sorry, Clara. But I was right about one thing, they don't eat people."

She giggled and threw her arms around his neck.

***

They landed at La Rochelle early the next morning, perfect winds guiding their way. While the crew unloaded their cargo, the captain struggled to tie Clara's shoes on her bouncing feet. Her hair certainly looked like she fell into the water, but she was safe and happy.

"Promise me you won't leave until I'm sure I like my aunt?" She hugged a dirty Theodore to her chest.

He sighed. "I promise, Clara. Now button up your coat!" He snagged her arm and sat her down so he could put on her other shoe.

She swung her legs while he did so, making it difficult for him to properly tie the laces. "What are you going to do now? Are you going to stay a pirate?"

He chewed his lip, unsure how to answer. He hadn't let himself think of a future when he thought himself a dead man. Did he continue to sail with his crew and rebuild the Williams & Co. name? Or did he retire somewhere south, perhaps in the Caribbean?

"Oh! Are you going to find that girl?" Clara giggled, as if the thought of him finding love too funny to bear.

His heart twinged as he thought of his long lost love. Perhaps he would find her again, but she had probably married a man with a steady job and had children of her own. She didn't need him disrupting her life. Perhaps it was best to stay far away from England all together, to avoid the possibility of encountering her. The Caribbean sounded more and more appealing.

"Beast?" Clara tapped his cheek, snapping him out of his reverie.

"Let's go." He took her hand, pulling her to her feet.

She skipped down the gangplank and onto the dock.

"I'll be back by sunset, Edison. You're in charge." He chased after Clara on wobbling legs. It had been five years since he had last stood on a solid surface. Luckily, she had a similar problem.

He had no clue how to locate Clara's aunt. He wasn't even sure how to talk to strangers after so long. But when he looked down at Clara, he knew he had to do something. Taking her hand in his, they walked through the town, asking everyone for directions. Finally, a kindly old man pointed them in the right direction.

When they turned down the correct street, Clara slowed. He nudged her forward, but soon he pulled her hand instead of the other way around. They stopped at the bottom of the steps, and the captain double-checked the address. He squeezed her hand. "Clara, don't forget my promise. If you don't like your aunt, I will take you with me." This time he meant it.

She tugged once on her braid then released it. "Okay." With a shaky breath, she made her way up to the door and knocked, the captain right behind her.

A young woman with dusty brunette hair opened the door and gasped, her hands flying to her mouth.

He momentarily forgot why he was there. "Rosemary?"

"Adam?" Behind her hands, a hint of a smile played around the corners of her mouth.

Clara scrunched up her nose and spoke through a fit of giggles. "Your name is Adam?"

"Oh, Clarabelle!" Rosemary dropped down and pulled her niece into a tight hug. "We've been so worried about you! Adam, how on earth did you find her?"

Clara pulled away and stepped back toward the captain, still nervous.

"She, uhh, she ended up on our ship, so we brought her here." He put a hand on her shoulder, feeling uneasy.

"How do you know my Aunt Rose?" Clara folded her arms.

The corners of his mouth quirked upward. "Remember that girl I told you about, the one who grew up across the street from me?"

Clara's wide gaze jumped between the two. "Really?"

Rosemary's cheeks reddened. "Adam, how are you alive? I thought you went down with your father and the *Swift Storm* all those years ago!"

"It's a long story." He ran a hand through his hair. "What are you doing in France?"

Clara tugged on Adam's sleeve. "She's not married, if that's what you're wondering."

Now it was his turn to blush. "I didn't… I mean…" He peered down at Clara. "Your name is Clarabelle?"

The little girl's eyes widened in terror, as if a great secret had been let loose.

Rosemary chuckled. "Would you like to come inside for a bit?" She opened the door wider.

He grinned as Clara pulled him inside. "Sure, I can stay for a while."

Bluebeard's Wives

Mae Baum

"Is he still out there?" Juan asked, rolling an unlit cigarette between his thick lips. The boss leaned his potbelly against the steel counter, a dirty dishrag draped over a shoulder.

The stranger had been coming for weeks, in the late evenings, and sitting at the back of the patio. Drinking only wine, the man left plates of untouched food stacked on his table.

"I think he's just lonely," Gina said. *It's a feeling I know well enough.* She flipped her blond ponytail back over her shoulder.

Sheila pushed up on her tiptoes to peer through the small window on the upper part of the door. Her apron dangled over her bird-like legs. "Man, he gives me the creeps."

"I don't mind him," Gina said, picking up the dish laden with tacos. "He probably doesn't have anyone or anything to go home to." *I don't either.* Gina frowned. Her rundown, box-like apartment was all she could afford in Atlanta, and there wasn't room for a cat, much less a roommate.

"Get him on his way," Juan said gruffly, scraping a fat hand across his chin. "Can't have him taking that table up all night."

Gina nodded, although she knew if she tried, the man would only order another plate. Pushing out the door,

Gina glanced toward where the man sat.

His swirling blue eyes met hers, and she smiled.

The corners of his full lips turned up, and he raised his wine glass.

Gina's grin widened. Momma would have told her to be careful, men like him only want one thing, but Gina didn't think he meant any harm. Of course, Momma rarely dealt with any man who didn't come to the bar or live in the trailer park. Momma wouldn't know any one as well-dressed and polite as this gentleman.

He followed her movement across the deck as she brought the food to the couple at table eight. His dark hair and neat beard seemed almost blue under the white string lights that crisscrossed the patio. He wore a gray suit tailored to his athletic body; the crisp white collar of the shirt framed his chiseled face. His skin seemed pale. Must be all the long hours in the office.

After taking down the order for the family at table two, Gina tucked her stubby pencil behind her ear and dropped her notepad into the pocket of her waist apron.

"I'll put your order right in," she said, heading back toward the kitchen. Her gaze darted to the back table. He was still there, sipping his wine and watching her.

When she opened the door, the smells of corn tortillas, chili peppers, and burnt grease wafted out into the warm night air. Even though it was September, the Georgia heat lingered into the evening hours.

Sheila nudged Gina's shoulder. "How're your classes?"

"Great." Gina grinned. She'd worked hard for her scholarship and loved her classes, even if she had to work nights and weekends to afford living in Atlanta. "We're reading Shakespeare's sonnets. They're fantastic."

"Why anyone in their right mind would choose to be a librarian is beyond me." Sheila raised her dark eyebrows, wrinkling her forehead.

Gina laughed.

"Not a librarian yet," Juan said, jerking his head toward the waiting food.

***

Just after midnight, Gina stepped out through the tall wooden gate. "Good night," she called back.

"G'nite," Juan hollered.

The streetlights pooled on the cracked sidewalk as Gina headed toward the light rail station at the end of the deserted block. She passed some blooming flowers and sniffed, but all she could smell was chili pepper and grease. Pausing, she dug around in the front pocket of her messenger bag for her transit card. *Where is the dang thing? Did I leave it at work?*

Her fingers brushed along the familiar creased edge as a dark limo pulled up along the sidewalk. Gina startled, backing toward the building behind her. Shaking, her fingers released the card and groped for the pepper spray instead. The window slowly rolled down, and she met the storm blue eyes of the man from the back table. He'd followed her?

"Gina." His deep, smooth voice rolled over her, and she trembled.

"You know my name?" Her eyes darted around the quiet, empty street. She glanced back toward the restaurant. Juan was totaling up, so he wouldn't be leaving for a while.

A gentle smile stretched the man's face, and he gestured toward her name tag. "I didn't mean to scare you."

Of course, he didn't. Gina blushed and stared at him, her eyes wide. Her stomach turned over, and she took a couple of deep breaths. She didn't think aggressors were usually this polite, but she didn't let go of the pepper spray.

"I'm Louis." His eyes pulled her in, swirling in the gray and blue depths. "I only wanted to offer a ride home, but I can see you're uncomfortable."

"Yes," Gina said slowly. She didn't know if she was supposed to admit that or not. *What's wrong with me?* She shook herself. "I'm taking the train. It's not far."

"Of course." He perused her, and he quoted, "'Unthrifty loveliness, why dost thou spend, upon thyself thy beauty's legacy?'"

His voice filled her mind. The street lights burned brighter and the flowers' scent invaded her nose. She gasped. "What?"

He chuckled, warm and low. "The Sonnets." He gestured to the book peeking out of her bag.

Gina's heart tripped. "You've read Shakespeare?" A lonely man who read Shakespeare? How more perfect could he be? Gina swayed toward the limo. He wasn't like Momma's men; he was cultured.

"I've read a great many things." His lyrical voice lured her closer. "I have quite an extensive library."

She leaned forward. "You have a library?" Gina swallowed.

The door opened, and he held out a hand. "Come, let me tell you about it."

Gina held her breath, staring at his hand. When had she dropped her pepper spray? She rubbed her head. How could she have been nervous with him?

"I promise to be a perfect gentleman."

She released her breath and took his hand, climbing into the limo.

***

Meeting her by the curb, Louis ferried her home every night that week and they spoke of the books they'd read. The dark confines of the limo created their own little world. Gina was thankful that he played the perfect gentleman as promised although she twitched under his sensual gaze.

Momma had brought enough men home to their run-down trailer, usually drunk or high, that Gina knew that look. As Gina grew, the men had started to turn their eyes to her and she'd taken to hiding in the closet. Even when boys from school had started asking her out, she'd turned them down one by one, unable to bear their gaze.

But somehow, when Louis watched her, she didn't mind.

"Why'd you choose your major?" he asked.

"I've always loved books." Gina blushed. "Well, obviously." How could she tell him that when Momma caught her nose deep in a book during a cookout, she'd hollered that Gina was wasting her youth and beauty? That it only comes around once, so she had better go out and find herself a man? "I'm the odd one in my family."

"I'm the only one left in mine," Louis said quietly.

"That might be preferable." Gina grimaced. When her mom's latest guy had reached over and stroked her leg, she knew then that she had to get out. That home wasn't safe for her anymore.

She glanced up at Louis's face. "I'm sorry though, for your losses."

"It's all right," he said. "It was a long time ago."

Gina reached out and squeezed his hand. He seemed so much older than his thirty-something years.

***

The following week, when Louis offered to show her his library, she squealed and hugged him. Her nose filled with the spicy scent of his cologne as she buried her face in his silk shirt.

He stroked her hair and a shiver slid down her back. Gina tensed, holding her breath. But this was Louis. Somehow he seemed to melt away all her reserve, and she wanted more than she'd ever wanted. She exhaled.

"I'll send the car for you on Saturday," he whispered in her ear. His thumb traced the edge of her neck, and her heart fluttered.

"Oh, Louis!" Warmth uncurled in her stomach. He was unlike any man she had ever met. She'd known that, if she waited, someday her Heathcliff would show up.

He kissed her gently on the forehead and then patted the seat. "Let's get you home."

Gina's eyebrows drew together. Why was he dismissing her? Didn't he think she was a real woman? "Don't you like me that way?"

"Modern woman," he growled. A grin spread across his face, and he yanked her to him. His deep kiss sent shockwaves through her whole body.

***

On Saturday afternoon, the limo pulled to a stop at the curb. She'd worn her best, a pale blue sundress worn thin before she'd bought it at the thrift store. She'd carefully done her makeup. Her blond hair was piled on her head in an attempt at sophistication.

She'd been so confident stepping into the limo, but now, peering out the window, Gina stared at the tall, white columns that seemed to reach for the sky. Gina had never seen a house so enormous; it was bigger than the campus buildings where she took her classes. Brushing imaginary lint off her dress, her cheeks burned. How could she be seeing a man who owned all this? It was a long way from the trailer park. She knew he was rich, but this was way more than she'd ever imagined.

The chauffeur opened the door, and she stepped out onto the hot sidewalk. The cool of the air conditioning faded immediately in the Georgia sun. Sweltering heat washed over her and sweat sprung up on her back.

Reluctantly, Gina climbed the steps. *I'm an invited*

guest, she reminded herself as she approached the white double door with the large brass knocker. It was shaped like a lion with a ring through his gaping mouth. She reached for the ring and the door swung open.

A suited man held the door open. "Welcome, Miss Gina, we've been expecting you."

Gina's heart squeezed. She didn't belong here. She wanted to turn and run down the steps, but she plucked up her courage and stepped inside.

Despite the big windows on the house and the bright sunshine outside, the interior seemed dim. Her eyes took a moment to adjust. The foyer led to two large staircases that swept up to the second floor and a crystal chandelier dangled above.

Why is it so dark? She peered at the high windows, just making out the gauzy curtains that dampened the light filtering in. *Odd.*

The butler closed the door behind her, and she jumped at the sound. Her gaze slipped around the room, taking in the heavy old furniture and a light coating of dust. Her eyebrows drew together.

Louis stepped out from a side room. "Gina! So glad you are here."

His energy swept over her and she relaxed. This was her Louis. She smiled. He grasped her hands and pulled her deeper into the house. The elegant furnishings swept by, but she only had eyes for him until he opened the door at the end of the hall.

The book-lined walls of the library rose around her. A colorful variety of books sat on the dark wood shelves; antique leather-bounds stood next to modern paperbacks. While the long windows were covered with green velvet drapes, recessed lighting and round lamps lit the space and a pair of oversized armchairs looked inviting. Two circular staircases rose in the middle of the room, leading to the second and the third tier. Her mouth dropped open, and she spun in a circle, her skirt floating around her. "It's beautiful."

"Take as many as you like," he said as her fingers lingered on the spines.

Gina grinned and pulled down book after book. "You have all my favorites and more."

Louis chuckled. "Gathering favorites is one of my specialties."

He carried her books to a fluffy armchair. She settled in, tucking her skirts around her and started reading. "Would you like tea?"

She glanced up at him. "Oh, yes, please."

Gina read all afternoon. Louis hand-delivered jasmine tea and small almond scones, even though she was sure he had servants for that sort of thing.

Late in the evening, he invited her to dinner. Real hunger that couldn't be satisfied by scones and tea was the only thing that tore her away from the precious books. That, and Louis's promise that she could come back any time she desired.

He led her up another flight of stairs and out onto the balcony. A round table was set with service for two, along with lit candles and a fragrant bouquet of white roses. She shivered in the cooler night air, and he swept a shawl around her shoulders. His fingers lingered along her neck, stroking, and a different kind of shiver spread through her.

Sliding into the chair he pulled out, she licked her lips at the fluffy rolls in front of her. The sweet cream butter melted in her mouth. Perfectly grilled lemon chicken and a salad that was so fresh it must have been picked that day. Somehow he'd guided her through the whole meal without making her feel like an idiot. His subtle cues had let her know which fork was for the salad and what knife to use for the butter.

"Prosecco," he said, filling their glasses. "It's Italian sparkling wine."

She smiled at him. "You're amazing."

He inclined his head. "And you are lovely, my dear."

They sipped their Prosecco silently. Then, he snapped his fingers and classical music filled the balcony like magic. He stood and bowed to her. "May I have this dance?"

She laughed. "Of course." Taking her hand, he swung her into a waltz. Gina had never danced before, but he somehow made it easy. Louis made everything easy.

The stars struggled to peek through the smog-filled skies above them. As if they, too, wanted everything to be perfect.

***

Gina woke in a tangle of blankets on an elegant four-poster bed. Her eyebrows drew together as she looked around the unfamiliar room.

Where am I? Sitting up, she swung her legs over the edge of the bed and looked down at the white nightgown that covered her body.

She thought back over the events of yesterday—the library, the dinner, the dancing, but she didn't remember anything after that.

Why hadn't she gone home? The wine must have gone to her head and she'd passed out. Warmth flooded her cheeks. What an idiot he must think her. Passing out after a little wine.

She stretched her arms out and rubbed her sore neck. *Must have slept on it wrong.* The smooth cotton of the nightgown slid along her legs. Who'd changed her clothes? A maid? Louis? Her cheeks got even hotter. She looked around but she was all alone. Biting her lip, she searched her memory but after the dancing, the evening was a blank. She hoped they hadn't done anything. No, Louis wouldn't. He'd been so sweet to her.

Gina sighed. At least she didn't have anywhere to be this morning. She slid off the bed and her feet landed in the thick blue carpeting. The sunlight streaming in the glass doors beckoned her, and she strode over and flung them open. The warm breeze slid over her and she sighed.

A knock sounded at the door. "Come in," she called.

The door opened and a rotund woman pushed a rolling cart ahead of her into the room. Glancing up, her round face broke into a wide grin. "I've your breakfast for you here, dearie."

Gina's stomach rumbled, and she smiled back at the woman. She felt like a fairy tale princess, with a castle and servants and an enormous library. "Can I eat it on the balcony?"

"Of course," the woman said, pushing the cart across the thick carpeting. She set out a full breakfast of eggs, toast, and berries on the wrought-iron table. "Coffee or tea?"

"Coffee. Thank you." Gina sat down and stared at the food. "Is Louis up yet?"

Pouring out a cup, the woman laughed. "No, dearie. Not yet." She pushed the cart back out the door and closed it behind her.

Gina dug into the food. The scrambled eggs were perfect, light and fluffy, and the berries tasted like they'd just been picked. After breakfast, she took a luxurious bath in the giant tub and put on her dress from the night before. If Louis still wasn't up, she might as well go explore the library some more.

***

Curled up in Louis's library chair, Gina looked up when a shadow fell across her book. "Louis!"

A lazy smile stretched across his face.

Her lips parted as she met his blue eyes. They burned like the hottest part of a flame. Her heartbeat echoed in her ears.

"I'm glad to see you've made yourself at home." His

voice flooded her. "Did Mrs. Peterson see to your needs?"

Her mind blanked, and she blinked up at him. What had she been doing?

"Yes," she said breathily. Joy laced through her; she'd made him happy. "It's wonderful."

Taking a steadying breath, she gestured toward the books. So many more than she could read in a single lifetime. "Your family must have been collecting them for generations."

"Yes, we've always been collectors." His stormy eyes slid over her.

Gina shivered.

He dropped down and took both of her hands in his. "You're beautiful, intelligent, and well read. How could I resist falling for you?"

"I've never met anyone like you," she whispered, trembling.

"Nor I, you," he said. "I feel like I've known you forever."

Heat suffused her chest and radiated into her limbs. He was so perfect. Louis washed away all the ugliness of her life with his presence. Tears pricked at her eyelids. "Me too."

"I love you, Gina, and I want you to stay here with me always as my wife." He pulled a small box from his jacket pocket and popped it open. An elegant diamond cupped by an antique setting intricately wrought and surrounded by smaller jewels glittered in the velvet nest.

Gina gasped. "It's so lovely!" Her eyes blinked rapidly as her thoughts raced. She didn't deserve this kind of happiness. "But we're only just starting to get to know one another."

Louis stroked her arm, and delicious trembles skidded down her nerves. "I know it seems fast," he murmured. "But it feels right, doesn't it?"

Gina's head lolled back against the overstuffed chair, thoughts fleeing. "Yes…"

Louis slid the ring on her finger. "I love you."

Staring at her hands and the enormous ring, she smiled. "I love you too, Louis."

***

Gina'd barely had time to catch her breath with all the wedding plans, but she hadn't wanted to miss her shift at the restaurant.

The heat of the kitchen swept over Gina as she clipped her sheet to the ticket holder. She wiped the back of her hand across her forehead and sighed. "Why are you staring at me, Sheila?"

"Girl," Sheila said, scooting over and peering at Gina's hand. "There's a rock on your finger bigger than I've ever seen. Where'd it come from?"

Juan looked up from his receipts. "A rock?"

"Oh, it's from Louis." Gina glanced back and forth between Sheila and Juan. "He's amazing!"

Sheila's dark eyebrows drew up her forehead. "Who the heck is *Lou-ee*?"

Blinking, Gina frowned at them. Had she really forgotten to tell them about the most important man in her life? "He's, um, the man from the back table." Gina twirled in place, her skirt lifting like a cheerleader. "We've been seeing each other."

"The creep?" Sheila dropped a hand on Gina's arm. "Oh, honey."

Shaking off Sheila's hand, Gina frowned. Why were her friends acting this way? "He has the most amazing library."

"You've been to his house?" Juan stared at her, his voice dropping into a growl.

Gina grinned. It was so sweet how protective they were of her, like family. "Of course I have. We're engaged!"

Sheila's mouth dropped open, and she backed

toward Juan. "I think she's ill."

Gina raised an eyebrow. "Why are you two acting so weird? I thought you'd be happy for me."

Sheila stared at Juan and shook her head. Then she turned back toward Gina. "We are."

Juan grunted.

"We just think it's kinda sudden, honey," Sheila said.

Gina laughed. "Yeah, I did too, but…" She sighed. "Louis is irresistible."

Sheila stared at Gina.

"Oh, I almost forgot," Gina said, running over and pulling a pair of cards from her purse. "We're getting married on Sunday. Here're your invitations."

"Sunday!" Sheila's voice squeaked. "You've known him, what, two weeks?"

"What?" Juan asked. He stood, his stool falling over behind him. The metal rang against the linoleum floor.

Gina laughed and pressed the invitations into their hands. "I know it's fast, but it's just so right." Then, she turned and danced out into the restaurant.

***

The night of their wedding, the stars did their best to light up the large balcony and the Atlanta skyline glowed in the background. On one side, a vine-draped archway had been set up for the ceremony, and on the other were white-clothed tables, topped with silver candelabras and white tapers clustered around a small dance floor. Across the back, Mrs. Peterson had arranged a long table with a feast of artichoke mousse puffs, miniature Reuben sandwiches, and a chocolate fountain. Gina peered around the doorway. Her mouth watered just looking at it.

She stroked the soft silk of her wedding gown. Her shoulders and arms were covered by lace sleeves and the sweetheart neckline was dotted with pearls. Gina tried not to think about how much it cost; more than she'd make in a whole year at the diner she was sure.

Tugging on the lace and pearl choker that encircled her neck, she looked out at the guests. She'd insisted on inviting only a few close friends and family and Louis had agreed. Her mother was propped against a post, wearing a black dress with trailing roses, a glass in her hand and a smile pasted across her face. Louis's staff had done a great job at making her look somewhat presentable and possibly, Gina sniffed, halfway sober. What had she done to deserve such a man?

Sheila and Juan had come too despite their vocal misgivings. Juan wore a blue zoot suit that had seen better days, and Sheila's pink gown flowed over her thin form. They perched nervously on the white folding chairs that had been set up for the ceremony.

Other than a couple of her college friends, the rest of the guests were Louis's. Three couples, the men in silk suits and women in elegant gowns. They moved with unnatural grace across the balcony, ignoring her friends and speaking softly. Gina's stomach sank. How was she ever going to fit in? She didn't belong in Louis's world.

Then her husband-to-be strolled onto the terrace. Gina's heart beat faster as she watched him greet everyone with grace and kindness. Sheila blushed when he kissed her hand, and Gina giggled. Even gruff old Juan seemed charmed.

Mrs. Peterson shooed her back into her room. "The groom mustn't see the bride before the wedding, Miss Gina."

***

The ceremony was short and simple, just as they'd wanted. When the minister announced her as, "Mrs. Louis DeLuce," she almost missed her step on the path. Gina hadn't thought it possible to be this happy. Louis tucked her hand under his arm and introduced her to his friends. Gina was nervous, but she didn't seem to have any reason to be. The men kissed her hand and said they were enchanted. The women hugged her and kissed her on each cheek, welcoming her to the family.

Gina raised an eyebrow at Louis. "Family?"

Louis smiled. "Sometimes friends make better family than blood."

Glancing over at Juan and Sheila dancing, Gina agreed. "Absolutely."

"Let me get you some champagne," Louis said, releasing her arm. "I'll be right back."

Gina watched him walk away.

"Now that's a man," her mother slurred, stumbling into Gina's side. Her wine glass sloshed and red liquid dripped down Gina's white lace-covered arm.

"Momma!" Gina cried. "My dress!"

Her mother rubbed a tiny cocktail napkin against the stain.

"Oh, leave it alone," Gina said.

"I wanna tell you," Momma said, gripping Gina's arm. Her accent thickened with the drink. Momma's bloodshot eyes met Gina's. "You done good, baby."

Gina sighed. "I know, Momma. He's a good man."

Her mother glanced around, hair sliding off her neck, where a purple and blue hand-shaped bruise discolored the skin. "An' rich too!"

Ignoring her mother's words, Gina stared in horror at her throat. "Who did that to you, Momma?"

"What?" Momma squinted her eyes at Gina.

Gina gripped her mother's upper arms and shook her. "The bruise! Who did it?"

"Don't you go talking to me like that, Missy," Momma slurred, "when you have your own injuries."

Sighing, Gina asked, "What are you talking about?"

"You ain't hiding nothing with that fancy choker." Momma crossed her arms. "You winced when he tilted yer head for the kiss."

"You're crazy." Gina rubbed her neck. It had been sore, but she'd just slept on it wrong. "And drunk."

"Too good for yer momma now that you snagged a rich one."

"Why do I even bother?" Gina shook her head sadly. Her heart ached for her mother. Couldn't Momma, just once, stand up for herself? "Go home, Momma."

Motioning to the staff, Louis stepped up next to Gina. "Mr. James would be happy to call you a cab, Madam."

Gina turned her head into Louis's chest as the butler led her mother away. Louis murmured softly and stroked her hair. Her tears were hot against her cheeks.

The rest of the evening passed quickly. Mrs. Peterson applied some stain remover to Gina's sleeve, and they opened presents. The best one was Louis's gift for her— plane tickets for their honeymoon to Europe. He'd booked private evening tours of the best libraries. Gina had grinned and clapped her hands, putting her mother out of her mind. She did have a good man, and she wasn't going to let her trailer trash mother ruin it.

The honeymoon was a blur. Louis had bought her a new wardrobe, arranged for her classes to continue online, and they flew on a private jet. Gina soon found herself adjusting to Louis's schedule; he didn't wake until late and stayed up most of the night.

So she slept in, feeling spoiled, ate a late breakfast, and read until he woke up. The only odd thing was that he insisted they sleep in separate beds, saying he had too long been a bachelor and didn't sleep well with company. Still, the suites he provided her were luxurious and comfortable, and he was romantic and attentive the rest of the time. He'd been as gentle on their wedding night as she could have hoped. It was all so perfect.

As soon as the sun set, they were off and exploring the libraries and then sometimes to a late party or dinner with his fashionable friends. Gina grew more at ease with his crowd as the days passed, and Louis made sure to smooth the way when she wasn't clear about polite protocol or the right fork to use. She appreciated his kindness more and more every day.

She'd been swept away in a fantasy, and Gina could barely keep up. The only blight on their time was the persistent headaches that plagued her. She blamed them on too much rich food and drink, and her new schedule. She found it hard to concentrate on her studies and she knew her grades were slipping. Louis insisted she eat as much red meat as she could tolerate, saying it would keep her energy up.

Despite their adventures, she was grateful when they returned home. It was time to sort out her new life. Louis introduced her to the staff. Other than Mr. James and Mrs. Peterson, there were just a few other maids and gardeners. Really, the bare minimum for a house this size, Mrs. Peterson insisted.

Louis insisted that she didn't have to worry about a thing. Gina could continue her classes or she could play lady of the manor and spend her days reading and eating crumpets. The library was always open to her, and he showed her through dozens of rooms throughout the house that she was free to explore. He told her to feel free to invite her friends to visit or even her mother. He didn't mind. She'd hugged him and gave him a big kiss.

Gina settled into her new life quickly, and while the headaches persisted they seemed easier to manage here at home. "Do you think I ought to see a doctor?"

Louis looked up from his book. These afternoons in the quiet library seemed to suit them both. "I thought the headaches haven't been so bad."

"No, not so bad," Gina said, absently turning the

pages of her book. It was a mystery, which she usually loved, but she couldn't seem to follow the plot today. She rubbed her temple.

He stood, stretching his legs. "I've been meaning to tell you that I have a business trip planned and will need to leave tomorrow."

"What? So soon?" Her heart dropped.

Setting aside her book, he took her hands and pulled her to her feet. "I'm going to miss you too, my love."

Gina leaned her head against his chest. They had just been married; she had hoped they'd have more time. "How long will you be gone?"

"A month."

She gasped. "That long? What am I going to do without you?"

He smiled. "You'll be fine."

She nodded, although she wasn't as confident. Since they'd gotten back from the honeymoon, she felt like she'd lost something, some spark that her life had had before. She hadn't even logged into her librarian classes lately. Maybe it was just the headaches.

"I have something for you," Louis said, picking up a ring of old-fashioned keys from his desk. "These are the keys to my heart." He pressed them into her hands.

Gina laughed and looked at the keys. Each of them was different—gold, silver, bronze, polished iron, and so on. "They're beautiful."

"They fit all the doors in the house, so if there's anywhere you want to explore, just ask Mrs. Peterson, and she'll tell you which key fits what lock."

"Why are they locked?"

Louis shrugged. "We're a small household and don't use many rooms. The unused ones are locked so guests don't get lost."

Gina nodded.

"There's one thing you must do for me," Louis said,

taking her hands and looking into her eyes.

"Of course, anything."

"There's one room I don't wish you to explore." Louis pulled out one of the oldest keys, an iron one on a blood-red ribbon. "You may have free rein anywhere else in the house, but do not enter this room."

"Why?" Gina asked, her eyes gleaming. She always loved a mystery.

"That room has some old memories that I'm not quite ready to share." Louis kissed her hands. "I will though, soon, my love."

Gina could understand that. There was plenty of time for them to share their whole lives. If Louis needed time, she could give him time.

***

"This is wonderful," Sheila said, sipping the sparkling wine.

"Thank you for coming," Gina said. She'd been so bored since Louis had gone away. Even though Gina could go back to school, she'd continued to take classes online. She hadn't wanted to step out of the house as if it might evaporate like a mirage. The longer Louis was away, the less sure she became that this was anything more than a dream. "I know you had concerns about Louis, but I appreciate that you're still my friend."

"Of course, honey, can't let a man get between us." Sheila chuckled. "We chicks gotta stick together."

Gina grinned. She felt so much more grounded with Sheila here.

Sheila tripped on the patio stones and caught herself. She'd insisted on dressing up, in heels and a black dress, to have dinner with the "Lady of the Manor."

Laughing, Gina had played along with her own fancy dress, blue taffeta with trailing ruffles that matched her eyes.

Louis had presented her with a closet full of perfectly fitting clothes, all in finer fabrics than she'd ever seen. She'd never had so many new clothes, and she felt as if she were playing dress-up, as much as Sheila was.

"So what do you do for fun around here, girl?"

"Besides read?" Gina shrugged. "I've been exploring the house. There're so many rooms, each more beautiful than the last."

"Sounds good." Sheila grinned. "Let's go."

Gina led Sheila to the library and pulled the keys out from behind the copy of Shakespeare's sonnets. Then she and Sheila headed up to the second floor and into the west wing. "Which one do you want to check out?"

The first room Sheila chose was a bedroom decorated in shades of red including a rich mahogany four-posted bed covered with maroon bedspreads and thick red drapes. It was too dark and luxuriant for Gina's taste, but Sheila oh'd and ah'd over every piece, stroking the fabrics between her fingers.

Sheila twirled in the hallway, her hand pointing through the air as she went. When she stopped, she looked at the door she pointed to and said, "That one next."

It was a sitting room, done in white and gold. Gina liked the overstuffed gold armchair near the window, perfect for reading, and the landscape of a deep forest over the mantle.

Sheila lay on the fainting couch and draped her arm over her head. "Jeeves, bring me my champagne!" she said dramatically.

Gina giggled.

The third door was set back into the wall. Made of heavy oak with iron latches, none of Gina's keys fit the lock.

"Why won't it open?" Sheila asked, her dark eyebrows pinched.

Gina shook her head. "I don't know. I can't find the key." The keys rattled as she flipped through them. Then she saw the red ribbon. "I wonder…"

"Wonder what?" Sheila leaned toward her, alcohol on her breath.

"There's one room Louis asked me not to open."

Sheila put her hand flat on the wood of the door. "Why?"

Gina shrugged. "Some memories he wasn't ready to share."

"Oh!" Sheila waggled her eyebrows. "You think he has an ex? I knew there was something not right about that guy."

"Hey!" Gina glared at Sheila. "He's my husband."

A guilty look flitted across Sheila's face. "Sorry, honey."

Gina sighed.

"Yeow!" Sheila yanked her hand away from the door. "It's freezing."

"It's a door," Gina said. "How can it be cold?"

Gina reached out and laid her hand on the wood. It was cold. A shiver trailed down her hand toward her shoulder. *That is creepy.* Butterflies whirled in her stomach, and she dropped her hand. Backing away, she pulled Sheila along.

"Aren't you gonna open it?" Sheila asked.

Gina shook her head. "Come on, let's choose again."

***

Night after night, Gina dreamed of the icy door. She opened it again and again but she couldn't see what lay beyond it. The darkness was too deep. Her white nightgown billowed around her as she stood there and shivered.

She wanted to go and open it, dispel all her fears, but she'd promised Louis. He'd been nothing but good to her. How could she betray his one request?

The dark circles under her eyes became deeper every

day. She wasn't sleeping well. Every night she woke in a cold sweat, dreaming of the locked room. She should wait. Louis was coming home soon and then she could ask him what was there.

Despite the lack of sleep, the headaches were less frequent now and her energy increased. She still hadn't logged into her library classes, but she'd read several books.

Still, the door worried her. The coldness was weird, but it was just a door, right? When she woke up from the nightmare, for the third time in one night, she decided to go and see what was there.

She put on a t-shirt and jeans, and they felt like armor compared to the gauzy nightgown. The jeans were from before Louis, jagged rips along the knees where they had worn out long before she got them at the thrift store. Pulling her long hair into a ponytail, she felt more like herself than she had in a long while.

The moon outside was full, and the light lit up her bedroom. The now familiar shapes looked spooky in the odd light. She reached for her cell phone, but it wasn't on her nightstand. She frowned. That's where she'd always left it.

Her mind had still been cloudy lately. Maybe she had lost her purpose since she stopped going to classes on campus. She needed to be around other students. That would get her back on track. She reached for her purse and dug around in it, pulling out her phone. It only had a quarter of a charge; when had she last plugged it in? Gina shook her head.

The soft carpeting sank under her feet as she crossed the room. She pulled the keys from the drawer of her desk, wrapping them in the bottom of her t-shirt so they wouldn't clank. Not that the servants would hear her at this time of night. She peered at the clock on her nightstand. Two in the morning, and yet she felt wide awake.

She opened the door and peered into the dim hallway. There wasn't much light to see by so she clicked on the flashlight on her cell phone. Even though there didn't seem to be anyone about, she closed the door as silently as she could and then laughed at herself. It was her house now too. She should be able to go anywhere she wanted no matter the time.

Making her way through the halls, she wondered if she would even recognize the door. Then it was in front of her, and there was no mistaking it. She touched it and a cold shiver slid up her arm and down her spine.

Unrolling her t-shirt, Gina pulled out the keys and flipped through to the one on a red ribbon. She took a deep breath and slid the key into the lock. To her surprise, it turned easily. The wooden door swung open on well-oiled hinges despite its weight. A cold breeze and foul smell wafted over her from the depths of the room.

Gina brought up her cell phone, flashlight first, and stepped into the room. The floor was bare wood planks. A large metal tub lay in the center of the room. She held the back of her forearm against her nose and mouth and then crept forward.

The light from her phone bounced around the room as she moved, shadows appearing and disappearing on the plain walls. When she neared the tub, she closed her eyes briefly. Then, she peered over the edge. A dead goat lay in the tub, stuck with tubes that seemed to be pumping fluid out of it and carrying it across the room. Bile rose in her throat and she coughed.

Gina held her breath and followed the direction of the tubing to a large box laid out on the floor. Walking around it, she traced the shape and frowned. It was a coffin! Flipping her light up, she peered across the room. Seven coffins in a line and tubes of goat's blood pumping into each one. She shuddered.

Was this just another dream? Was she going crazy? She gulped the stale air. Maybe it was an experiment. Or maybe her husband was a killer?

Gina walked around each of the coffins and inspected them. Some seemed older than others, the wood darkened with age, but they were all in great condition.

They had been well cared for.

Her light glinted off something metal on the top of the current casket and she looked closer. It was a nameplate: Isabella DeLuce. She checked each of the seven caskets, and each one had a different woman's name and Louis's last name—Margareta, Colette, Isabella, Francine, Emily, Kathrine, and Jane. Were they sisters?

Did Louis keep his dead family members here in this room, instead of in a mausoleum? It wasn't like Atlanta was going underwater any time soon. Why would he keep them above ground? And what was with the goat's blood?

Trailing a hand along the edge of Colette's coffin, Gina bit her lip. Did she dare open it? She glanced toward the tub with the goat. It couldn't be any grosser than that, could it?

He told her not to come here. Her mouth was dry. She swallowed several times trying to wet it. What secret was he hiding in these coffins?

Curiosity burned in her gut. Pushing her questions back down, she flipped the latch on Colette's coffin. Lifting the lid, she shined her light down on the corpse. An emaciated female lay in the casket, wearing a long dress, a veiled hat, and gloves. The tube fed directly into her mouth and her eyes were open and staring.

Gina smothered a scream. Impossible. Vampires weren't real. She closed her eyes. Was she having some sort of hallucination? Holding her breath, she inspected the body.

Colette wasn't moving and didn't appear aware. Although Gina's eyes watered at the musty smell of old clothes, there wasn't any scent of decay. Mostly the woman seemed dried out, like a piece of beef jerky.

Modern fluorescent lighting flickered to life and exposed the whole room. Gina jumped and scraped her hand on the edge of the casket. Blinking, she turned and stared at Mrs. Peterson, whose portly form filled the doorway.

"Now, dearie, what are you doing in here?"

"Um…" Gina stuttered, her gaze darting to the large kitchen knife in Mrs. Peterson's hands. "Who are they?"

"The Master's wives." Mrs. Peterson smiled. Her grin seemed oddly vacant.

"Louis is a vampire?" Gina blushed at the squeak in her voice.

"Of course, but I don't think…" Her smile faltered. "The Master will be unhappy." Mrs. Peterson advanced across the wooden floor. The blade of the knife glinted.

Gina backed along the edge of Colette's coffin as slowly as she could. Her hands raised palms out in front of her. "I'm sorry. I know I'm not supposed to be in here."

"No, you are not. The Master told you."

Gina flinched. "I know, and I'm sorry. I truly am."

Mrs. Peterson raised the knife and charged at her.

Gina stepped back quickly and tripped over the decorative side of the coffin. Flailing her arms, she barely managed to stay on her feet.

The old lady swung, but Gina was younger and faster. She dodged the blow. Then, Gina shoved her shoulder into Mrs. Peterson's side. The woman toppled into the open coffin.

Gina watched in horror as the dried-out hands curled around Mrs. Peterson, holding her in place. A slurping sound echoed in the room, competing with the angry buzz of the fluorescents. Gina's breath came fast and heavy. She wanted to scream, but she couldn't get the sound to come out.

Mrs. Peterson didn't scream either. Her limbs thrashed as she fought the vampire, the knife dropping from her grip. Her eyes were wide and round in their sockets.

Gina's heart tripped as the woman ceased struggling and a beauteous smile crossed Mrs. Peterson's face. Gina knew she should run, but she couldn't seem to get her legs to move. The lividity drained away from the old woman's face and hands. The feeding seemed to go on forever.

Then Mrs. Peterson's body was released and a young woman rose from the coffin, her skin pale and long black curls streaming behind her. The woman's bright eyes stared at Gina. "Hungry," she whispered.

Gina gasped, backing toward the door. Her eyes darted to the knife, but she didn't think she could get it fast enough.

The vampire stepped over Mrs. Peterson's corpse toward Gina.

"Stop right there, Colette." Terrified, Gina waved her hands in front of her. "I'm not a meal."

The vampire cocked her head to the side and frowned. "You wear his ring." Reaching out, Colette caught Gina's arm and stared at the wedding ring. "You married him?"

Gina gulped, staring at the diamond. "Yeah."

Colette smiled sadly. "Then you'll soon be one of us."

"No way." What had Mrs. Peterson called them? *The Master's wives.* Had Louis been married before? Had Louis somehow made all these vampires? Gina's heart ached.

Gesturing to the coffins behind her, Colette said, "We are all Louis's wives."

"No." Seven times, he'd been married. Gina swiped her hand across her wet eyes. But Louis was different. He was kind and loving and…just as much a liar as her mother's bar hookups. Every one of them told Momma that they loved her and this time would be different, then they walked away as soon as they got what they wanted.

Colette patted Gina's shoulder awkwardly. "Je suis désolé."

Louis was a vampire. She didn't want to believe it, but the headaches, the cloudy thoughts, and the bruises ran through her head. "There's no way I'm gonna be a vampire."

Colette's delicate eyebrows drew together. "But you are just a puny human. He's centuries old and strong."

"But what if we wake them up?" Gina looked around the room. "Then there's seven, er, eight of us. Some of you are old too, right?" This wasn't the first time she'd had to fight for herself, but now she had to do it for all of them too.

"But we are starved." She frowned, her hands stroking the front of her ragged gown. "Louis has kept us locked up for so long."

Gina smiled. "I have an idea about that."

***

Tummies full of all the sleazy barflies Momma could provide, the now pink-cheeked vampires had raided the full closets of the mansion for fresh clothes. Now they were waiting less than patiently for Louis's return in the early hours before dawn.

Gina called out when his limo pulled around, and the vampires trooped upstairs to hide. Smoothing her dress, Gina pasted a smile on her face and tried to act normal. Colette assured her that Louis wouldn't have expected his enchantment to have faded.

The butler opened the door, and Louis strode in. "Gina, my love," he said, pecking her cheek.

"Oh, Louis, I've missed you." She injected her voice with as much syrup as she dared. "Mr. James has a lovely breakfast prepared for us." Gina led him toward the stairs.

He paused mid-step. "Mr. James? He's never cooked a day in his life."

No kidding. The taste of half-cooked eggs and burnt toast rose in the back of her throat. Gina maintained the insipid smile on her face.

"Where's Mrs. Peterson?"

Trying to keep her heartbeat steady, Gina swallowed.

"She's not feeling well."

Louis sniffed the air, and then he rounded on Gina, glaring. "There is much blood in this place."

"Did Mr. James cut himself?" Gina squeaked. The energy of his fury rolled over her, and she panted. Now that she knew what he was, she didn't know how she could ever have thought he was human.

Narrowing his eyes, Louis grabbed her forearm.

Gina cried out, "Don't bite me!"

He inhaled. "You're frightened."

"Y-yes."

"You've been in the forbidden room." He sneered. His teeth glinted in the low light, and Gina looked for fangs but didn't see any.

She nodded, trembling.

Louis opened his mouth wider, and his fangs descended. "Is this what you were looking for?"

Her whole body shook. It was real. Her Louis was a bloodsucker. "You've been feeding on me."

"Stupid humans can't follow simple directions." Louis's voice was thick with irritation. "Now, I'm going to have to kill you."

Her eyes darted around the foyer. The others were upstairs, and Mr. James was hiding in the kitchen. She yanked on her arm, but his grip was unbreakable.

"Why do you keep them?"

"My brides?" Louis pulled her against him.

Gina gasped. "Yes."

"To keep me company in my old age." Louis laughed.

She shuddered at the harsh sound. Gina glanced up the stairs and caught Colette's eyes as she peeked around the corner. *Help*, Gina mouthed.

Stall, Colette mouthed back.

Gina sighed. "Will you make me one too? Will I get a coffin?"

Louis leered. "Little Gina from the trailer park? No, my dear, you are just a snack."

"What?" Her lungs constricted and she couldn't catch her breath. A snack? Spots erupted in her vision and she bowed her head. She'd loved him, and she'd thought he'd loved her. But she hadn't meant anything to him.

Stiffly, Gina looked up. The color drained from her face at his amused expression. He was toying with his food.

"Maybe if we had had more time together, you would have made a fine addition to my collection." He traced the curve of her cheek. "But you've ruined that."

"Some collection, starving in a pine box." Colette strolled down the stairs.

"Mon trésor," Louis said, opening his arms. "You look ravishing as always."

Colette raised a perfect eyebrow.

His eyes perused her form. "Mrs. Peterson seems to have been quite a meal to restore you to your former beauty."

Colette laughed, like the tittering of champagne glasses. "As sharp as ever."

Gina looked back and forth between them. Her chest burned. There was so much history here. Little Gina from the trailer park could never hope to compete. Gina blinked. Not that she wanted to. He wanted to *eat* her.

Louis gripped Gina's shoulder. "Would you like to join me for a taste of little Gina?"

Colette smiled and came down the last few steps to stand in front of them. "Oui, mon amour."

Had Colette abandoned her? Gina's heart raced. She couldn't fight off one vampire, let alone two. She gazed at the sky, through the wide windows above. The sun had risen and its light filtered through. Had she fought her way out of the trailer park, only to die here?

Louis tilted Gina's head to the side. "A fragrant bouquet."

Colette leaned down, sniffing Gina. Her eyes on Louis, and her hand pushing against Gina. Colette shoved a small, rectangular box into Gina's fingers.

Tracing the edges, Gina forced her brain to think with these two predators leaning over her. *A lighter.*

"She smells delicious," Colette said, stepping back into a curtsy. "But you must have the first taste, my lord."

Trying to keep her body still, Gina flipped the lighter around in her fingers and opened the latch. She squashed a scream as Louis's teeth bit into her neck and her blood pulsed.

Pushing her thumb along the spark wheel, Gina held the flame against Louis's shirt. The heat burned her thumb but she didn't let go until the clothing caught fire.

Louis's teeth released her neck, and he pushed her away. Staring down at the tiny flames, Louis chuckled. "Silk doesn't burn well, you idiots."

The other wives rushed down the stairs. Colette grabbed a decanter from one of them and opened it, tossing the brandy over Louis. "But alcohol does."

Raising an eyebrow, Louis smirked. His shirt was soaked, clinging to the muscle beneath, but there were no flames.

Gina's stomach dropped. They were all dead, well, deader. There had to be something. Her eyes surveyed the room. If only they'd thought bigger. The empty hearth mocked her.

Then she had it. It was the only chance. Gina willed Colette to look at her and, when she did, motioned her head slightly to the right.

Colette nodded.

"Come on, my dears," Louis said, stepping toward them. "Time to return to your coffins."

The vampire wives rushed him, pushing him back across the room. Louis stumbled in the wave, and they carried him along. Their hands grasped his limbs and lifted his body.

"Stop. Put me down," he commanded, his eyes widening.

The group wavered, but they pushed on. Their sheer desperation overrode his magic.

Louis growled.

Gina sprinted for the door. Closing her hand on the brass knob, she yanked it open.

Not even pausing at the doorway, the vampire wives swept Louis out into the sunshine. Gina gasped. She'd thought they would throw him, not immolate themselves.

Screams burst from their throats as their skin blistered and fell away. They writhed in pain but held their course. Louis flailed against them, and Colette wrapped her arms and legs around him like a lover. She glanced back at Gina, her hair aflame around her head, and smiled.

The Veiled Queen

B. C. Marine

From within the darkest corner of the candlelit hall, Barbenia took a long sip of cider, marveling as the golden prince of Boscada reduced another maiden to tears. Barbenia couldn't understand a word of their conversation, but the meaning was clear enough when the offended woman covered her prominent nose and fled the room.

The next woman Prince Elio approached wore a golden tiara—probably a princess—and after they exchanged a few words in yet another foreign tongue, her sturdy frame shook with anger. Not the wisest move. Even at his considerable height, he only had a few inches on her, and she looked more than capable of bashing in his flawless visage.

Without a hint of concern, he turned toward Barbenia. The luster of his fair hair dulled as he stepped into the shadowy nook. He crossed his arms, silently looking her up and down, then cleared his throat.

With the fascinating display of self-destruction, she'd forgotten the advisement to let him hear her speak once before their first conversation. Otherwise, he would continue speaking in the last language he'd heard. She held out her hand. "Good evening, Your Highness. I am Barbenia, Queen of Uskev."

"Hiding from me in the dark?" he asked in perfect Uskevi.

"The view is better from here."

He smirked. "I cannot say the same."

She would not take the bait. "Your palace is lovely."

"Are you sitting back here to hide because of that scar?"

"I am not hiding from anyone," she said coolly.

"You should." He spun on his heels and looked around the room—likely searching for his next target.

Barbenia had not lied. The thin line that ran down the left side of her nose had not bothered her since it healed. Not enough to hide it, anyway. The darkness protected her sensitive eyes, nothing more, but he clearly would not care for the explanation. She had known people like him before, and such reasoning was irrelevant. He would only look for a new scab to pick.

An older version of Elio rushed to her side. "A thousand apologies, Your Majesty," King Lehen said. "Whatever offense he has caused, I shall correct it forthwith."

"I am fine, thank you, but you may want to catch him before he starts a war with a less forgiving queen."

Lehen nodded, and in a few long steps, reached Elio and grabbed his arm. "What do you think you're doing?"

Elio tried to pull away. "Leave me alone."

Strangely, they were not speaking Boscadan. They had both been speaking Uskevi to her and, by a fluke in their shared Gift of Speech, continued speaking it to each other. Unless someone pointed it out, they never could tell what language they were speaking. For all the father and son knew, they were speaking their native language now. If she didn't let on that she could understand them, and nobody interrupted in another language, she could listen indefinitely.

"You can't keep insulting these women. Placating noblewomen is one thing, but the foreign dignitaries?" Lehen shook his head. "For pity's sake, Elio, we'll be lucky if we only lose a few alliances."

"I told you not to press me," Elio said smugly.

"This isn't a game. These decisions affect whole kingdoms."

Elio rolled his eyes. "Why am I part of this? I'm at least sixth in line—no, soon to be eighth. You told me I wouldn't have to concern myself with all this."

Barbenia knew Elio was the youngest of Lehen's four sons, but not that his brothers were so productive.

"You still have a role to play," Lehen said.

"As a stud for hire to the finest b—"

"Enough! I cannot abide this anymore. If you keep this up, then, by the Giver, I *will* treat you like a dog." Lehen jabbed his finger into Elio's chest. "And I expect better than this from one."

Elio scoffed. "You wouldn't dare."

"You're spoiled, son. I've coddled you for too long. The future you so disdain is one of luxury, and you spit on it. Since you cannot appreciate what you've been given, I will not waste any more resources on you."

Elio cocked his head back with a sideways glance. "What is that supposed to mean?"

"I'm cutting you off. You will no longer enjoy the easy life of a prince. You can work from now on."

Elio waved him off. "You aren't serious."

"The first employer seeking manual laborers can take you. I expect you to be gone by this time tomorrow." Lehen flagged down a servant and, in Boscadan, began directing him to write something down.

Elio sputtered and let out a stream of angry Boscadan, but Lehen ignored him.

Barbenia finished her drink and walked out onto the terrace. With only the light of the crescent moon, her Night-Sight revealed the palace gardens in stunning clarity, as well as the harbor at the bottom of the bluff. Ornamental trees and grasses filled the garden above, with nary a berry bush or fruit tree in sight. Below, opulent galleons, schooners, and brigs occupied most of the slips. Though Boscada had no shortage of beauty, she hadn't come to see the scenery.

On paper, Elio was the perfect choice for a future consort. Boscada was strong and stable enough to make a valuable ally, but the prince was far enough from the throne to neither be needed here nor threaten the autonomy of her own kingdom. In more capable hands, Speech should have been his greatest asset. And to top it all off, he wasn't bad looking—who was she kidding?—he was gorgeous.

If only his arrogance didn't turn everything to rot.

Barbenia sighed. Would Lehen go through with his threat? He seemed serious enough, but she doubted he could so easily grow a spine after years of caving to Elio. Lehen would change his mind by morning. If Barbenia were in his position, she would've cut Elio off without delay to sooner undo the damage of a lifetime of favoritism.

She had plenty of means to teach him. When she was younger, her father would take her to either the woods or the bay every few months and make her catch dinner for the night. Not born into royalty himself, he never let her forget the humbler side of her roots.

She smiled. They were overdue for another outing, and she'd promised to catch a few salmon on the return trip. He wouldn't have to wait long for it. At the rate things were going here, her three-week trip would be over in a few days. Besides the disappointing prince, Lehen's need to put out Elio's fires would distract him from making trade agreements with her.

Ha. Hiring out Elio herself would be a more productive use of her time.

Wait. Could she?

She had the time to spare. If it worked, it'd be worth the effort. And if it didn't…well, she'd appreciate the entertainment.

***

Barbenia adjusted her daylight veil as Lehen inspected the deed to her newly acquired ketch.

He frowned. "Such a small vessel. Are you sure this is safe?"

"My men checked its seaworthiness when they purchased it, and I inspected it myself an hour ago. We will stay near the archipelago, deep within the Sound and far from open waters." She took back the deed and handed him two contracts. "As I am using my own time and funds for this…venture, I have drawn a trade agreement that I believe you will find fair."

"What about Elio's labor? How does that factor into your equation?"

Barbenia chuckled. "I think we both know what that's worth. Besides, I do not deal in slaves. He will be paid the same as any green deckhand, according to his work. As for the trade agreement, should Prince Elio come to any significant harm in my care, it shall be void."

Lehen raised an eyebrow. "*Significant* harm?"

"This is not a leisurely voyage. I will not void an entire trade agreement if your son gives himself rope burn while manning a sail."

"And this other contract?" He held up the paper. "Who is Thrush?"

"That is my father's surname. The prince will see that contract, and I believe this will work best if he does not know I am a queen."

"But he has met you before."

"Briefly. The veils that guard my vision against the sun will hide my face, and I do not wear a gown to fish. I will be shocked if he makes the connection out of context."

Lehen stroked his chin. "I need to read over these contracts. Meet me here in three hours. Elio will be ready for you then, if I agree."

"If? Am I not the first willing employer?" Barbenia put a hand on her hip. "Or are you reneging on your original offer?"

"You expect me to accept this without question?"

Barbenia smiled. "In essence, you wrote it. This is the same proposal you drew up for any royal willing to marry Elio. I simply replaced any references to marriage with employment."

His eyes widened. "And what will that leave me to offer if he does marry?"

Such a silly, short-sighted question. "He has no marriage prospects now. If you let him continue, his insolence will cost you much more than I am asking for."

He sighed and looked over the contracts again, then turned to one of his servants. "Bring Prince Elio to me."

***

Elio sauntered into his father's office. As if last night's public beratement wasn't enough. What did Father want this time? "You summoned me?"

"I would like you to meet Captain Thrush." His father gestured to a small woman at his right.

She looked more like a deckhand than a captain. The faded green scarf tied around her hair anchored a gray veil, which shielded her face from the top of her forehead to just past the tip of her nose. Saltwater stains spattered her sun-bleached brown tunic and slops.

"Hello, Captain… Father, why have you called me here?"

"Captain Thrush is your employer now."

Elio laughed. Father had outdone himself this time. Using an actual person to make his point? Elio wasn't a gullible child, easily cowed into submission.

"You have been hired onto her fishing boat."

"Yes, yes, very funny, Father. Was there anything else, or may I go now?"

Captain Thrush held out a stack of rough brown

cloth. "You'll need to change into these before we depart."

"I am not putting on those rags."

She shrugged. "If you wanna ruin your fine clothes, suit yourself. You'd best make your goodbyes now."

"Oh, goodbye, Father," he said sarcastically. This farce was becoming annoying.

Father teared up, then turned around and leaned against the window frame, bring a hand to his face. "Have a safe voyage. I will miss you."

Did he think pretending to wipe away a tear would be more convincing?

Thrush clapped a hand to Elio's back. "Come along, greenie."

Elio gasped. He didn't know which was more repulsive: the lack of honorific or the audacity to touch him. "How *dare* you! I am a prince!"

"Not anymore." She brandished a document. "'Cording to this, you're my new deckhand."

He snatched it from her. She was lying. The document couldn't be real. He looked it over and—no, no, no, no, no… "You cannot enforce this. I am not willing."

Father crossed his arms. "Your alternatives are to find another employer yourself or take up begging."

Elio's blood ran cold. "Are you banishing me?"

"You will leave with Captain Thrush, or the guards will escort you out," Father said in a tone he reserved for delivering unfavorable edicts. A tone he'd never used with Elio before.

Elio picked up the ugly clothes. Better to walk out with his head held high than to face the humiliating attention the guards would attract.

Father and Thrush waited outside while he changed. The tunic and slops hung loosely. They might have been comfortable in a proper fabric, but he'd never worn anything in such an atrocious cut. The open air on his calves felt downright strange, as if someone had either forgotten to add the last foot of fabric to his pants or stolen the garment from a much shorter and fatter man.

When he exited the office, Father was already gone. Without a word, Elio followed Thrush out of the palace. They wound through the streets, and for the first time, he had to dodge other people; they did not make way for him. The crowds thickened as they walked downhill, suffocating him with their nearness.

Within twenty minutes, they reached the wharf. A pungent low tide punctuated the briny wind. Sailors, dockworkers, and merchants bustled about, shouting over lapping surf and fluttering sails. A sweaty group of workers unloaded fish one by one, using their Ice to freeze them solid with their bare hands. A black and white eagle screamed overhead at a flock of barking gulls. A shining fleet of tall ships, twice as grand as his father's, were moored across a quarter of the docks, all bearing the same blue and yellow banner.

"I wonder whose fleet that is?" Elio said.

Thrush glanced at the ships without breaking stride. "That'd be the Uskevi flag. With a fleet that size, Queen Barbenia herself must be traveling here."

"How do you know about politics?" Such knowledge seemed above a commoner.

"I know boats, and I know the Sound. 'Tween the mainland on both sides and all the islands in the archipelago, different ports usually mean different kingdoms, too. Everyone's sailing the same water out there."

As they walked alongside the great ships, their glorious size and sleek paint grew more impressive. "I could have ridden on one of these ships."

"Well, you ain't now. Our boat's just a few yards up ahead here."

She turned down a ramp to a floating dock and stopped in front of the saddest boat in the world. It had only two small masts, the one in front relatively taller than the other. Nets and baskets filled most of the pitiful deck, and several patches dotted the sails.

Elio wrinkled his nose. "*That* is our boat?"

She smiled. "Hop aboard, sailor."

"Where is the rest of the crew? For that matter, where is the rest of the boat?"

She boarded effortlessly. "You *are* the crew."

He crossed his arms. "You lied. You said you were a captain."

"Where's the lie? I've a vessel." She patted a mast. "And I've a crew." She gestured to Elio.

"Of one."

"Still counts." Thrush grinned and held out a hand. "Need help boarding?"

He waved her away and held up his head. "I have boarded a ship before. It is only a foot from the dock."

As he took a large step, the dock shifted backward. He pitched forward into the boat. It tilted downward. He leaned to compensate. His feet slid across the deck until he landed on his rump.

Thrush covered her mouth and snorted. She thought this was funny? Impudent sea-wench.

Elio glared at her. "You moved the boat!"

She held up her hands. "I didn't touch nothing. This ain't as stable as a ship. The dock and the boat move with the water. You'll get used to it."

He didn't want to get used to it.

She fiddled with the sail, tying and untying ropes. "Watch for the boom."

"The what?"

The sail swung around overhead, and the boat strained against the lines holding it to the dock.

She fastened another part. "Work starts now. Throw the lines."

When he didn't move, she pointed back to the dock. "Untie us."

Elio reached for the nearest cleat and began pulling on the knot.

"Ah-ah. Not that one. You'll lose the rope that way. The dock first."

He stretched out to the farther cleat and tugged on the loops. "How was I supposed to know that?"

"Common sense?"

The knot was impossible. No amount of tugging helped. The boat just pulled it tighter again.

With a sigh, Thrush leaned next to him. "Look." She took hold of the rope end that wasn't attached to the boat and yanked the knot free in one motion. As they glided away, she hauled the rope in and coiled it at their feet.

"How did you do that?" Elio asked.

"I'll get there, but let's start with the basics." She pointed to the front of the boat. "That's the bow." She pointed at the back. "That's the stern. We're at starboard, and…"

For half an hour, Thrush taught Elio nautical terms, adjusting the rudder and sails throughout. His head ached from trying to keep up. When she finished zigzagging out of the harbor—or tacking, as she called it—she sat at the stern.

"That wind should be good for a while. You've had a nice little break." She tossed a short length of rope onto his lap and held another aloft. "Now for something more difficult: knot tying."

***

Elio's fingers throbbed. He couldn't tie another knot.

Thrush frowned at the misshapen mass of rope. "It'll do. I've a more important task for you now anyway."

He leaned his head against the rail and groaned. How could there be more? "Have I not done enough? When is lunch?"

"We need to haul it in first. Up you get."

"You cannot be serious. My hands are ruined!"

She lifted a lid from a large wooden box near the stern. "I let you man the rudder while I set the nets. Consider that your break."

Elio gaped. "That was hours ago." This woman was trying to kill him.

She crossed her arms. "It was only an hour. We're pulling it early so you don't get overwhelmed on your first haul." Steadying the tiller between her knees, she hoisted in a rope over the stern, and a line of wooden buoys moved toward them. "The wind's perfect to gently back us over the net, so I can help with the net this time. As I bring it in, pull the fish and put 'em in that box of ice. You'll need to move quickly."

"But—"

"Here they come." She lifted the end of a sheet-like net over the rail, dripping water at their feet. Two-foot salmon hung by their gills at intervals, their heads wedged into the square openings.

He grabbed at one of the fish, but it flopped, and his hands slid over the wet scales. Again he tried, using a firmer grip this time. Its gills ripped and bled.

"Ugh!" Elio yelled and dropped the fish. It bounced off the rail into the water with a plop. The same happened with the next two fish.

"Hey! Don't be dropping my catch," Thrush barked.

He shuddered. "They were moving."

She rolled her eyes. "Living things do that. Quit dropping fish overboard, or you'll go with 'em."

Once more, he took hold of a fish. It flopped out of his hands again, but this time, he leaped after it and batted it back before it went over the rail. While the salmon flopped around the deck, he repeated the process until the gillnet was empty.

Thrush turned around. "Get the lid and— Why are there fish roaming my deck?"

"I did not drop them overboard."

She growled. "You incompetent sponge—" She removed a knife from her pocket and flicked it open. "I said to put 'em on ice."

Elio backed against the railing and clutched at it. His feet slid on the wet surface, refusing to flee as he required.

She slashed the knife across the gills of the nearest fish. "All this stress'll ruin their taste. We need to put 'em out of their misery." She handed him another knife. "Cut the gills and put 'em *on the ice* this time."

He took the knife from her, and they set to work. The first several were easy enough; they were barely wiggling. But many still flopped around. He poked at one with his knife and missed.

"Put the knife down, and grab it with your hands," Thrush said. "One of us is bound to lose a finger if you stab randomly like that. We need to chill the livelier ones to slow 'em down."

They chased the fish across the deck, throwing them on ice and occasionally bumping into one another.

Elio wiped his brow with his sleeve. "This is madness. How do you do this all the time?"

"I don't." She dropped a fish into the box. "The fish ain't supposed to be on deck." She covered the box of ice then sat on it.

He moved to join her but slipped on the briny, bloody deck and landed half on the box with his arm across her shoulder. A slow grin spread below her veil until she cracked up. The melodic noise caught him by surprise, and he found himself laughing with her.

"Oh, Elio." She sighed. "What am I gonna do with you…" She lifted a hand to his face.

He tensed. Was she making an advance on him? The nerve.

"You got fish guts on your cheek." She laughed again as she wiped the offal away.

His face warmed. His dignity was slipping from him like the fish. "We still have a catch, at least."

"This?" Thrush patted the box. "Ain't worth much. It's a small haul, and with the poor handling, only the dogs will eat 'em."

"Surely, we can rest after all that."

She produced an oilcloth bag from behind the box and reached inside. "I'll get lunch ready, but first"—she pressed a bundle of rags into his chest—"you're gonna scrub down this mess. I ain't laying my bedroll in guts."

He sighed, then did a double-take. "Excuse me. Did you just say 'bedroll'?"

***

Elio squinted and rolled over on the salty bedroll, which did little to cushion him from the wooden planks below. Around him, inky waters melded into spiky profiles, serrating the starscape above. As the boat glided silently through the abyss, only the gentle creak of Thrush's footsteps broke the isolation.

He glanced in the direction of the sound, but the moonlight was too weak to see by. Thrush might as well have had Invisibility. Nothing but himself and the shadows now. Elio shut his eyes once more.

At home, he'd fought for power over his life. Now he was truly powerless. Perhaps the key was not in fighting.

Perhaps it was in surrender.

***

Barbenia inhaled the fresh, salty air and gingerly picked her delicate veil off the line where she'd left it to dry overnight. She enjoyed the breeze on her face, but the dawn would soon blind her if she didn't replace her eye cover. Elio didn't concern her. For all his whining that he couldn't sleep on deck last night, exhaustion had faded him in tandem with the sun, and he didn't look close to waking anytime soon.

Without the veil or Elio in her way, the night sailing had been pleasant. A few stiff winds had let her get some real speed. She would have to manage the sails more today and leave the nets to Elio. Given his ineptitude thus far, she didn't have high hopes for his success.

Barbenia stole one last unfettered look at his sleeping form. The fine layer of stubble and grime did little to mar his looks. If anything, it made him more ruggedly handsome. Ugh. Good thing there were no reflective surfaces on board. That was the last thing his ego needed.

She fastened the veil. It didn't matter how pretty his face was; the man ruined everything he touched. Barbenia reached into her tunic and pulled out a whale pendant, kissing it for luck as Father had taught her, then tucked it back inside.

With her pocket knife and flint, she lit the small pile of cedar chips in her ceramic cooker. When the flame was steady, she laid down pieces of salmon and shielded it with a lid. If the smell didn't wake him, she wouldn't try to. Better that he sleep through cooking. He might set the whole boat ablaze.

Barbenia checked their heading while breakfast cooked. Thanks to the favorable winds overnight, they weren't far from Uskev now. But he wasn't ready for that yet; she was nowhere near finished with him.

Satisfied with the cooking, she suffocated the fire. "Elio," she singsonged, "time to wake." Barbenia dangled a piece of grilled salmon over his nose.

He groaned and rolled over. She poked him in the back with her foot, but he groaned again and swatted at her.

"So much for a pleasant 'good morning.'" Barbenia leaned over the rail and dunked a cupped hand in the frigid water. "Last chance."

Elio didn't stir.

"Suit yourself." She flung the handful of water in his face, flicking her fingers a few times for extra measure.

He gasped sharply and flung himself upward, then sputtered and flailed.

Barbenia smiled. "Gooooood morning, sleepyhead."

"Flaming frog nuggets! I thought I was drowning. You're sadistic."

"Tsk, tsk. Not very princely language."

"I thought I was a sailor now."

She gave a hearty laugh. "True enough." Perhaps she was getting through to him better than she thought. Barbenia offered him a fillet. "Breakfast?"

He wrinkled his nose. "Fish again?"

"I'm sorry, we're all out of roast elk."

He took the proffered food with an apologetic grimace.

Barbenia wolfed down her own breakfast and sat at the stern. "We're coming up on a good spot. Get ready to drop the net."

Elio gulped. "I'm not done eating."

"Hurry up then. If not, you can finish after we drop the gillnet. You'll have more than enough time later."

He shoved the last, large piece in his mouth and joined her at the stern. His cheeks bulged out like a squirrel stuffing nuts.

She covered her smile. Better not to mock him when he'd finally demonstrated a will to work. She cleared her throat. "Feed the net in slowly, starting with this flag. We need the floatline on top and the leadline on the bottom, so don't twist it. And take care over the rail. Lift it over. Don't drag it."

He nodded and picked up the end of the net. To Barbenia's surprise, he followed her directions to the letter. When the sails demanded her attention, she felt secure leaving him to finish on his own.

Elio dropped the last buoy. "Now what?"

She handed him a line. "Let's try your hand at sailing."

***

Elio tied down the boom and smiled at Thrush. Now that he'd given up railing against his situation, he found the experience…exhilarating.

Even Thrush was more pleasant. Had she softened toward him, or was it the rush of coastal wind and sea spray making him giddy? Away from the palace, she looked at home on the bow, with her face to the wind. Her rough nautical clothing flowed in the breeze. A midnight braid coiled in and out of her headscarf at her nape. There was a strange, wild beauty to her.

She bounded down the deck. "You're learning well now."

He leaned back on the rail. "I must have a good teacher."

"Now *that* sounds more like someone with Speech. I always thought flattery was second nature to your kind."

"Ha. It's just easier to grasp when you're not worried about translation."

She crossed her arms. "Guess the same goes for insults as well."

He hung his head. "Did my father tell you why he hired me to you?"

"He didn't tell me why you did it. You had every privilege in the world. Why'd you throw it away?" Thrush sounded curious, not accusatory.

His father didn't understand. What were the chances that she would? He inhaled and let the breeze wash over him, imbuing him with its freeing exposure.

"I felt trapped," he said. "Growing up, Father sheltered me, showered me with praise. He favored me. When I turned twelve, it only increased his favor."

She nodded. "You got his Gift. Reminded him of himself."

"Exactly. Boscada was prosperous, our neighbors were peaceful, and I was already far from inheriting. I didn't have a care. He ensured that."

"Sounds like you led an easy life."

"It was. When Father heard about the war on the mainland, he changed his mind. Suddenly, it was my responsibility to make an alliance or shore up the loyalty of one of our lords. I was excess personage, too far removed to matter in succession and not trained for anything of consequence."

"He prepared you for nothing and punished you for living up to it," Thrush said matter-of-factly.

Elio gaped. "Yes. I tried to explain it to Father, but he never listened. He only cared when I sabotaged his plans." He had never felt such a sincere connection before, and he fought a peculiar urge to hug her.

She put a hand on his shoulder. "Well, you're not gonna be useless anymore. Fishing's a fine, respectable trade. We're in the Strait of Keesvoy now. You know, a fisherman in these waters once caught the eye of a queen."

He shook his head. "You don't need to make up a legend for my sake."

"No, really. A Baythroan crew was fishing here when an Uskevi fleet passed through. The Uskevi were hungry, and their meat had spoiled unexpectedly early, so they offered to buy the Baythroans' whole haul."

"What about the queen?"

"She was so pleased with her meal, she wanted to thank the fishermen personally. One of 'em made the queen laugh, and she requested to see him again and again and again until, eventually, she made him her consort." Thrush had the smile of someone retelling her favorite story.

The tale sounded so far-fetched to Elio. He'd met an Uskevi queen, and unless she was different than her ancestors, she seemed far too regal to take an interest in the affairs of fishermen. "Do you think it really happened?"

"Every sailor from Baythroas to Uskev will swear to its truth." Thrush looked out over the water. "Ready to circle back to our net?"

"I can try."

She smiled. "Good. You take the sheets. I'll take the tiller."

They tacked back to the net, and Thrush dropped anchor. "The wind's much stronger than before, so I'll need to focus on keeping us steady while you haul. Do you think you can handle it?"

He wanted to get it right this time. "All the fish will be on ice." Elio took hold of the flag buoy. "Ready when you are."

Thrush trimmed the sails again and stood by the tiller. As soon as she weighed anchor, the boat drifted back. Elio heaved the net over the rail, pulling fish out and icing them as quick as he could.

After a few good heaves, his muscles ached. He pulled the net again but failed to lift it high enough, letting it snag on the rail. A palpable ripping sound informed him of his mistake. He panicked, looking for the tear.

"Don't stop." Thrush tugged on a line. "I'm going as slow as I can in this wind. We'll run over the net if you don't pull."

He kept working, taking extra care to lift the net high over the rail, but his strength flagged again and again. By the end of the net, he was ripping it as often as he cleared the rail. He dropped the last fish on the ice and closed the box, then slumped on top of it.

Elio had failed again.

"How's the catch?" Thrush sat down next to him. "I don't see any fish on deck. That's a good sign."

He couldn't look at her. "I—I ruined the net."

"Let's see." She got up and lifted the gillnet, one yard

at a time. One to two-foot holes slashed the netting throughout. She whistled. "That's gonna take a long time to repair…if it's even worth it. We may need a new net."

Disappointing her hurt worse than the blow to his pride. "I'm so sorry. If I knew how, maybe I could do the repair."

Thrush sat next to him. "We can get another net. You're not the first fisherman to destroy one, and you won't be the last. Do you know how many have been lost? They drift away with the current, or the buoys sink, or a whale makes off with it. It happens."

Elio looked at her. "You're not angry?"

"Let me see the haul," she said calmly.

They stood up, and she lifted the lid. Countless salmon filled the box, covering the ice completely.

She grinned and closed the box. "They look to be in good condition. You did well, Elio." She gave him a playful shove. "Not bad for a greenie."

***

Barbenia pulled the boom tighter and secured the line. The southeaster was in perfect position for blowing them straight to Uskev. The angle pushed them into higher speeds, bringing faster winds across the deck than they'd experienced yet. She took the blankets from their bedrolls and approached a shivering Elio at the bow. Wrapping one around him, she said, "You're too cold. Come with me."

He followed her back to the stern, where they sat on the deck in front of the tiller. "What's the plan when we reach port?" he asked.

"We'll offload the haul, buy a new net. We're making good time, but if it's late when we get there, we'll stay overnight." She waited for him to make a fuss about the possibility of a real bed.

He continued shivering under his blanket. "Then I

hope we're not late. I don't want you to lose time as well as the net."

Barbenia didn't know what to say. It was the most empathetic thing he'd said since she met him. She moved closer and wrapped her blanket around them both.

Elio looked at her. "It's funny. You've seen me lower than anyone in my life, but I've never seen your face." He slowly brushed his fingers along her jaw, ruffling the edge of the veil as he grazed her ear. His gentle touch called to a deeper craving within her, beckoning her to satisfy it.

Barbenia wrapped her hand around his and lowered it. "It's too bright outside." Though she could have closed her eyes, she wasn't ready to reveal herself yet. She wanted to believe this other Elio was real, but she needed to see what he would do in Uskev.

He laced his fingers between hers. Were his eyes always such an intense pine green? The gray of her veil hardly softened the vibrancy of his gaze, as if he could see right through. He leaned in ever so slightly, his gaze traveling down to her lips, and Barbenia's breath quickened.

"I can wait for starlight," he said.

"Not if you fall asleep first," she teased.

A brief, quizzical frown passed over his face. "Why are you up all day? Surely, you work better at night."

"Who says I don't work at night?"

He leaned back and tilted his head. "But when do you sleep?"

"I rested for an hour after you fell asleep."

"You must be exhausted."

Barbenia shrugged. "I can't let the boat steer itself. We'd run aground in the night."

"Why don't we stay in the harbor tonight, even if it's not late?"

She yawned. "That's tempting."

If the wind kept up, they could sail for an hour without changing tack. Barbenia stretched out her legs and settled back, expecting to feel hard wood against her back. Elio's arm cushioned her instead. She hadn't noticed he was leaning on it.

"Oh, here." He grabbed a bedroll and tucked it behind her.

She smiled. "Thanks." As she sat back, her lids grew heavier. After a few minutes of relative comfort, the weight of her head became too much. She could not deny her body rest for much longer. Like it or not, Barbenia would have to rely on Elio. "Wake me if we…if we…"

"I'll wake you when we're near the harbor."

"But what about…what if…"

Elio chuckled. "Or if we veer off course. You can trust me. Just sleep already."

Her head lolled onto his shoulder. "Don'touchm'veil…" she mumbled.

"I wasn't planning on it."

Sleep overtook her desire to press the issue.

***

Elio reached up behind his head and steered a little farther east. Thrush still rested against him, her warmth filling him with contentment. True to his word, he hadn't tried to peek at her face—not that he wasn't tempted.

Ahead, a bright and colorful city perched atop a long wharf. At its peak, a blue and yellow palace spread across half a mile. Lush evergreen forests surrounded it all.

Thrush nestled closer, and Elio smiled. He would have to make larger adjustments soon as they approached the shore, but he hated to wake her. She needed the rest. He laid the second bedroll out on her other side, then gently eased her onto it. Until they made berth, he could continue handling things.

Elio made it to the mouth of the harbor and eased the sails, letting the boat slowly glide toward the docks. Signs pointed the way to docks designated for unloading seafood. He had the boat under control, but it occurred to him that Thrush hadn't taught him how to dock yet.

Dare he try? He'd failed at fishing, but sailing had gone well. He rolled up the mainsail, letting momentum carry them to the pier.

As the boisterous clamor of the wharf overtook them, Thrush bolted upright. "I thought you were gonna wake me."

"I was doing fine," he protested.

She rushed to the bow. "How'd you plan to dock by yourself?"

"The same way I sailed by myself?"

She shook her head. "You can't steer and catch the dock at the same time." Leaning her whole torso over the rail, she reached her arms out and took hold of the edge of the dock, pushing against it and swinging the starboard side toward the pier. "Take the other end."

Elio rushed to his right and followed her movements.

The harbormaster walked over to their section. "What do we have here today?"

"We've got a large catch of salmon for Chef Anja," Thrush said.

He wrote in his ledger. "And you are?"

"Thrush."

The man's head snapped up. "Oh, I didn't realize…"

She shook her head slowly. Even for a woman who covered her face, it was an oddly mysterious gesture.

He cleared his throat. "Ah…uh…I'll get some men to unload for you… Have a nice day?" The harbormaster scurried off and flagged down two burly men.

"I'll get the net. You tie up the boat," Thrush said.

Was she going to pretend that was normal? Elio raised an eyebrow. "That was an odd exchange."

She lifted a full armload of netting. "How so?"

"He acted strangely when you told him your name."

"I just share a name with a more popular captain here." She stepped onto the dock. "Are you coming?"

He quickly looped some rope around the dock and the boat and followed her onshore. The harbormaster watched as they passed, but he turned away when he saw that Elio was watching back.

There was something weird about that man.

Not far down the wharf, Thrush led Elio to a net-maker. The little old man looked over the damage. "I could repair it," he said, "but the time'll cost you more than a new one. I could buy this one off you for scrap and—"

Someone shouted. A crowd had formed on the pier they'd just left. Elio and Thrush ran to see the cause of the commotion.

Two dockworkers held the box from Thrush's boat aloft, and the dock beside them was empty.

The boat was drifting into the harbor.

Frog nuggets. Was there nothing he couldn't foul up?

Elio took off toward it. He couldn't let her boat get away.

Thrush jumped in front of him, arms outstretched. "What do you think you're doing?"

He reached for the hem of his shirt. He'd want it dry when he got out of the water. "This is my fault. I'm going to get it back."

She pressed him back. "No, you're not. That water is deep and, more importantly, cold. You can't swim in that."

"But—"

"*No!*" She took his face in both hands, forcing him to look at her. "That boat's not worth drowning for. Either another boat'll catch it, or high tide'll wash it back."

He dug his hands into his hair. "I lost the boat."

"I know."

"I lost the boat." He couldn't fail any harder than that. The fish. The net. They were nothing compared to the entire boat.

What was worse: he'd lost *her* boat.

She took his hands. "Just breathe, Elio. Come with me." She led him a bench, far from the crowd, and sat him down. "I know you already feel terrible, but I'm afraid I'm gonna have to end our contract," she said gently, putting a hand on his shoulder. "Without a vessel, I don't have any work for you."

He went numb. "I have nowhere to go," he murmured.

She reached into her tunic and pulled a thin gold necklace over her head. "Take this." She pressed the pendant into his palm. Time and hands had worn the white jade orca smooth. "My father works in the palace. Go there, and ask for Thrush. Show them this pendant. He will help you."

More strangeness from his mysterious captain—or former captain—but he had no right to demand answers now. "You won't come with me?"

"I've got my own matters to deal with."

Elio put the necklace on. "Will I ever see you again?"

She nodded. "I'm sure of it. Just promise me you'll go to the palace and ask for Thrush."

"I promise." After all he'd done, he couldn't believe she was helping him. He would have promised anything to thank her. He would make this right someday...somehow.

"Until we meet again, Elio." Thrush walked away without looking back.

It took all of Elio's willpower not to chase after her.

***

As Barbenia stepped into the welcome dimness of her private wing, she peeled away her veil and scarf. "I brought your favorite dinner with me," she said in Baythroan.

Father's face lit up as he hugged her. "You're back

awful early."

She shrugged wearily. "Plans changed."

"Should I be worried?"

"Not at all. Lehen signed the best possible agreement. Uskev got everything it needed." Despite the overwhelming political success, a sense of incompleteness nagged at her.

He cast a wary glance over her shoulder. "If that's the case, why are you alone? I thought he'd only sign that in exchange for a marriage."

"We struck a bargain. There's no marriage," she admitted.

He grinned.

Barbenia put a hand on her hip. "Why are you smiling?"

"I'm sorry. You know how I feel about those kinds of arrangements." He'd always reminded her that she never would've been born had her mother married for politics. He wanted Barbenia to find love as they had.

She sighed. "Yeah, well, you might be right. I may have…I don't know." Elio was attractive, and she'd felt *something* between them, but she couldn't dare to speak her emotions into being. What if she were wrong?

Father's smile turned bittersweet. "You look so much like your mother just now."

Barbenia squeezed his hand, blinking back the threat of tears. She cleared her throat. "I have a favor to ask— Well, a few, actually."

✳✳✳

Pausing to catch his breath, Elio ran his thumb over the whale pendant and looked around the courtyard. It'd taken at least a dozen wrong turns to get this far, but he'd finally made it to the palace. Though many winding paths had led upward, it was difficult to judge where they'd end from downhill.

He caught the attention of a helpful guard, who directed him to the servants' entrance. There, another guard with Speed zipped in front of him as Elio attempted to step inside.

"I don't recognize you, and you're not delivering anything. State your business," the guard said.

"I'm here to see a man named Thrush. Someone told me he works here."

"I'll let him know you're here to see him. And you are?"

"He wouldn't know me." Elio removed the necklace and held it out. "I was told to show him this."

"Wait here." The guard ducked in and whispered something to a servant before turning back to Elio. "He should be out shortly. You can have a seat for now." The guard gestured to wooden stool a few feet out of the way outside.

Elio sat with his back against the yellow siding. Before long, a simply dressed man with black hair walked out. As he approached, the fine quality of his plain attire became more apparent. He must have held a respected position here.

The man stopped in front of Elio. "You asked to see me?"

Elio lifted the pendant. "My name is Elio." His title was irrelevant now. "Your daughter sent me. She said you could help."

"With?"

"She hired me onto her boat, but I'm afraid I bungled everything…" He recounted their whole voyage— omitting the part about snuggling under a shared blanket, of course. "…and I have nowhere else to go."

"I see," Thrush's father said. "Come with me."

Elio followed him inside. The first corridor was the same painted wood as the outside, but the interior grew more grand and detailed as they ventured deeper in, far past where a man dressed in fishy rags should be allowed to wander. They walked for ages until they reached a dimly lit passage.

Thrush's father knocked on a door and entered. "Wait here."

It seemed everyone was saying that. Elio couldn't remember waiting for anyone in his life until today, but change itself had developed into a pattern lately—as had failure. Only one of those things was worth fighting.

He rocked on his heels and took in his surroundings. Even in the soft candlelight, he could make out the fine wooden inlay of the panels on the wall. His father would envy such a beautiful palace.

What kingdom was he in? He'd never thought to ask, and it seemed a silly question now. His inability to distinguish what language people spoke did not help. He should've paid more attention to the flags he'd passed along the way.

The door opened, and Thrush's father beckoned him closer. "Her Majesty has graciously agreed to an audience and is, fortunately, free to meet right now."

Elio gaped. "Her Majesty?" Who would have guessed Thrush was so well connected? Elio wished he'd thanked her more profusely for such a favor.

"The Queen of Uskev is a busy woman. Best not to keep her waiting."

Elio stepped forward stiffly. Uskev? That would be Queen Barbenia. His breath caught in his throat. Oh no. He hadn't been kind to her in the brief time they met. She would be justified to throw him out on sight. But he needed to atone for all his mistakes, not just the ones against Thrush. He took a deep breath to steady his knees and pressed himself into the shadowy room.

Sumptuous jewel-toned fabrics draped around the darkened room. Queen Barbenia occupied a rich blue armchair at the center. A red satin gown flowed over her. Raven hair fell in tousled waves around an elegant face. The hairline scar he'd disparaged before was of little consequence to her striking appearance.

Elio bowed low. "Thank you for your time, Your Majesty."

She regarded him coolly. "I have been informed of your plight. What skills do you have?"

"I have Speech and recently learned to fish and sail, though my proficiency in both is severely lacking."

"I currently have little use for an interpreter."

Elio clasped his hands together. "Please, Your Majesty. I will do whatever you ask, but I must work. My request is not for my own sake, but for the woman whose boat I lost."

Her expression softened. "You ask nothing for yourself?" Her tone was so familiar.

He lowered his head. "I have not earned it."

"On the contrary. You did well, Elio. Not bad for a greenie."

Impossible.

He looked up gradually. Her mouth. He knew that mouth. He'd caressed that jaw, wanted to kiss those lips.

Elio turned to Thrush's father. He had the exact same shade of dark hair as his daughter—and the queen.

Elio blinked. It wasn't real. A dull ache lodged in his chest. She wasn't real…

"I apologize for hiding my title," Barbenia said, "but I promise everything else was true. Speaking of which, I don't think the two of you have been properly introduced. This is my father, Hector Thrush."

Hector held out his hand. "Pleased to meet you, Elio."

Elio shook it cautiously. "The fisherman who married a queen?"

"They call me Prince Hector or the Prince Father

now, but yes."

Elio turned back to Barbenia. "This was revenge for how I treated you, wasn't it?" The Giver knew he deserved it, but it didn't fit with the woman he'd come to know.

"No, not revenge," she said softly. "I did not wish to strike you down. I gave you a chance to grow, to become a better man."

True. She could have been much crueler if revenge were her aim. "Why the ruse?"

"If I came to you as a queen, my orders would have been a show of power. So I humbled myself by your side."

"And my father?"

She took a deep breath. "He signed a trade agreement in return for this arrangement, but my end of the bargain is fulfilled. You are free to do as you please now."

"What do you mean 'free'?" His father had used that word too many times in reference to his so-called choice of marriage.

"If you want to return home, I will order a ship at once. If you wish to stay in Uskev, you may stay. My father has generously offered to teach you more fishing and sailing, if that's what you desire."

Hector stepped forward. "We can have a boat ready by tomorrow."

"If you want something else instead, simply ask," Barbenia said.

"Anything?"

She smiled. "Within reason. If you wanted to take up pickpocketing, I couldn't help you."

Elio knew what he wanted. The desire had been with him before he stepped foot in the palace. He'd thought his chance had sailed away with the boat, but here it was again.

"I now realize that even as a prince, I did not deserve to ask, but I come to you, even less deserving now as the worst fisherman in the world"—Elio dropped to his knees and bowed his head—"and humbly request your hand."

The silence was interminable. He had overstepped his bounds. Her gown swished quietly. Why didn't she answer?

A red satin hem appeared at his knees. Barbenia knelt down and took both of his hands in hers. Elio lifted his head.

She smiled as tears trailed down her beautiful face. "I would love nothing more."

The Thief and the Spy

Katelyn Barbee

Once upon a time in an unhappy kingdom…

Theo pulled his hood lower as he approached the seedy tavern. He scratched the doughy skin of his cheek, rubbing the sagging tip of his nose. The masking potion had done its job, but left his face hot and itchy. Though he was unlikely to be recognized so far outside the city, he still wasn't taking any risks.

He skirted around a puddle, his boots squelching through the fresh mud.

Inside, he strode over to a thickset man wiping down a table. The owner, based on the missing ring finger and pinkie. Just as he'd been told.

"I'm here for Mr. Smith," Theo demanded, using a gruff voice. "He's expecting me."

The man jerked his thumb toward the rickety-looking staircase. "Room eight."

Theo ascended the steps, keeping his breathing steady. Drunken laughter boomed, and emerald smoke crawled from beneath one door. The lanterns lining the walls flickered, and a noxious, heady odor stung the back of his throat. He coughed.

Nothing like being in a den of illegal magic. Hopefully, it meant people would mind their own business.

He rapped twice on door eight.

"Who is it?" a familiar male voice called.

The tight coil around Theo's chest eased. They'd sent Paul. It wasn't a trap, then.

"Mr. Brown," Theo answered. "I'm here to settle an account."

"Which one?"

"Three-eight-one-seven-two-two."

The lock clicked, and the door opened a crack. "That is an *ugly* face." A hazel eye peered at Theo. "And you're late."

Theo pushed the door wider and slipped inside the room. "Abandoning my classes for the day would've looked odd." He bolted the lock, then settled into the chair across from Paul. "This isn't about recruiting, is it?"

"The safe house in Kingshire was burned down last night, courtesy of Emperor Ignatius. He sent a battalion of revenants, not that the papers will mention them." Paul's voice lowered, his face darkening. "Left more than ten of our people dead."

Theo inhaled a shaky breath. So many... How many of the dead did he know?

Paul's flinty gaze locked on Theo. "We need more people to compensate for those we've lost. Preferably those with unique abilities who can also hold their own among the aristocracy. Amelia's orders."

"And she wants me to do that *now*?"

"Of course now. Your father's annual Festival ball is the perfect opportunity." Paul leaned forward, tapping a finger on the chair arm. "Use your Persuasion on the crowd. Uncover people's allegiances and turn a few of them to our cause."

Theo's face grew hot, though not from the potion. He might as well try to steal eggs from a dragon's nest. "But I'm unregistered. If they catch—"

"So are most of the other nobles. I doubt anyone will notice unless you prod them too hard, and I know you won't. You're too smart for that." Paul flashed him an encouraging smile. "You're the best we have."

I'm the only one you have. Using his ability to sniff out people's loyalties was a good way to get caught. Or worse, executed and forced to serve in Ignatius's growing and unstoppable undead horde. But gathering dissenters was another chance to avenge his brothers. He grimaced. That, he could not pass up, but it meant visiting Father.

Paul laid a hand on Theo's shoulder and squeezed. "We need you…"

Theo stood abruptly. It was worth the risk. "I'll do it. You'll have your new recruits come Festival's end." *Or I'll be caught and this whole operation is doomed.*

***

Theo stared at the palatial house that was no longer home. The white face and ivy-wrapped columns looked the same as when he had left two years ago for university.

"Here we are, Viscount Townsend." The yellow-clad Blinker released his arm. "Will you be needing anything else?"

"No, thank you." Theo handed the man a small wad of notes, the world drifting at the edges of his vision. Despite frequent Blinking, he still wasn't accustomed to the sudden jolt of starting in one place and ending up in another, sometimes hundreds of miles away.

The man nodded and vanished as the front doors opened.

Ancient Mrs. Kingsley, the housekeeper, toddled out. "Young Master Theo! You've returned!"

She threw her arms around him, the top of her head grazing his chin, and laughed. "You've grown taller."

He grinned. "Or you've shrunk."

"Still all cheek, I see." She patted his face, clucking her tongue like he was a naughty five-year-old. "How long will you be staying? Until Festival is over, I hope?"

He matched her slower pace as they headed inside. "I think so."

Her steps faltered. "It'll be good for your father to see you. Help ease his mind."

She led him toward his father's study.

He kept his eyes straight ahead when they passed his brothers' old quarters. Not that long ago, they'd been putting toads in each other's beds or using silly charms to fill each other's rooms with purple smoke that tasted of pond water or stale socks. Heaviness settled in his chest. Those days were no more.

In the study, Father sat at his desk, reading *The Gazer*. Wispy smoke issued from the ivory pipe clenched between his teeth. When he looked up, the corners of his eyes crinkled. "Theo," he said softly.

Theo inclined his head. "Father."

"I'll put the kettle on," Mrs. Kingsley chirped, whisking out of the room like someone half her age.

When her footsteps had faded, Father chuckled. "She's excited to see you."

"And you are not?"

"Of course I am." Father's smile faded, his mustache twitching. The paper crinkled as he set it aside.

Theo sat across from Father, trying not to grip the armrests too hard while he read the headline: ELEVEN KILLED IN FIRE! ACCIDENT OR ARSON?

"I have to admit, I didn't think you'd come after your last letter." Father's eyes glimmered with happiness. "But I'm glad you have."

"About that..." *Let's get this over with.* He took a breath. "I have a request for the ball."

Father puffed on his pipe before speaking again. "Which is?"

"I want to invite everyone in the city to attend. Not just the highborn and wealthy merchants." Theo chose his next words carefully. "A ball truly worthy of Saint Andrew and his giving spirit." He glanced at Father. "Like the one where you met Mother."

Father's brown eyes scrutinized him, clearly trying to determine if he'd been attempting Persuasion. He hadn't, of course. Accidents still happened but he never intentionally used his ability on Father. He would not stoop so low.

"I will agree. If you do something for me in return."

Should have known there'd be a condition. "And what would that be?"

"There will be many lovely young noblewomen in attendance, including the Duke of Eddington's daughter."

"Her?" Even if Bridget had been against the emperor, she was still a spoiled, empty-headed brat.

Father glared at him. "I know you dislike her but the duke is very well off and close to Emperor Ig—"

"I will not court someone who supports that usurper."

Is this what his brothers had dealt with once they'd come of age? Father nagging them to marry well and produce an heir? Growing up a third son, Theo had been allowed to do as he pleased, but now, with his new, unwanted position, that was no longer possible.

Father flushed a bright red the way he always did whenever the subject came up. "Keep your voice down." His gaze darted to the door. "You shouldn't speak about the emperor that way, not if you want this family to survive."

Theo scoffed. *What family?* Henry and Ben were dead because of that imposter's foolish campaign to take the continent. He took a breath and held it until the urge to shout faded. But he shouldn't be angry with Father. After all, he was only trying to protect him from the Emperor.

"I'm not doing this to be cruel, Theo." Tapping the ashes of his pipe on the nearby tray, Father leaned forward. "I only want to know your future is secure before I part this life. Please, make a serious effort to find a bride, and you may invite whomever you wish."

Theo resisted the urge to roll his eyes. Father always made it sound like he would die before the year was out. "All right, but if I don't find anyone, you'll allow me to complete university before I search for a wife again." There, two years was reasonable, wasn't it?

Smoke rings floated into the air. "As long as it's clear you've genuinely tried. And no Persuasion." Father's voice was stern. "If the Emperor found out—"

"He'd force me into his service or kill me," Theo finished the unneeded reminder. "I'm aware."

Father held out a hand. "Do we have an agreement?"

Theo sighed but shook it. This was going to be tricky. "Very well."

***

Asha slipped off the leather glove and pressed one of her wooden hands against the safe door. If it weren't for lines across her wrists where flesh and wood met, no one would be able to tell the difference. They were even the same bronze shade as the rest of her.

She exhaled slowly as she turned the dial. It was a newer V-series model and supposedly uncrackable. A faint smile tugged at her lips when she felt the gentle vibration of the first number beneath her fingertips.

A sudden, impatient pull within Asha's mind made her startle and turn the dial sharply. *What is it, Dove?*

Cecilia's having trouble keeping Mr. Benson downstairs. Dove's words were clipped. *How much longer?*

Asha let out a long sigh. *I'll be quick.*

I'll tell Cecilia. Dove's presence slipped away.

A knot formed in Asha's gut as she refocused on the safe and turned the dial slowly. Another vibration at thirty-eight. Then fifty-one. Thirteen. Nine. Her stomach calmed.

She turned the handle and opened the safe door.

Well, that was eas—

Empty shelves greeted Asha. Nothing?

Her spirits fell, spiraling away like water down a drain. How could there be nothing? Mother would be furious if she didn't return with the jewels.

The heavy thud of Mr. Benson's boots and the sharp staccato of Cecilia's heels ascended the stairs at the end of the hall. Asha froze, forcing her breathing to remain steady.

"Oh, what a handsome painting!" Cecilia's smooth voice dripped with practiced awe and surprise. "That can't be you!"

"Yes, I was quite a looker in my youth, if I do say so myself."

Asha imagined Mr. Benson's throat ballooning like a giant bullfrog's as he chortled. The man certainly had enough chin for it.

Cecilia let out a high, girlish laugh. "I'd have to agree."

Laying it on thick today. Asha rubbed the space between her eyebrows. The dull but growing headache signaled Cecilia was losing her grip on him but she would regain it soon enough. None of their marks could ever resist Cecilia for long.

"And this one here?" Cecilia's heels tapped along the hardwood floor, moving away from the vault room. "Is this you?"

The pain in Asha's head lessened.

"No, my eldest," Mr. Benson said cheerfully. "Come, the piece is this way." His footsteps and voice grew distant.

When their voices became a faint murmur, Asha gently shut the safe door and slipped on her glove. She peeked out into the empty hallway and crept to the bedroom beside the stairs. Mother would probably confiscate her hands for a week, but she couldn't skulk around with Mr. Benson so close. Perhaps if she explained what had happened, Mother would give her another chance.

She opened a window, using the clinging ivy to climb to the ground.

Dove appeared from behind a rosebush. She beckoned Asha to follow, her blond braid swinging as she jogged to the tall, thick hedges sheltering the property from the main road.

Bright afternoon sunshine forced Asha to squint as she trailed Dove. "The safe was empty."

Dove whipped around, her pale blue eyes widening. *But I thought—*

"I did too." Asha slipped through the narrow gap between two shrubs, ignoring the branches tearing at her loose tunic and trousers.

What are we going to tell Mother? Dove's terrified voice rattled around Asha's brain as they hurried along the mercifully empty road, a rare stroke of luck with the Festival of Saint Andrew only a couple of days away.

In town, the streets were already flush with newly arrived vendors and rich, starry-eyed foreigners from every corner of the ever-growing empire. Easy marks. Mother would likely have her and Dove pickpocket when the hour grew late and the cider and mead had gone to the newcomers' heads.

Asha chewed the inside of her cheek. "The truth. Maybe she'll allow us one more try."

Dove gripped her braid, tugging on it. *You really think that will work?*

"No, but it's better than no plan at all."

***

Asha's throat constricted as they entered the recently repainted townhouse she and Dove called home.

Mother glided down the stairs, one of her dainty hands trailing the polished banister. "Back so soon, girls?" Her voice was sweet. Too sweet. That always meant they were in trouble.

Dove's grip on Asha's arm tightened.

"We ran into a problem," Asha murmured. "The safe... It was empty."

"Oh?" Mother's eyebrow lifted a fraction, along with her voice.

Reluctantly, Asha removed her gloves, stuffing them into a back pocket. Better to save herself the tongue lashing that would follow if Mother had to remove them instead. "But if you just give me another day, I'll—"

"No need." Mother headed into the drawing room.

Dove's lips pressed together. *Something's off. She's never this calm when we fail her.*

Asha silently agreed and followed Mother with cautious steps. She perched on a cushion of the new, plush sofa beside Dove.

Mother held up an envelope with a red Townsend seal. "The Earl of Fleetford has issued a general invitation this year for his ball. Rumor is he's hoping to find a wife for his son."

"Why would he ever want to do that? We're not of noble birth or rich." Asha shook her head. "We're terrible prospects."

When the emperor had taken over after King Albert's murder, Townsend parties had become exclusively upper crust. One hard look at Asha or her sisters was all it took for the veil of deception to fall away and reveal their lack of funds or proper breeding, despite Mother's efforts for them—well, Cecilia—to appear otherwise.

Mother smiled. "I doubt that will matter. The earl's late wife was as common as they come."

Dove stiffened, crossing her arms. *So what's the job?*

Probably wants us to steal something, like always. Asha licked her dry lips. "Are we going to find husbands?"

Mother laughed harshly. "Not you two. You're going to gather secrets we can exploit, but Cecilia... If she could

Persuade the viscount…"

And there we go. Dove sighed.

Mother's sharp gaze narrowed on Dove. "Anything you'd like to share, darling?" Her icy tone meant she was not in a testing mood.

Dove folded her hands in her lap, eyes downcast.

"That's what I thought." Mother stood, tapping the letter against her palm. Her voice became honeyed. "Go make yourself useful in the kitchen. Dinner needs cooking."

Dove's eyes glazed over as she stood and drifted out of the room.

Pain sliced through Asha's skull. She gritted her teeth. At least she had the illusion of choice, something Dove never had. Persuasion had never worked on Asha, so Mother had found an alternative to ensure her obedience.

Mother gestured to Asha. "You know the price of failure."

With a sharp yank, Asha removed one of her hands. Mother would only keep them longer if she hesitated. The wood returned to its lifeless state.

Mother yanked her other hand free. "You can have them back for Festival."

Two whole days? Asha kept her gaze on the ground. Complaining about the unfairness of her stolen hands wouldn't get her anywhere. A fae had gifted them to Asha as thanks for her family sheltering her during one of the emperor's raids. Only faint wisps of the cherished memory remained now, much like those of her real parents. They had died not long after, and Mrs. Gladstone—Mother—had taken her in.

Mother waved her away. "Get out of my sight."

***

Asha huddled under her blankets, trying to fight off the autumn chill invading the attic. She shivered, goosebumps rising along her arms.

A knock on the door made her sit up. She squinted as light from the hall and Dove's lamp flooded the room. In Dove's other hand was a tray.

The mouthwatering scent of fresh pea soup wafted over to Asha. She wiggled out of her blanket cocoon. "You're a lifesaver."

Dove sat down on the bed and stirred the soup. *It isn't right for her to take away your hands like that.*

Asha shrugged. "It is what it is. Where's Cecilia?"

Picking through the new dresses with Mother. Dove held out a spoonful to Asha. *I don't know how she expects you to starve for two whole days before Festival and then help find our next mark.*

Asha's stomach rumbled in approval as she tasted the soup, the pleasant heat warming her. And though she hated being reduced to helplessness, unable to feed or relieve herself, she appreciated Dove's help. Dove was the best sister she could've hoped for, even if they weren't blood-related.

"At least we'll get to eat some decent food there," Asha half-joked. Mother never bothered to feed them well unless someone important was visiting.

Hey, my soup's not that bad. Dove grinned. *Maybe we'll find husbands.*

Asha laughed harder than she meant to at Dove's hopeful tone. "Always a romantic."

The rest of the girls their age would certainly be looking for husbands, that was true, but not them. No one wanted a handless girl or a mute.

"Maybe Cecilia will," Asha whispered. "But not us."

I know, but I can still dream, can't I? Dove offered another spoonful.

"I suppose dreams are all we have," Asha said, more to herself than Dove.

Cheer up, Asha. Dove smiled. *You never know what the future might bring.*

***

Theo's eyelids drooped as Bridget droned on about the latest fashions in the capital. Father murmured something to his neighbor, the Duke of Eddington, while he and the other members of their small circle nodded approvingly.

"Theo, did you hear me?" Bridget's lips pressed into a thin red line.

"You were talking about silk from the Azure Isles. Prices are much too high, but the quality is worth it." Thank goodness university had taught him to regurgitate facts when he was only half-listening.

She leaned in, placed a hand on his arm, and whispered, "I shouldn't say this, but the emperor plans on making my father governor there. The fae are hostile and can't manage the country properly. Best we take over and put them in their place." She released him, smirking. "But, as I was saying, the change in color is so fluid. Superior to anything we have here."

She twirled, sending nearby ladies into envious twittering as her gown shifted from turquoise to blood red.

An appropriate color for all the lives it had probably cost.

Theo locked away his rising anger. He took her empty wine glass. "Allow me to get you a fresh drink."

Bridget fluttered her eyelashes and giggled. "Very kind of you."

"I'll be right back."

So the emperor had taken the Azure Isles, one of the last fae strongholds. He'd probably enslave them, or more likely try to exterminate them, if his record with the goblins and giants was anything to go by. At least some of that horrid woman's incessant babbling had proven useful.

Now if he could just find more recruits. He'd managed to convert four common folk to the cause already, but more were needed. Still, it was an impressive number given how many times Father had pulled Theo away to meet noblewomen and their wealthy parents.

Theo's stomach grumbled uncomfortably. Perhaps he could have a quick bite before he was missed. He hurried toward a long banquet table. Father had really outdone himself this year with the roasted dragon. It was a blue Whiptail—no bigger than an ox, but just as delicious as larger, rarer species.

"Excuse me, Viscount Townsend?"

Theo turned. A mother and daughter—the resemblance was too uncanny for them to be otherwise— approached him. The younger, lovelier creature wore a rich plum gown embroidered with pale pink roses that emphasized her generous bust. She smiled and dipped into an impressively low curtsy.

The mother did the same. "We wanted to thank you for the opportunity to attend. Extraordinarily gracious of your family to think of the little folk."

Theo inclined his head. "It's my pleasure. Everyone should be able to enjoy the festivities, Mrs...."

"Gladstone." She placed a delicate hand on the younger woman's shoulder. "And my daughter, Miss Cecilia Gladstone."

"It's a pleasure to meet you." Cecilia curtsied again, her voice warm and inviting. She brushed a copper curl away from her face, smiling with lips the color of rose petals. The perfect shade for her porcelain complexion. And those smoldering eyes, so green, like—

Theo had to stop himself from groaning. *Not another one.* She was Persuading him. Well, trying to. Three other noble girls had tried already, but her ability was the strongest he'd encountered tonight. He hadn't felt the pull, the magnetism initially, but once he'd recognized it, the spell had broken. Few, he suspected, could escape her charm, unless they already knew how to break free. "I'm sorry, if you'll excuse me."

Cecilia's smile waned. "Of course, my lord."

He wove around a pair of giggly young women trying to catch his eye, then inched past the massive gut of a foreign ambassador deep in discussion with local tradesmen.

Bridget's shrill laughter sounded. He craned his neck. Father was speaking with her, probably regaling her with old stories of—

Wham!

Theo nearly tripped but caught himself. The young woman he'd slammed into fell, her plate of food smashing against the hardwood. A couple of pumpkin tarts rolled away, settling at the feet of a nearby dignitary.

"I'm so sorry! Are you all right?" Theo's hand shot out. "Here, let me—"

"Not necessary." The girl ignored his hand and stood, picking crumbs from her curtain of ebony hair before brushing them from the front of her silver gown, staining it orange. She frowned at her satin gloves, covered in the gooey crushed remains of a tart.

Most guests ignored the girl. A couple laughed, only falling silent under Theo's glare. A servant attended to the floor as Theo grabbed napkins from the closest table.

His cheeks burning, he offered them to the girl. "I can have your gloves and dress cleaned. Or would you prefer new ones?"

"Neither." She snatched a napkin, wiped her bronze face, then handed it back. Her skirts swished as she glided toward the courtyard doors.

He blinked. Well, that was curious. A girl who didn't want to talk to him. Still, he needed to make things right and it gave him a legitimate excuse to stay away from Bridget that much longer.

Theo made his way through the crowd. Cool autumn air blasted him as he went outside. Rising on his tiptoes, he caught sight of her near the hedge maze of midnight suns.

The glowing yellow blooms shook as she swept past them. He headed into the tall shrubbery, following the glimpses of her silver gown, but every time he almost caught up, she managed to lose him again.

He turned a corner and came face to face with her. Theo halted.

She wore a deep scowl, her arms crossed over her chest. "Is there a reason you keep pursuing me, Viscount Townsend?"

He cleared his throat. "I only wanted to make things right. I didn't mean to offend. As a host, it's my du—"

"As I said, it's not necessary." Her hard expression dissolved into a frown. "I appreciate your intentions, but perhaps you should return to your other guests. I'm sure there are dozens of young ladies who would be thrilled by your attention."

Well, at least she's not afraid to speak her mind. Perhaps she was from one of the smaller surrounding villages, then. Noble women rarely gave him their true thoughts on anything, too afraid to offend and hurt their chances with him.

"I have had more than my fill of their attention this evening, miss. Would you at least allow me to send someone to your home tomorrow to repay you for the damages?"

"Are you always this persistent?" Was that a hint of amusement in her voice?

"Generally." He chuckled. "You would not be the first to find it one of my more irritating virtues." Father certainly did.

That got a fleeting smile. Perhaps he was wearing down her defenses.

But the frown returned. "I'm afraid I cannot give you an address." She walked away.

"Wait!"

Theo's magic crawled its way to the surface and forced itself behind his words. He shoved it back down. The amount released had been small and the effect negligible, but the burst had been unintended. *Need to be more careful.*

She faced him and the fury burning behind her dark eyes made his insides shrivel.

"How dare you."

"No, wait, I—"

She disappeared behind a hedge, the steady clip of her heels fading quickly.

That had gone splendidly. Not only had he ruined her dress, but now he'd offended her.

He shook his head. But she couldn't have been aware of the magic, could she? No one could detect a burst that small unless...

Unless she's a Nuller.

His heart thudded against his ribs, panic spreading like a poison. He only knew of two Nullers in Albion. One worked for the emperor's secret police to sniff out Persuasion users among the royal court and upper classes. The other... He was either dead or in hiding.

New energy flooded his veins. He jogged down the path she'd taken. She could be an asset to the resistance...if she wasn't already working for the emperor.

***

Asha walked faster, twisting down several empty maze corridors.

She glanced over her shoulder. *The nerve!* Asha scrubbed her forehead with the back of her hand. It hadn't hurt, just a sudden tingling between her brows, but she knew Persuasion when she felt it. A pity too. Stubborn and even a little charming, he'd been doing quite well until he'd tried it on her.

But the Townsends weren't known for any magical talents. *Probably unregistered then.*

She turned another corner, following the brightly

colored paper lanterns strung above her. Maybe if she kept following them, she'd find a way out.

Dove's presence entered her mind. *Are you all right?*

Fine. She huffed. *Just had an encounter with Viscount Townsend.*

Mother saw him run into you. Dove's voice was filled with dread. *She says you're to return home and wait for her there. She wants to know what happened.*

Asha scoffed, shaking her head. She'd be blamed for taking his attention away from Cecilia. Unless she told Mother about his Persuasion. But then Mother would blackmail him so he'd marry Cecilia.

She shuddered. Even he didn't deserve to be under Mother's thumb for the rest of his life. No one did.

***

When Mother arrived home past midnight, she grabbed Asha's arm, dragging her into the drawing room. "What did Viscount Townsend say?"

Asha obediently recounted most of what had happened, leaving out the part about his Persuasion. The hairs on her arms stood on end at Mother's wicked grin.

"I do believe I've got an idea." Mother went to the drawing room door and opened it. "Come, girls! We need to have a chat."

Asha settled on the sofa as her sisters entered.

Dove plopped down beside Asha while Cecilia took her usual place beside Mother.

Cecilia's eyes narrowed. "What were you thinking, talking to Viscount Townsend? You were supposed to be—"

A glare from Mother silenced her. "Never mind what she was supposed to be doing. Fate has dealt us a stroke of luck. Cecilia, you will leave Townsend to Asha."

Cecilia's expression soured like old milk. "Her?"

"*Me?*" Mother couldn't be serious. She was only

supposed to follow people and uncover their secrets. Interacting with marks was Cecilia's job.

Dove's face fell.

"Yes, *you*. Tell him you've reconsidered his offer and invite him to visit our home after the second ball tomorrow." Mother's smile turned smug. "It's too risky to try at the party, but I doubt he could resist the two of us together."

"But—"

Dove squeezed her arm. *Don't, Asha.*

"But what?" Mother's eyes narrowed.

Asha shook her head. "Nothing. Of course, Mother."

***

Theo kept smiling despite his aching feet. The endless dancing hadn't helped, nor the long hours of standing listening to politicians, nobles, and common folk. At least recruiting was still going well. He'd managed to convince another three, giving him seven in total. Paul would be pleased with that number, even if they were common folk and only a couple of them had useful abilities.

He twisted around Princess Astraia of Ionia, the latest girl Father had set upon him. Happily, Bridget had already moved on to other prospects and Astraia was agreeable, though perhaps a little too enthusiastic when it came to dancing. The woman had incredible stamina.

He waited with the other men as the women circled, and he scanned the crowd for the girl from yesterday. Although he'd spent every spare moment this evening searching for her, he hadn't spotted her yet. His heart skipped a beat. What if she wasn't here tonight? Worse, what if she came back and had him arrested? It would kill Father.

The music slowed and the dance ended.

Theo clapped and bowed to Astraia. She grabbed his

hand, jerking him back into the mix of dancers. "Let's go again."

"Perhaps some refreshments first?"

"Oh, just one more."

A lively fiddle tune started up, with people clapping to the beat.

He inclined his head. "Very well."

One more dance and then he'd excuse himself.

A bronze face in the crowd caught his eye. Her raven hair was coiled at the base of her neck, decorated with tiny blossoms a few shades lighter than her golden dress, a gown much finer than the one she'd worn the night before, oddly. She kept her chin held high as she drifted past the line of dancers, unaware of him or, more likely, ignoring him. *At least she's here.*

A mix of relief and excitement twisted within him. If she was going to turn him in, she would've done it already. That ruled out the spy angle…unless she hoped he'd incriminate himself. Either way, he needed to test her allegiances and perhaps even recruit her.

The dance quickened, and Theo took Astraia's hand, switching places with her. As she moved further down the line, he vanished into the crowd. Astraia would be annoyed, but he could deal with her later.

He caught up with the mystery girl near one of the feast tables. "I need to speak with you."

She kept moving, hurrying past servants carrying trays of cider.

He pushed his way through the crowd, following her. "Please. Just a moment of your time and then I'll leave you be," Theo promised.

Her steps slowed. "If I agree, will you stop following me?"

"Yes. I won't try anything again."

She glanced around the room. "All right. But perhaps somewhere…away from the noise?"

***

Asha followed the dark-haired viscount upstairs into one of the rooms. Books lined the mahogany walls, the scent of tobacco clinging to the air. Old newspapers were strewn across a small table with an ashtray.

He closed the door behind them. "This is my father's reading room. No one will bother us," he said in a reassuring voice. "Only members of the household have access, and the enchantments will zap any eavesdroppers. We can speak openly."

Asha paced to the window, chest tightening. She'd meant a quiet corner or outside in the gardens, somewhere she would be visible to Mother, yet far enough away to talk freely. Not alone with him in a private room. It wasn't proper, and Mother wouldn't like Asha being out of sight, though perhaps this would be easier without eyes on her.

Dove, perched on a bench below the balcony, stared up at her with wide, fearful eyes. Strange she hadn't contacted her yet, though maybe the enchantments were interfering with Dove's telepathy. Asha flashed a reassuring smile, hoping to ease her sister's mind.

Soft footsteps approached, and she turned sharply, crossing her arms over her chest.

He held out a hand. "Can we start again?"

She didn't budge. A handshake was too risky, even with gloves on. Regret burrowed beneath her skin. Luring men into traps was Cecilia's job, not hers. She was supposed to gather information and report back, like Dove.

He cleared his throat, hand finding the pocket of his blue waistcoat. "I'm sorry for last night. I wasn't trying to make you stay—well, not like that. Sometimes strong emotions bring out my ability."

That was surprisingly honest of him. Perhaps too honest. What was he playing at?

"You're forgiven." She touched her necklace,

twisting the chain around a finger. "I…overreacted yesterday. Viscount Townsend, I—"

Just say it. Get it over with.

Her breath came faster, but the words stuck in her throat. Her gaze fell to the wrinkled newspaper, the headline proudly proclaiming the emperor's latest victory over the northeastern countries.

She grabbed it. The emperor had almost reached the other side of the continent now? No wonder so many young men had gone missing in the last few weeks. Though Mother had always discouraged her from doing any sort of reading, she picked up bits of news running errands in the market and during jobs. *Why can't I just do as Mother asks?*

"Rather sad, isn't it?" His posture stiffened, jaw set. "So much death."

"Yes…" Asha's lips pursed. At least she could be honest with him about something. She'd only been a child when the king had been assassinated, but life had become worse under the emperor. Mother often resorted to selling people's secrets when they were desperate enough for funds. Occasionally, when she was in one of her fouler moods or they'd displeased her, she threatened to hand over Asha or Dove to the police.

He studied her. "I didn't take you for someone interested in politics."

"What the emperor does affects everyone. But his luck will run out. No man can win every battle."

Viscount Townsend wore a grim frown. "He can if every soldier that falls is added to his army."

"Revenants?" Bile rose in her throat.

He picked up the paper. "Supposedly, the emperor takes care to deploy revenant forces discreetly—small groups, under the cover of darkness. That's why we never hear about them, I imagine."

"Oh." She'd heard the rumors, but one necromancer commanding so many dead at once…it should've been impossible. But Townsend was a noble, and they knew more secrets than anyone else, which meant it was probably true.

"I'm in no position to ask anything of you, and I know I'm being rather forward for asking it, but would you meet me tomorrow?" He smiled warmly, making the dimples in his cheeks stand out.

Asha's gut clenched as she went to the door and opened it a crack. She threw a teasing smile at him over her shoulder the way she'd seen Cecilia do. *Mother's going to kill me.* "Maybe."

***

"You stupid girl!" Mother ripped off one of Asha's gloved hands. "I ask you to do one thing and you cannot do that properly!"

"Let me try again, please." Asha winced. *Why can't I follow simple directions?* "He's meeting me tomorrow. I'll ask him then."

Cecilia scoffed. "I told you she couldn't do it. She's too soft. Let me at him again."

"He resisted you last time," Mother snapped. "We keep to the plan. Asha *will* convince Townsend to come here after the final ball."

Tell Mother you'll do it so she'll leave. Dove's voice surged with barely contained excitement. *I need to tell you something, alone.*

Asha started. Dove rarely entered her head without warning, which meant this was important. She kept her gaze low, hoping Mother hadn't noticed.

"Of course, Mother. I won't fail you."

Dove shrunk back against the wall, slinking toward the stairs.

Mother yanked Asha's remaining gloved hand free. "You can have them back tomorrow for the ball."

Once Mother and Cecilia had disappeared into the

kitchen, Asha followed Dove upstairs.

Sorry about that. Dove took her arm as the hallway lights bloomed into life. *I thought I might burst if she stayed any longer. I listened to Townsend's thoughts after your encounter with him tonight and I learned something interesting.*

Asha's chest tightened. *What is it?*

Dove led her into the attic, shutting the door behind them. The bed wheezed as she sat on it and grinned. *He's a spy for the resistance movement.*

"Townsend?" Asha fought to keep her voice low. She'd thought the last of the rebellion had been quashed for good years ago. "You've got to be kidding. He's a nobleman. His family has always been loyal to the emperor."

Dove shook her head. *A carefully constructed façade. Townsend's been recruiting resistance members for two years. Why do you think he won't leave you alone? You're a Nuller. He wants you to infiltrate the courts with him.* She grinned. *He rather fancies you. Cecilia would be furious if she knew.*

Asha's head spun. "How did you keep all this from Mother?"

Easy. I gathered enough secrets on other people to satisfy her and never brought up Townsend.

A smile tugged at Asha's lips. "And she thinks you're not clever."

Dove took her forearms gently, eyes going round. *You would be free of Mother if you joined Townsend.*

"That wouldn't end well." She was already in enough trouble. One more mistake and she'd never be allowed outside the house again.

Dove's eyebrows rose. *So you'd rather Townsend be under Mother's control for the rest of his life? You'd let him share our fate? Cecilia nearly Persuaded him the first night. I'm not sure he could fend off both her and Mother.*

"It's too much of a risk." She lifted her arms to show her stumps. "I'd never get my hands back if she found out."

Dove's face fell. *Then what good is living?*

"I'm sorry…" Asha's heart jumped up into her throat. "I don't have a choice."

You do. Dove's eyes flashed with defiance. *Don't let fear choose for you.*

***

On the final night of celebrations, Theo waited in the gardens for the mysterious girl. Fireworks shot skyward with a scream, the first bursting into the shape of the mighty river dragon Skurra, the second taking the glittering knightly form of Saint Andrew. The two battled fiercely for several moments before they both exploded into sparks and rained down on the oohing and ahhing crowd like a shower of starlight.

Where was she?

The hour was growing late, nearly midnight. Once the fireworks were over, everyone would go home and he'd lose his chance. *Maybe I'm in the wrong area. Why didn't I tell her a place and time? Oh right, because I'm an idiot.*

Theo passed through the manor doors into the stuffy interior. At least recruitment had been a success. Ten new recruits would please Paul even if he wasn't able to convince the girl to join. True, most of them were common folk and possessed no abilities, but they were more passionate about the cause and easier to turn than his fellow nobles.

Unfortunately, doing recruiting had probably cost him university. Theo's disappearances hadn't gone unnoticed by Father. Worse, though he'd explained he'd been meeting the mystery girl, Father thought him a liar when he couldn't name her.

He squeezed past the large crowd surrounding an illusionist, entranced by the vine-like snakes lifting off her fingers. The snakes twisted to form the weathered trunk of a tree. A kaleidoscope of enormous glowing butterflies landed on the wood, their wings shifting to a new color with each flap.

His gaze darted from face to face, stomach in knots. Still no sign of her. What if she hadn't come after all?

*****

Asha pulled up her glove again so it covered her bicep. This pair was looser than the others, but Mother had insisted on them because they matched her new dress. This gown, made of light, airy fabric and the pale blue of a midday sky, was even more exquisite than last night's.

A firework burst above the crowd, filling the smoky, sulfur-tinged air with a brilliant flash of red light.

Mother tugged a strand of Asha's hair, making her wince, and secured it back into place. "There. You look perfect. He won't be able to resist you."

"Yes, Mother." Asha's voice came out as a whisper.

Dove crossed her arms. *You still have a choice.*

It's not so easy. Asha bit her lip. *Mother will find out. She always finds out.*

Dove turned away and disappeared into the crowd. *Not if you run. Just think about it.*

Mother took Cecilia's arm and glided toward the garden. "Go, Asha. Make me proud."

Bitterness stuck in the back of Asha's throat. Make her proud. That was the last thing she wanted to do. And yet, she still shuffled toward the manor. No matter what she thought or felt, she had to obey. She had no choice.

Asha pushed through the crowd. Townsend, being nearly a head taller than the women hovering around him and wearing a vibrant green waistcoat fringed with gold, was easy to spot. She approached and tapped him on the shoulder.

He spun, breaking into a dazzling smile. "I was beginning to think you might not show."

Her chest tightened. He was so pleased to see her.

No one, except Dove, was ever that thrilled by her presence. And here she was, about to lead him into a trap.

"Sorry I'm late." The constant dread of her task had made her prolong getting ready for the ball. Well, until Mother had threatened to remove her hands for the next few days if she didn't speed up.

He offered an arm, lowering it when she refused.

Asha pulled at her glove again. "Can we go somewhere less crowded?"

"My father's reading room is available again."

"No, somewhere else." She glanced toward the garden. Mother and Cecilia were watching her from the crowd. "Maybe somewhere outside? I rarely ever have a chance to see fireworks."

His blue eyes brightened. "I know the perfect spot to view them."

He led her out of the crowded manor, heading toward the surrounding woods. "It's just this way. Not much fur—"

"Theo!" commanded an angry voice.

Townsend halted, blanching.

A mustached gentleman in his fifties emerged from the crowd. When he caught up with Townsend, he grabbed his arm and began to drag him away. "Where have you been? The Duchess of Rouen has been looking for you everywhere."

"Forgive me, it is not my place to speak, my lord, but the viscount was only being a good host." Asha kept her voice soft. "I am to blame for his recent disappearance."

The man startled, quickly releasing Townsend's sleeve. He inclined his head to Asha, cheeks reddening. "My apologies, miss, I did not mean to intrude."

The muscle feathering in Townsend's jaw relaxed. "If you'll excuse us, Father, I promised the young lady some fireworks."

"I see." With a curious twinkle in his eyes, and

mouth hinting at a smile, the earl said, "I'll leave you to it, then."

When the earl had gone, Townsend leaned over to Asha. "Thank you."

"For what?"

"For saving me from being thrown at another noblewoman. My father's rather keen on finding me a bride." He smiled. "I think he expected to find me shirking my duties, not with you."

"Oh." Warmth crept up Asha's neck and she laughed nervously. If Dove hadn't told her about Townsend wanting to recruit her, she might've thought he meant to propose.

A weight dropped into her stomach. But she wasn't here to join the resistance or marry him, only to betray him.

Another dazzling explosion of light burst above them as Townsend motioned to the trees. "Did you still wish to see the fireworks?"

Her breath hitched but she nodded.

Townsend led her into the woods to a small pond on the edge of the property. The steady croak of frogs and rhythmic chittering of beetles greeted them. Fireworks boomed in the sky, their blue and white reflections exploding across the water.

Asha ducked under the branch of a hazel tree. "How much farther?"

"We're here." Townsend pried a stone loose from the soil. He flicked it across the water, grinning when it skipped several times.

"It's lovely." If it had been a different day under different circumstances, she might've found it romantic. But not today.

"I used to play here with my brothers, before the emperor pressed them into service." He tossed a pebble. It landed with a heavy plop.

Asha chewed on her lip. "What happened to them?"

"Killed in action two years ago, or so my father

wrote me. I had just started university when it happened." His gaze fell, voice growing softer. "Their bodies were never returned. We can't even bury them in the family plot."

"But you were spared?"

"A way to keep my father in line."

It was a common enough tale. If the emperor suspected your family to be disloyal, he soon tested your faith. Sons were sent off to war, rarely returning, while daughters married into loyal families far away from their homes.

"I'm sorry, Viscount."

He smiled at her. "Call me Theo, if you wish."

"I'd rather not." *I don't deserve to.* "I…wanted to talk with you about something. The first night we met, you offered to have my dress taken care of."

Dove's presence pressed against her mind. *Don't do it, Asha.*

Asha started. She glanced around. *Where are you, Dove?*

"Are you all right?" Townsend cocked his head.

"Fine." She waved a hand in front of her face as if she were swatting away a fly. "Just a bug."

You always have a choice. Dove's voice was forceful.

"What were you saying about the dress?" Townsend gestured to her gown, eyeing her with curiosity.

She took a breath. "I've changed my mind."

"I was only supposed to be in town for festival, but I could call on you. Where do you live?"

Stop making this so hard. Her heart thumped against her ribs. "It's on… I…"

He frowned. "Are you certain you're all right? You look pale."

I can't do it. He doesn't deserve it. "I have to go." Maybe if she could return home before Mother and Cecilia, it would give her enough time to gather her things and escape with Dove.

"Wait!"

She twisted away, but he caught her hand. She felt the tug as it detached, and the silken glove slid along her skin.

Theo made a choking noise.

Idiot! Asha ran without glancing back to see if he followed. She'd ruined everything.

***

Theo stared at the gloved hand in his. Carefully, he slid out the hand.

He squinted, running his fingers over the hard, smooth surface. It looked exactly like a real hand, but closer inspection revealed it to be carved of painted wood. The same golden shade as the girl's skin, and no less elegant or delicate than the rest of her. As if it had been made for her. Probably magical too.

Viscount Townsend… A female voice at the back of his mind called.

Branches shuddered and leaves whispered as someone moved through the bushes.

For a fleeting moment, he thought the girl had returned, but instead, a petite blond woman emerged from the deep shadows. She pointed to the hand in his. *I can help you find the owner if you're willing to trust me.*

Theo took a step back. "Who are you?"

My name is Dove. The girl you seek is my sister. She tapped her throat. *I'm sorry for the mental intrusion, but I cannot speak.*

He clutched the hand. *What a strange night this is turning into…*

The girl smiled. *If you want explanations, I can provide them, but we must hurry.*

"You heard that?"

Of course she had, she was a telepath. A cold shiver crept over him. What if she told the authorities about his connection to the resistance? What if he'd just ruined not just his own family, but everyone else's as well? In one stupid, careless mistake, he'd killed the revolution.

You can stop worrying. If I had wanted to turn you in, I would've already done it. All I want is freedom for myself and my sister.

He stared at her. "Just how long have you been listening?"

Long enough. She put her hands on her hips. *Now, do you wish to find your mystery girl or not?*

Theo ran his thumb over the smooth wood. *Explains the gloves and the reluctance to shake my hand.* Though he'd started out pursuing her for the resistance, it had grown beyond that. *No point in stopping now.* "Take me to her."

***

Asha stuffed a coat into the bag on her bed. Her chest heaved as she tried to catch her breath. If she were quick, she might be able to avoid Mother's wrath. Better to leave with one hand than let Mother take the other.

Downstairs, a door crashed against a wall.

"Asha!" The raw anger in Mother's voice and fast footsteps ascending the stairs made Asha work faster. She snapped the bag shut and went to the window. With her forearm, she pushed on the latch. If she could just get it to—

"What do you think you're doing?" Mother appeared in the doorway, fuming.

Cecilia leaned against the wall and smirked. "Running away, it looks like."

"One simple job…" Mother advanced toward Asha. "Can you do nothing right? You wretched, useless girl!"

Asha took a step back, wrapping her fingers around her stump. "I'm not useless."

"Oh? No longer a mouse, are we? Found a little gumption?" Mother thrust out a hand. "Give it to me now, Asha, and maybe I'll be generous. Or else you will never see the outside of this room again."

"No." The word flew out of her mouth before she could stop it, but she meant it. She would find her own way in life. Dove had been right. This was no way to live. "I won't."

Mother lunged at her, but Asha sidestepped her grasp. She snatched the bag off the bed, inching toward the door. "I'm leaving."

***

Theo followed Dove down the narrow cobblestone street of an upper-class neighborhood, head still spinning from everything she'd told him. His mystery girl was a thief! And she'd been supposed to lure him to her home so her sister and mother could Persuade him! No wonder she'd run. *Leave it to me to find the most interesting girl at the party.*

Part of him still wondered if this was some sort of elaborate rouse, but Dove exposing her family's small-time thieving operation seemed too much of a risk for it to be a lie.

Dove led him into a well-kept townhouse. Lights flickered to life when they entered the foyer.

She's up there. Dove motioned to a set of twisting stairs.

"Hello?" Theo called. "Are you here? Your sister, Dove, brought me."

Soft footsteps sounded above him. One, then two sets.

Mrs. Gladstone and Cecilia appeared at the top of the stairs.

Theo's gut clenched. Dove had warned him there was a chance of running into either of them. That they would try to Persuade him, but he could handle them. Hopefully.

Uh-oh. Dove's head snapped to Theo. *Run!*

It's all right. I'll deal with them. Just get your sister out of here and wait for me.

"Viscount Townsend, what an unexpected surprise." Mrs. Gladstone's voice sweetened as she descended the stairs with Cecilia.

"Dove? Theo?" The mystery girl appeared behind her mother and sister, clutching a carpetbag. "What are you doing here? You need to leave. Now!"

Theo held up her wooden hand. "We will. But I thought you might need this."

The mystery girl ran down the rest of the steps to embrace Dove, pressing their foreheads together. "You were right. This is no way to live."

Mrs. Gladstone's gaze narrowed on Dove, a smile spreading across her lips. "Thank you for bringing him, darling. You're dismissed now."

Dove's eyes began to glaze over and the mystery girl pushed Dove behind her. "She's coming with me." She stood taller, her remaining hand curling into a fist.

"She will do no such thing." Mrs. Gladstone let out a low, cruel laugh. "Neither of you are leaving me."

Theo slowly inhaled, focusing on Cecilia while Mrs. Gladwell was distracted. Tapping into the well of magic deep within, he let it ooze from every pore.

Cecilia met his gaze, her eyes widening. "Viscount, what are you doing?" Her melodious voice rang in his ears. *Beautiful…*

∗∗∗

Asha moaned as pain erupted in her skull. Her heart flip-flopped when Townsend staggered. Cecilia was overpowering him. "Fight her, Theo!"

She advanced toward Cecilia. If she distracted—

"Dove, restrain Asha!" Mother screamed.

Dove's eyes began to glaze over again.

Oh no. Not her too! "You have to resist. Don't let her

control you."

But Dove's glassy expression remained as she rushed at Asha, catching her wrist. She wrapped her arms around Asha's waist, dragging her off the stairs.

Asha wiggled, trying to break free of her sister's tightening grip.

Mother spoke to Dove in a smug voice. "Keep her quiet but I want her to watch."

Dove's hand clapped down over Asha's mouth.

Mother came close, her face inches from Asha's. "You can't win."

Fiery anger raged in Asha's veins. *Forgive me Dove for what I'm about to do!* She bit down hard on Dove's hand.

It was enough.

Dove's grip on her loosened.

She pulled Dove's hand away from her mouth. "Think of the resistance, Theo! Think of what the emperor did to your—"

Stinging pain across Asha's cheek stole the rest of her words.

"That is enough out of you!" Mother pointed to the hall. "Take her away!"

***

Heavy fog invaded Theo's brain. All the tension in his limbs melted away as he sank down into bliss. The mystery girl struggled against her sister's grip, yelling at him.

"Viscount, look at me." Cecilia grabbed his chin, forcing his head back toward her.

He stared into her eyes, two vibrant green pools. She was so very lovely. What had he been thinking, pursuing her sister? Clearly the best choice was in front of him and—

More shouting. Something about brothers… The emperor… Slowly, her words drew him back to reality.

Theo glanced down at the wooden hand in his. Why

did he have this? The smog began to dissipate. The mystery girl… He'd come to return it. And something else. He fought against the fog, hacking back the invading tendrils trying to wriggle deeper. The resistance! The emperor! Henry and Ben. Father.

"Cecilia…" His voice hummed with the magic, exuding all the charm he could muster. "Sit. Down."

She blinked, and the intense haze retreated from Theo's brain. Slowly, and as if half-asleep, Cecilia sank onto the steps. The muscles in her face relaxed, and her eyes glazed over, giving her an almost wistful expression.

Mrs. Gladstone finished shouting something at Dove and the mystery girl before glancing from Cecilia to Theo, her confusion quickly morphing into fury. "How dare you—"

Fog tried to cloud his brain again, but he forced it out, closing off his mind to her. The mystery girl shoved her mother and the invading tendrils instantly retreated. Mrs. Gladstone tipped back onto the steps, landing on her rump.

When she tried to stand, Dove forced her to sit again.

"What do you think you're doing?" Mrs. Gladstone screeched.

Seeing his opportunity, Theo quickly pushed out another burst of magic, directing it toward Mrs. Gladstone. "Do not move."

Her body shuddered, stare going vacant.

"Good." Theo took a steadying breath. He could make them do so many things with the right words and they wouldn't know he'd planted the idea there.

"Do either of you"—he waved at the mystery girl and Dove—"have a punishment in mind?"

"Us?" the mystery girl squeaked.

"Yes. Name it." It wouldn't do to just let them go after all the suffering they'd caused.

Anything? Dove's voice was filled with glee.

"Within reason."

The mystery girl folded her arms. "Make them leave town and start fresh somewhere, only not as a thieves."

And make them forget us too! Dove piped up. *The last thing we need is them coming after us.*

Theo focused all his energy into his words as he gazed at Mrs. Gladstone. "You will flee the city to avoid imprisonment and find a respectable occupation wherever you settle. You never had any daughters. Should you for some reason return, your many crimes will be reported to the authorities and you will be locked up for the rest of your life."

He turned to Cecilia. "You never had any sisters. After much thought, you've vowed to move far away and to use your abilities only for the good of mankind."

He inhaled slowly. "Do the both of you understand me?"

Mrs. Gladstone's and Cecilia's heads bobbed several times.

***

"Any final requests before I release them?" Theo asked.

Asha and Dove shook their heads, Asha's headache dulling.

"Very well."

Slowly, the glazed look in Mother's and Cecilia's eyes faded; replaced with something Asha had never seen: fear.

"Leave." Theo loomed over them. "*Now.*"

Mother and Cecilia scurried down the rest of the steps and out the door without so much as a glance.

Asha stared after them for a long moment.

A pinch on her arm made her jump. She rubbed it. "What?"

Dove nodded to Theo.

He presented the wooden hand. "Dove explained everything… So your mother had you opening safes, huh?"

"Among other things, but I don't want to do that anymore." She secured it to her wrist and wiggled her fingers. It felt good to be whole again. Even better to be free.

"Actually, I was more interested in your ability to block Persuasion. Highly useful skill, especially among the crowds I'm a part of, but there's no obligation to join—"

Without thinking, Asha pulled his face to hers and kissed him.

When she finally released him, he beamed at her. "What was that for?"

"Everything." Happiness bubbled up inside her. "If I did join, what would that entail?"

"Well, for one, a name. Unless you prefer 'mystery girl,'" Theo said with a laugh.

"She never told you?"

Dove shrugged. *Your name is the one thing that is truly yours. I thought it would be best if you told him.*

"It's Asha."

He smiled. "Asha… It suits you."

Dove put her hands on her hips. *Are you two going to stare at each other all night, or can we discuss joining this rebellion now?*

"My apologies, ladies." Theo offered her and Dove each an arm. "I know a few people who would love to meet you both."

Story Index

"Vanity" was inspired by Snow White

"The Measure of a Princess" was inspired by The Princess and the Pea

"Monsieur Puss" was inspired by Puss in Boots

"Rapunzel and the Toad" was inspired by Rapunzel and The Frog Prince

"The Scarred Shepherdess" was inspired by The Dirty Shepherdess

"Reed Girl, Fire Girl, Cloud Girl" was inspired by The Reed Girl

"Goodbye, Gigi" was inspired by Goldilocks and the Three Bears

"Cursed Winds" was inspired by Beauty and the Beast

"Bluebeard's Wives" was inspired by Bluebeard

"The Veiled Queen" was inspired by King Thrushbeard

"The Thief and the Spy" was inspired by Cinderella

Author Biographies

Kristy Perkins – Vanity

Kristy Perkins is a nanny, and a writer whenever she can find the time. Ever since she could write legibly, she has created stories. She writes fantasy and sci-fi stories to satisfy the need for more dragons and spaceships in her life.

Having grown up with fairy tales, she wanted to write one of those classic stories from her own viewpoint. Her story came from one question: What if Snow White's evil queen didn't mean to kill her stepdaughter? She took that idea, some oblivious self-interest and a new villain, and thus "Vanity" was created.

Kristy's short story "Childhood's Last Nemesis" was published in *Between Heroes and Villains: A Superpower Anthology*.

Follow Kristy on Twitter (@KristyEPerkins), her blog (nocluewritingplatform.wordpress.com), or Pinterest (perkinswhatif).

Rebecca Mikkelson – The Measure of a Princess

Rebecca Mikkelson has been writing fantasy stories since her early teens for fun and is thrilled to turn her dream into a reality. She currently lives in Hawaii with her husband of six years where they enjoy not going outside and avoiding the scare ball on the sky.

You can connect with her on Facebook (@RebeccaMikkelsonAuthor).

Heather Hayden – Monsieur Puss

Fueled by chocolate and moonlight, Heather Hayden seeks to bring magic into the world through her stories. A freelance editor by day, she pours heart and soul into her novels every night, spinning tales of science fiction and fantasy that sing of friendship and hope.

She chose to retell "Puss in Boots" because she loves the fairy tale, especially the main character, Puss. Inspiration for Pip came from her asking the question, "Why was the miller's boy so lazy?" Heather believes the answer is a simple one: Pip is a daydreamer like herself. "Monsieur Puss" is dedicated to Echo, a beautiful kitty who left her paw prints on Heather's heart.

Heather's other publications include *Augment*, a YA science fiction novel, and several short stories in the JL Anthology series. She is currently working on *Upgrade*, the sequel to *Augment*, as well as a gaslamp fantasy series titled *Rusted Magic*.

You can follow Heather's writing adventures on her blog (hhaydenwriter.com), Facebook (@HHaydenWriter), and Twitter (@HHaydenWriter).

Renée Harvey – Rapunzel and the Toad

Renée Harvey is a wife and mother, historian, and author in Iowa, USA. Her novels are historical fiction—stories based on the lives of little-known people with messages of their own to share.

"Rapunzel and the Toad," while not based on history, reflects elements from both the original Grimm "Rapunzel" and "The Frog Prince" stories. Her inspiration for this retelling came from the simple desire to tell a Rapunzel story, preferably a mash-up.

You can follow Renée on Twitter and Facebook (@PRHarvey6), or through her website: storytellerreneeharvey.wordpress.com.

Kelsie Engen – The Scarred Shepherdess

Kelsie Engen is a part-time editor and author, and a full-time wife and mom. She grew up in North Pole, Alaska, where the winters are harsh but beautiful, and Santa Claus was only a five-minute drive away. (Those winters may or may not have inspired her fairy tale world of Canens and the Seven Kingdoms.) In her spare time, she huddles in front of the fire and reads fairy tales to herself or her two children--if they'll listen. If the weather's -20F or above, she might be found outside on a run, listening to an audiobook.

She can also be found through her website for writers (KelsieEngen.com), Instagram (@KelsieEngen), Facebook, (www.Facebook.com/kelsieengenauthor), and Twitter (@KelsieEngen), or hunched over her laptop working on her fairy tale series, the Canens Chronicles, set to release in 2019.

Current information on her newest releases can best be found at her author website: KelsieEngenAuthor.com.

Lynden Wade – Reed Girl, Fire Girl, Cloud Girl

Lynden Wade spends as much time as possible in other worlds to avoid the dirty dishes piling up in her home. Her writing is inspired by fairy tales, legends, and history. She has had stories published in *Fairy Tales for Unwanted Children*, *Ink Stains 9*, *The Forgotten and the Fantastical 3*, *The Forgotten and the Fantastical 4*, and the JL Anthologies *From the Stories of Old* and *A Bit Of Magic*. She is still hoping for a house elf.

"Reed Girl, Fire Girl, Cloud Girl" was inspired by motifs from Eastern European legends, particularly those in *The Kingdom under the Sea and other Stories*, retold by Joan Aiken and illustrated by Jan Pienkowski. The plot, however, is original.

You can find her on her website Queens, Quotes, Quills and Quests (lyndenwadeauthor.weebly.com), and on Facebook (@lyndenwade.author).

Louise Ross – Goodbye, Gigi

Louise Ross is a writer from the greater Kansas City area. When not quilting and working, she lives in a fantasy world where ordinary creatures build everyday lives outside the major battles and politics.

"Goodbye, Gigi" is retelling of "Goldilocks and the Three Bears". To Louise, Goldie was never a sympathetic character. She broke into the bears' home, used, broke, and stole their stuff, and in Louise's version jumped out a window and broke her neck. She is her own antagonist. Therefore, this story is about Gigi, a cat burglar, who is her own worst enemy and headed down a negative path.

You can connect with Louise Ross on Facebook (@ALouiseRoss), Twitter (@A_Louise_Ross), and her blog (83louross.wordpress.com).

Allie May – Cursed Winds

Allie May is a dog lover, mom, and Dr. Pepper addict who turns her caffeine-fueled dreams into believable fiction. She fell in love with the impossible at a young age and has been telling stories (some fiction, some mostly non-fiction) ever since. In high school she won two poetry contests, and in college she started the blog, Hypergraphia to combat her uncontrollable impulse to write. She married her high school sweetheart because he takes her to Disneyland (oh, and because she loves him). Together they have a dog child and a human child. On the weekends, you might catch a glimpse of her in the shadows as a lightsaber-wielding superhero.

"Cursed Winds" was inspired by a question after many viewings of "Beauty and the Beast"—Why would his servants stick around to take care of him if they didn't love him? And if they loved him, why didn't that break the curse? After the birth of her son, she decided to change the romantic love to parental love.

You can follow Allie on her blog (alliemayauthor.blogspot.com), Facebook and Twitter (@AllieMayAuthor), and Goodreads (Allie May).

Mae Baum – Bluebeard's Wives

Mae Baum grew up among the snow and birch trees of upstate New York, but now makes her home in the urban jungle of Atlanta with her husband, daughter, and two cats. Always to be found with her nose in a book, she enjoyed exploring fantastical worlds and now loves making up her own. She currently has several other short stories out in anthologies and is currently hard at work on a novel series.

Mae has always wondered why Bluebeard killed his wives because of their curiosity. Forever curious herself, she firmly believes that inquisitiveness should be rewarded, not punished. Through her retelling, she explores a different angle of this well-known tale.

You can follow Mae on Goodreads (Mae Baum), Twitter (@MaeBaumWriter), her website (maebaum.com), and Facebook.

B. C. Marine – The Veiled Queen

B. C. Marine's Ballads of Carum Sound are heavily influenced by the beautiful Pacific Northwest, where she lives with her husband and two sons. The scenic views of Puget Sound and the Cascades provide plenty of inspiration for her superpowered romantic fantasies. A Western Washington University alumna and former cosmetologist turned work-at-home mom, she writes in between family life and work for A4A Publishing. She loves knitting and spends far too much time researching for her stories.

If the name didn't give her away, Queen Barbenia Thrush of "The Veiled Queen" is a female version of King Thrushbeard from the titular Grimm brothers' fairy tale. Though controversial, the core of the original was a beautifully dramatic love story that this author could not resist. A special thanks for this story goes to her father, Joe Marine, for his fishing knowledge. Look for her other retellings in *From the Stories of Old* and *Of Legend and Lore* as well as her debut novel, *A Seer's Daughter*.

For information and updates on future stories, connect with B. C. through her website (www.bcmarinebooks.com) and Twitter (@Meriverian).

Katelyn Barbee – The Thief and the Spy

Katelyn Barbee is a Phoenix college student by day and a writer by night. When not working on her fantasy series, you can find her at the cinema catching the latest flicks or enjoying a nature walk when the weather is nice. The story "The Thief and the Spy" was inspired by the many variants of Cinderella.

Her other publications include "The Miller's Daughter" in *From the Stories of Old* and "The Solstice Beast" in *Whispers in the Shadows*.

You can connect with Katelyn on Twitter (@WriterBarbee) or Facebook (Katelyn Barbee).

About the Illustrator

Heidi Hayden was raised in the forests of Maine and graduated from the Maine College of Art as an Illustration major. A bookworm by nature, she reads copious amounts of questionable fiction by unpublished authors, in the few moments of spare time when she is not writing and illustrating her own books. She works in gouache, ink, pencil, and fabric, and enjoys repurposing materials for her art.

She drew inspiration for the anthology's illustrations from a variety of old fairy tale books, such as those depicting the tales of the Brothers Grimm. The medium—ink on paper—was chosen in order to capture both the essence of the retellings and the timelessness of black-and-white illustrations.

You can see more of her work on her website (haydenillustration.com).

About the Just-Us League

Hailing from all corners of the globe, the members of the Just-Us League share a common passion for words and worlds.

The League can be found on Facebook (@jlwriters), Twitter (@JL_writing), and our website (jlwriters.com). Follow us for updates, giveaways, and new releases.

Also by the Just-Us League

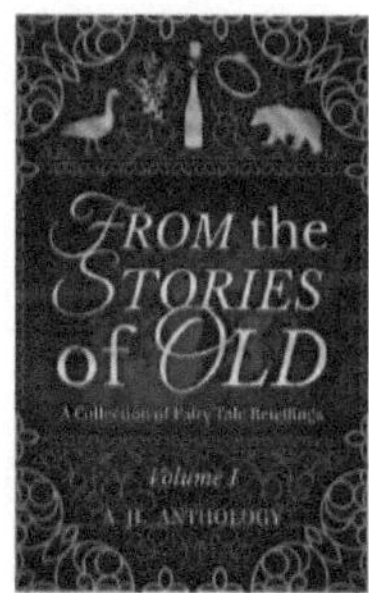  

  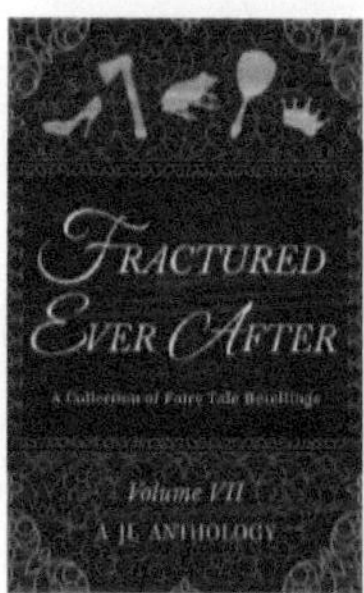